Mother Sea

LORRAINE WILSON

Fairlight Books

First published by Fairlight Books 2023

Fairlight Books
Summertown Pavilion, 18–24 Middle Way, Oxford, OX2 7LG

A CIP catalogue record for this book is available from the
British Library

1 2 3 4 5 6 7 8 9 10

ISBN 978-1-914148-33-0

www.fairlightbooks.com

Printed and bound in Great Britain

To Jared.

With gratitude. And not just for the sunsets.

*And the selfsame well from which your laughter rises
was oftentimes filled with your tears*

—'On Joy and Sorrow', Khalil Gibran (1923)

Chapter One

Sisi

Sisi de Mathilde had thought herself reconciled, until today. An hour after dawn, she stood in the doorway of her house gazing westward across the bay and the blue ocean, and wished herself gone more terribly than she had wished it for years. Away from loyalty and ancestors and the parameters of their island; away to the Seychelles or South Africa beyond. Anywhere, she thought, other than here with children's voices lonely on the beach, and beyond the reef her husband fishing. Anywhere other than here, today, with this secret.

Chickens were squabbling behind her house and somewhere a coconut fell to the ground, but Sisi barely heard them, the way you barely hear your own heartbeat or the voice of the sea. And yet when the two children laughed down on the beach, she flinched.

'Oh Mother,' she whispered. That they were the island's only children, and still laughed. That they, and her secret, all translated into heartbreak in a thousand different ways.

*

Wrenching herself away from her dread and the view, she walked inland, passing the store where Mama Mandisa was sitting in a patch of shade, hemming cloth with her strong, old fingers as the radio murmured weather reports.

'Sisi de Mathilde,' Mama Mandisa said, smiling with every muscle of her face and tilting her head in a way that she had done since she was very young and very beautiful. 'Mother Sea is calm for our fishers, is she not?'

The cliff-forests were dense with morning shadows, and above them lay the plateau of Les Hautes where Sisi's work was waiting. Sisi came forward to press her cheek against the old woman's, smiling into her milk-skimmed eyes. 'She is, Mama. All is well with you?'

'All is well,' Mama Mandisa answered, but Sisi heard the lie and forgot about her work, forgot even about the secret that was not yet a truth.

'It is not Manon?' Her dearest friend, carrying a baby so nearly ready to be born.

'No, no,' Mama Mandisa shook her head, the tower of her braided-up hair swaying. 'Nuru has news from outside, and I do not like it.'

She called through the dark doorway of the store for Sisi's sibling by marriage and Nuru stepped out, their immaculate white shirt glowing against their skin, brighter even than the strung shells around their neck, the traditional shells that said they were Sacere, neither male nor female but history-keeper, faith-leader, guide. They came to Sisi and, just as she had done with Mama Mandisa, pressed their cool cheek to hers, then sat. Mama Mandisa's hands worked without pause and above them a flycatcher, streamer-tailed, called to its children.

'Alors,' Nuru said. 'The Commonwealth Office are sending a new Administrator.'

'Because of—' Sisi cut herself off abruptly. The babes, the babes.

Mama Mandisa made a low humming sound in the back of her throat and Nuru said steadily, 'Perhaps. Doctors are coming once again. But I think a new Administrator would not visit us so soon only for this.' Would not, because they were an ocean-speck atoll in Britain's shrunken empire, far east of the Seychelles and further still from anywhere else. 'It is not for your work?' they said to Sisi.

Sisi shook her head.

'Child, this Administrator visits us so soon because they wish to take something away.' Mama Mandisa dropped the cloth, brushing creases from her wrap impatiently, her breath full of the tides as if Mother Sea were reclaiming her. 'And what do we have left to give?'

The British government and doctors. Perhaps they wished to take Manon away for the sake of her unborn child, and Sisi would want them to but Manon would not. A gecko flat-toed along the wall behind her, its slit-pupilled eyes merciless.

*

By the time she left the store to climb up through fields, then forest, then out into the thorn scrub and karst of Les Hautes, the sun was high overhead. Heat fierce on her uncovered hair, but the breeze was trade wind flavoured and smelled of iodine and distant rain. From here at the edge of the plateau, she could see a slice of fields and village, then the long beach and arc of atoll enclosing the lagoon. L'Ambre's red peak rose to her right but she would not look at it, not today, and her gaze was drawn helplessly westward instead, towards the Seychelles where she had gone for school and then come home, certain that she would soon be leaving again. Before she had understood.

Out there a ship was coming bearing outsiders and, in Mama Mandisa's eyes, also trouble. For now, though, the sea all around their tiny, lonely island was silk-ruffled and quiescent, the crescent of reef blemished only by its anchored dock. To the south, a constellation of seventeen white stars was the fishing fleet, one of which would be her husband, Antonin. Sails heeled their pirogues into the wind and they were like Sisi's own restlessness, she thought; also pulled, and also tethered. She had chosen to stay, though – even if the choice had not been for herself – so there was nothing to be done except strive to make her work worthwhile, love her husband inadequately, walk and climb and let the ocean bear her up.

Alors, enough of that, Sisi thought, turning away. She followed a track between karst and thorn bushes that snagged at her clothes, until she reached the white-washed cool of the old lighthouse where she worked.

Instruments hummed subliminally as she downloaded the numbers coming from her offshore buoy, entered yesterday's data from the crop fields, connected to the erratic internet to send updates to her distant colleagues. Today, the solar panels did not need cleaning of salt and dust, but next time, or in a few months? Stretching to lean over the awkward construction with an awkward body? Above the door was a web of termite tunnels and Sisi could almost hear the insects feasting infinitesimally, eroding the timbers bite by minuscule bite.

It was only returning home, as she saw the fleet again from the top of the path and counted them absently once more, that she thought, *seventeen boats*. Seventeen? Sometimes the fleet separated, sometimes a damaged boat or a full one returned early. But still... but still... a gecko called from a tree below her and Sisi went down the path frowning, her sandals slip-sliding on the dusty earth.

*

Sisi did not mention the missing pirogue to Manon because logic told her it was nothing of concern, and her friend's optimism would have said the same.

'I think that they will not be back until tomorrow,' Manon said, missing her husband even that much. Sisi was sitting on one of the fine tight-woven mats that Manon had made for her married home, and she was rubbing coconut oil into Manon's feet, massaging the skin upwards to ease the swelling. As she poured more oil onto her palm and lifted Manon's other foot into her lap, her friend was reading aloud from a blog about spa hotels, laughing at it as she stroked the rise of her belly. The pregnancy had been difficult for her, sickness gripping her hard until well into the sixth month so that flesh fell from her arms and face and only now with weeks to go did she look well again. Rounded and brown as a fresh nut, contented in a way known only to pregnant women and cats. Despite everything.

A bowl of shelled beans lay on the table beside her, their cast-offs in a basket near Sisi's hip, and the room smelled of the pods' broken skins as well as the oil.

'Here,' Manon said, reaching for Sisi's slippery hand and placing it on her stomach, her smile like a sunrise. Beneath Sisi's palm, the baby kicked once, twice, then pushed both feet hard into Sisi's touch, as if the child were searching for the world.

'Oh, little fish,' Manon said, a laugh turning into a groan as she pressed her own hand into the base of her ribs on the opposite side. 'Every minute he grows bigger, I swear.'

Such dangerous love on her face, dense as honey. Sisi took her hand away, holding the feel of the baby's movements between her palms. *Give me joy*, she prayed. *Scorch my smile clean.*

'He?' she said gently.

'I am sure of it.' Manon rubbed at her ribs, soothing. 'My first was not at all so...' She tried to make her flinch into nothing, a gesture like the falling of a leaf.

Manon's first, her daughter whose name was known only by Mother Sea, her tiny weight borne in their hands up to the red cliffs with their hearts in ashes. Sisi had no words because language was not made for this, but she laid her fingers on Manon's calves, traced courage and love onto her skin.

'This one, he will live,' Manon said after a moment. She had said it before.

'Yes,' Sisi said. What else could she say? Not epidemiology or statistics, not today. No mention of drug resistance, or tetanus. If you spoke a thing with enough faith then perhaps it would come true. If you did not speak a thing, then perhaps it would not. The Mothers said that they must have hope, and that Mother Sea would not let her children suffer forever. The Mothers said to guard your heart.

'The mailboat will come tomorrow,' Sisi said, wiping her hands on a cloth then taking the beans to the sink, setting them to soak. 'There should be the new buoys for me. The ones that are to monitor the artificial reef.'

'Luc ordered a new laptop,' Manon said and Sisi smiled. The monthly thrill of deliveries, of currency arriving from their small exports of vanilla and cloves, traded for an increasing list of things that the island could not give them but that the outside could. Their atoll alone in the wide, wide sea.

There were things, she thought, that you were certain of long before there could be certainty. Nuru said these were the times Mother Sea whispered one of her infinite secrets to you, for one of her infinite reasons. But Sisi thought it was simply the eighty-six billion neurones in your mind knowing far more than you chose to believe.

*

One more night and one more day, then, suspended between knowing and unknowing. And in the evening Sisi went down to the beach with Manon as the fishers returned. The pirogues' masts groaned as their sails were bound, the fishers jumped into thigh-deep water and ran their boats up to the goat's foot vines. *Seventeen*, Sisi thought. Then Luc was there, his hand reaching for Manon but his eyes on Sisi, and she could not move. The others carried fish baskets from the pirogues up to the mats beneath the tamarinds, dripping salt water as if the fish had died weeping, but Sisi could not move.

'Sisi,' Luc said.

'Where is he?'

'He went further beyond Les Soeurs, but the wind is now against him. He will be in on the morning tide, no?'

The sea and the day's sweat were tidelines on his shirt and he had been her friend every day of her life. It was easy to forget what that meant, sometimes.

She might have believed him, if not for that *no*.

*

'We saw the mailboat,' Luc said. 'Antonin will be back before it arrives.'

Old Abasi left his boat to pat her arm gently, damp-fingered, and she could see on his face and on Luc's that they had searched before coming in. A frigatebird cried, its long silhouette whipping across the sand, and Sisi turned to join the others beneath the tamarind trees. Shadows were gathering purples there and the lights strung between trees turned everyone's faces burnished and the scales of the fish into jewels.

*

Sisi's hands had done this since she was a girl, parting belly flesh with a thin blade, a hooked finger pulling out guts that drowned the smell of the tamarind with that of iodide blood. The fishers went to hang their nets and wash, and someone turned the radio on, a seggae song reaching them from Mauritius like a heartbeat.

'They will go out with the dawn,' Mama Mandisa said. 'Do not fear, Sisi. It is as Luc has said. The wind and tide are against him and he knows it is better to wait.'

Faces turned to Sisi and then away, and Manon was there even though she was not permitted to gut the fish, her shoulder touching Sisi's. The radio paused; another song began. Nuru set a coral grouper aside then laid their hands in their lap, and soon everyone else's hands paused too, waiting. Sisi reached for another fish.

'Many years and many years ago,' Nuru began, their voice tonal, the shells at their neck reflecting the lights like a string of tears, 'a great ship sailed on Mother Sea, laden with sorrow...'

'Aie,' someone hummed, a tiny grief for those long-dead griefs still living in their bones.

Sisi listened more to Nuru's voice than she did to the words. The story was their oldest, and that of course was why Nuru spoke it now with their brother still out on the sea. Because the story that tells you how you came to be, against the odds, reminds you of Mother Sea's mercy.

*

Sisi refused to think of mercy or wreckage, though. She threw discarded innards to the hermit crabs and the flightless rail that crept, stilt-stepped and head jerking, between them. She did so without thinking, children of Mother Sea sharing with other children. Nuru spun their story from slavery to shipwreck to survival, conflict to faith, and Sisi shivered. It was beautiful in a way, that Nuru could keep their face so serene with Antonin unreturned. But terrible too, Sisi thought, that the role of Sacere subsumed Nuru so completely there was no space left within them to belong only to themself. How did they do that? Find contentment in that? Perhaps they were simply stronger than her. Their hands, she realised, were clenched as tightly in their lap as hers were around the knife.

She worked with Antonin in her mind in fragments: the sight of his face half-averted, the sound of his laughter, the salt-sweat remote smell of him that filled their house whenever he returned. Then the two children, Chicha and Katura, bent beside her and Manon, and their startling youth made Sisi's hands unsteady as she passed them the gutted fish.

Manon ran a palm over the mound of her belly and reached out blindly to hold Sisi's hand in the shadows. As she let her knife fall and tilted her face up to the sky, Sisi's heart was full of Manon but her mind was on Antonin's hand on the back of her neck, the empty space on the beach where his boat ought to be, the secret she wanted not to be real. The night watched her through a filigree canopy and a bat swept across the sky, obscuring the stars. The sea told truths to the sand and helplessly Sisi listened.

Chapter Two

Kit

Kit Benedict half-slept his way across the empty ocean from Mahé to the island, aware of the cabin and the sea's rise and fall only distantly. He was on a boat; and he wasn't.

Because he was still in the hospital, waking.

Over and over, waking and waking, and knowing he'd failed. Again, waking in the hospital, and failing and being alive. Again, waking and failing; again.

*

His bed rocked and the motion made him open his eyes. Blurry blankets and a wall of white-washed chipboard. The boat, he remembered, sailing away for a year and a day to a land of money and honey and monsters, exiles all dancing on the sand, and he pictured falling into waves, watching his breath trail upwards as he sank. The peacefulness of it was something akin to hope. His phone rang, muffled, but he didn't move and it fell silent, and he lay staring at the wall, his body oceanic as the boat stole him further and further from the moment he'd lived rather than died.

*

'Kit,' someone said, like a shout through water. 'Kit, we're here. Get up.'

Here? Kit opened his eyes, struggling to focus on the blanket that lay over his face. The weave was coming loose in a couple of places, threads hanging free.

'Come on, mate. We're here now – you need to see this place, it's like paradise.'

It was his uncle, Kit realised. Uncle George, the Englishness more marked than in Kit's father and too loud because the room was too small. Kit could taste fetid air from his own lungs and didn't understand why this foreign uncle was here; then did.

His parents and a hospital, his parents and his aunt, his aunt and uncle, an airport, a boat; a second-hand son sent away for repair.

'I'm coming,' he said, the medicines they'd given him slurring his words.

A sigh and a creak, the blankets pulled away in one rough move, Geo's face looming over his. Kit squinted at it through searing light. 'Mate,' Geo said again. His eyes moved from Kit to floor to wall to Kit. 'Let's get you up now, hey? You need to give this a chance, mate. Come on now.'

He straightened but didn't leave, and Kit, for lack of anything else to do, stood, a hand against the wall as the world swam. 'Good man,' Geo said, moving back towards the door then hesitating. *Poor Uncle Geo*, Kit thought faintly. Such an... *emasculated* nephew forced upon him by his brother. Why had he ever agreed to it?

'Do you want to get dressed? Or I suppose you can stay as you are. No one will mind.'

Geo was in a linen suit, expensive and a little rumpled; Kit stayed in shorts and a T-shirt that he might have been wearing since they'd boarded the boat, or before. But now they were climbing steps so steep they were almost ladders, the air full of engine fumes and salt, light exploding inside his cranium, and as he reached the deck, around them was every possible shade of blue. *Langebaan*, he thought dazedly, but no, it was too bright and too hot, and the sea far, far too vast for their west coast holiday house. *We sailed away for a year and a day*, he thought, *to the land—*

'Don't stop yet,' Geo said, and Kit winced. He hadn't known it was possible to be so tired, and he couldn't remember what this land was, or why they'd sailed to it in their pea-green boat. His parents hadn't cared about the *where*, though, only the *away*.

'This way, mate,' Geo said. Not a slow man, or a... *quiet* one. Kit tried to move but his body weighed universes and seemed beyond him, like he had been disassembled.

'You go on ahead, G,' Rachel said, appearing beside her husband so slim and cool that Kit became half-aware of how he must look and dropped his head rather than see her pity. Her hand on his arm was so light that he felt like weeping. 'All right, sweetie,' she said. 'It's not far, and we'll get you straight to the house so you can rest. You can do it.'

He moved where Rachel moved him, rust under the handrail catching his skin and the sun scorching the crown of his head. There was a stretch of metal dock then a smaller boat, an orange rib with its outboard roaring. Then land in a blur of white dust and flowers and the sound of a bird singing. Sand beneath his shoes, his head swimming in darkness. Did the owl and the pussycat mind where they had ended up, or that they'd gone so far from home? Did they worry about not being able to find their way back?

'Not much further, and at least we're out of the sun now,' Rachel said. She was right, he realised distantly – the fire was gone from his shoulders; trees, flowers, the ghost of a lawn, a doorway and someone talking and Rachel answering. He wanted to stop moving, to ask her something, anything, that would anchor him to this moment in time. *Where are we?* would be a good start, or *Why are you being so kind when you barely know me?* But she kept moving through the cool shadows of the hallway, and into another room, saying, 'There you go, darling. Someone will bring your things and I'll get you a drink in just a tick. It's time for your tablets, remember.'

She went, and even though the curtains weren't enough to shut out the light, they softened it. He sank onto a bed where the sheets were stiff and thin, and lying down just then was the closest he'd come to happiness in as long as he could remember. He still felt like he was on water, or falling through it, falling towards a half-dreaming sea-green memory of swimming through a kelp forest at Langebaan with his regulator trailing air bubbles, starfish on the rocks beneath him in reds and golds. He remembered how he'd stopped swimming to hang there in the jade water, startled by his own wonder. How his brother had been bored within minutes, the great columnar jungle not nearly as exciting as sea caves or the beers awaiting them on the yacht, but Kit had pretended not to see his signalling, had swum down to the rocks and roots where he'd watched a cuttlefish send untranslatable messages to him as it fled.

'We should go shark diving,' Charlie had said when they'd hauled themselves back aboard. 'Those caged ones, you know, more exciting than seaweed.'

Kit had shrugged. He saw nothing particularly tempting about sitting in a cage watching sharks baited to come to them like trained dogs. He'd gone, though, and laughed with his brother's friends about the blood in the water, about Heinrich, who had jerked back from the bars too quickly to mask with bravado. That had been before he'd started resisting, or before Charlie had started pulling away; he couldn't remember now which had come first. Not that it mattered – not now with sleep tugging him back beneath the waves.

*

He was woken by his uncle's voice again. The light and his viscous limbs telling him he'd slept for hours.

'Beautiful place, Kit, mate,' Geo said, silhouetted against the windows. A breeze was making the gauzy curtains slither inwards, and Kit could smell the foreign island that he'd been sent to. To recover, his mother had said, and make himself useful to this English, Commonwealth Office uncle; such a polite exile.

At least the smells of rock, heat, nectar were better than engine oil and his own breath. Something was making a long chattering call like an unbroken code, and he wanted to fumble his way to the bathroom, drink endless water from the tap then return here and sleep.

'Rach just spoke to your mum,' Geo said. Kit closed his eyes. 'Let her know we'd arrived safe. You need to ring her though, mate, all right? She'll want to hear from you.'

Kit made a noise that was mostly disbelief.

'So, I could use a hand, mate,' Geo said, still standing by the window, gazing at a point above Kit's head. 'Use some of that law education of yours, you know?' He hesitated, then added more firmly, 'Here's the deal, Kit. You get up, you come downstairs for something to eat, then we'll... ah, we'll take it from there, hey?'

Kit looked at his uncle through slitted eyes, nodding automaton-like. Law education? If he'd had the energy he might have laughed. Did his uncle know how little of that he could lay claim to, how he'd deliberately, merrily forgotten all of it when he'd switched courses? Ice cores and bathymetry, methane emissions and time-series models rather than statutes, case law, *mens rea* and arbitration. If they'd brought him here thinking he'd be any use as a law student they were going be quickly disillusioned. He wondered if they too would send him away.

'Great,' Geo said. 'Lunch in half an hour, mate.'

*

Get up, come downstairs for something to eat.

Kit wrenched himself out of bed and moved to the window, meaning to simply shut the things and draw the curtains again, but standing with one hand on the frame, he hesitated.

Passing just beyond the house on a beaten earth track were three figures. One woman old and broad, her feet shuffling, another woman and a man carrying bundles of dried leaves and flowers. Wine-red flowers and scarlet ones, fiery against the colours of their skin. The younger woman's fists were tight and Kit stood watching them until they were out of sight, his mind furling and unfurling around the bloody flowers. He turned away and ran a hand over his face and hair, grease beneath his fingertips making him grimace. If he had died, he thought, then nothing in the world would have changed. His uncle and aunt would still be here, preparing food in a house on a rock in a vast ocean. His parents and brother would still be at their practice in Jo'burg or in court; his friends in Cape Town would be in lectures. The seas would still be rising, the Arctic burning, and his mother would not want to speak to him until he was acceptable once more.

Kit pushed away from the window, wanting suddenly to be clean.

*

'There you are!' Geo said as Kit stepped through a doorway leading onto a veranda. Of course they were eating out here, he thought, in the incendiary light and with birds calling from the bushes, everyone wearing pale linen and bright smiles.

'Kit, darling,' Rachel said, gesturing to a chair and modulating her voice to a tone she might use with children and nervous dogs. It irritated him, but only fleetingly. Three strangers sat watching, all white, uncheaply dressed, relaxed; type specimens that he would once have matched perfectly. How odd, to hate what he was now and still feel grateful that he was no longer what he had been.

'This is Geraldine Adler and Matthew Freshman. Geraldine is a paediatrician and Matthew is a biomedical researcher, both based in Cape Town like you, dear. They've been seconded to the Commonwealth Office; they were on the boat but I think you missed them. And this is Euan, of course, Geo's assistant. Here, have some water, sweetie.'

'Matt,' said Matthew. Geraldine nodded, the smile on her face small and analytical. Kit looked away.

'I'm probably more Euan's student here,' Geo said, laughing, and the ghost of a wince passed over the assistant's narrow face. 'He's the expert on this whole situation – I'm just the government ballast, you know?'

No, Kit thought, he didn't. He concentrated on taking slow sips of his water, tearing bread into small pieces, crumbs forming pixellations on the table and his lap. The narrow-faced man smiled at him with such incurious neutrality that Kit echoed it without meaning to.

'I come here every few months,' Euan said, 'for a short stay, help out with formalities, that sort of thing.' His voice was more cricket and less rugby than Geo's. 'I'm not sure I could claim to know the place any more than you will in a couple of days, but we can certainly manage between us all.'

Geo said something, then Rachel did, and Kit turned his head towards the trees and a slice of sea without really seeing any of it. Sleep crawled behind his eyes. *How do I endure this?* he wondered. *Where do I begin? And why?* There were boats out there, he realised. White sails against the searing azure of the lagoon, and just like with the memory of a kelp forest he was suspended again, hiked out as far as he could, sails close-hauled and salt on his face, gulls calling and his father shouting instructions into the wind. Laughing because they were beating his brother and friend in their overpriced catamaran, laughing because it wasn't often he and his father were aligned in victory and it made him both invincible and dizzy.

'Well, first meeting tomorrow,' Geo said loudly and Kit blinked. 'Lots of prep to do, Euan, mate? Got to teach me how to walk on eggshells, hey?' He laughed, throwing a glance at Kit but Kit's face was numb with sedatives and remembered laughter, and Geo looked away.

There would be a tomorrow, Kit thought. There were flowers in the hedge that matched the ones the woman had been holding as fiercely as if they were keeping her alive.

Chapter Three

Sisi

The children came to tell her mid-morning, while she was picking at a meal that Manon had put in front of her, a little of last night's rice and beans, coffee brewed dark and latent. Sisi had not seen the mailboat arrive, but an hour ago the pirogues had returned and she had watched them, bleak and hollow and unsurprised.

'The Mothers have called a meeting,' Katura said, Chicha waiting behind them restlessly, the sunlight staining Katura's eyes older than they ought to be. People had begun calling Katura the Last Sacere, the place where all their people's stories came to an end. It was, Sisi thought, a terrible burden to put on a child.

'Thank you, Katura,' she replied and they nodded gravely, then they and Chicha were gone, four bare feet raising the sandy dust.

*

The island hall lay close to the beach at the western end of the village, only a slim line of coconut trees between it and the rocks of Pointe Basse stretching beyond. It was the oldest of their buildings, an open-sided, low-roofed space filled with pale woven mats and the handful of benches and desks for the school. Some of the beams in the roof were so salt-smoothed and desiccated that perhaps they really were remnants of that first ship, the ship that died so they could be free. Today with the wind in the east, the wall screens on the lagoon side were lowered, concealing the Administrator's newly re-occupied house across the wide arc of the bay, and concealing the fishing fleet.

Sisi noted that, and wondered where the pain was. Surely now there was no doubt, there ought to be pain. But her heart was adrift in the confines of her chest and perhaps, she thought, it did not yet know.

The three elder Mothers sat together – Mama Mathilde diminutive with age and Mama Anouk keeping her eyes closed because they would be full of tears, and Mama Mandisa stringing shells onto thread with her mobile hands.

'Mother Sea,' Mama Mandisa said, 'has taken one of ours for her own. Antonin de Sabah, husband of Sisi de Mathilde, and brother of Jomo and Nuru. He is gone to Mother Sea as we all go when she calls us.'

'Nuru de Sabah,' she said, 'Sisi de Mathilde, we are here with you. We know your sorrow.'

Everyone echoed the words. Manon held Sisi's hand and Mama Anouk unclasped her fingers and raised her head. She was paler-skinned than most, and so the smile she gave seemed paler too. 'Tonight we will hold velasa to ease our son's passing over into Mother Sea's embrace. We the Mothers witness Mother Sea's tithe and ask our fishers to take care because we love them. We ask the Sacere,' with a tilting nod towards where they sat, 'to advise whether there is meaning in Mother Sea taking this man at this time.'

Sisi, everyone, looked to where the Sacere sat together at the side of the hall. Nuru's eyes were fixed on something Sisi could not see, and the eldest, Berhane, rose slowly, blue cotton billowing around them then settling.

'We shall look for these answers, Mama. We hope' – they paused; their fingers twitched – 'that Mother Sea has sent us this sorrow in place of others.'

Manon's grip shook and she turned blindly to Sisi. The kernel of Sisi's secret burned, everyone beneath the quiet roof took a breath.

'I am here with you, Sisi-si,' her friend whispered again. 'I know your sorrow.'

She meant both condolence and apology, and Sisi wanted to say that there was no need. Because everyone knew Mother Sea's love was constant, but never soft. No need, because anyone there, even Sisi if she believed in such things, would accept the fairness of one man taken if it meant the children would live.

'Thank you,' Sisi said. 'I hope...' But she stopped. Silenced by too much faithlessness and guilt because how could the Sacere offer such promises and how could she, Sisi, keep her secret now? How could she tell Jomo any of this at all?

'It was surely peaceful,' Manon said.

Which was perhaps what Sisi had meant, but she said only, 'The Sacere will be right this time.'

The hall was a sea of murmurs. Manon bent forward over her stomach and made a sound like a wounded bird that broke Sisi's drifting heart. 'Oh Sisi-si, forgive me, it is a terrible thing, but I hope this too.'

Mama Mandisa spoke once more. 'The outsiders,' she said. 'We will talk of them after we have held velasa for our son.'

*

As everyone else returned to the fields, or the boats or whichever task they had set themselves, Sisi, Nuru and Mama Mandisa made the slow walk up to the tombs in the red cliffs below L'Ambre's summit. The wife, the newly brotherless Sacere and the Mother. Tonight, they would do it again with everyone and by torchlight. Now, with the early afternoon sunshine just reaching the rock face, the stone was cooler beneath Sisi's hands than the bruising air, grit gathering on her fingers as she trailed them over fissures and pioneering plants.

*

As they passed the first of the tombs Nuru spoke from just behind Sisi. 'The red cliffs are our haven here on Brother Island. But they are not our home, yes?'

'Yes,' Sisi said, understanding what they were not saying. 'I think he would have chosen the sea, if he could.' It was true, and also perhaps what Nuru needed to hear.

'I think that you are right.'

Sisi took a breath, smelling rock dust and the coconut oils from Mama Mandisa's skin. A second tomb opening yawed on their right. They passed on.

'Are you well?' Nuru asked and Sisi stumbled, thinking momentarily that they had guessed, her fingers curling on the rock before she gathered herself. But how to answer? What was the truth when neither mind nor heart wished to speak? Was it dread, this numbness, or grief, or a fond lovelessness she had never allowed herself to scrutinise?

'As well as is possible,' she said. 'And you?'

'He was my brother,' Nuru said. Sisi stopped, turning on the narrow path to face her sibling. She tried to read their face but nothing in the calm eyes, the edge of smile, showed the heartbreak she had heard.

And without warning Nuru's other, absent brother filled her mind. *Oh, Jomo*, she thought sadly, *it was not only me that you abandoned.*

'Tonight I will lead the ceremony, if that is well with you,' Nuru said, and Sisi nodded, turning away again to follow the slow-moving form of Mama Mandisa, who had only the rock face beneath her hand, and her memories, to keep her from the cliff.

*

There were bats in the cave that would be Antonin's symbolic tomb. Their guano had accumulated in piles in several corners and as Sisi swept the floor clean, she could hear wings resettling above her head. She could have reached up to touch their tiny, clustered bodies, but that might drive them out and the thought of them here, contentedly watching over the sleeping bones of her husband's ancestors, pleased her, so she kept her head bent and they barely stirred, their black eyes reflecting the light like constellations of stars.

Mama Mandisa prepared traditional torches made from coconut husk fibres and tightly padded bolls of tamarind seeds, wrapped in raffia and soaked in oil. Nuru lit bundles of herbs and the tomb filled with the airy scent of lemongrass, the bittersweet of cloves. If Antonin had died on land then he would lie here, but Sisi thought again that he would be happier where he was. If he could rest beside his first wife, Afiya, then that was what he would have chosen. But between his mother's tomb and the sea, he would have wanted the sea.

The thought was not bitter. There was only ever a tiny, weary ache to accompany all Sisi's thoughts of that first and undefeated competitor for her husband's heart. If competitor were the right term. Sisi had also lost her own love, after all, and she had never truly tried to win his.

They walked back down the way they had come, Mama Mandisa whispering greetings to the ancestors and friends and family in the tombs that they passed. Despite her eyesight, she never said the wrong name, and Sisi tried to imagine becoming old here. Being Mother and mother, as well as aunt and grandmother and friend and wife. How many people had Mama Mandisa helped pass over to Mother Sea? How many of those had been nine days old? How many times could she, or any of them, retain their faith and protect their wary hearts?

The rock had gathered the day's heat now, throwing ochraceous light back up into their faces. Basking lizards tilted canny heads to watch Sisi pass and the tombs breathed age and shadows, but never decay. Despite knowing about desiccation and ants, Sisi had always liked to imagine that this was because Brother Island took his people into himself so completely there was simply the body sleeping, and then the bones.

She paused at the tomb of Manon's family and yet even here the cave breathed only stone and the cold of deep places, perhaps a ghost of cloves or cinnamon. She imagined tiny finger bones resting in their scarlet wrappings, and pressed her hand against the rock, fireworks in her fingertips, an anger singing in her blood that made faith and patience into betrayal.

Such familiar fury.

She held her hand against the rock, nailbeds whitening, then walked on, wearily knotting her rage back away.

*

Later, in the lengthening shade of her house, Sisi sat beside her new research buoys, weaving a figure from raffia and cotton thread. Once in a while, someone would come to sit with her, giving her a strip of bright cloth to be woven in, or a length of supple twine. Manon brought her a tiny, dark scallop shell with a hole in its base that might have been from a sea urchin, or from a needle. Sisi threaded it onto a length of black cord to tie around the figure's neck like a charm.

'He is well done,' Manon said, and Sisi studied the work of her hands. The attenuated limbs and wide torso bore poor resemblance to Antonin, but it was not meant to be exact, only a repository for their farewells. 'Are you well?' Manon added when Sisi did not speak.

Sisi looked up at her friend. Berhane that morning had said that perhaps Antonin's death would pay for the life of Manon's babe, and all of Sisi's thoughts were terrible.

Frowning, reaching awkwardly forward to take the figure from Sisi's hand, Manon folded her warm fingers around Sisi's own and said, 'You were... Sisi-si, you were happy, yes? At least a little.'

'Yes,' Sisi said quickly. 'It was... we were friends and kind to one another.' But she remembered their wedding day, looking into his eyes and seeing resignation there, a determination laid thinly over grief.

'The Mothers should not have put you together.'

Manon had said the same at the time but when Sisi then talked of leaving, or of refusing, Manon's face had spoken abandonment. *Perhaps you will find love together*, she had said. *We need you. Stay.*

A year before then, Sisi's mother had died from a stonefish sting while diving for clams. Sisi had been alone and lost, and the Mothers had pointed out that she was the last of her line, that Antonin came from a large family and their people needed hope. Besides, everyone younger was away at school and everyone older was married or gone back to the outside for university or work. She had emailed Jomo to tell him but he had not replied and it was this more than anything else that had made her agree.

Sisi shrugged now. It no longer mattered and as she had chosen to accept her marriage, she could hardly now resent *this*.

'He was my friend, and a good man,' she said. He deserved to be mourned unconditionally by his wife. Like he mourned Afiya, like Afiya would have mourned him.

'Yes,' Manon agreed, rubbing a hand over her stomach and shifting her weight as if the child inside were restless. 'I wish I could come with you tonight.' But she could not. The Mothers would not allow her even within sight of the evening ceremony however much Sisi wanted her friend's hand in hers. Pregnancy forbade her from contact with this death as much as it had the glittering deaths of the fish.

Pregnancy forbade her.

The hairs rose on Sisi's arms.

Pregnancy forbade her.

Because swimming half-entwined with Mother Sea, a babe might still choose to return. Especially now, with death so hungry.

A magpie robin hopped towards their feet, its head angleward as it scrutinised the debris of Sisi's work, and Sisi stared at it blankly.

'What it is?' Manon asked. 'What is wrong?'

Sisi should have told her days ago when first she realised herself. Why had she not?

The robin tossed a piece of raffia aside with a flick of its beak, swallowing some morsel and eyeing Sisi sidelong as it did so. It would go to roost soon, just as the bats in the tombs awoke.

'I only' – speaking as much to the sharp-eyed bird as to Manon – 'wished for my life to be *mine*.'

'It is,' Manon said.

'It is not.' But the robin flew away, chattering as someone approached, rapidly enough to be a child but too heavy-footed. Sisi and Manon looked up and Nuru appeared. They were a little breathless and although their face was calm, there was a line of perspiration around the border of their headwrap, the whites of their eyes shining like an eclipsed moon.

'Nuru,' Sisi said, tensing.

Nuru stood in the damson shade and took several breaths, their hands on their hips and their head bent. Sisi said their name again and this time they looked up.

'Mother Sea told me,' they said.

Manon looked between them, bewildered. 'What did she tell you, Nuru?'

'Sisi?' Nuru said, another step bringing them into the sun, and their face wrung out Sisi's heart.

This, she thought, *this* was why she had not said, even to herself. Because she could not bear to carry so much hope.

'Sisi-si?' Manon asked, and it was to her that Sisi spoke.

'I am pregnant,' she said quietly. And quietly, again, her life ceased to be her own.

*

She and Manon sat in Manon's house that evening, when everyone walked up to the red cliffs. As the singing faded, the only sounds were gecko calls, fruit bats squabbling in a lychee tree and the slow breathing of the sea, the tide high enough that if she listened carefully, Sisi could hear sand hissing in the backtow.

'Oh, Sisi-si,' Manon said after a while. 'It will be well, you know.'

Sisi looked at her but did not answer. She felt scoured out by the afternoon; by the joy and fury and bustle of the Mothers, the rushed debates about re-cleansing the tomb, the touch of people's hands on her shoulder as withheld pity and withheld hope made their eyes so contradictory it hurt. Endless talk of all the things she must now do, and all the things she must not; of how this was truly Mother Sea confirming Berhane's words in the morning and how childish, how reckless she had been to go up to the tomb with this secreted inside her when she knew what was at stake.

Yes, she wanted to shout, yes, she knew what was at stake.

Her life, *her* life and *her* choices and all the dreams she thought she had surrendered the morning she married Jomo's brother but which had not gone at all, had only lain down beneath expectation and compromise. If Sisi could have said one thing alone to Manon just then in the dark of Manon's house, it would have been this: *Have I not given enough?* Or no, perhaps this: *Just because you want this thing, why must I?*

But how do you say such a thing to a mother who has buried her child? To a mother carrying a second who would also – oh, there were too many ghosts here beside them – a second child who would also likely die.

Doctors had come again, though, and looking into Manon's loved face, Sisi thought, *This time, let it work. For her if for no one else, let the science succeed.* She reached for Manon's hand

and pulled her around, standing behind her to unwind the wrap from her hair. They stayed like that while the village was up at the tombs, and then while everyone was on the beach, watching the drifting lights of the pirogue that bore Nuru and one of the Mothers out to the far side of the lagoon. Sisi smoothed out her friend's dense curls, oiling them, and then as Nuru gave gifts to Mother Sea, she silently rewove Manon's hair, pulling it into tight braids that made Manon wince but only a little, and without a sound.

When a song began again on the shore, they took a deep breath together and unsteadily, and after their long silence this made them both laugh as quietly and as sadly as shorebirds far away.

'Alors, it is done,' Sisi said, and Manon ran her hands through her braids, which were also finished, smiling gently at Sisi in the darkness.

'Tomorrow,' Manon said, kissing the back of Sisi's hand but not understanding at all. 'Tomorrow you start again.'

Chapter Four

Kit

Kit had left his windows open through the long afternoon because the room was an oven, so the constant sea wind had outweighed the sense of falling out into the world. He lay on the floor where the wooden boards held a vestige of coolness, and from there he could see nothing but the room's white walls, ceiling beams, and a trapezoid of sky drifting from blasted cerulean to a pale damson that seemed almost unreal. Then, so rapidly he wondered if he'd fallen asleep, the sky was indigo, stars winking into existence, undrowned by sunset. Someone in the village began to sing, other voices joining in, then a drum and something stringed but odd, all distorted by distance so Kit couldn't make out any words. They sang call and response, the caller's voice a contralto, the responses a chorus that might have been five or fifty strong. As the voices came closer Kit rose to his feet unwittingly, like this was a dream. He stood in the window with the curtains lethargic against his shins and watched torches drift up the path from the village. It *was* a dream, he thought. He'd fallen asleep on the floor and hatched in his mind red-gold flames in woven cones flickering in time with the song, the song in time with the footsteps, figures outlined by firelight and starlight and shapes in the rising smoke that might have been bats if this was real life, but right now in this dream were djinn. He leaned his head against the bricks. Gold-bronze figures, two of them carrying something other than torches, a pallet borne on their shoulders, cloths hanging over it like a bier and on it... on it lay a small figure.

This is me, he thought. Dreaming his own death made pagan, the strange smells and the heat, the drugs turning his broken brain back into children's tales.

This is me, and my longing.

He leaned forward over the sill, straining to keep his dead self in sight as they moved away past the house. But this was a dream, so he could follow. He was bracing his weight, lifting a leg, when the door behind him opened.

'Oh good,' Rachel said.

Kit jerked back, elbow catching the window frame and blood rushing to his head then away again so fast his vision blackened.

'I brought this in case you were awake.' She held out a plate and a glass opaque with condensation, but Kit didn't move. *I'm awake*, he thought sadly. *I'm awake.*

'Did you see them?' Rachel put the food down and came to stand beside him. She smelled of flowers and tea, and Kit stared out at the garden, empty again except for stars. 'It's a funeral, apparently, or velasa, Euan called it. One of the fishermen died.'

Kit turned to stare at her, surprised by how close he'd been after all. A funeral; just not his.

Rachel held his gaze for a moment, and her face fell and softened like she'd seen far too much in his expression. Reaching a hand out to touch his forearm, she said quietly, 'Oh, Kit. Darling. Please come back to us.'

He turned from her and closed his eyes until he heard her walk away.

*

The night swallowed him whole, slow and salt-hot, dreaming of the sea and torchlight until the heat of the morning woke him. At lunch he slipped bare-footed out onto the veranda where Rachel patted the chair beside her and Geo grinned. If only, Kit thought, other people were not exhausting – that was almost the worst bit of all this. There were memories in his head of rugby matches, laughing loudly with friends in bars, unfraught conversations with his parents; odd fragmented flashes of a person he barely recognised.

He remembered an evening, spilling out from a bar, someone saying, 'I'm for bed. Nine o'clock damn lecture tomorrow.' And him slinging an arm around his friend's shoulder, saying,

'Or... the beach. Midnight swim.'

'Or sleep.'

'Or the beach,' he'd repeated.

'The beach,' others had chanted. 'The beach!' And they'd gone, and stripped naked in the city-lit dark of the shoreline, plunged laughing into the high tide, gasping and swearing at the cold, someone asking if sharks were nocturnal, him answering that they were all more beer than blood at this point so no shark would be interested. They'd wandered home afterwards shivering and halfway sober, leaning on each other and talking about girls, of course, about the coming exams, rugby, the exams.

'Why did I ever take law?' he'd moaned. 'Who fucking cares about the law of delict, for Christ's sake?'

'But you're a Benedict,' someone had said with grave pomposity. 'Benedicts do law, young man, otherwise they wouldn't be Benedicts.'

'Yeah,' he'd said. Strange how he could remember his friend's voice so clearly, the familiarity and jostle of them all, but he couldn't remember who had said that. Who had encapsulated his entire upbringing in one beer-tinted sentence.

*

'I'd like you to come to the meeting later, mate,' Geo said, and it took Kit a moment to focus his eyes on his uncle, the drugs in his blood making him oceanic. 'You don't have to do anything, but it'd be handy if you could just watch, all right? Let me know later what you make of it all.'

A black-and-white bird, pert-tailed, hopped a random search pattern across earth and scrappy grass, its head canting this way and that as if everything that had ever existed was vital and important and fascinating.

Rather than slip back into those unwilling memories, Kit said, 'What's it about?' He imagined he was already supposed to know. Still couldn't quite believe he'd come placidly way out into the Indian Ocean, self-stranding on a speck of rock, with no idea why.

'Well...' Geo braced his forearms on the table. 'It's gonna be a bugger, that's for sure. There's their Climate Plan, you know, which is going to be a knotty old problem, but first thing is to get them to give the docs access. From what Euan said, it's a toss-up which one'll be the toughest battle.'

Kit nodded, the words creating more gaps in his understanding than filling them. Climate Plan; he should know about this, then – he should be interested. It had infuriated him how they'd dodged the subject when his parents' home had burned last year. Wildfires and moisture indices, they'd said, and 'bad luck'. But beyond the garden the sea whispered and he spotted another bird sitting among hibiscus flowers the colour of poppies. This one was black with tail feathers so long they bent in the breeze, a blue ring around its eye making it look intent, predatory in a too-beautiful way.

'What's that bird?' he said. Geo frowned, but Rachel turned.

'Oh, gorgeous!' she said. 'Look, Geo, it's a paradise flycatcher. They're endemic.'

Geo made a noise that might have meant anything then turned as someone came up the veranda steps. 'Euan, great timing, mate,' he bellowed. The flycatcher vanished in a blur of wings, its tail feathers tracing sine waves.

Kit tried to concentrate on the talk over lunch, because compliance was camouflage, but also because those gaps in his knowledge were like splinters and even if someone handed him a map now, he couldn't point to where he was.

Euan's fox-like smile and Geo's familiar one were both taut, but the more Kit tried to listen, the less sense it made. Just as he discovered the angle at which it held meaning, he would remember waking in the hospital or his nameless friend's voice.

'I don't get why they aren't welcoming the doctors, though, if I'm honest,' Geo was saying. Kit thought that there were many reasons for not welcoming doctors, and he doubted Geo would understand any of them.

'It is vital we remain aware of the sensitivities,' Euan said, his voice calm and slow. 'This is about trust as much as it is about tradition, sir, regrettably.'

'Geo, Euan. Geo.' Geo leaned back, interlocking his hands on his stomach and Kit watched a bee crawl across the surface of the table, abdomen flexing. Rachel poured more coffee, putting a cup in front of Kit without asking him, adding milk to it and sugar, even though he didn't take either. The bee encountered a droplet of spilled lemonade and uncurled its tongue.

'We need to win the Mothers over,' Euan said. 'Even more than the Sacere. We'll try to speak to them individually afterwards—'

'Shouldn't we do that first? Have them onside before going to the wider public? And why the mothers – oh, do you mean—'

'Yes, the elder Mothers, uppercase.' Euan was rocking a teaspoon back and forth over the finger joints of one hand, beating an almost inaudible timpany on the table. 'Before wouldn't work. They do everything openly so it would look' – setting the spoon aside – 'divisive, covert.'

The bee refurled its tongue, lifted a foreleg to clean an antenna then raised its wings and flew away. Kit tracked it for the distance of the garden, picturing it returning to its hive, sharing the taste of lemons and sugar with its sisters and then dancing them a map. Was it altruism or conjoined joy?

'Everything openly, apart from healthcare and childbirth!' Geo snorted a laugh that might have been contemptuous but was probably not. Kit looked at him with his mind full of honey and sisterhood.

'You can hardly blame them, darling,' Rachel said mildly, holding her coffee below her nose with steam concealing her eyes, and something moved in Kit's ribs like a snake, the taste of pity on his tongue.

'No, love,' Geo said quickly. 'No, of course not.'

You idiot, Kit thought, with a clarity that surprised him.

Euan pushed to his feet. 'On that note, shall we prep the doctors, Geo? See if we can smooth the way.' He smiled, his canines sharp and his eyes reflecting sunlight already reflected off the sea. *Tertiary light*, Kit thought, *folded twice.*

The two men walked away and Rachel began to clear the table then paused. 'Have you been able to check your email?' she said softly.

Kit wanted to tell her he was sorry, but doubted she'd welcome his sympathy.

'Your mum said she'd write.' She stacked one plate onto another with exquisite care. 'I thought email might be easier just now.' The paradise flycatcher returned to his perch, blue-ringed eye watchful, and any answer Kit gave would be wrong. When Rachel touched the back of his hand, he stiffened, but she didn't draw back. 'When you're ready, darling,' she said and rose finally, gathering more plates. He should help her or follow the men, or do something, but the air in his lungs was the temperature of a warm bath and his muscles, for once, weren't aching. The flycatcher fell to the lawn then lifted up again, a cricket within its beak.

Chapter Five

Sisi

The outsiders sat like ghosts within the island hall. It was so easy to forget back here on the island how pale skin could get. With all the screens raised, sunlight and shade turned Sisi's people's skin into satin and mysteries, but made the outsiders oddly double-layered. As if beneath their red noses and smoothed hair, the afternoon light revealed their skulls.

Although Sisi and Manon were not late, or at least no later than most, Nuru had already arrived and when they saw Sisi they rose from the low bench where they had been sitting with the other Sacere – Berhane, Krish and Sable, and Isolde with their wife behind them – and came to sit on the floor beside her. She looked at them cautiously, her hands stilling on the mat where she had begun worrying at a loose fibre.

'In case,' Nuru said, reaching out to tuck a frangipani flower into Sisi's hair, and then a small cloth bundle into her hand. She lifted it to her nose inhaling cloves, salt and the woody tang of pepper. 'Protection?' she said.

Nuru gave her a small, contained smile and said again, 'In case.'

'You have one for Manon also?'

'Of course.'

Looking back down at the bundle, Sisi had to force herself to slip the thing into a pocket rather than fling it away. She ought to be grateful that Nuru wished to safeguard her from the restlessness of the newly dead, or perhaps it was the taint of the outsiders that the amulet was for. Either way it was to protect the kernel of life within her, the cluster of barely differentiated cells that rendered her irrelevant and only secondarily precious.

The bitter salt she smelled would be from a tiny cone shell – there to lend its fierceness, but instead she felt only its slow, poisonous hunger. She watched the outsiders again, thinking of the email she had sent Jomo to tell him about his brother. Thinking that perhaps he was more figment to her now than real, a totem of merciless choices, and a heartbreak that had felt insurmountable but was now only one part of a byzantine tangle of resentment, loneliness, guilt... and now grief.

*

Mama Mandisa spoke, and everyone fell silent. She sat aslant from the strangers, Mama Mathilde beside her. 'We shall listen to the British this morning, and Mother Sea shall listen also, she who sees everything and will guide us to the truth.' She lifted one hand and the bangles on her wrist clattered like the claws of a crab. 'Administrator Benedict,' she said. The coconut trees whispered beyond the hall.

'Thank you, er, Mama Mandisa, and thank *you* all for coming today,' one of the outsiders said unmelodically; not Euan, the assistant whom they knew and almost liked, but the new Administrator. He rose to his feet and the silence tasted of such suspicion that Sisi almost pitied the man the job of telling them what distant experts wanted to do about the... about the tombs and the childless homes.

Not particularly tall, and more solid than perhaps he had once been, he would have been forgettable if not for the way he held himself, as if by assuming he was remarkable, he made you assume so too. He was a natural speaker, though, his hands relaxed and his tone inviting, enthusiastic, talking of how pleased he was to be there and how he hoped to achieve so much working with them. And braced as she was for words like 'tetanus epidemic' and 'medical care', her own name caught Sisi unawares.

'You'll remember that our resident scientist, Sisi Mathilde, *de* Mathilde, sorry, has been sending soil and water samples to the, um, University of Durham for further study.' He scanned the room and Sisi's blood hummed in her ears, but the few furtive glances were not enough for him to locate her. 'Well, I'm afraid the results aren't as positive as we'd hoped, and I'd like to open a discussion with you about the long term, and how to safeguard your community for future generations.'

Sisi felt the seated mass take a tiny, collective inhalation. *Future generations.* Dear Mother, how dared he?

'We have two issues we need to focus on,' the man was saying. *We*, Sisi thought, *we?* He spoke and everyone's eyes showed caverns.

'The first is an acceleration of the Community Migration contingencies in your Climate Plan,' the man said. He clicked a device in his hand, making the image on the screen switch as the projector fan hummed determinedly in the still air. The screen showed smiling children, white houses with green lawns.

Voices rose like the waves of an incoming tide. *Community Migration*, he had said. Sisi thinking confusedly of plovers and lobsters, the yearly arrivals of shearwaters at night, thinking, *What does this have to do with us?* But Manon gripped her hand; people were shifting noisily and Nuru was staring at their fellow Sacere across the hall, and finally Sisi remembered.

Migration.

'But we have decades,' Manon was saying, 'Sisi-si, n'est-ce pas?' Nuru touched her shoulder then crossed the hall, the other Sacere also moving towards the Mothers, a gathering of leaders, and everyone leaning towards them saying in a hundred different ways, No. *That was only a last resort!* And, *We are managing this, we can survive this, they cannot make us go!* And, plaintively, angrily, *Why now?*

The Administrator was trying to throw his voice over them all and Euan was speaking to him without rising from his chair, and Sisi could not seem to gather her thoughts.

*

It was all of course already known. They could all see the yellowing of the crops; they had all seen patches of their reef turn white. And they had of course taken advice and taken steps. Investments and renewables, Sisi's own artificial reefs, flood barriers, shoreline planting. *Leaving* only ever far away and worst-case – not this year, not this decade.

It had not once occurred to Sisi, even being the one who ran the data, that the Administrator would be here for this. Walking through the village to the hall she and Manon had not even talked about the reason for his visit, because they had assumed, everyone had assumed, that it was about the babies, perhaps also about trade but mostly a cursory, courtesy visit to acknowledge the epidemic. To support the doctors once again coming in the hope of solving it.

*

Sisi found her voice because Manon's hand in hers was trembling. 'They cannot make us, Manon. It is some bureaucratic nonsense only. We do not need to leave – we are safe.'

But the two doctors were still sitting at the end of the hall with their heads bent together and Manon's great stomach was a reminder that *safety* was not a thing that they had anymore, not really. Because without a future, what was a nation, an island, a village, a person, if not only a collection of endings?

'They cannot make us,' Sisi repeated, and Luc came over from where he had been sitting to take Manon's other hand in his, rubbing a palm over her shoulder with his eyes furious.

'This is our home,' Manon whispered.

'It is only talk,' Luc said. 'You know outsiders are like this, and politics, and this is both. We have our Climate Plan and this is only talk. The Mothers will chase them off, n'est-ce pas?'

'And the doctors?' Manon said. 'What about them?'

Sisi looked over at them. Behind the Sacere, the woman doctor had spotted Manon and Sisi knew she was thinking Subject A, even if only unconsciously. But her face was alert and clever and Sisi examined it and thought that yes, surely here was enough hope to save Manon's heart.

'We will...' Luc hesitated, himself looking to the Mothers and Sacere. 'We will see what the Mothers decide,' he said.

A response perched on Sisi's tongue, one that Antonin would have disagreed with, and all her labyrinthine emotions at his death choked her until she thought she might heave. So she stayed silent, thinking, Where is he now? The man who had fathered this tiny nebula within her? How could he lodge himself within her when they had shared so little, and how could he, even after his own death, still parameterise her life? But then Manon moved and Sisi tightened her hand.

Sisi heard, just, Administrator Benedict say, 'If we could all...'

Mama Mandisa touched a hand to Mama Anouk's shoulder and turned to face the room. 'My family,' she said, having barely to raise her voice for everyone to hear her and fall silent. 'My family,' she repeated. 'We will tread carefully so that the rocks do not cut our feet, yes? We will learn what Administrator Benedict has to say...'

He came to stand beside her.

'...but not today,' Mama Mandisa continued, her eyes reflective, and Sisi knew that she had heard the outsider move. 'Go home, talk to your ancestors, to each other. The meeting is finished.'

Administrator Benedict half-raised a hand but then dropped it again, giving a wry, resigned smile as he turned towards the others, the two doctors, his assistant, Euan, and the fourth man who had not spoken. Sisi ignored Euan, even though he was the one she spoke to about research and collaborations, because she wanted to watch the doctors instead, measure their competency and determination. And what of the other man? Sisi tried to study him, assign him degrees of hope, but between moving bodies she could only assemble him patchwork. Long legs too thin and pale as the bones of whales, downcast face, hair falling into his eyes and too-long nose, the angle of his shoulders speaking such constrained fatigue that it was a marvel he was upright at all. No, she thought, he does not matter. Manon's salvation could not lie within someone so weary.

The crowd thinning, Manon pulled Sisi away, saying, 'Sisi-si, come on. You asked me to help with setting up your data logger things, yes? Come away.' She was right, and also if Luc was going back out fishing tonight then Manon would want to be finished before the tide. But just at the edge of the hall, her feet in the afternoon sun and her face still in shade, Sisi looked back over her shoulder, searching for the doctors but finding that fourth man again, watching her.

'Oh,' she said. His eyes were sea glass and hopelessness, and recognition fell through her as if she had leaped from high rocks into the sea.

*

In the afternoon-battened shade outside her house, Sisi lined up all four buoys, batteries loaded into their compartments, covers peeled from solar panels, and then listened as Manon read aloud from their instructions.

'To calibrate the DO_2 meter – Sisi-si, what on earth is that? – access meter settings, then reset. Ready? Yes? So then, when screen reads a flashing *oo.oo*, insert the probe into control...' Manon's voice drifted to a stop and Sisi looked up from her position bent over the equipment.

'You are well?' she asked quickly. How did they come to this? Always one step away from heartbreak.

'Yes,' Manon said, smoothing a hand over her stomach because she knew exactly what had been in Sisi's mind. 'Yes, it is only... They are really wanting us to leave? Why now, when before they did not?'

Sisi leaned back. Nearby a cricket was calling, amplified by the walls. They had talked themselves silent about this in the hour after the meeting, and been pretending not to think of it since. 'Yesterday I heard there is no more funding for the soil analyses,' she said. 'Convenient, n'est-ce pas? That I hear this just as the outsiders come with this... *acceleration.*'

'It is not happening so fast, though. Are we not...' Lifting out a hand in a gesture that said, *Look, look at all the life, and the beauty, the two hundred shades of green. How can this possibly be dying?*

'It is not only from the storms, though,' Sisi said. 'We know this. The soil would perhaps recover from them, but it is the groundwater. Those core samples we drilled – there is salt coming in from underneath, through the rock. There will come a day when the wells are not pure.'

'Mother Sea coming up underneath us,' Manon said, half-laughing, half not. 'But that day is not here. We still get a harvest. We are building more reef, planting trees.'

'Yes. And there are crops being bred for salt tolerance,' Sisi said. She had checked, last year and then again, and again, watching the slow trickle of research papers appearing online like promises. 'We could contact the scientists, volunteer for trials. We have our Climate Plan and people will help us, outsiders. Not everyone will agree with this one man.' But he was not just one man. She did not say this.

Manon's eyes tilted upwards at the corners when she smiled. 'Yes, you will find us our answers and we will stay,' she said, hands on her stomach, running her palms over the patterns of her wrap.

'Yes,' Sisi said again. She would make it true. Her knowledge and her work enough to tip the balance; justify everything she'd given up, allow Manon to carry hope like a beacon with her heart so obstinately tender. And the doctors, too, were forearmed this time, so were poised surely to prove Sisi's convictions and Manon's faith.

She heard the shuffle-step of Mama Mandisa making her slow, sure way towards them.

'Children,' Mama Mandisa said, and they both replied so that she knew where they were as well as whom. Sisi rose to take Mama Mandisa's hand in her own, kissing her cheek and then helping her to sit on the empty chair. Manon retrieved a glass and poured out juice that the children had made after school, and Mama Mandisa drank it long and slow, as if all the pleasures of her life were distilled into this one taste.

'Ah,' she said, resting the glass on her knee and tilting her head as Sisi settled on the ground beside her laptop, close to it but not touching. 'Ah, now. We must talk, Sisi de Mathilde.'

'Mama,' she said, and waited. Manon leaned back in her chair and closed her eyes. She was not sleeping well, Sisi knew, and today was become such a long day.

'These buoys that you want to put on the reefs...' Mama Mandisa looked at the hulking shapes, perhaps seeing a mass of unnatural orange, perhaps seeing nothing but smelling their complex alienness the way a shark might smell blood. 'I think that we should not put them out, Sisi child, not at this time. I think that Mother Sea may not like being measured and watched and tested in this way, now.'

Antonin. Sisi fought a flinch, curling her hands in her lap.

'We need them,' she said carefully. 'To monitor the reef and the trials better. We agreed when I was writing the proposals. Nine months ago.'

'Yes, yes we did.' Mama Mandisa took another drink then held the glass out. Sisi took it and set it in the sand just beyond the edge of the mat. 'But we agreed to the measuring of our wells, our tides and soil also, and see now how that is turned against us.'

Guilt coiled in Sisi's stomach. It was she who had requested permission, and she who had gathered the data. 'It is not like that,' she said, reaching out to touch the nearest buoy with her fingertips. 'It is all... I'm doing it to help us stay.'

'What if your studies show that the new reefs fail, or that our reefs are dying the way the Barrier Reef is dying?' Mama Mandisa said implacably. 'Will this not let the outsiders say to us, *Your land is poisoned and your fish are dying – there is nothing to keep you here anymore?*'

'Mama,' Manon said, surprising Sisi, 'the things Sisi-si does are good for us, I think.' She leaned awkwardly forward to take Mama Mandisa's bent hand in hers. 'We need the truths, so that we can judge for ourselves, yes? And also, it is good to say, *Look, we are neither naive nor helpless; we know all of the challenges we are facing and we are taking action, and we are not afraid.* N'est-ce pas?'

'We are not afraid,' Mama Mandisa repeated slowly, rubbing her thumb back and forth over Manon's knuckles. 'Sisi child, do you too think this is true, that the knowledge from your work will help us?'

Sisi did not answer straight away, knowing that Mama Mandisa wanted honesty, not conviction. 'Yes, Mama,' she said eventually. 'Even when the truths are hard, it is only by knowing them that we can try to change them.' She hesitated, then added, 'The outsiders can help us, yes? I would do nothing to risk our home.'

'Mmm-hmm,' Mama Mandisa said, releasing Manon's hand and touching Sisi's hair briefly. 'Even though you still wish to leave?'

Sisi recoiled. 'I know, child. I know,' Mama Mandisa said, pushing herself to standing with the aid of her stick and a grunt. 'But I do not believe things are as simple as you wish them to be. Ah, well. This is anyway bigger than one woman's wishes – Mother Sea is troubled and there are storms ahead.' She shook her head, the knot of her hair unmoving, and began to walk away.

Sisi and Manon watched her, and when she paused beneath the lychee tree to look back at them, her voice was soft and fierce all at once. 'Remember your pregnancy, Sisi. You live by the fadys now more than ever.'

'Yes, Mama,' Sisi said. A day gecko as long as her forearm moved around the trunk of the tree into the sun, red spots along its green sides and a black stripe through its eye. They were the keepers of secrets, the geckos, always watching, gathering up all the things she had not said. 'The fadys,' she whispered with enough bitterness that Manon threw a shell at her.

'Hush. They are our protection,' Manon said. 'They are to protect the babe.'

They do not work, Sisi thought, the blasphemy searing her as if all the salt in her body had become needles.

Chapter Six

Kit

After the meeting, Kit had drifted away from the others and down onto the beach. The sand beneath his feet was half-molten, heat so viscous he had to lean into it as he walked, fire on neck and forearms, calves and thighs. But he'd rather this searing light than slinking behind his uncle back through the village, watched by people who so patently didn't want them here.

It added another layer to the mystery. What was he supposed to do here on an island he didn't know, with people who didn't want him?

Kit's feet followed the tideline, finding comfort in its linearity, its illusion of destination. Shells and bone-branched coral shifted against his sandals; a crab sprinted sideways away from him, long-eyed. Up ahead those boats he'd seen before were pulled up to the trees, strange wooden things with single outriggers and white sails wrapped around the stubby masts. A world removed from the sleek and shining yachts his father had taught him and Charlie to sail, but perfect here, as much a part of the sweep of the bay as the trees and the sand. His fingers twitched, furling around the memory of sheets slipping cold and wet within his grip, around the memory of joy. He looked from the boats to his empty hands, baffled by how unfamiliar he was to himself.

Perhaps, he thought, they'd sent him here kindly, understanding that he just wanted to sleep without judgement and until the world ended. Or perhaps they'd sent him here to give inevitability free rein.

He knew even while thinking it that it wasn't true. More, that it was unfair, however much his parents wanted him and his failings hidden away. *When you're ready*, Rachel had said, about emailing them. But if they cared how he was, why had they sent him here?

If he squinted against the glare, he could see cliffs rising in a half circle around the village, huge and rust-red in the east, then forested and lowering westward until behind the island hall they became simply a ridge, stretching out into the sea. The peak in the east was where they had gone, he thought, the three islanders. In the burning day, and then by firelight they had climbed those red, precipitous rocks. Cliffs, he thought.

Oh god, *cliffs*.

His eyes were watering with the light, and he started walking again, seeing benedictions and thinking, please, please.

Not a full thought, not pictured or made into words, just a feeling in his stomach and the empty expanses of his lungs. Second chances, silences. Hope.

*

Could he do it that way, here? He didn't know, he didn't know. Certainty stolen by drugs or apathy, the sun liquefying his muscles – and this seemed a lower place to be than before. At least then he'd had purpose. Faith that if he could just see this one act through then everything that was too much would no longer matter and the world would spin on without a murmur, either to die itself, or not.

A small flock of terns lifted off the sand ahead of him, becoming indistinguishable against the sky. The back of his neck and the gaps in his sandals were scalding. He imagined the sunlight like a weapon, searing through cell walls, making his skin a layer of tiny, individual mortalities. He imagined clifftops and veered down over rippled white sand towards the sea. It was cold against his hot feet, the cool of a first sip of beer or a distant cloud, and then quickly, sensuously, some perfect temperature that was wholly inviting.

'Oh,' Kit said, and his voice unfathomably reminded him of the woman in the hall, the one who had walked up to the cliffs clutching flowers. She'd had a flower in her hair today too, petals like cream and honey, and she'd looked surprised to see him, as if she knew him but had thought he was very far away.

'Oh,' he said again, as the sea licked his ankles, gathering itself beneath his heels. The terns wheeled overhead then off across the water. There were islets over there, he saw, squinting against the light; perhaps that was where they nested. He moved forward until the water reached his knees, tiny black-striped fish parting around his legs. The birds and the water, they reminded him of another time, a moment sat on the soughing deck of a boat watching seabirds diving like thrown swords; a pod of dolphins passing by, cresting the waves then vanishing again so completely it was easy to believe you had imagined them. That was the moment he'd known he was going to change degrees, watching those dolphins with a surge of joy and fascination and... desperation. He'd nearly said it aloud then, turned to his parents and told them that he hated law, with all its machinations, that he wanted to become someone who could fight for a better future, not sit at a desk exonerating failure. But the dolphins had surfaced again and he'd only watched them, holding the decision to himself like a rising star.

How blindingly optimistic he'd been. So full of relief at his own revelation that he hadn't braced himself for their reaction, not really, not as much as he should have done. Perhaps it would have made a difference if he had. The fish at his feet darted away then back again, forming patterns that verged on the edge of meaning. He could duck beneath the surface to watch them, he thought; he could swim out deeper and... and what?

What was he meant to be here? A tourist splashing aimlessly in the sea, or an accomplice in his uncle's work, a sideline errand boy? Or was he here, between the sea and the cliffs, to be set free? His chest ached and he stepped back quickly out of the waves. Off to his right, two children dashed between houses and onto the sand. They saw him and waved thin arms, then hurled themselves high-kneed through the shallows before diving sleek as otters. Kit walked away past the boats, wanting to pause and run his hands over their salt-smoothed hulls, but scared to do so. As if the memory of sailing was more dangerous than the presence of the cliffs.

He wanted to ask the woman what she'd recognised in him. She here in flowers and cheap cotton; he come from privilege, certainty... uncertainty, invisibility. The thought of being *seen* startled him, of being *known* at all – it was like having a secret note folded into your palm.

It was an assurance, he decided, her coming from the cliffs and recognising him. Her, and the funeral held in the dark. He reached the shade of three wide-canopied trees and felt the separation of sun and shadow like a knife skimming over his skin, like an exhalation. Something moved in the branches, but as he looked up, a voice called his name.

Rachel. Of course it was Rachel. He wanted to resent her coming back along the path towards him, her neat hair and expensive sunglasses, her sheer collectedness where he was uncollected, ungathered. But the animosity didn't come. Perhaps it required more energy than he had to give, especially with the cliffs hovering in his mind like a bird.

'There you are, Kit, dear.' She scanned him quickly. 'You went down to the shore? Unbelievable, isn't it? I feel like I've...'

Kit smiled, or thought he did. *Died*, he finished for her, *and gone to heaven.*

'So what did you think of the meeting?' she carried on quickly, turning to fall in with him as he walked through burnished shade. 'Geo feels a little frustrated, as you might imagine.'

He glanced at her, the trees and the sunlight reflecting from her glasses like an inkblot painting. The sea murmured on their right and two chickens were scratching around the base of a palm tree, ignoring them. They'd passed the last of the village houses now, so even if he hadn't escaped Rachel, he was at least unwatched by strangers.

'They don't want us here,' he said, because she honestly seemed to be waiting for an opinion, although he had no idea why that was. He hadn't been sent here for that.

She tilted her head, watching a butterfly weave a drunken path past them. He wondered if she knew what it was, or had brought a book to help her find out. He didn't ask.

'No, they don't, do they? Or at least, they're very wary. I suppose they're right to be.' She sighed, then shook her head as if by that alone she could cast off the thought. 'Anyway, you don't need to worry about all that. You're here to relax. We should go swimming once the heat has died down a bit – what do you think?'

But then the trees ended in a flurry of red flowers and they were in the garden, Geo and Euan sitting on the veranda, both turning to watch them approach.

'Ah, there you are. Thought you'd got yourself lost.' Geo laughed, and Kit slipped past them towards the doorway. 'Think they'll go for it, Kit? Our plan?'

Kit turned and looked at him blankly. *Which plan? The doctors or the…*

'I reckon we can convince them to agree to the relocation, or climate migration or – what are we calling it? I can never remember.' Looking at Rachel and then saying, 'Community migration.'

Euan sipped at a cup of tea, its steam barely visible in the scalding air.

'I don't know,' Kit said blankly. He wrapped one hand around the doorframe, one step away from solitude and yet unable to quite make himself move, as if he was waiting for permission.

'I don't suppose any of us thought it would be easy,' Rachel said, pouring Euan more tea, resting her fingertips on the cafetiere then pouring coffee for herself.

The line of her nose was just a little burned, Kit realised, although probably not as much as his own. An anticipatory pain swarmed his skin and he blinked away the spots swimming across his vision. *Sleep*, he thought. He wanted to sleep and drift and dream of kelp forests and black-eyed seals.

Geo snorted softly. 'The economics of it will make sense to them, once they've got over the shock.'

'That may not carry much water, I'm afraid,' Euan said. 'It's the inevitability that will have to be the clincher, and the promise of keeping community integrity. I would present it as simply an acceleration of their own plans, with the benefit of better access to healthcare. I'd keep repeating that, sir.'

The inevitability, Kit thought. Yes, yes – that was what would carry him now.

Chapter Seven

Sisi

Euan and the new Administrator met Sisi on the shoreline as she waited for Luc to take her new buoys out to the reef. She stood with her hand resting on the bright flank of a buoy and even though she liked Euan, talking to him felt different today, either because of the man with him, or because of herself.

'Sisi de Mathilde,' Euan said, smiling slightly. 'All is well with you?'

'All is well,' she replied. 'And with you?' Unfairly resenting how he spoke her words as if she did not know theirs.

'Quite, thank you.' He half-turned, lifted a hand briefly. 'May I introduce George Benedict? Sir, this is Sisi de Mathilde, the scientist.'

The scientist. Pride, and longing.

'A pleasure,' the Administrator said, his pale eyes squinting against the light, fine sweat on his forehead. He reached out a hand towards her, but the fady on her forbade contact with outsiders so Sisi shifted uneasily, keeping her back straight and her hands at her sides. He glanced at Euan and Euan gave him a tiny nod. 'I've heard good things about you, of course.' But what had they said of her? Praise or condescension? Did they see her as an ally just as Mama Mandisa saw her as complicit?

'I saw you at the meeting,' she said. She wanted to tell them what the buoys by her side were for, to explain the work her people were doing to save themselves. But the data were not yet ready and she refused to give them reasons with which to dismiss her.

The Administrator tucked his hand into his pocket as if it had not been spurned. 'I wanted to ask if you would meet with us, actually, and the Mothers and... and the...'

'Sacere,' Euan said softly.

'Yes, yes, Sacere. I hope your training might allow you to interpret the information for the others better than we can.'

Interpret the need for relocation? He did think her an ally, then. He thought she knew enough science to be useful yet not enough to prove him wrong. That her position made her automatically a traitor to her people and her home. Luc would be here soon and Sisi pulled herself straighter.

'If the Mothers ask for my help, then of course I will help them,' she said. 'We would be interested to see your analyses and compare them to our own.' And maybe her qualifications paled against his, but this was still her part in the whole. One of her parts. Luc appeared behind Euan. 'I am sorry, Administrator – I have work to do.' She smiled again and Euan winced.

She turned, walking towards Luc, who ignored them completely.

*

They sailed without speaking beyond a few words, until Luc said, 'Ici?' with the GPS in his left hand, his right letting the pirogue's sail slacken.

Sisi checked the position and nodded. 'Perfect.' Looking over the low side of the boat she could see reef a few metres down, the movement of fish blurred and refracted by the swell. One last check of the buoy, then she and Luc between them lowered it over the side. Sisi followed it into the water, accepted the coils of anchor rope from Luc, took a few deep breaths and inverted herself, pushing downwards, the weight of the anchors helping. It wasn't essential to set the anchors in place by hand, and she was meant to wear a tank, but today more than ever she wanted her presence here to be as gentle as possible.

Antonin in her mind, she swam among angel fish, a stonefish only half cryptic against old corals, trigger fish and a slowly curious peacock grouper. In between the branches of a fan coral, two glass shrimps wove their elaborate legs in the current and Sisi reached a finger out to give a message they might pass on and on again through the sea. She tried to summon the memory of Antonin's smile, but could think only of tangled weights and ropes floating, the mercury of rising air bubbles. Her husband's face evaded her; his eyelashes in sleep, the contours of his arms – they were already slipping from her grip as if she had never in their three years together looked at him fully.

A ray larger than herself rose over a ridge of reef and passed so close that its slow wing brushed her leg and Sisi smiled, choosing to read comfort in that touch rather than fearless chance. Perhaps farewells from Antonin, or forgiveness. Or was this not him but Mother Sea, making promises? Making promises, or asking for them?

Sisi hung motionless in the embrace of the water watching the ray. If she did not swim at all, the currents would dash her against the reef. The sea demanded effort; it was not a passive thing. So why, she thought, should her children be?

*

When she hauled herself back into the boat, water streaming from her skin, the first thing Sisi said was, 'Luc, what will you and Manon do about the doctors?'

He did not reply immediately, studying the GPS again, pulling on ropes so that the pirogue heeled and began slipping forward towards the next deployment spot. Sisi almost regretted the way she had asked, but then remembered the ray's touch, so she waited, wringing oceans from her hair.

'It is Manon's choice,' Luc said eventually. 'But they could not help last time.'

The sea sang against the sides of the boat and Luc's eyes were full of Manon's face. Sisi's hands were switching the next buoy on, yet her attention was on her friend. 'Things change,' she said. 'You know this. New research, new medicines.'

The buoy's electronics activated, but she ignored it. The wind tugged at them, making Luc shift his weight.

'The Sacere think we must have faith in Mother Sea,' he said slowly. 'That we must solve these things ourselves or... no longer *be* ourselves, no?'

'It is not faithlessness,' she said, 'to need technology from outside to fight climate change, or a disease that has mutated beyond our drugs.'

'I do not know, Sisi.' He closed his eyes for the length of a wave then opened them again. 'I know only that Mother Sea took your husband just as you found you were carrying his babe. That surely means something, n'est-ce pas? It must.'

But Manon's babe would be the next one born. In a week, perhaps, and then it would begin again. Counting the days, the hours, the minutes; measuring the strength of their feeding, the volume of each cry. How were they going to bear it? How did you endure such a thing once, let alone again and again?

Luc misinterpreted her silence. 'I am here,' he said quietly. 'I know your sorrow. I miss him too.'

The pirogue skipped and her heart lurched and she shook her head. Antonin had been older than the four of them – Luc and Manon, her and Jomo – returning from high school the very year they all started it, so he had been almost a stranger when they in turn had finally returned. Perhaps that had made it easier to marry him in a way, despite his relationship to Jomo.

'He was proud of you.'

Her head jerked up and she frowned at Luc's averted face. He corrected one of the ropes, and although she felt no difference, that meant little. He and the pirogue were almost chimeric.

'He talked about this.' Luc nodded at the buoy. 'He was proud of you for doing it.'

'Mama Mandisa wanted me to stop,' she said, because she did not wish to talk about Antonin, not out here, not to Jomo's closest friend.

Luc grinned at her unexpectedly. 'No, she did not. If she wished for you to stop, you would not be here now. She only wished for you to think about whether you should.'

And for a moment, with both of them smiling, it was easy to forget everything other than a thousand childhood memories of believing you were defying Mama Mandisa only to later be disillusioned. Then Luc bent forward to check the GPS, glanced up at the angle of the sun, and the moment was gone.

'He would have wished you to take care. Most especially now.'

A gull cried overhead and as if in answer, plovers rose up from a sandbank, alarm calling.

'There is no danger,' Sisi said. It was true. She did not want to think about what she might choose even if there *were* a danger in doing this.

Luc glanced at her, frowned, then looked back to the sea. 'I did not mean diving with the babe. I meant the outsiders and... I meant only that he would have been wary of them, yes?'

Sisi hissed in a quiet breath. 'Even the doctors? Even now?'

He shrugged uncomfortably. 'Mother Sea must have her reasons. I trust her more than I do outsiders who have already failed us half a dozen ways.'

With the sea evaporating from her skin Sisi was cold, and wanted only to slip back beneath the waves. Away from the look in Luc's eyes, and the presence of her own anger. But she could not help herself: 'And if Mother Sea is waiting for us to *seek* answers? If she means for us to look for them beyond here?' Gesturing out over the teal-blue lagoon to the great mass of their island, their houses, their entire people.

'Then it is people like you who will find them, Sisi. Not me. What can a fisherman and a farmer discover other than that the harvests are poor and the storms are crueller? What can a father do other than hope?'

Fight, she wanted to shout. *We can fight.*

But he loosened the sail and said, 'Voilà, we are here.' And seeing the expression on his face she said nothing, only took the anchor ropes up from the floor of the boat to slide noiselessly into the water. Sea surrounded her again, the cries of the birds vanishing, ropes slapping wood, Luc's faith.

Chapter Eight

Sisi

The next day, anyone with time was helping to prepare nato dye for the screens that were being woven to replace worn ones in the island hall. Sisi, with Nuru, was tying strips of bark into small bundles, building a pile that would see them through the eight days of boiling and reboiling the dye pots until the water was a red that hung between sunsets and blood. Others were burning cactus down to a fine ash, and the sun was fierce but the work in the shade was easy and no one minded the smoke because it kept the flies away.

Sisi wished she'd gone up to her lighthouse, though. Agathe and Mahena had their heads bent together over the ash pile, whispering words that Sisi did not need to hear because the sidelong lozenges of their eyes slipped her way too often to be mistaken. It was not, she thought, any accident that she and Nuru were working just a little separately from the others.

'What are they saying of me, Nuru?' she asked eventually, her fingers struggling to pull the twine tight enough around the bundle in her palms. 'Is it about the soil core data?'

Nuru looked up at her then back down to their hands. Sisi could not interpret the expression on their face.

'Do people say that I am... on *their* side, the outsiders' side, because I do my job? It helps us, Nuru, and it was not our *knowledge* that salted the soil—'

'No?'

'Pardon?' Sisi stared at her sibling until Nuru sighed and looked up.

'You are so sure that it was not your... our meddling that turned Brother Island against us?'

'Yes—'

'Because we have never driven cores deep into the earth before, or tried to build our own reefs. I worry, sister, that it was wrong of us to do so.' Nuru threw a glance over their shoulder at the others. 'But if so, then it is the whole of us at fault, yes? And no one blames you.'

'Yes they do.' Again looking over to the two women sieving ashes into the dyeing pots, meeting Mahena's eyes and seeing the way her cheeks sucked in against her teeth. Bitterness coiled upwards through Sisi's lungs like smoke, but then it was gone because Mahena had borne three babies in the last eight years, and Agathe had borne two, and only Katura had lived.

They were two of very few who had continued to try. There was immense courage in that.

'They are not talking about this, Sisi,' Nuru said eventually, reaching out to remove a hermit crab from the mat, straightening the pile of bark bundles although they did not need it.

'Alors—'

'They talk of Antonin.' A flicker of shadows in Nuru's eyes. Sisi's heart beat an irregular pulse but Nuru had not finished. 'Sister, they say that he would wish you to stop your job, now that you are...' They made a gesture that was both full of sorrow and cautionary.

Oh Mother, Sisi thought, *how can you do this?*

'They say too that this is the second time Mother Sea has taken your closest kin from you, and perhaps this holds meaning.'

Sisi closed her eyes and wondered whether it hurt them, to be so cruel.

'I do understand,' Nuru said.

'Do you?' Sisi watched their dual hands dually tying bundles with twine, Nuru's a little lighter than her own, their fingers stronger.

'I know that you and my brother fitted well, even if you did not find together the happiness that everyone hoped for you.'

Did you hope for happiness, Sisi thought, unfairly and sadly, *or did you only hope for children?* But Antonin's absence was as vast here as it was in their house and Sisi did not know how to navigate it; besides, he was not here to defend himself, so she had to.

'We were friends,' she said.

Silences full of strange compassion, making love while avoiding one another's eyes.

'I wrote to Jomo,' she added eventually.

A sand lizard skipped from the bole of a tree onto their mat, head bobbing, ignoring them completely as if they, mountainous, were a landscape without souls. Nuru was watching the lizard too, but not for messages. The geckos with their secrets and the skinks with Mother Sea's wishes, the rays and the cuttlefish and so many others might give them. But not this little thing built purely of aggression and speed.

'Will he come?'

'I do not know.' He had not replied. She understood, of course. He was a thousand miles from home; her words in an email would need time to become truth to him. She told herself that she understood and yet this was their first contact in the three years since her marriage to his brother. When he first saw her name, what did his heart do? Did it fear, knowing what it would take to make her reach out? Did it fear, or did it not?

The thought was pointless and far too old. Sisi willed it silent.

'He should come,' Nuru said. 'He is needed here.'

'Not enough to make him stay,' Sisi said before she could stop herself. She winced at her hands, pulled the twine tight over her fingers. If it had been Manon here, she would have touched Sisi's hand, said something about Jomo being feckless. It would have hurt despite being meant as praise that Sisi chose her people over the outside. But then, Jomo had not been asked to do that – he had only been asked to choose Sisi.

Nuru studied her face, but she could not look at them.

'He is not like your father. He will return.'

Sisi nodded wordlessly. Her father had left in search of work when she was seven; she heard from him perhaps once a year, often less, and his face in her mind was a mutedly fond blur of shining browns. Whereas Jomo's face was as clear as a photograph and too painful to look at.

'You should ask Mother Sea to bring Jomo safely home. Rum and rice at the next high tide.'

She set her tied bundle aside, reached for more bark, wanted to say, *Why me? Why not you?* But did not, because this was the Sacere asking, and not the sibling; Mother Sea's chosen weighing Sisi's faith.

'I will,' she said. Even if neither belief nor hope were enough to make her, the familiarity of compliance was.

Nuru nodded. 'The others – they have asked me to be the people's Voice.'

Sisi wrenched herself back from far away.

'Oh,' she said, smiling. 'For the talks with the Administrator? This is wonderful, Nuru. You will be wonderful.' But she wondered as she spoke if the other Sacere were giving Nuru this responsibility as a distraction from grief.

'The Administrator is wrong, you know?' she said. 'In saying that we must leave. There are many more things we can do to help us stay.' They had tied up the last of the bark, and soon the dye pots would be ready, but Sisi made no move to rise. 'And if they do not help us then others will. N'est-ce pas?'

'What I think no longer matters, sister,' Nuru said, brushing the mat clear of debris and the ever-gathering sand. 'If I am the Voice, I am the wishes of the whole, not my own.'

'But your own count as part of our whole.'

Nuru's eyes drifted over her shoulder towards the sea. 'And yet I have no idea what to do,' they said very softly, then frowned and said more loudly, as if they had not meant her to hear, 'I am Sacere, and now the Voice. That is what is needed of me.'

No, Sisi thought, *no, I need* you *more than I need the Sacere, Nuru. You, Antonin's sibling.* But she said only, gently, 'So what are our wishes?'

Nuru took a long slow breath that lifted their collarbones. 'I feel we are a long way away from being together on this,' they said. 'Everyone has different ways of seeing their fears or their angers.' A tiny stumble over the last word, and Sisi thought, *Et bien, so they* are *blaming me, some of them.*

'But everyone wants to stay.' It was not a question. 'So we show this Administrator that we are adapting.'

Nuru's lips twitched and they looked over to the fire, the people sitting there, the radio a tinny undertone.

'Nuru?'

They shook their head a little and said, 'We need time to think.'

'And information.'

Nuru gave her a wry smile and Sisi saw Antonin in the line of cheek and jaw and mouth. 'You will obey the fadys, yes?' they asked instead of answering.

'Of course.'

'Really?' Nuru asked, and if it had been another Sacere, or one of the Mothers, then she would have hidden her annoyance better.

'Of course, yes.' She would not touch any man who was unknown to her. She would not eat shellfish or shark, or drink the dense, dark rum. She would not go beyond the reefs; she would not eat tern eggs or climb the coconut trees. She would not use iron tools or speak the names of the newly dead, and she would not go into the tombs, not again. Sisi shifted under Nuru's quiet gaze and sighed. She would not go out under the new moon, nor would she walk in another's shadow. She would not raise her voice in anger nor shed her blood for the sea.

'But, Nuru,' she said eventually, her voice sadder than she had hoped, 'we can do more for Manon. We must, yes? She cannot... We must stop *resigning* ourselves.'

'Those are the fadys for pregnancy. Manon has abided by them and you must also.'

'I do not mean the fadys.'

Nuru's mouth opened but then shut again and they rose to their feet, bending to gather up the nato bundles then straightening, their eyes squinting with the light. 'Come,' they said.

They set the bundles beside the dye pots and Nuru murmured something to the women there, then Sisi followed them down to the sea, unfinished words like a tether. As the tide was falling, they cut across wet sand with their heels leaving tiny pools in their wake, and only when they were halfway across to the island hall, furthest from land, did Nuru speak again.

'You must not talk like this, Sisi,' they said, and Sisi realised how much hope she had imbued into that long silence. 'Like you did to Luc yesterday. Like you do not believe.'

'Why? We reject the doctors and the help they offer, and instead we tell Manon not to love her children because they may die?'

'Sisi.'

They were walking beside one another, their strides matched so that from a distance it must have looked like harmony. Sisi's jaw muscles ached. 'What if Mother Sea wishes us to—'

'Stop,' Nuru interrupted. 'Why did Mother Sea choose to save us, Sisi?'

Sighing, because the teacher in Nuru brought out the child in her. 'Because we trusted her. But Nuru, she provides us with food and safety because we work for it – we go out to fish, we farm the island. And we have taken in things from outside to help us before...' Seeing Nuru shake their head, Sisi rushed on: '...goats and wheat, and medicines. We go away for high school, we use the tele-medical support, the internet. Solar panels, the well pumps. We have accepted these things, sought them out, so why not also help from the doctors? This is no different.'

Nuru stopped walking and turned to face her, the sun catching their face slantwise so that one eye appeared tawny and the other black. 'Perhaps it is because we accepted these things that Mother Sea is angry with us.' They must have seen all of Sisi's arguments in her face because they sighed and in the space of that breath became just a person again, not a role. As worried and tired and heartbroken as everyone else. 'I do not know, sister. I do not know. But the doctors came before, and they failed us. Mother Sea is everything – our faith in her is all we have to make sense of our... our lives. If we lose that faith, we also lose ourselves.'

They had lifted their hands in a kind of entreaty and now studied their own palms as if looking for answers there, or as if remembering all the tiny bodies they had wrapped and blessed and bid farewell to. Did Nuru know, Sisi wondered, how alike their hands were to Antonin's?

Reaching out to take one of those hands in her own, Sisi said, 'It is not losing faith, Nuru. It is not. Manon is so close and it is possible that they can treat the tetanus this time. That her babe would then live. How could Mother Sea resent us this? I cannot believe she is so cruel.'

'And if the babe would have lived, but died because the outsiders tainted it?'

Nuru's hand in hers weighed oceans. 'That is so very unlikely,' she said, but why did this argument sound weak when it was founded on numerical risk and probability and logic? *Faith has no truck with numbers*, she thought, *and neither does fear.*

'Do not do it,' Nuru said. 'You must act as one of us, Sisi, not as yourself. We are *one people* – do not divide us at such a time as this. It is not fair to anyone, but least of all to Manon.' They released her hand and began to walk again.

Sisi stared at their back, then turned sharply towards the high-tide line, leaving Nuru to carry on alone. The lost argument set fires burning in her lungs. 'Where is the difference,' she whispered to the scalding sand, 'between faith and defeat, when they both mean doing nothing?' It would be better to belong nowhere than to live with this. Manon had so little time and look where all her obediences had brought her; look where it had brought *them*.

Chapter Nine

Kit

Kit thought he saw her again late on another morning, walking a different path north towards the forested cliffs. Just a distant brown figure, red T-shirt and black hair, fabricated significance.

From here, standing at the edge of the garden with hibiscus flowers like explosions in his peripheral vision, Kit could see the island hall and the far half of the village. The woman had passed the house that lay furthest inland, and was now an intermittent shape moving through patchwork fields. He lost her behind a tree smothered in red flowers, so watched instead the movement of a man in between rows of some thigh-high crop, bending and straightening, bending and straightening. Where did the paths lead? Two paths and one woman piloting his imagination up to the cliffs. Is that where the paths went? To the great red-tinted cliffs behind the house? He could walk up there until he was high enough.

He could follow the birds back down.

The muscles of his legs ached at the thought of the climb, but once he was up there...

Kit tipped his head back, the sun high and behind so all he could see were a hollow blue and the cliffs; three white birds, long-tailed, crossed his vision looking less like living creatures than like slivers cut out of the sky. It would be so easy. Just a step, just one step and then the sea. No paramedics to haul him back from the brink, nothing but the fall and the relief.

*

Kit sank down into the shade of the hedge, gritty earth pressing into his knees, yesterday's sunburn stinging. Ants were running pathways between glass-edged grass, Escher-esque.

Rachel's voice drifted out of the open doors, and what would Rachel do, and Geo, once they knew he was missing? He pulled a grass stem free, its minute teeth sawing at his skin. They'd ask the islanders to help, at a guess; the fishing boats with their outriggers and their white sails would ease along the coastline looking for his body in among sandbars and tide-pools. Perhaps people would walk up to the clifftops, but in his mind the land up there was a plateau as smooth as a desert, so they'd not stay long. They'd leave him in peace.

Someone – Euan? – had told him that they worshipped the sea here, so perhaps they'd leave his body for the fish and crabs to feed on. Perhaps Geo would want to insist on his retrieval, but would weigh that against his own task here and his stalling career, and stay silent. The tide would take him away eventually, Kit figured, or the crabs would. Pincers would excise his flesh and pick him clean. The image condensed, overlaying garden and house with red carapaces, fish that were toothed and swivel-eyed, his muscles exposed but his mind quiet. The air became oceanic and he swam through it, terrified and full of hope.

What would his parents do, his brother? He couldn't fathom it, couldn't reach past the enormity of their disappointment to anything else. He stopped trying, returned to the ocean and the hungry crabs and the quiet of the fall. Perhaps dolphins would find him; perhaps they would know he'd wanted to be more than he was. Perhaps they would think he'd succeeded.

*

What was she doing up there, anyway? He imagined her poised high above the sea, her hair a cloud and her hands red with rock dust. What was she doing?

An ant, then two and three, found the skin of his toes and he jerked, brushing them off reflexively, coming to his feet so fast that the world swam with black light.

'Oh, there you are, Kit, sweetie,' Rachel said and he turned, still half-blind from the dizziness and the transition from shade into sun. 'Come have a drink with me.'

He wanted to be alone with cliffs and crabs, shut off from anyone's judgement, even his own, but she held two glasses and a jug silvery with condensation and he didn't know how to say no.

'Euan is taking us on a tour this evening, when it's cooler,' Rachel said. Kit made a noise in the back of his throat, keeping his eyes on his drink, turning it and turning it, his fingers leaving trails on the glass. Euan would know the woman's name.

'Apparently there's the most stunning view from the top, if you want to come,' she said. 'I quite fancied watching the sun set up there, but Euan says the track is a bit risky in the dark. Still, maybe next time, don't you think?'

She didn't expect him to answer and he was repeating her words to himself. Unfurling them like a wing.

From the top. From the top.

Just one step, an intermission filled with sunlight and white-feathered birds, and then the sea.

He took a sip of the lemonade, wincing at the bite of it, acid in the roof of his mouth and sugar on his tongue. There should be a word for that, he thought, something stronger than *bittersweet*, something fiercer for moments that were both cruelty and kindness, victory and defeat.

Lemonade? He laughed and almost choked at the sound of himself in his own ears.

'I'll come,' he said to Rachel and she replied, sounding gently pleased. 'I like the lemonade,' he added and laughed again because cliffs were waiting bittersweetly, his heartbeat clattering like startled birds; he wanted to laugh and laugh and laugh, fill his skull with sound because he could taste it, the lemonade and the sea, the sensation of putting one foot out into nowhere. The thought of an end.

He pushed his chair back, heard it fall behind him but didn't stop, half-tangling himself in its legs then lurching towards his bedroom. Hiccupping laughter and relief, sinking back against the closed door so Rachel couldn't follow, hiding his face, lungs spasming and the palms of his hands filling with the sea and the sea, and he was crying. He was crying in huge jagged sobs that tore at the muscles of his stomach but he cradled his head in his arms and couldn't stop, his mouth wide and the sound of himself terrifying. He rocked and rocked, self-soothing like an orphan, cracking open with the ocean flooding out through the wounds.

*

A knock on the door woke him, and he pushed himself up off the floor onto his elbows, staring around the room bewildered, crusty-faced, with the sunlight painting portals on the wall.
'Kit, darling, can I come in?'

'Um...' Scrambling upright, wavering on his feet and rubbing hands over his face, memory coming back jaggedly. 'Um, no, not just... give me a minute.'

A pause, and then more hesitantly: 'It was just to say it's time to take your next dose, and we're off for our tour in about half an hour, if... if you still fancied coming.'

'Okay,' he said, and her footsteps receded down the hall. 'Jesus.' He rubbed at his face again, salt moving under his fingers. He was so hollow a stray wind might make him resonate to the point of shattering.

'Okay,' he said again, to the square of sunlight on the wall and to himself.

*

Rachel covertly watched him swallow his tablets and the thought of what she might have heard made him turn away from her, glad he'd scrubbed cold water over his hair. He wanted to tell her there was no need to worry anymore.

'Wonderful,' Geo said and Kit set the glass down. 'Good job, mate. This'll be a sight, I reckon.'

'You left your phone out,' Rachel said and Kit realised that she was talking to him, holding the thing out in the palm of her hand. He took it, moving in slow motion, his mind swimming and far away. There was an email alert. He dismissed it.

'We all set?' Euan materialised, giving the room an indiscriminately mild smile. Rachel picked up a small backpack, then Euan turned and everyone followed him out of the house, down the garden towards the village.

Kit paused at the garden entrance, looking at the path that led off behind the house, the way the funeral procession that was not his had gone. 'I thought...' he said, and although he'd spoken quietly, although Rachel was up ahead with Euan, she stopped immediately and both of them turned back.

'What is it, dear?' she said.

Kit waved at the path, trying to find words.

Euan tilted his head. 'Oh, sorry, I wasn't going to take you that way. Did you see them go past the other night? That's the red cliffs, you see, it's where their tombs are. We can go up there, it's fascinating, but only once a Sacere has appeased the ancestors.' He waved a hand in a gesture that managed to be disparaging of his own explanation and nothing more. 'I was going to take you up to Les Hautes, the central plateau, if that's okay?' Not a question, more giving Kit the opportunity to back out if he wanted to.

Kit wondered who had told Euan why he was here, and whether the look in his thin face was pity or simply disinterested, instinctive tact.

Les Hautes.

Okay, Kit thought.

They went the way he'd watched the woman go earlier that day. Plants that might have been eggplant on one side of the path, some crawling vines on the other. They were all yellow-edged, reminding Kit of the meeting the other day, salt and harvests and water tables, benign words full of spectres.

Like him. Everyone talking to the Kit they thought they knew, everyone ignoring the ghost of what he'd tried to do even though it wasn't gone.

Lemonade, he thought, but the humour of it had vanished. He wasn't sure where it had come from to start with.

*

The track started to climb, turning from sand to scree to rocks, until they were walking a switch-back path between ridges of pale stone that were as sharp as scalpels. A voice in his head whispered *volcano atoll, limestone karst, old uplifted reef*. These were not red cliffs full of tombs, but they were glass-edged bones.

His muscles wept with the effort of the climb, his lungs were drowning, and he remembered running up and down hills for team stamina training, running and laughing, sweat on his temples and the thud of their feet as regular as their pulses. When had he stopped playing rugby? He remembered them banging on his door, grabbing him in lecture theatres, but he couldn't remember what they'd said to him, or what he'd said back. He couldn't remember the last time he'd been sailing, or diving, or anything at all, but it was still a shock to realise his own body's attrition.

'Bloody hell,' Geo swore from just ahead of him, coming to a halt with one foot raised up on a ridge of stone, elbow on knee and head bent forward. 'Higher than it looks, hey, mate?' he said, gasping.

Kit carried on past him, not stopping in case he couldn't start again. It was so sordidly visceral, to be panting and straining, sweating inside their clothes. How could people stand it? How could they endure within something that hurt and broke, that held no escape?

Soon, he thought. *Soon*. Pulling his useless limbs up, staring at the trodden dust and blue shadows at Rachel's heels, his head full of hungry fish and the sea.

*

'So these are Les Hautes,' Euan said, making Kit realise they had stopped. He looked as neat and contained as he had back at the house, and smugness might have been justified, but there was none of it on his face. 'They don't grow anything up here – it's just used for the herd of goats and the odd bit of charcoal, you know?'

It wasn't the blank desert space Kit had imagined, so they would search up here after all. They'd push through the patchy thorn scrub, call his name into the sharp hollows and hunt for clues on the rocks.

Today, then. It had to be today.

That way they'd know, and was that a kindness? Maybe. Maybe he simply never wanted to experience again that moment of waking in the hospital and seeing his parents' faces. So instead there would be the empty air and then the sea, no more *enduring* and no more doubt.

Geo exclaimed over the strange jagged landscape and Rachel's camera imprisoned the souls of lizards. Somewhere out of sight he could hear bells that must belong to the goats he hadn't yet seen. He never would, would he? He'd never see the goats that climbed these rocks, nibbling dark leaves delicately from the thorn bushes. How strange, to hear something you'd never see. The others' voices were an old radio and his eyes were playing tricks, showing polaroid pictures of all his failures in between the scrubby plants, in the shadows behind rocks. Here that scene with his parents and their disbelief, here them again in the hospital; here that photo of his childhood bedroom with scorched walls and his old toys melted beyond recognition, here his brother laughing when he'd told him about changing his degree. *It's as good as dropping out*, he'd said. *Admit it, you're failing.*

I'm failing, he thought. *Yes.* Not in the way his brother had thought, but yes.

'Kit?' Geo said.

Kit staggered out from faded arguments and smoke-black rooms. Lost chances and lost houses and lost homes.

'Kit, mate, you okay?'

'Water, sweetie?' Rachel said.

Kit coughed on cinders and took the bottle. Water. That was what he wanted now. 'Thanks,' he said.

'This was decommissioned in the nineteenth century,' Euan said. 'They aren't on any shipping lanes, so it's an oceanic weather station now.'

Kit had come to a halt but the others went ahead again, hands visoring their faces to admire a tower crouching cankerously in among the blades of rock.

'That's some impressive gear for a place like this,' Geo said but Kit wasn't looking at the aerials or satellite dish or solar panels. He was looking past to where the land… stopped.

There were pale rocks as thin as glass with silvery leaves in between, and then there was a distant sea, trammelled satin and eternity.

'It's manned, for scientific research.' Euan's voice was thin and distant. 'We'll see if she's in here…' He carried on talking as they moved into the building and Kit drifted in their wake and then past along the side wall where termites had built dusty tunnels over the paint. He kept walking, the ground in front of him spooling shorter so he wasn't moving at all, really, he was just here, waiting, while the world spun itself away. The ridges of rock between him

and the edge shrank from twenty to ten, to five, four, three...
the earth slowed and his lungs heaved like he'd been running but
he hadn't, he'd been here waiting for months, maybe for years.
Waiting for peacefulness, for just these two more steps, and no one
was shouting for him, no one had turned to wonder where he was.
Because he was already gone, and had been for so long that the
world would let him do this last thing gently. One more step, wind
reaching up over the edge to grab at his shirt and the air full of
salt; he could hear the sea now quieter than his heartbeat, quieter
than his lungs, whispering absolutely nothing at all. Yes, this was
where it was; everything he needed was here and all he had to do
was look up at the sky and close his eyes.

Thank god, he thought. *At last. Thank god.*

He stepped forward.

Chapter Ten

Sisi

Sisi was up on Les Hautes, kneeling in the dust between ridges of rock fifty metres from the station, working and thinking of Nuru and Manon, and coming to a decision. The wind and her thoughts had deafened her, so she only looked up from her equipment when movement at the cliff edge caught her eye; the cliff edge and the nameless outsider poised, half-falling. She screamed.

But she was too far away. '*Wait!*' she shouted again.

He stopped. Standing right at the very edge of the west cliffs and motionless. He could not have heard her, though, because he did not turn.

Maybe, she thought, she had misread and he had always meant to stop just there at the last moment, but the way he had been walking was the way you walked towards home. She stood in the hollow where she had been crouched, only thirty metres from him. The soil probe in her hand flashed three times then switched off, but she did not move, watching the man whose eyes had held so much desolation it had felt like falling – and now here he was, standing half a breath from the long drop to the sea.

But what could he possibly have to be desolate about? What reason could someone like him have to walk towards a cliff as if he did not intend to stop? A thin anger stuck in her throat and she put a hand on the muscles of her stomach, pressing against that tiny thing that contained all the reasons in the universe to despair. What could he possibly know of that?

His body swayed forward and despite her, her heart screamed. But he would not welcome her intrusion, and anyway it must be only a dare, the adrenaline-seeking of the affluently bored, so she bent down to her equipment determinedly trying to remember what she had been doing. Testing whether they could create pockets of soil in these hollows to grow things far above the water table and sheltered from the sea.

A skink wound itself up out of a hole in the rock, light reflecting topaz and indigo from its smooth skin, and Sisi said the words unthinkingly: 'Dear sister, what would you have me do?' The skink tilted its head, black eye sharp as a frigatebird's, then turned to run up out of the hollow, towards the cliff.

She sighed.

*

She was ten paces from him when he lifted a foot again and began to lean forward, and *Oh, Mother...* stumbling over rocks, her hands reaching forward... but she was too far and his eyes were closed. He hung there supported by the wind rising up the cliff, and then he put his foot back down. She saw stillness, and then an enormous rise and fall of his chest. She saw him open eyes that were already dead, and she forgot he was an outsider, and a man, and white; he was simply broken.

'Hello,' she said softly.

He spun, jerking away from the edge, and stared, perhaps trying to remember how to see. She spoke again, pushing her hands into her pockets because she thought they were shaking. 'You will take care, yes?'

Jerking his head towards the sea and then back to her, he took a step towards safety, lifting his hands between them as if fending her off. 'I wasn't... I mean, I don't...' Stopping and seeming to gather himself with immense effort, he ran both hands over his face, then dropped them. 'I saw you earlier,' he said. The cliff yawed and he was still too close, but she did not dare to move. His voice had the edges that meant South Africa, but muted, like he was half one thing and half another.

'Did you?' she said. Tipping her head towards the old lighthouse: 'I run this. I am up here often. Are you here with the... the others?' She could still see the ghost image of him half a breath from falling. But what was she supposed to say? *Were you about to jump? Why did you stop? What can you,* you, *possibly have to bear that would drive you to that when I, with a dead husband and a doomed child and perhaps the death of my people, have not come to this?*

He was frowning at her, but then looked away. 'My uncle and aunt, and Euan, yes.' They appeared at the corner of the building just as he spoke, the Administrator and his wife halting there abruptly, momentum making them stumble. From here, Sisi could see the terror fading from their faces, and maybe the man beside her saw it too, because he bent his head, shoulders curving as he took another two steps away from the edge.

Euan reached them ahead of the others, perhaps because he did not need first to breathe. 'Sisi,' he said, his clever eyes catching the sunlight. 'I didn't see you here, sorry. All is well with you?'

'All is well,' she replied, remembering Nuru. 'And with you?'

'Thank you, yes. You've met Kit? And this is Rachel Benedict.'

His name was Kit, then, this strange man, with his pale eyes and his desolation. The Administrator's wife had a smile that spoke of kindness, and Sisi saw how she had come quietly to stand between Kit and the cliffs.

'Can we...?' the woman said, gesturing at the empty air. 'I'm not good with heights.'

The Administrator laughed uneasily and Kit seemed to shrink very slightly. Sisi turned, taking him in with a passing sweep of her gaze, relieved that there were people here now to whom he belonged. Everyone walked back towards the weather station, with Sisi dragged along in their wake, because once their backs were turned there seemed no way for her to say, *I am working, I must get on.*

*

That evening Sisi sat watching flames curl around the base of the rice pot like painted lovers, listening to the last gulls calling out on the arms of the bay, a gecko laughing in the tree above. She could have cooked on the stove inside, but preferred it out here. Soon the fruit bats would be out and the lychee tree would become a battle and feast and parliament all in one. She would laugh up at their hidden fox-faces because their lives were so utterly important to them and it was a relief to know that her life, and her trials, were not. She remembered the outsider, Kit, walking towards the cliff as if reaching for someone beloved, and Nuru standing on wet sand saying, *Mother Sea is everything – our faith in her is all we have*, and wondered if the two were the same.

Nuru was with Isolde and their wife, and Manon would come by as Luc was out on the water, the fishers one soul's worth more careful with their ropes and knots and weights. Sisi thought that Antonin would be angry with her for what she was about to do, but Antonin was no longer here. Nuru would be angry too, and Sisi shied away from that thought because Manon's needs outweighed theirs, surely. Nuru and the Sacere would give rum and rice to Mother Sea in the hope that she might give them answers, but Sisi would sit here cooking and waiting for the bats, the gecko hoarding her secret; waiting for Manon. The sky above her was a damson and charcoal eye, the horizon slow-blinking towards the darker sea.

If, three years ago, she had refused all the arguments of her friends, her kin, the Mothers – refused to put the whole before the self – she would be out there now over the rim of the sky and in a life so far from this one it seemed laughable. Would she and Jomo have survived? Would she and Manon? Would she ever have come fully home or been here for this, tonight?

She would not, that fantastical self, be mourning a half-loved husband, nor carrying his child like a chain.

*

Old palm leaves skittered and Sisi thought it must be a bird, but then *skrit-scratch* and *skrit-scratch*, faint as whispers. If Manon had already arrived, likely she would not have heard it.

'Oh,' Sisi said, her stomach tightening as she came to her feet.

Skrit-scratch, skrit-scratch, down the parabola of the palm trunk, the light of the fire rendering glimpses of movement prehistoric, sinister, and Sisi's toes curled into her sandals, her hands flat on the cloth of her wrap.

The robber crab reached the ground and realigned the points of its legs into the sand, great pincers held heavily in front of it and antennae moving ponderously. Sisi watched it, hating the moisture on her palms and all the inescapable stories in her subconscious.

'You mean nothing,' she whispered to it. But it only flexed its claws, stretching foretellings between serrations as if testing them for doom. 'Go,' she hissed, stamping her foot in the sand even though to chase away one of Mother Sea's messengers was fady strong enough to scald. But *this* one, a robber crab who had abandoned Mother Sea and broken her heart, so now must carry ill omens; could she not spurn this one? Furiously thinking, *Birgus latro*, its deep colour making it perhaps as much as forty years old. Endangered, eaten to extinction wherever humans lived, other than here where superstition made them spectres, only safe to see if they did not see you.

This one twisted the tiny columns of its eyes and watched her. Conservation through fear. Dichotomies like her own split self.

Then a noise: far away Chicha's mother calling for him to come and eat, *Come eat, you wild child*, and here footsteps. The crab lifted its balletic feet, tasting tremors in the sand, and as Manon appeared, the old beast turned a strange pirouette and vanished beyond the light.

'Oh, Mother,' Sisi whispered, smoothing her hands on her wrap and shucking off tradition because the night-waking meeting with a relic crustacean was nothing but a random intersecting of two beings coexisting on a scrap of land full of days of not intersecting, and surrounded by the sea.

*

'What is it, Sisi-si?' Manon asked, and Sisi realised she was still standing, the rice boiling angrily by her feet.

'Nothing,' she said, sitting and reaching to stir, Manon sitting also, gathering her feet beneath the edge of her wrap as though she were cold. Above, the branches of the lychee tree clattered and Sisi could just make out the silhouetted bat, wings half-stretched. When it called to the next arrival she remembered to smile. 'Nothing.'

They ate together just as they had done a million times before. At street cafés as students in Mahé, the four of them high on freedom and homesickness, Manon and Luc halfway in love, Sisi and Jomo already there. And then the two of them here, just like this, when their husbands were out at sea, only this time the emptiness in the house behind them was as loud as the ringing of a bell. And there was this, too: the ticking clock of Manon's womb, and also Sisi's, quieter and secretly less precious.

'Manon,' Sisi said eventually. Voices were audible from other houses, but their little circle of light was a small, private star in the wide night.

'Mmm.' Manon was toying with the last of her food, breaking the chicken into smaller pieces with her fork, full but not full. Tired but not sleepy.

'I was thinking of going to the doctors.'

'But the Sacere say no, Sisi-si. You must not.'

Sisi spread her hands on the mat in front of her, thumbs touching. 'And if the doctors can help?'

'This time.'

'Yes. If they can help this time?' She looked up from her knuckles to her friend. 'Would that not be worth anything?'

'And if the doctors cannot help but only interfere? Nuru says that they cannot be trusted.'

'I think they can help. The Sacere are not always right, Manon.'

Manon did not answer, one hand on her belly and for once no laughter at all in her face. Her mind, Sisi knew, drifting up the red cliffs to a tiny shroud on a bed of grasses and rock; the imprint of heartbreak on every part of her soul, and Sisi would honestly do anything at all to spare Manon that again. She would give her whole heart for Manon to wake ten days after her child was born and hear it crying. What an exquisite thing it was, a child's cry.

'Come with me,' she said. Probably Sisi could bully Manon into anything if she chose, and she thought this was worth bullying for.

'But the Mothers agree—'

'—with the Sacere, yes, I know. But it is not enough, Manon. We have carried this thing for nearly ten years and nothing we have done is enough. Now the sea brings us a new thing to try, should we not *think* about it at least?'

'Sisi...' Manon hesitated. 'They failed us before, and... and they are *outsiders*.' The word encapsulating so much more than just the miles of water.

'So were our ancestors, once,' Sisi said, smiling a little to try to soften her desperation. 'Why are we so distrustful of people who we lived alongside in high school? It makes no sense.'

'This is different.'

'Manon, I do not care if they come from the moon if they can help you.'

'And you also.'

Looking down but failing to see her flesh grown and fecund in the way Manon's was, failing to see the life within her womb as anything other than the vestiges of a marriage that had been a firmly closed door. This thing nestling in the cup of her bones like treasure, and yet she didn't treasure it even though she ought. 'This is not for me,' she said. 'It is... Manon, you let yourself love them, so let yourself fight for them also.'

'You are being cruel.'

It was true. Sisi laid her palms skyward on her knees. 'I only want us to fight for the things we need. For answers and our children and our home. Mother Sea accepted us as her children because we fought for ourselves, so how could she now begrudge us doing the same?'

A small smile. 'Have you said this to Nuru?'

'Yes.'

'And what did they say?'

Sisi could have prevaricated, but Manon would know. 'They said I lack faith.'

That earned a huff of laughter, a passing smile as beautiful as the stars. 'You do,' Manon said without condemnation. 'The you that is a scientist deconstructs our stories like algebra.'

Was that it? She, two distinct people in one flesh? Not one complex person, but instead one perfect islander, content; and one wilfully separate, tainted by her expertise.

'The scientist in me knows the doctors are our best chance,' she said eventually. 'The islander believes that Mother Sea wishes for us to fight for ourselves again.' Shrugging: 'I will go tomorrow. Will you come?'

'Sisi-si.' Pleading or remonstrating or both.

'Please.'

The night carried on around them, bats flying in or away. The sea reaching high tide as close as a second skin, breathing longer than their own breaths. It was almost cold now, the warm air beneath the trees having slipped away towards the stars, the shadows smelling of iodine and mystery.

'Manon, please.'

'Alors,' Manon said after the longest time. 'Yes. I will.' And Sisi's relief was so strong she could taste it.

Chapter Eleven

Kit

Every step Kit took sent shockwaves up his spine, his feet expecting air and hitting earth until his head ached with the reminder of what he hadn't done.

He'd stepped out, and then he hadn't.

Christ, again he'd tried, and again he'd lived.

*

He was walking around the garden barefoot, miniature earthquakes in his heels, tracing and retracing his own steps, bewildered. What had happened between eyes closed, relaxing into the fall; and the next? What had erased *let go*, and become *wait*?

It was harder on the body to set a foot against the earth than it was to set it on the air; it was harder to walk away from the cliff than it would have been to fall. So where had it come from, the foot returning to rock when his heart was already out in the void with the birds?

Walking and walking, the soles of his feet catching twigs and stones, pain a proof of the ground. Kit's hands were in his pockets and the tiny blue-brown bird berating him from the lantana finally stopped to dip the glossy curve of its bill into flowers. From inside the house, plates rattled together, voices mingled and this meant it would soon be lunch. They would come out onto the veranda to call him and he'd either have to hide in the breathless cage of his room or sit with them. But then Uncle Geo would ask for his help or Rachel would suggest coming with her to the village to take photographs or force stilted conversations on the locals. She would still have the echo of that look that had been on her face when she came out of the lighthouse and saw him standing with the woman, Sisi.

He swung sharply out of the garden and downhill, not really caring where he went as long as it was *away*.

There were people everywhere, sitting outside houses in the shade of trees, walking along the beach with baskets balanced on their heads, gathered by the store and all of them talking. Talking. Their eyes on him dark and unblinking. What had his parents been thinking sending him here? And Geo and Rachel, on their way through Cape Town between postings, why had they ever agreed? Had he been right the other day – was it a test? Surround him with cliffs and the sea, give him quasi-obsolescence, and see if he would finish what he had begun.

He kept moving. Breathing raggedly, wanting to ask them which choice would have passed the test, and which would have failed it.

*

Only when the path leaped vertically, turning to razor rock infilled with bone dust, did he recognise where he was going. He nearly stopped but then carried on, pursued by the creep-crawling, spider-legged shadow that was his defeat. Up, calves and thighs screaming, but he wanted them to hurt today, wanted them burned in their own acid, punished; achilles, quads, tibia, instinct.

Rather than fail again, he swerved away from the defunct lighthouse, sweat sticking his shirt to his back, sweat on his forearms, salt stinging his eyes and lips, his city-soft, inertia-soft feet being cut and stabbed in so many places that they were an aurora of pain. He realised he was snarling, lips pulled back, teeth clenched and his breath coming in hot explosions. The pain freeing his anger, drowning out catatonia and shadows and letting him gorge on punishment like a flagellate.

There was no path so he stumbled along lines in the rock, led by the placement of shrubs and cacti and the open, startling maw of an ancient giant clam. Then, with one foot in the air, the other in the dust, a smell hit him.

He stopped and stood very still, his eyes closed as the scent quartered his lungs.

Charred wood and old cinders.

Kit sat, lowering himself gingerly onto a cusp of rock. He couldn't see the fire, or even its smoke; there was only old coral and dwarfed scrub, the red hill rising ahead and a sliver of the sub-horizon sea.

Ashes in the air; and loss. He rubbed his hands together, tendons moving over bone, trying to scrub away the ghosts of charcoal and melted plastics. He wondered what his bones would smell like if they burned. And had they smelled it, the firemen? Beneath charcoaled boards and furniture, beneath burned paint and exploded tins, had the firemen smelled bones?

His lungs were full of smoke, but it was fraudulent because he hadn't gone back. When they phoned to say the house was lost, he hadn't gone back. When they said that Jingo... Oh, the poor dog, they couldn't bear to think of it, if only they'd had more time, if only the wind hadn't picked up that morning, if only, but the smoke must have killed him first, they just had to hope, didn't they? Hope that poor old sweet, silly Jingo died from the grassland smoke before the fire reached the house.

Dad had said there was nothing to go back for – the insurers had it in hand. Mum had said he mustn't miss out on classes just to poke through ruins and trash. Kit sat in the furnace of the sunlight, heat on his head and shoulders, rubbing his hands, grit and salt and the texture of Jingo's fur gathering beneath his fingernails. It was a struggle to stop, forcing his palms instead against the sharp rock, understanding now why people might take a razor to their skin, shallow cuts for shallow pains that distract you from the deep ones. Penitence. He breathed slowly, the scent of smoke still there but now he couldn't tell if it was real or imagined. Ghost images of his childhood home husked, cindered rubble that hinted at tables, pictures, microwave, a bookshelf half-filled with books, a thousand tiny memories unnoticed so it was ridiculous to mourn them now. But he'd scanned the photos over and over anyway, hunting childhood and not finding it.

No bones either. No empty blue collar reduced to a buckle and threads. Nothing to say goodbye to. *And it was only a dog, Kit, for Christ's sake, and a house you didn't live in anymore. Just bricks, son. Just bricks and* stuff, *and Jings was old, poor boy, so he wouldn't have had much longer anyway. And you can't blame your poor grades on* that. *Stop this rubbish about changing courses, stop making excuses for your failures. You can't mess up your whole future, Kit, on some pointless degree. We expect better of you. No son of mine... No son of mine...*

The ground beneath his feet was immutable but if he couldn't fall, then how could he possibly stand?

*

When he finally came back down, bloody-footed and mute with exhaustion, Rachel was angrier than he'd thought possible.

'Where were you?' she said, her voice rising on the middle word so sharply that it cracked.

'Out.' He stared at her blankly. 'Walking.' Being haunted by burned childhoods and failure.

'*Walking!*' Effort rippled through her body like an earthquake, a hand held delicately over her eyes for a second and then rested on the counter top. 'You were walking.' Her eyes so bright they hurt to look at. 'You're barefoot – your feet are bleeding. You were just walking, Kit? Really? You were just walking?'

'Yes,' he said. The connotations in her questions making the whole thing somehow sordid. He looked down at his feet. 'They're just scratched.'

'Kit, that's...' taking a long breath. Kit thought of flies in amber, of pinioned birds. 'Sweetie, that's great. But darling, you have to let me know if you are going out anywhere. Please?'

Muscles moved on his face, weariness battened down by something else. 'Why?' he said. 'I can hardly run away.'

Her hands slapped the counter, the sound echoing in his ears like wingbeats. '*Why?* Jesus, Kit. Why do you think? So I know you haven't—' Cutting herself off with a sound like a bird. 'So I know you are *safe*, and I know not to send everyone out searching for your...'

Body, Kit finished for her. *For my body.*

But what about me? he thought, and did not say. *How do I get to know that I am safe? Why should it be so easy for you, when it's impossible for me?*

'I just wanted to walk,' he said. 'That's it. I didn't think you'd mind.'

'I don't, honey, I'm glad. Really. I just...' Another sigh. Why did they say emotion came from the heart, when so much of it was in your lungs? 'Darling, please, just leave a note or something, so I know you're okay? Will you?'

Heat had wrung him out, slow thoughts and fast ones blurring. *You aren't the one dying by degrees instead of by choice. You wouldn't mind that much, and neither would my parents. I'm lost. I'm sorry. I'm tired.* 'Fine,' he said to the floor halfway between him and her, and then footsteps and Uncle Geo rushing into the room as if he'd run for miles.

'Ah, Rach,' he said. 'No worries, then, hey? After all?'

Kit took a step backwards, towards his room where the quiet of the sea would be coming in through the window.

'He was just walking,' Rachel said. 'Sorry.'

'Walking, hey?' Geo looked at Kit, nodding quickly. 'Good on you. But if you want something to do, there's more than enough work and I'd like your input, Kit, mate. Use that expertise of yours, you know?'

'What expertise?' he heard himself say, then took another step back. 'I was studying ocean and atmosphere science, not law.' Waiting for the same disappointment, the same denials.

'Ah, um, yes. Your dad said.' Geo winced, but then smiled in a way probably meant to be winning. 'That's exactly what we need, though. Come with me tomorrow, mate. We need to explain to these people what our crop yield models mean and I'm damned if the graphs don't confuse the hell out of me. You'd do far better, Kit. That's why you're here.'

Is it? Kit thought, briefly startled. Did Geo really think that? There was still a pressure in his head and if this was anger, if this was what anger felt like then he wasn't sure who it was for.

'Maybe,' he said, to escape. It wasn't true, about the graphs. Geo was perfectly capable of understanding them, and they both knew it. A kind lie, and unsubtle; and incredibly cruel.

*

Kit went up to Les Hautes again the next day. As if compelled. He'd left a note; he'd even sent a text to his mother without looking at his emails. *I'm ok*, he'd typed, *Kx*. Just that. What else was there to say that wouldn't make the lie even bigger? Then he'd come up here with his cut feet stinging, a backpack making his back itch with sweat and friction. Walking around the clifftop from the lighthouse and then away towards the red hill that must be the old volcano. Not consciously searching for fires, and not consciously staying away from the boats that reminded him of joy, or the cliff edge that reminded him of failure, but still doing all three.

He walked. It was better than being in the house, his mood simmering beneath Rachel's claustrophobic gaze and Geo's lies, feeding on his parents' disdain and then their platitudes. Here instead there was nothing but heat, salt in his wounds and the off-kilter memory of that woman, Sisi. In his first blind-sided moment of not-falling, she'd been there, looking up at him with eyes that were brown, but also green. The colour of buried moss. Him still half-falling, those eyes full of shock and scorn.

Who was she, to look at him like that? What could she know about losing everything that defined you, of weighing too much even to fall? Excised from your family by failure, your childhood erased. But then he remembered, and stopped walking. Of course she knew. Wasn't he here to throw her and all her people off this island? To make them climate refugees, homeless. That was what Geo wanted him to help with – convincing her and all the others that it was better to live as strangers than die themselves.

It didn't matter. They would still have each other and their belonging. He would give anything for that.

He bent over slowly, hands on knees and eyes closed, wanting numbness and isolation, not envy, and definitely not compassion. Straightening up and taking long, painful gulps of water, he set off again, faster. The red hill filling his vision, sparse trees on it making a noose. He didn't know how to stop feeling, or how to start, but he pressed his hands against his chest anyway, listening to his heart.

Chapter Twelve

Sisi

Sisi and Manon spent the early morning collecting papaya. The fruit trees grew in the western valley, beneath the great edifices of the baobabs, where some mysterious alignment of strata meant that fresh water lay close to the surface and thousands of years of fallen leaves had bred an improbable fertility in the soil. The vanilla vines grew there also, the precious vanilla that went out into the world and sent back all the paraphernalia of semi-westernised life.

With papaya in their baskets, long as their forearms and yellow as flowers, Sisi and Manon began the short walk back over the ridge towards the village and the bay. 'Now?' Manon said with a hand against the base of her spine. 'Or later?'

The promise, and Manon's doubts, had hung over them both like thunder all morning. *Now*, Sisi was about to say, because if she said later then Manon might not go at all, but then two people came around the corner of a house and Sisi did not need to say anything. If she were Sacere, would she read Mother Sea's wishes in this? Would she be right?

'Good morning,' Euan said. 'All is well with you?'

'All is well,' Sisi murmured. 'And with you?'

He gave his narrow smile but only turned to the woman at his side to say, 'This is Geraldine Adler, the paediatrician. Dr Adler, Sisi de Mathilde and Manon de Oni.'

Impressive, Sisi thought, that he always remembered their full names through the months between his visits. Perhaps he did not, perhaps somewhere there was a folder of their photographs, listing their matrilines and their histories like a stock-book. She and Manon both nodded and smiled and said nothing; the woman's pale clothes were the colour of mourning.

'I was hoping to meet you,' the woman said, to Manon and the dome of her unborn babe. 'Would you be willing to talk with me about how you are, and how I might help?'

Manon looked at Sisi, and Sisi wanted to look for Nuru, but didn't. 'We would,' she said. Euan's clever eyes noting her own inclusion, and almost, almost not reacting. Hidden behind sunglasses, there was no way of knowing whether the doctor also realised, but Sisi did not care so long as she did not have to see that same twist of pity on another outsider's face.

'But not here,' Manon added, her hands clasped on her stomach and her knuckles as prominent as mountain-tops.

'Can you come to the clinic?' Dr Adler asked, angling her body in that direction as if about to lead them headlong into her experiments. Sisi recognised the keenness in her voice, wanted to lift Manon up herself, carry her into the clinic and stand watch over every single thing the doctors did until her friend was saved.

'Later,' she said eventually. 'After lunch.' When most would be resting through the heat of the day, and perhaps it was cowardly to plan it like this, but Sisi was so tired of being told what she must not do, and so tired of being told that if only she were someone entirely other, then her life would fit. 'After lunch we will come to you.'

*

'We do not have to agree to anything,' Manon said later, walking up under tamarinds and screw pines towards the Administrator's house and the clinic beside it, built by the French long ago. Thwarted men come to save their souls and leaving only a flag and hostility. 'We go only to listen, n'est-ce pas?'

'How much longer do you think you have?' Sisi asked in a convoluted form of answer.

A couple of slow steps, and then, 'Not long. Ten days? Maybe less. My first was late.'

Reaching out to slip her hand into Manon's, Sisi nodded. Not long. Not long to find an answer that had hidden from them for eight years. Not long to find a way for her friend to be happy, and perhaps she was fixating on this in place of analysing her own unhappinesses, but how much was too much to care about the life of a child? How much was too much to care about the heart of the person you loved best in the entire world?

'They will be able to help,' she said. Faith. And desperation.

*

'Our options are,' Dr Adler said, leaning forward in her chair, counting fingers, 'one: identify the source; two: isolate the new mutations of the toxin and try to formulate a drug regime that will work; and three: begin developing a targeted drug.' She had taken off her sunglasses and in the flat concrete light of the clinic, her eyes were the colour of wet sand. Brown, but a thin brown, like cloth that had almost worn through. No one on the island had eyes so pale and to Sisi she almost looked blind. Sisi thought of the man, Kit, on the clifftop with his oceanic eyes – but he had been blind in a different way, she thought, and almost envied him.

'The source?' Manon repeated. 'But I thought you knew this.'

The door behind opened to let in the other doctor. Manon sat straighter in her chair, braced against forbidden contact, and Sisi remembered to do the same two heartbeats later. 'We know it's a new strain of tetanus,' Dr Adler said. 'We know *what* it is, but not *where* it's coming from.'

'The last research team was trying to find out,' the man said – Dr Matthew Freshman, who was not a doctor but a scientist. 'But they... didn't have much luck.'

Sisi remembered. She remembered them talking with the Mothers, negotiating access to the birth of a child, wanting samples of placenta and blood, oils and water and cloths. Sacere Isolde handing sample jars to them with sterile fingers.

'It was not from the mothers,' Sisi said, 'or from the birthing equipment.' She lifted her chin and met Dr Freshman's eyes; he blinked and nodded. She wanted them both to see the scientist in her, not complicity but understanding.

'It wasn't,' he agreed.

'Then you have brought new antitoxins or antibiotics?'

Manon looked at her. Sisi took a breath, the unfamiliar equipment surrounding her both thrilling and bittersweet.

'We have some drug combinations that worked well when tested in the lab against modified forms of the toxin, yes,' Dr Freshman said.

But, Sisi thought, *but...*

'But until we know exactly what strain is infecting new cases, we can't be sure what will work best.' The doctors looked at one another and it was the woman, Adler, who spoke next, as if they would swallow her words more readily than his. Which was true, probably, measuring out the precise distance of the fadys.

'We would like to carry out some basic tests before baby is born, and give you some inoculations. Then immediately after birth start regular testing of both mother and baby, and start preventative treatment which we can adjust alongside the labwork.'

It sounded so simple. Give them blood, take their drugs. It had sounded so simple every other time too. It is neonatal tetanus; eliminate the source, take these drugs. And yet their drugs and their sweeping answers had saved no lives. Their vaccinations had done nothing, their frown lines and their vials of blood, their blue-gloved hands and computer screens. None of it had stopped the babes from weakening, from dying.

'You have new things to try, yes? You have worked on other cases like this?' Sisi asked and Manon hissed quietly between her teeth, perhaps at the word 'cases'. But Sisi needed to talk this way. 'Drug-resistant tetanus – you have seen this elsewhere?'

Hesitations as loud as a shout. 'Not in tetanus, no,' Dr Adler said, drawing the word out. 'But Matt and I both specialise in disease outbreaks, so we have covered epidemics with very similar characteristics and of course have worked on lab simulations, so—'

'Dr Adler,' Manon said, cutting across the woman with a smile that almost overrode the rudeness. She rose to her feet and touched a hand to Sisi's shoulder, saying with all the dignity of a queen, 'Tomorrow I will return for your first tests. Sisi will also.'

The man's eyes widened and Sisi stood. Manon inclined her head with utter finality and Sisi discovered that one day Manon would make an indomitable Mother. She had not realised it up until this moment.

*

'You are well?' Sisi asked, outside the clinic, in the shade still but with the day's heat engulfing them.

'Yes,' Manon picked up a trailing edge of her wrap and tightened the whole over the rise of her belly. 'He settled.'

'He...' Oh. *Oh.* The babe had settled, readying his tiny mass for the struggle to come. 'Oh, Manon.' Tears in her eyes that she had to blink furiously away.

'So you see, I have to try them.' Manon voice was calm, but she was placing her feet into the sand, toes and then heels, toes then heels, tiptoeing into her future, and Sisi's eyes filled all over again.

'I thought, when you stood—'

'I trust you, Sisi-si. And because you believe them, so then will I, but this does not mean I will be with them any more than I must.' Manon tilted her head sideways to look at Sisi uncertainly. 'With Luc, and... and with everyone, it will go easier I think, if we do as much as possible through someone else.'

'Isolde? Nuru?' They were the most trained and Manon was right. Also, perhaps Manon could soften Nuru where Sisi had failed. Her handful of remaining days giving her will a sanctity that Sisi was still some way from. Or perhaps it was that Manon, loved and loving and unutterably *present* here on the island, would be listened to in a way that Sisi, half-present, was not.

'Yes, either of them. Perhaps Nuru, as the Voice, n'est-ce pas? We have a few days, I think.'

Sisi looked down at her dusty feet. So, they were committed. The doctors would take Manon's blood, and they would save her child.

'This is the right thing,' she said.

Manon did not answer. Toes and heels, toes and heels into the sand.

Chapter Thirteen

Kit

Another walk. Kit lost count of the days, and of the ways he could avoid helping Geo. His muscles were no longer agony when he climbed up to this place. His breathing easier, which made him uneasy; this proof of his body reverting to someone he couldn't remember being, and didn't want to be.

So don't think. Smell the sea instead, rock-tinted; study the strange decurved flowers, defiantly pink...

...Listen to that sound, a hollow moaning that he couldn't identify, resonating in his bones, and if it had been dark, or foggy, he'd have been terrified but beneath the sun it was hard to be frightened of anything.

He was walking again towards the red hill – L'Ambre, he'd learned – faintly wanting to reach its summit this time. Wanting to do so without really setting out to, because the idea of trying and failing was overwhelming. But if he walked, and breathed, and did nothing else, then the summit might be there waiting like it had waited for several million years.

The strange sound stopped. He breathed. You didn't have to *feel*, he decided, you only had to *be*.

A bird flew up from the bushes in front of him, alarm calling and catching the wind to flip away over his left shoulder. Rachel would have known what it was. Kit tracked the improbable parabola of its flight, caught unawares by pleasure.

That moan rose again, almost a boom but softer and more diffuse. He was closer to its source, close enough that the next time it came he felt it first beneath his feet. Thirty metres ahead, perhaps less, was the point where dead coral karst shifted to reddish earth; way off to his right was the long, forested slope down to the village and the bay; fifteen short metres to his left were the cliffs of the island's northern shore; and the next wave of sound pressed up beneath his feet like a huge drum, consuming his whole body.

'Oh my god,' he whispered, his blood echoing. 'The sea!' The sea underneath him, reverberating with the swell.

He crept warily to the edge of the cliff, but it turned out to be nothing like the sheer drop back at the lighthouse. Less an edge than a castellated, fractalled, jag-toothed slope from old volcano to risen reef to sea, promising neither fall nor peace but instead footholds and ledges that to a goat would have been a highway but to him still looked deadly.

He didn't care. The cave moaned again and he wanted to see it. The opening was directly beneath him, the pale rocks vanishing and the sea all white-streaked and cerulean, surging inward and out of sight. He wanted to climb into that hidden space; actually, he wanted to *dive* into it. His brother would have loved it and for once he agreed. He wanted to be tugged and lifted by the resonant waves, but if that wasn't possible then he still wanted to *see*, and it was a rush, a heady, giddy rush to want anything at all, so he sat, and swung himself down onto the first ledge, one hand on a crenellation of rock.

'No!'

Kit looked up, his head spinning. Back the way he'd come the woman, Sisi, was half-running towards him, a red cloth coming loose from her hair. 'Wait!' she called.

He climbed back up as she approached him; the void sucked at his back and he took a few steps inland while the cave soughed and hummed. 'Hi,' he said, his hands feeling strangely empty, wanting to hold on to something. 'Sisi, is it?'

'Kit,' she said, frowning. 'All is well with you?'

'Umm, yes.' He looked at her, at the tension in her jaw, her dark eyes. 'What's the matter?'

She blinked and then shook her head. 'I... you cannot go down there. I am sorry.'

The sea boomed beneath their feet, and Sisi put a hand over her heart as though she too could feel it there.

'I can't?' He didn't understand. Fascination and the blue water still running in his mind.

'It is...' She sighed. 'It is fady. It is forbidden.'

'Forbidden?'

'Yes. Sorry. It is a special place to us – you cannot go there.'

It hurt, stupidly, like a rejection. 'Like the red cliffs?'

She flinched, and he remembered too late: the place that was just a mystery to him was a litany of loss to her. He reached out one of his empty hands towards her in a kind of apology, and it hurt all over again when she stepped sharply back like she was dodging a blow. Was he really so unwelcome? Anger uncoiled itself, whispering bitterness.

'Why? Why's it special? I won't go in – I just want to see.'

She looked away, towards the red hill and her dead, then down at her own feet, and his anger subsided, subdued by the movement of her escaping hair when she bent her head. 'Come with me,' she said, glancing at him then turning inland towards the dividing line between coral and volcano. He threw one last glance at the sea then followed her slowly, but very soon, she stopped and knelt in a dusty bowl where plantlets clung to the surreal, tunnelled karst. Not far from where he had been standing when he had recognised the sound of the sea beneath him. As soon as Kit knelt beside her she began to talk, her voice soft enough that if he'd stayed standing, he'd not have been able to hear.

'Many years and many years ago, Brother Island was a powerful and greedy child,' she said. 'Not satisfied with all the oceans, he looked above the water and wished to taste the air and the stars. Mother Sea told him he must not leave, but he was stubborn and became angry, and rose up in a great fit of rage. When his temper had cooled, Mother Sea welcomed her son back and forgave him. She sent other children to keep him company so that he was not alone, and seeing her kindness he was sorry for his anger.' Sisi paused, running her fingers lightly along the ridges of rock. 'But soon Brother Island forgot gratitude and thought to himself, *I have tasted the air but I have not yet tasted the stars.* Once more and twice more Mother Sea said no, but in his hunger and his anger he rose up again, taking her children up into the air with him so that they died. When he saw what he had done, he was so filled with sorrow for killing his siblings that he opened up his own chest and said to his Mother, *Please, live within my heart and wash out my anger so that I do not do this again.*'

She fell silent and the story left afterimages in Kit's mind of time, wonder, regret, but he still didn't understand until Sisi's hand moved again over the rock and beneath them, the sea cave spoke, softer now as that crucial tide-point was passing.

'This is the heart of Brother Island,' she said. 'This song is his rage that Mother Sea is washing away.' Looking sideways at him and smiling without warning, she added, 'It is fady to climb inside a demigod's heart, Kit Benedict, but you can see it, if you like?' She bent forward, turning her cheek and pressing her face against the scalloped ridges of rock.

What? Kit thought, the movement so unexpected that he couldn't parse it.

'Come,' she said. 'You wished to see.'

So he copied her, pressing one cheek against the sharp rock, and looked down. Down through fretwork rocks that extended – *my god* – they extended only a foot below him. There in a cut-out window was the sea. Turquoise and white-streaked, breathing far beneath him in a constant susurration. The island's heart, whispering.

'Wow,' he said. His whole body was off-balance with the movement of the water beneath them, the thin honeycomb of rock holding them up.

'The story,' he whispered, 'what does it mean?'

'I do not know,' she said. 'That we are all one and that your selfishness will damage those you love? That Mother Sea forgives? I do not know, I am no Sacere.'

He felt her stiffen. He looked up.

'Mother,' she whispered. It sounded like a curse.

'What is it?' he said, and she sat back, gesturing with one hand to the spot where she'd been looking. He bent towards her and pressed his eye to the rock where her cheek had just been. It was awkward to bend sideways like this, so it was a moment before he registered the streaks coming from a fissure on the far wall of the cave, tracking bent-backed paths down to the tideline.

'The red stuff?' he asked, thinking, *Leached water from the volcanic rock – why does it matter?*

She didn't answer and he realised his shoulder was touching her knee. Perhaps she realised it too because she jerked backwards so fast that he was knocked away from her, away from the peep-hole that looked into the island's innards.

'Sorry,' he said, because her eyes were wide with what he thought was dismay. 'Sorry, what's—' But she cut him off, windows closing in her face and her gaze returning to the rocks.

'It is new,' she said. 'The red water. I do not… why did we have to find it now?' Her lips thinning; looking away from him so he couldn't see her face at all.

When he spoke, it took so much effort that he sounded oddly formal. 'It's probably just iron oxides from that,' lifting his chin towards L'Ambre even though she couldn't see him. 'Perhaps there's been a tiny tremor that shifted things, or erosion has just opened up a new path or whatever. It's not dangerous. It's not toxic or anything.'

'I know this,' she said curtly, and he winced.

'Of course, I'm sorry, I didn't mean...' He was no good at this. 'Is it a problem for the... the fady?'

She looked back at him, and rested both of her hands over the rock like she was trying to hide the thing she'd seen, or heal it. 'What does it mean when Brother Island's heart bleeds just as you outsiders come telling us to leave? Just as Manon...' A soft sound strangled. 'And why did I have to find this?'

A yellow and green day gecko ran up out of the rocks, paddle-footing its way across the hot ground, skimming Sisi's fingertips and then vanishing up into a shrub. Kit heard her laugh, her fingers flexing. 'So, Mother,' she said. As she caught his eye he'd have sworn a flush deepened her brown skin. She shrugged and waved a hand in the direction of the shrub. 'The geckos, they are Mother Sea's secret keepers. They see everything and some of them have eyes the shape of locks, you see?' Perhaps she could see he didn't, because she added, patient, a little embarrassed, 'When one comes to you, it is because Mother Sea is telling you a secret. That is the story.'

'The secret is... she wants that to be secret?' Nodding his head towards the rocks.

'Yes, I suppose. She knows that I will keep it.' She looked at him like a cat might, eyes full of impenetrable colour. 'Geckos carry secrets, skinks carry messages when Mother Sea wishes you to act. There was a skink the other day – she told me not to let you jump.' He recoiled. 'But I did not need to,' she continued quietly, still watching him and seeing too much, peeling away his thin skin and studying his bones. 'You yourself stopped.'

He had almost forgotten himself, talking about rocks and legends, but couldn't look at her now for fear of what she might see.

'I am glad,' she said and again he held his breath, because the world swung on what she meant and what she didn't mean. He had no idea what the right thing for her to say would be, but she said nothing at all, pushing to her feet and leaving him half in pieces. She'd shown him a god's heart, rendered him down to bones and now brushed rock dust from her bay-brown knees as if all of this was the easiest thing in the world.

'I must go back,' she said, looking down at him but her eyes already in the village. 'You will not tell? It would not be good for anyone, I think, to know this thing at this time.'

He didn't understand and didn't know which he resented more, that she had taken him away from his failures or returned him to them. But he was abruptly so tired he could have slept here in the roasting heat and needle rocks, so he nodded anyway, the movement graver and more thoughtful than it felt.

Chapter Fourteen

Sisi

The sea today lurked in the corners of Sisi's mind, in the corners of everyone's minds; the flat silver of it, the way the tide barely moved over the sand, thickening until it was as supple and dense as mercury.

Storm is coming, people whispered to each other, talking quietly because the absence of the sea's voice made their own too loud. *Storm is coming*. People checked roofs and carefully dismantled the frames holding the partially painted screens; they hauled the boats way up into the coconut trees, tying them there with multiple ropes. They sealed drying vanilla, cloves and fish tightly away and brought the goats down from Les Hautes to shelter in the woods. The sky was the colour of tin and the temperature scorched eyelids and fingernails, made every movement like swimming. The edges of shadows melted until you did not know whether you were in sun or shade, walking through half-worlds that hung between realities like a prophecy.

Manon knelt by her doorstep, stroking her belly against the tiny forewarnings that rippled across it, and watched as Sisi rolled up her outdoor mats to store up in the rafters. Over the lagoon, frigatebirds grappled one another with their forked tails and hooked bills foreshortened by the light into dual-headed jaws. Sisi shivered and looked away, foreboding in her blood; the presence of the sea and the circling birds, the blood in the island's heart.

She knew it was a simple leaching of iron; but so was bleeding.

'Nuru took a blood sample this morning?' she asked, because she had to say something.

'Yes.' Manon sighed and pressed a hand into the small of her back. 'They are not happy.'

'No, I know.' Sisi had experienced all of Nuru's disapproval over dinner yesterday and told herself it did not hurt, or at least that she did not mind. Probably one or all of the Mothers also wished to speak with her, but between her staying in the weather station and now the storm, they had not yet found her.

'Mama Mandisa will blame the storm on us,' Manon said.

'Mama Mandisa will not dare be angry with *you*,' she said, and Manon laughed because it was true. The laugh morphed into a groan and Sisi turned from pushing the last mat into place to see Manon bent forward over her stomach, face contorted and hands splayed over her skin like stars.

'Manon?' Kneeling by her side, one hand on her friend's back, rubbing circles and circles, the other laying itself over one of Manon's to feel what she was feeling. 'They are beginning?'

'Mmm-hmm.' Manon's teeth clenched, breath hissing, and then like a switch flicked, she relaxed, leaning back against Sisi's hand and blowing out hot breath on a laugh. 'I would say yes, Sisi-si.' Her face – her wide, unblinking gaze – made Sisi's hands tighten. 'Can you get them? I will walk around, yes? Wait, pass me my watch, and help me up. Go, Sisi-si, go on.'

Sisi ran. The sea watched her and the frigatebirds rose, broken-bladed. Each footfall was a wish, each flex of muscles and breath a wish. Her whole mind and whole heart and whole soul a single wish.

Let this one live. Let this one live.

*

Nuru came, and Isolde. Mama Anouk sat herself outside and Luc stood by Manon's shoulder, and when Manon called for Sisi, she joined them. But when the contraction passed she ran to the door of the house, seeing Chicha and Katura there who ought surely to be in their own homes with the weather pressing heavier every minute. She understood, though, why they would want to sit here, playing mysterious games with hermit crabs and empty shells, their heads tilted to listen to another hope. *Please*, Sisi thought.

'Katura,' she said and the child looked up. 'Will you take this to the house of the Administrator? It is for Dr Adler, the lady doctor.'

Katura studied her, black-eyed and pensive, and then reached a decision that was wholly their own. They stepped forward to take the slip of paper from Sisi's outstretched hand.

'Thank you,' she said.

Katura nodded and then said to Chicha, 'Coming?' Running before the word was finished, gone from adult to child in the turn of a head. Sisi stood on the threshold and watched until they were hidden by walls and trees, then she looked at the sky.

It had darkened from tin to lead but there were still no clouds, only the heat syrupy in her lungs, syrupy and metallic. She shivered again. It meant nothing, the birth and the storm. Nothing other than bad timing and the season, just as the iron in Brother Island's heart meant nothing; because the doctors, this time, would change everything.

But her own heart beat painfully, losing its rhythm and then finding it again. And the life in her own womb had never been more present than it was in this moment, scaring her more than ever. *If there is a choice*, she thought, *then please choose Manon's*. If poor Antonin was a tithe, then let it be for this. For Manon who was loved and who so very much wanted to be a mother, Manon who deserved to be given all the happinesses that life could grant one single person.

Sisi turned and went back inside, collecting ice cubes from the freezer and a stack of fresh cloths from the cupboard in the hall.

'Sisi,' Manon said when she came back in, groaning as Sisi wiped an icy cloth over her face and collarbones, reaching out to grip hands so hard that Sisi's finger bones realigned themselves. She thought it was another contraction, but it was not.

'Sisi-si, he will live, yes? They will save him?' Her eyes so wide and so full of stars that Sisi thought the universe might crack open just to grant her wish. 'You said this. Say they will.'

'Yes,' Sisi said, fear in her stomach, her spine as cold as the cloth in her hand. 'They will. They will, Manon, I know it.'

'Yes,' Manon whispered. The pains came again and her eyes closed, breaths puffing, all her weight held between Sisi and Luc, who met Sisi's eyes without blinking.

*

Sisi was there through each pain and each endless, ticking minute. Manon's voice rose with the wind and the cloth in Sisi's hand was forgotten, the rain roared and Luc's low voice was as calming to Sisi as it was not to Manon.

'Aie, shut bloody up, Luc,' Manon said, spitting the words out between pants, but Luc's face showed no response and Sisi almost smiled.

Then Isolde's voice rose over the cacophony of the storm: 'Push now, Manon. Next contraction, you push down hard, you hear?'

Manon growled and Sisi dropped the cloth, folding both her hands around the one that Manon reached out, squeezing back with all the force that Manon was squeezing. There were sudden voices in the room outside, shouts and instructions, the clatter of furniture, but they faded, the wind and drum of rain faded, everything narrowing down to Manon's curved spine, her white-boned hand, her roar and roar and roar, Isolde's voice steady as a song, then Manon going limp so abruptly that Sisi's heart stuttered and failed and stuttered again. But Manon was gasping, half-laughing, and Nuru, kneeling beside Isolde, hands hidden, said, 'Wonderful woman, Manon. You wonderful woman. Like this once more and you are done.'

So once more, Sisi's whole body echoing Manon's, straining when hers strained, pain like a fire, a flood, a fury, and Manon's voice – oh, her voice – such a primal thing daring the world to deny her, and Sisi thought her heart might burst at the fear and wonder, the majesty of her friend.

Then it was over. Manon slumping backwards, heaving breaths and tears spilling over from the corners of her closed eyes. Isolde and Nuru bent double, faces hidden, hands moving, and Sisi hanging suspended between relief and terror, waiting, waiting...

A cry spun a web in the air. Indignation and shock; and the storm paused to let that sound, for a moment, rule the world.

'Your child,' Isolde said, handing the slick-wet, scrunch-faced, tiny scrap of a thing into Manon's arms, Luc propping her up, and them, the three of them, utterly perfect.

*

'Stop it, or you will make me start also,' Manon said and Sisi realised that she was talking to her, and that it was because she was weeping.

'Sorry,' she said, laughing, reaching out a hand to touch a fingertip to the balled fist of Manon's son. 'You were amazing,' she said.

'I was, yes.' Manon smiled downwards, and when the child opened the flower of his mouth to cry she fitted him onto her breast with an ease that made the world surge back into Sisi's heart, because she had done this before.

For a while it had been easy to forget, to pretend there was no reason for Manon to shield her helpless heart. *Oh,* Sisi thought, *oh, how vast can one hope be?*

*

'What—'

Nuru stood up sharply from where they were kneeling on the floor, folding up soiled cloths and laying clean linen beneath Manon's hips. 'Mama Anouk?' they called through the closed door. Sisi realised what they had realised and gasped.

The floor was flooded. Water a thin skim over the tiles, reflecting the lights like a lake full of eyes.

'What is it?' Manon said as Mama Anouk slipped through the narrowly opened door.

'Ah, you goddess,' Mama Anouk said, bending to kiss Manon on the temple, brushing a hand over her wet hair and then bending further to kiss the back of the babe's head where he fed with a concentration that the old lady's touch didn't break. 'You do not worry, yes? It is a little water, that's all. You stay in your bed and let the child feed.'

'Mama?' Sisi asked, and Mama Anouk straightened, her face still holding the smile but the skin around her eyes tight. She tipped her head and Sisi followed her to the doorway.

'It is not high tide for another two hours,' she said, her face hollowed out by the light, her voice subterranean. 'We are bagging around the storm doors.'

*

They worked with the rain pouring over them like rivers, numbing their senses, dissolving their skins and forcing them to gasp for air in the shelter of their own bodies. The knee-high storm barriers in the doorways of their houses were meant only to stop run-off, to stop sand and leaves and debris from drifting in. But the sea was still climbing, licking at their heels as they sloshed between houses, the light bruised, the village becoming flotsam.

They filled bags with wet sand that ran like blood from their shovels, and then, slick-fingered, bent-backed, passed the bags along and along and along, protecting one house, then the next and then the next. Checking the ropes of the pirogues, where the tide was heaving them back and forth between the weeping trees, wiping water for the thousandth time from blinking eyes, mouths swallowing floods. Sisi did not know how long she worked, handing off bags along the chain until her shoulders throbbed and her hands stung, with the rain falling as if it would only stop when the ocean rose up above L'Ambre. Perhaps this was what Mother Sea wanted, to reclaim the bones of her lost children, carry them back down to the depths. Perhaps finally she had come to drag Brother Island home. Perhaps if this happened, those who had broken this climate would spare a moment for regret.

Then, when it was unthinkable to continue one more second, the wind died away faster than it had risen, and this was worse. Because with the rain silent and the tide cool around her calves, it was peaceful, and so she was free to think.

About the damage being done to their houses. Their carefully woven mats swollen, their sofas and beds and chairs all sodden-footed. Manon and her tiny child, wet air and wet soil making heavens for bacteria, viruses, amoebas. Born into a storm, and what would everyone foretell in this flood and his birth, once the rain had stopped and they could breathe without drowning? She had seen the slip-twitch of fear in Mama Anouk's eyes; she had seen it and blamed it on the relentless sea. A mere coincidence of season and nine counted months, plummeting air pressure and a poised womb, but how many might refuse to believe it? Were they really so hopeless that they would leap at any chance to brace themselves against grief? Perhaps it was wisdom. Perhaps it was what Sisi had done every other time, but she could not do it for Manon.

She waded between trees trying to fathom whether the water level was dropping yet, the part of her heart that was not anticipating battles instead cataloguing the stems of legumes bent underwater, sweet potatoes invisible and drowned. She wanted to lean against a tree trunk and weep, because how could they fight this? And how could they pretend that Mother Sea loved them when she stole food from their mouths and babies from their arms, when she stole the land from beneath their feet, and please, dear Mother, cruel Mother, please let the outsiders find the cure that Sisi had promised. Please, whichever gods those pale doctors worshipped, Christian or Muslim, Darwin or their own two hands, please let them save this child.

Chapter Fifteen

Kit

Kit had been in the garden when the two children came. They bounded up the steps of the veranda, their physicality making him feel old and a mockery of himself, shabbily inhabiting his own skin. He had turned back to studying the sky, its terrible mass mesmerising in the same way as the sea cave. 'Storm's coming,' Geo had said, and he, Euan and Rachel had bolted shutters over windows, turning the house into a mausoleum, and even though that darkness ought to have been blissful to Kit, he'd escaped back outside, head tipped to watch the empty sky weigh more and more by the hour.

If he were still at university he might have learned about this, storms and climate change and oceanic cycles. It was a strange thought, neither good nor bad, but persistent. His mum had emailed, his father copied in, and he'd read it this time. Perhaps he shouldn't have done because it told him nothing he didn't already know.

We hope you are putting your effort into recovering from this episode, and making yourself useful to Geo. Use this time to take stock, Kit. You have a good life to come back to. I hope you can appreciate that once you've had time to think.

And, of course, this:

Your brother won that pharmaceuticals case. It's a big step for him and we're very proud. We went out for dinner with the family and your absence was felt.

It wasn't subtle. It never had been. He kept his eyes on the clouds, thinking of knowledge, and of not having it. Then Geo came out onto the veranda and the two children pelted back past him, raising tiny dust-clouds that settled so quickly again it was like the earth had sucked them back down.

'Hell of a time,' Geo said, perhaps to Kit, perhaps to himself or even someone out of sight in the black maw of the house. 'Hell of a time, poor woman.'

Kit turned, realising that even if Geo wasn't addressing him he still wanted to know. 'What's up?' he said, his voice flattened by the heat.

Geo grimaced, running a hand over his forehead to wipe at the sweat that made his hair stick out in dark spikes around his face. 'One of the women has gone into labour. Hellish timing, hey?'

That was what the children had come to say, which meant... 'They want Geraldine to help?'

'No,' he half-laughed. 'Jeez, I can barely breathe – the air's like soup!' Searching the emptied veranda before sinking onto the steps with a sigh. 'Won't let the docs in, but she's agreed to have samples collected or something. Tried not to listen too hard, to be honest with you, you know what I'm like with stuff like that.'

'Huh,' Kit said quietly, looking back out to sea where the horizon was condensing into a strange, boiling purple. His mind was full of unanswerable words, burned houses, barometers falling and tiny wooden boats, limp and vulnerable as moths. 'Oh, look,' he said. The storm front had materialised, distant but instantly galactic, light-rimmed, ponderous.

Geo pulled himself upright with one hand on the railing, coming out into the garden to look where Kit was looking. 'Bloody hell,' he said. 'Looks like the bloody apocalypse. Hey, Rachel!' Shouting to the barricaded house. 'Rach! Come look!'

The three of them stood in the tinny sunlight, wind picking up and that wall of fury coming towards them like the end of the world, the sea beneath it slicing up into whites and greys and blacks.

He'd expected thunder, lightning across the sky like veins in rock, but there was nothing. Just the purple cloud and the ragged sea, the line between pre-storm and storm as perfectly defined as the edges of a wound.

The wind rose again, shoving at them, rattling trees and bushes, raising dust. Then a crescendo of snare drums and opacity. Rain on the sea and then rain on the land, and all three of them fleeing for the swinging door, soaked in seconds; bent double by the weight of water; ears, eyes, skull full of nothing but the noise of it on ground and roof and their own skins.

Kit was laughing. Pushing water from his eyes, unable to hear himself but feeling it in his diaphragm and the muscles of his shoulders. Laughing because it was like they'd escaped a drowning; the air in his lungs was full of electricity and he was cold where seconds ago he'd been sweating. Every single nerve ending in his skin viciously, vibrantly alive.

Rachel handed him a towel and, still laughing deafly, he went to his room, peeling sodden cloth from his skin and standing naked in the dark, pressing his fingers to the window pane that vibrated with the energy of the storm outside. Shivering, water riveting from his hair, he leaned forward, laid his face and forearms against the glass with his whole body cold and overwhelmingly alive.

If he'd jumped, he'd never have known this.

The thought hung in his rain-filled skull like an afterglow. How ironic; he'd looked for peace in the sea but instead found jubilation in the rain.

He was glad.

Oh god, he was so glad. To be here and not there.

He hunched away from the window like he'd been punched, hands flailing in the dark, finding wall and windowsill as he clenched his eyes shut, rain running into them and then onward along the line of his nose, where it dripped onto the floor in a tiny irritation that ought to have been irrelevant but wasn't.

'Fuck,' he said. Gladness become nausea and he grabbed up the towel he'd dropped, scrubbing it over his torso in big, jerky movements, wanting to scour away this terrifying plummeting moment right here of realising it wasn't just that he couldn't die, but that he wanted desperately to live.

*

They had no electricity in the house because they'd covered up the solar panels and taken the island's one generator down to the village for the birth. So Kit ran his laptop's battery down trying to write an email to his parents, the fact that it wouldn't send making it easier, but still impossible. And he didn't know if it was his new realisation that forced him finally to write, or just the white noise and darkness around him.

Hello,
Thank you for the email.

(Too formal?)

Say well done to Charlie for winning that case – he deserved it after working so hard.

(Evenings and weekends not spent with his wife, not spent on anything, and was that laudable? Because Kit wasn't sure anymore.)

Thank you for arranging for me to come here, I think it was…

…cowardly of them, almost too easy for him to try again, perhaps the only place where he wouldn't do so; perhaps, because of that, the cruellest. How did you say that you no longer wanted to die, but that living was unimaginable? Living their version of life, anyway – but if not that then what, and where would that leave him? Familyless, unhomed, mapless.

It was only five sentences in the end, and only one of them about himself. It sat in his outbox and Kit was relieved to have written it, and relieved it wasn't gone. Then he wandered the house through surrealist, shifting shadows. Candle flames caged behind glass mounts stuttered and writhed; the storm pounded the house and Kit couldn't stay still. The doctors were working by battery power in their clinic and he envied them the focus, the activity, but not the weight of what they did. God, he could barely handle his own unexpected life, let alone be responsible for someone else's.

He paced the hallway and into the lounge. Geo sighed heavily on the sofa, papers dropping to the floor and his hand a puppet cut from its strings, twitching. Kit turned away, half-fearing what he'd see if he rounded the chair – a hung face, slack-mouthed – but why was he peopling his own imagination with ghouls? Was the idea of living really so terrifying? Walking and walking, his gaze on the slip-shod movement of his feet, the grain in the floorboards, the curls and talons of the unsteady light. It wasn't about *living*, he thought, but about *who* got to live, which version of himself.

Into his own room and out again, into Geo's and Rachel's and quickly out again, past Euan's unceremoniously closed door, onto the cool tiles of the bathroom, back into the hall, into Geo's office and around the large spread of the desk. Not one structure but a cobbled array of school desks and cheap ply, covered in a map and piles of paper, books, reports, three coffee mugs, four pens, a phone with its screen a blank rectangular eye, a closed laptop, a diary. Peering out through the slats of the window shutters, Kit saw only slices of black sky, flooded garden, the hedge dark and ominous. He turned away, straightened the pens and then the papers, trying in the lamplight to see the whole spread of the map, bending forward to trace Les Hautes and the thin scraps of yellow that marked the edges of the lagoon, bathymetry and altitude drawn in straying circles that made the whole, sea and land, look conjoined in a way that now, with the sky washing them away, made him shudder.

Death and life blurred.

He pushed the piles of paper back into place, hiding the dividing lines between water and air, and stopping to read a sentence. Then the paragraph, then pulling the sheet clear of the others to read it all. Reading it again, frowning, a stillness expanding in his gut in the exact place pain had been earlier, the two connected like land and sea, this stillness here, and the fear of living.

Sitting down in his uncle's chair, Kit rubbed a hand over his face to wake up his mind. The meaning was obvious but he read it again anyway, holding the pages gingerly. There were pencilled calculations in the margin, tallying pieces of silver.

'Holy fuck,' he whispered.

He thought he'd rediscovered anger, at Rachel for caring, at himself, at this whole island for forcing itself into his mind. He thought he'd felt something else too, at the sea cave and now before the storm. Curiosity, empathy, duality.

This, this here, though – it was shock, but also true fury.

Oh, he remembered this suddenly. Tearing posters from the walls of his university bedroom, hurling books from the bookshelf, rage forcing out a single throat-tearing howl. He'd forgotten doing that, and now, studying his hands minutely as if they held answers, he couldn't remember exactly *when* he'd done it. After being told of the fire where childhood and Jingo died? When he'd first mentioned not enjoying law? When they'd discovered his grades, or when he'd told them about changing courses and they'd tried to shame him into compliance?

There was nothing important of yours in the old house anyway. You're not thinking straight. You just need to focus more – you'll enjoy it once your grades are improving. He could remember the words but not the voice. Him squatting against the wall of his room, their disgust and their dictates on a loop in his head.

It had been a relief not to feel anything, after that. To watch himself retreating beneath his own skin and find it impossible to care. So how could he bear to be again the Kit who'd fought and lost and *felt*? So much safer not to feel. But the sheer *arrogance* of this, the... *expropriation*. Pushing away from the table, he dropped the sheet of paper without seeing where it landed, and turned the chair around so he could stare out at the hidden cliffs where he'd thought he had a choice, but hadn't.

*

'Kit, mate, where are you?' Uncle Geo's voice was slurred with sleep and Kit turned from the window as he appeared in the doorway to his own office, standing there with his face in shadow. 'Ah, there you are. Thought you were in your room.' An implied question, but Kit didn't answer it; he wasn't sure whether he'd say anything at all until he began to speak.

'What's this?' Picking up the paper he'd read, sliding it forward on a buffer of air.

'What?' Geo stepped into the room. 'Been catching up on the work, have you? Didn't realise all it would take was a good storm.' The accusation mild but then Geo lifted the page, tilting it to catch the wan light and although Kit still couldn't make out his face clearly, the whole line of his body shifted.

'Read this, did you?'

'Yeah.'

'Well...' Putting it back on the desk, Geo tipped his chin up, trying for teacherly but looking belligerent. 'What do you think?'

Kit was still sitting, and a part of him wanted to stand, to make use of the inches he had on his uncle, but it was what his brother would have done, so he leaned back, threw his legs out and folded his hands across his stomach. Perhaps this was worse, but Kit did not feel fully in control.

'I think,' he said slowly, 'this is a letter from some company that wants to mine the lagoon for sand and limestone, and has offered to pay to relocate the islanders.' Reaching out to pull the paper back towards himself, tapping a finger against the pencil marks, not recognising his own voice or his own hand, a buzzing in his ears that was almost but not quite the rainfall. 'I think that you are taking away these peoples' choices because of a business offer. I thought you were supposed be supporting them.'

The rain fell, but Kit could hear other sounds now too, water in the gutters and the surf. Perhaps the storm was passing. He thought of the court case his brother had just won, and which had made their parents so proud.

'Kit, son,' Geo said, exhaling slowly and coming to sit in one of the other chairs, forearms on the table. 'You've got to understand how this stuff works.'

'I think I do.'

'No, mate, you don't.' He raised a hand and Kit remembered it hanging lifeless in the lounge, saw his father in his uncle's gesture. 'It's complicated. Look, you think we should be recommending whatever is going to be best for these people long term, right?'

Kit nodded, meeting Geo's eyes, caught between righteousness and childhood.

'Well, you want to be some environmental hotshot, right? You know all about the climate change stuff. You *know* it's inevitable that islands like this will become uninhabitable.'

No, I don't, Kit thought. But then, did he? It had only been a semester from another life. That knowledge and that conviction, they didn't really belong to him now.

'They're going to have to leave at some point, it's just a matter of when, and how to get them the best possible life elsewhere.' Geo shrugged and leaned back. 'All these island nations have been preparing for years, you know. Buying up land elsewhere, investing in skills for when they leave so they've got options. But that all takes money, and to be blunt, there're just too few people here to save enough, and there's only so much that new internet and' – waving an arm at the window – 'coral restoration can do. So their choices are limited, and anything that'll give them a better settlement has got to be in their best interests, right? The government doesn't have bottomless pockets, after all, and they've had preferential trade for decades, not to mention subsidised telecom, education, the renewables...'

Geo stopped talking but Kit didn't move, the words had such weight. The sense of deals already done and momentum already gathering. 'It's all agreed?' he said slowly.

'Well, more or less.'

'You've sold the rights to the atoll to this... sand company.'

'Aggregates.' Geo shook his head. 'Not yet. But there's an application in, and we've got progress meetings scheduled when we return, so it would be useful to be able to bring something to that.'

'Wow,' Kit whispered, pressing his fingertips to the very edge of the table, the irregularities of the unvarnished wood tiny points of sensation when the rest of him had gone numb. 'Wow.'

'It makes sense, mate.' Geo tapped at the same figures Kit had touched, seeing in them something Kit hadn't, although his parents would. 'Look. Without the aggregates company, the immediate economic model is for the islanders to stay here and receive grants for mitigation work and to further subsidise food imports. But that sort of model is short-term, Kit, it's not future-proof. We're throwing money away. Relocating now is a real proactive investment for them, and this offer? It's generous and it's time-limited. We can't wait for the islanders to reach some crisis point – we have to pre-empt it.'

'But you're not just kicking them out of their home, you're destroying it as well. They'll never agree to that.' Cinders and blackened bricks, buried bones.

'It's only the lagoon and the sand spits, don't exaggerate. Like I said, sea-level rise and whatnot is going to destroy the place anyway; they may as well get money out of it and they won't care once they've gone.'

Kit had refused to go home because he'd not been able to bear either walking through the ruins of his childhood searching for ghosts, or facing his parents and their furious disappointment. The rain falling outside was definitely quieter now, although the room was darker, so somewhere the sun must be setting and he thought of the island's heart, of how it must be full of storm tides and white water now, the sea washing away all the rage. He didn't know what to say, but whatever he said he didn't think Geo would hear him. What were rocks and a stretch of water to Geo, whose own brother had shrugged off his burned home as soon as the insurance company had returned their call?

'It's just *stuff*,' his mum had said.

It's only the lagoon.

Kit's head dropped until he couldn't see Geo through his hair. Geo rose and came around the desk to stand beside him, putting a heavy hand on his shoulder.

'Don't get in a tangle over it, mate,' his uncle said, and he meant it kindly, that was the worst thing. If his father had spoken like this then perhaps Kit would have surrendered, complied, been forgiven. 'To be completely honest with you, there's a lot riding on this for me too. A governor post is coming up next year, and if I can sort this mess out it'll put me right in the running. It's now or never for me at this point, if you see what I mean. But we'll do right by them, I swear to you. I'll get them the best deal, 'cause that's what I'm good at, and you and Euan will convince the folks here, 'cause you're both honest enough for them to trust you.'

He meant it, he believed it, and when he left Kit didn't know what to believe anymore. Wouldn't they rather keep their home, or at least have the choice? Or did he think that only because he wanted to know what choice they'd make, what choice he'd make now, if it was him?

Chapter Sixteen

Sisi

'He is so hungry,' Manon said, one hand stroking her son's fine black hair, the other cradling his body, which was still curved into the shape of her womb. 'Look.' And Sisi looked. His eyes were open and the darkest imaginable shade of brown, fuzzily focused on Manon's face, his fist resting on the curve of her breast so incredibly perfect that the world was made more perfect by its existence.

'He is,' Sisi said. She would have given her heart and lungs for this moment to be devoid of the thought that this was day one. This was day one. And so while Manon read her reckless hope into each mouthful, everyone else held their breath. 'Dr Adler is coming down,' Sisi added, sitting beside Manon who was still in bed. 'How is the bleeding?'

'Oh.' Manon looked up from her boy and frowned at Sisi, not at the question but at the terrible irrelevance of her own body. 'Alors, it will quickly slow, yes?'

Sisi nodded, reaching down into the basket she had brought and pulling out jerky, dark chocolate, biscuits, placing them all within reach. 'So, eat,' she said. 'The biscuits are Philippe's, so you are safe.'

Manon reached for one and grinned at Sisi. 'Thank you for not baking for me.' And, dear Mother, it ought not be so hard to laugh, but all the muscles of Sisi's back were tight as wires and her arms were singing with the fury of impotence. If only it was her working in the clinic then she would at least be *doing* and not simply hoping.

The babe gasped and puckered up his face as Manon lifted him. 'Hush, my little fish,' she crooned. 'Patience. Here, see? Here you are.' He nestled onto the other breast and then a knock on the door sent Sisi hurrying to bring the doctor and Isolde and Nuru inside. Luc followed them in, his eyes moving from his tiny family to the outsider and back again, and Manon, seeing it, reached out a hand, saying, 'Luc. We agreed.' Sisi moved aside so that he could sit where she had been.

'I asked to be present so I can answer any questions you or your wife have,' Dr Adler said to him, staying against the wall, curtain-filtered sunlight turning her skin into a patchwork of colours. 'I won't do any of the testing myself,' she said, her palms open, and Luc's suspicion settled into a mask of acceptance that fooled no one.

Between them, Isolde and Nuru did everything, although it was only the full blood sample that they would not have otherwise taken. The babe's cry filling the room set all of Sisi's instincts into motion, the urge to soothe, to hold, to protect. But if Manon and Luc could bear it then Sisi could also. Then the babe was put back in Manon's arms, swaddled in bright cotton and hiccupping away all memory of his pain, and Nuru passed a slim vial of blood to Dr Adler, who took it between her thumb and forefinger as if it were made of glass or bone.

'Thank you,' she said. 'Are you happy to administer the vaccine and an initial antibiotic? We'll aim to create immunity and also kill off any bacteria before they can start producing toxins.' Putting the vial into a clasp-sealed box the doctor pulled out a syringe and hair-thin needle. 'Into the upper thigh, subcutaneous. Have you—'

'Yes.' Nuru cut her off. Sisi gritted her teeth to stop herself from talking. They reached for the drug, held it up to the light to prepare and then smiled at Manon. 'You are sure? You do not have to do this.'

Manon looked at Sisi, then at her husband and finally down at her second and only child. 'Yes, I do,' she said quietly, with her free hand parting wrappings to expose his thigh and the edge of his nappy.

The Sacere looked at one another, and it was Isolde who asked, 'Is this likely to sicken the child?'

'It is safe for newborns,' Dr Adler said. 'There's a small chance of some stomach upset from the antibiotic, but—'

'So it might weaken him?' Nuru cut her off again.

'It's a small dose. We'll fine-tune as we go along and monitor his health—'

'So it is a risk?'

Sisi stepped forward, putting a hand on Nuru's arm. They all of them were ruled by fear, and Nuru was also grieving. 'Nuru,' she said, waiting until her sibling turned to look at her, 'Nuru, it is all relative, n'est-ce pas?'

'It is also my choice,' Manon said from the bed making everyone look at her, all their hearts hurting a little more. 'Sisi understands this better than me, but I understand enough. I want this.' Luc breathed in and out slowly, taking his wife's hand in his own. Nuru stayed motionless for the space of three heartbeats, four, five, and then stepped back to the bed, raising the syringe again.

Another short, sharp cry like a falcon, and then it was all done, for today.

'I'll come again tomorrow,' Dr Adler said. 'We'll run screenings now to check for presence of the bacteria and if we get samples, we can incubate them for further tests. Just come and get me if you have any worries – you know where we are.'

She was more compassionate here than she had been in the lab. Perhaps she understood better now, or perhaps this was simply her way. The need to trust was galactic inside Sisi, all-consuming.

*

Once Dr Adler had gone, Manon leaned her head back against the wall and then tipped it a little way so that she could see Luc. 'You gave the first gifts?'

'Yes,' he said. At dawn of the child's first day, parent and Mother and Sacere had stood at the tideline with their feet in the sea, and given thanks of dark rum, fresh flowers and a handful of rice into the sea. Sisi had watched from the storm's tideline, catching ghosts of rum on the air.

'There is another gift-giving we need to do,' Nuru said, Isolde also nodding before taking away the paraphernalia of midwifery. Their voice was heard a moment later, and then that of Mama Mandisa, and Sisi moved again, pulling a chair from the far side of the room to be ready.

Mama Mandisa shuffled into the room and to Manon's side, her crook-boned hand finding the babe's head unerringly, cupping it. The contrast between her skin and his was both a thing of beauty and of sorrow. 'Yes,' Mama Mandisa said, settling herself into the chair Sisi had moved. 'Yes, Mother Sea will give this one a fine name.' Resting her stick beside her, she touched Manon's arm. 'But you, Manon. You will take care, yes? You must.'

Must resist loving too much.

Manon closed her eyes. Mama Mandisa looked towards Nuru, silhouetted by the soft light. 'Et bien. You have told them, child?'

Nuru smiled and Manon opened her eyes again. 'I waited for you,' they said, and then to everyone, 'We have gone through the oldest stories, our first years as Mother Sea's children when we were still finding our way towards her. We searched for ways that were perhaps important but became lost, and we remembered another gift that we used to give at the birth of a child.'

Everyone waited. The babe made a tiny sound and Manon handed his sleeping form to Luc, shifting herself against the pillows in a way that Sisi knew meant she was in pain.

'It was told that in a time of darkness, Mother Sea's eldest daughters hungered. They hungered for blood and with blood we sated them so that they turned away from our children. In those early famines, we gave to our eldest siblings, who are almost gods, blood from the air because this was unknown to them and so pleased them. So the darkness passed and our children grew strong.' Nuru closed their hands together in front of them, as though they closed the pages of a vast book or sealed shut the sky, and Mama Mandisa nodded her head, humming her agreement.

'So we will gift to Mother Sea and her eldest daughters a bird's blood, and this will please them,' she said.

'Why did we not know this story before?' Sisi asked, trying to make the words less than an accusation.

Nuru shot her a quick, brittle glance that told her she had failed, but answered calmly. 'We remember our stories through maps in our minds,' they said. 'This story was hidden on Les Soeurs in Berhane's mind. Mother Sea may know all, but we are not so lucky.'

'So then, I will go to Les Soeurs to capture a bird, a noddy,' Luc said, because that was what filled those two low islets, a thousand nesting terns and noddies, the sound and the smell of them like warfare. Nuru nodded but said nothing and Sisi could see Luc's urge to leave already piling up in his limbs; she understood that. If not for the fadys she would have gone with him or tried to help in the clinic – anything to stop herself watching Manon constantly, willing her not to love with such abandon.

'Tomorrow at dawn we will give the gift,' Mama Mandisa said. 'Mother Sea loves us best at sunrise.'

*

If there was one single good thing to have come from the destruction of the storm, then it was this: that there was more than enough work to keep Sisi busy the rest of that first day, and the next. They would not let her dig channels to drain the fields, or clear murdered crops away. But she gathered great armfuls of branches and palm leaves, coconuts and tide-washed, sea-smoothed relics from other places. Driftwood that had once been trees, plastic buoys and a metal barrel leaking unknown tainted water that was taken quickly from her to be stored safely until the mailboat came. Her house and Manon's needed sweeping out and washing and sweeping again, furniture dragged out to stand in the sun that seared clean the sky.

She missed Antonin in unexpected moments. His steady voice, his hands, the solace he would have been for Luc. But Nuru was here, and Manon. Always Manon.

'You are being careful,' Nuru said to her.

She felt her temper rise and some sharp word on the edge of her tongue, but when she looked up their face was full of something that she had no words for but that made her reach out instead and touch their arm. 'Oh, Nuru,' she said. 'Are you well?'

They held her gaze for a long moment, and she could see the battle within them between their terrible sorrow and their duty. The duty won, and she sighed before they even spoke.

'I am well. It is Manon and you yourself who matter, sister. And the choices we are making.'

'It was Manon's choice,' Sisi said, and the Sacere eyed her steadily, that moment of the sibling, the lost, gone.

'Was it truly?' they said, and then without giving her a chance to answer, 'Come, have you eaten?'

*

Once, she checked email, wanting and dreading a reply from Jomo. Because he still had not written and she was so perfectly torn between heartbreak and anger that she was not sure what he could possibly say that would straighten out her heart. But instead of him, there was this: a funded master's studentship for Commonwealth citizens sent to her by a colleague at Durham University. Sisi looked at it for a long time, then shut it down and went back to Manon.

However busy they all were, it was still not enough to halt the whispers. Sisi heard them as she washed salt and filigree crab skeletons from her floor; she heard them over the rustle of the palm leaves she carried.

'Mother Sea will surely take the child – she wanted him even as he was born,' said Mahena to her husband.

'It is because *they* are here, *they* carry the illness,' said Célestine, not seeing where Sisi sat in her doorway.

'Your Manon, Luc and the doctors. Luc, perhaps...' As Luc and Ghede upturned the boats to let them dry.

Then old Abasi: 'We must *do* something.' This at last was something that Sisi could answer.

'Yes,' she said to him as the light died on the babe's second day. 'We are.'

Chapter Seventeen

Sisi

It was the babe's third day, at noon, when Dr Adler came to the house with bad news on her face. Manon had her son in a sling and was hanging dripping clothes on the line, Sisi beside her, pegs in their mouths and Manon swaying in time with a slow song. They both stopped when the doctor came into view, Sisi turning to face her with a T-shirt hanging from one hand. Space in her stomach and the world falling through her as Dr Adler stood two metres away against a backdrop of milky lagoon and cerulean sky.

'There were bacteria in this morning's sample,' she said simply.

Manon made a sound like an injured bird, and Sisi went to her, slipping a hand around her waist. 'Sit down,' she said, because Manon was still losing blood and she did not need to be standing while the world betrayed her.

'What will you do now?' Sisi asked and Dr Adler took another step closer, bending beneath the half-empty washing line, lifting the bag at her side as answer.

'I want to switch to the immunoglobulin and change the antibiotic, give him a shot of magnesium, and take another blood test this afternoon, if that's okay. And give you another antibiotic as well, Manon.'

Manon was nodding but it was the gesture of someone agreeing because to agree was automatic. Sisi looked down at her friend and the crown of the boy's head and tried to deafen all of her thoughts except one.

'Tassa!' she called, and when the neighbour shouted a reply through the open window of their house, she added, 'Will you find a Sacere?' A faint answer came and then the sound of footsteps receding.

'When will you know if this will work? When will you know if the immunoglobulin is killing the toxin?' Asking the questions she thought Manon wanted asked. Demanding.

The doctor took another half-step forward, her instinct to touch fighting their agreement. They must also have been told about the fady against foreign men, Sisi realised, because no one had seen the other doctor for days. Unless he was working without pause, which was both what Sisi wanted, and also dreadful.

'We would hope to see a response by tomorrow,' Dr Adler said, 'but it might take longer. Will you... We can still airlift out to proper facilities. It could wait a day or two, but please think about it.'

But Manon would not be forced to choose, Sisi told herself, because they would solve it here, in their own home. Tomorrow, or perhaps on the fifth day, the tests would show an immune response, and none of the terrible toxin that wanted to poison the babe's nervous system. The antibiotics and the vaccine and Manon's antibodies would all protect him, because Sisi had been right, hadn't she, to go to the doctors despite everything that Nuru and the Mothers had said to her, and despite the whispers?

'Manon?' It was Nuru, kneeling quickly in the bare sand at her feet and taking a hand in both of theirs. 'Sisi,' they said without looking, 'Mama Mandisa wishes to know what news – go to her, please.' It was not a request, but Sisi waited, wanting to stay even though she was not needed, wanting to see in Nuru's eyes a clue to whether it was from condemnation or mercy that they were sending her away.

'I will come back soon,' Sisi whispered, bending to press a kiss to Manon's forehead and then walking underneath the inverted shapes of torsos that hung stiffening in the heat.

*

She found Mama Mandisa overseeing repairs to the hall roof, interwoven palm leaves being hauled across their tattered predecessors and bound and knotted into place.

'This is why it is better to do things our own way,' Mama Mandisa said to her, pointing her stick at the people up on the roof, the men's bare backs glistening like wetted stones. 'Where would we be now if we had decided to put up tiles? Roofless until the next ship brought us replacements from Mahé.' She smiled, her eyes the colour of pearls. 'And we already have new screens half-finished. This way is better, n'est-ce pas? Brother Island is happy and we are strong.'

Sisi rested her fingers on the old woman's arm and said with all the quietude she could muster, 'The babe has the infection, Mama. The doctor found it in the blood.'

Old muscles stiffened beneath her touch but Mama Mandisa carried on watching in the direction of the work with no expression on her face. 'He still feeds, though.'

'Yes. The medicines will work. It is early and so they have time for the medicines to work.'

'A little time.'

Taking her hand away from Mama Mandisa and folding her arms around her stomach, Sisi said, 'Yes, a little.' Her jaw was tense and an ache was behind her eyes like a dam straining. 'But it is more than we have had before.'

Mama Mandisa turned then, fixing her gaze somewhere on Sisi's face as the lines around her eyes gathered midday shadows. 'You are so sure, child. You have always been so terrifyingly sure.'

It was strange, Sisi thought, to live your life so close to others, secretless, and yet be unknown. *I am not*, she wanted to say, *I am not sure of anything, least of all my own heart.* But instead, and because she had to say something, she said, 'It will be different this time. It must.'

We fulfil our roles, she thought. Nuru was the voice of everyone but themself, Manon loved without limit, and she, Sisi, was certain.

'Alors, go,' Mama Mandisa said. 'Give me a little time with her. Chicha said that they found one of those buoys of yours on Pointe Rouge, below the house of the Administrator.'

'Oh.' She had remembered them at intervals, but between repairs and Manon, any thoughts of sailing out to check on them had been forgotten. She walked quickly, debris uneven beneath her feet where there ought to be only sand, but the lagoon was slowly clearing, shifting timidly from green-taupe to green, approaching turquoise.

Chicha and Katura were sitting in the shade of the buoy, laying out prizes gathered from the storm tide in strange mosaics of cuttlebone, pearl oyster, sea glass, urchin. Conches, tiny purple clams and the jaws of something from deep waters.

'Sisi!' Katura called, standing up, their face coming into the sun phoenix-like. 'It is broken?'

'I do not know,' Sisi said, smiling and touching her hand to Katura's shoulder. 'Thank you for telling Mama Mandisa. Can you find its anchors? Shall we see how it became loose?'

They scurried through the sand, unburying ropes and chains until they reached the folded metal of the anchors. One was bent from the forces that had pulled it free, but it was nothing that could not be corrected and Sisi ought to have been relieved, ought to have been keen to get the buoy back out there, especially now with cold water washed up by the storm and algae fighting to gain a foothold in the lagoon. An extreme event sample.

She brushed her hands over the red curvature of the buoy, sand shucking off it in avalanches, and tried to remind herself of all the reasons why this mattered just as much as it had before.

*

'Oh, oh my god, Sisi.'

Sisi looked up and Kit was there and the children began inexplicably to laugh. He was standing beneath the half-stripped palm trees, staring out across the sand to the village. The tide was coming in again and the next time it receded the beach would be a little more healed.

'It looks worse than it is,' she said. 'We have done most of the repairs already.'

'The houses,' he said as if she had not spoken. 'It... I didn't see the houses.' Muscles were twisting in his face as if he was in pain and Sisi almost reached out to touch him, before remembering that she could not.

'The houses, they are nothing,' she said and for the first time he turned to meet her eyes, startled and confused. 'It is the seawater in the crops.' She shrugged because it was odd to put into words what had been left unspoken among her people, less important than Manon's babe. 'It kills off this harvest now, and makes it harder to grow the next.'

'But your homes.' He was clenching and unclenching his fists, breathing hard with his eyes still narrowed in a distress she could not fathom but that made her sad all the same.

'Mostly they need only drying, replacing bits of roofing. The storm tide was worse than the wind and it is the wind that is hard on the houses. In a cyclone twelve years ago we lost half of our homes, so this is nothing.' Which was a lie, and besides every word she said only made the angles of his body more acute, so she stopped speaking, stepping past the buoy and the watching children, up to the trees. 'Kit?' she said.

'I'm sorry,' he said. 'I'm sorry, it's... I know how it... Jesus, you should have all come up to the big house. This is—' Cutting himself off, throwing his arms out in a strange, desperate gesture and then recoiling when his shadow did the same. 'It's worse,' he said, almost to himself. 'It's not just your houses, is it? It's your... it's your whole *world*. How do you keep going? ...What do you *do*?'

Sisi frowned at him, his proxy despair making her stiffen. She nearly spoke but he swung away and launched himself long-legged through the trees towards the path that led up to Les Hautes.

'We fight,' she whispered. 'It is our world. Would you not also fight for yours?' Remembering the children too late, and dredging out a smile. 'Come,' she said, 'we will tie this to the trees so it does not escape again.' Up the path, the two doctors were walking between the clinic and the Administrator's house, their heads bent and their mouths moving. It was both a nightmare and a blessing that she could not hear what they were saying, that Kit had taken his own despair away. In the old stories he would have carried bad spirits with him when he came over the sea, and it was harder than usual to suppress superstition, to tell herself that Kit's shadows were illness and not a tangle of ghosts. Perhaps, if Manon's child were safe from all harm, she would have had room to spare in her heart for pity.

*

The buoy's electronics woke contentedly as soon as the solar panels were cleaned and turned to the sun. The children went back to cataloguing their finds, and Sisi, after tying the anchor chains around a tree, did not know whether she could go back to Manon yet. She lingered in the sluggish air, beneath the palm yet in the sun, watching the curved spines and cricket-bent legs of the two children and trying to paint Manon's son into the picture, fat-kneed and laughing; if she could only picture the scene with all her heart then it surely must come true.

'Sisi, c'est quoi?' Chicha asked her, holding up a tiny thing, trailing weed, and Sisi came closer, crouching to look.

'Oh,' she said. Startled by grief, her eyes filling with the sea and her fingers glass-like as she reached out to take it. It was a charm carved from green stone into the shape of a great ray, spirals on its back and the slim tail curved like a hook. What had looked like weed was the remnants of its leather cord, threaded through the hole at the top, and cold where she touched it. Her fingers knew the lines of this thing. Her breastbone knew the weight of it when it rested between their bodies; her eyes knew the patch of paler skin in the hollow of his throat where it lay.

'Oh,' she said again. Missing him all over again. More than that. It *was* love, she realised finally, simply to know someone so well and to have forgiven them and been forgiven. And it was not, after all, a betrayal of herself to miss the kindness and finite scope of their marriage.

The children were silent, looking at her with eyes wide and full of sunspots. 'It was Antonin's?' Chicha whispered. Sisi looked at him and nodded. The movement released rivulets from her eyes but because she was with children, she laughed a little.

'Yes,' she said. 'He wore it always.' She had threaded it onto new cord for him just months ago, handing it over silently and shrugging away his thanks. She hoped that it had mattered to him, her doing that tiny thing.

Katura reached out and touched it with their fingertip so lightly that the weight of it in Sisi's palm did not change. 'And Mother Sea gave it back to you,' they said, already half the Sacere they would become when they were older. The last Sacere, unless things changed. Unless Manon's child lived, and was one too.

It was almost a relief to be reminded, allowed to abjure some of this sorrow. 'Not to me, I believe,' she said, smiling. 'It was his first wife who carved it – this is why he loved it so much. I think Mother Sea brought it back so that we could give it to Afiya.'

Katura thought about this and Chicha leaned absently against them, tipping his head onto theirs. Sisi's heart ached.

'Yes, I think that you are right,' Katura said. 'I could...' More tentatively, 'I could carry it up for you, being as you...'

'Cannot go up to the tombs?' Sisi closed her fingers around the charm, the wing tips of the ray digging gently into her skin, the cord now as warm as her blood. 'Yes, thank you. I would like that very much, and I think my husband would also. I will tell Nuru.'

Metres from the sea, it was hard not to picture him out there, tossed by the storm and dragged into the dark. Watching to see if her heart was big enough to let this part of him lie with the bones of the woman he had loved most.

They hungered for blood and with blood we sated them so that they turned away from our children.

Would he be content if his blood saved Manon's babe, or would he choose...? Sisi shook her head, coming to stand. He had not known about that.

She left Chicha and Katura to their storm spoils and walked back to Manon and her unnamed boy.

Chapter Eighteen

Kit

He ought to offer to help Sisi, Kit knew that; or to help *someone*. But he couldn't. There was soot in his throat and the beach was a cemetery of broken coral. Reality wavered; flames burst into life at the edges of his vision, licking at the houses, and here was Sisi watching him as his mind broke apart. So he ran. Past contemptuous faces in doorways and under trees, flames chasing him towards Les Hautes. But they were haunted too. Bones and ghosts and broken things. He couldn't bear it. Murdered corals and the island's tainted heart, the roar of excavators and explosions shaking the ground beneath him as the cliffs sang love songs, holding out their dusty, weightless hands. He stopped, surrounded by fields, fingers against his temples, his lungs heaving and heaving. None of it was real. The fires in the houses and the ghosts, the pending ruin, his mind fabricating nightmares. They were imagined, they were imagined – but still he couldn't breathe and stumbled and ran away from them again, all the drugs in his veins not enough to stop his mind from shattering.

He turned back to the house, the breath in his throat like a vacuum, and paced the perimeters of the garden, sucking in air, his neck burning and his eyes shying away from the broken village. He couldn't stop moving, or breathe without it hurting, or stop seeing ruin.

*

Flames and panic, and drugs. He didn't know if it was the medicines making him hallucinate fires and ruin, or his own mind, and even once the visions stopped, once the world returned to blue sky and sea and tattered island, he felt that breathless fear crawling under his skin. As though now that he no longer wanted to die, the world was too fragile for him to navigate.

He retreated into sleep, but that too was full of nightmares and nothing at all. Drugs, panic and dreams. Losing track of everything other than the grip of these three things around his chest.

Was this where he broke again? Not death but fear and exhaustion and breathlessness.

He slept for two days; he avoided the village; he slept.

*

The fifth day after the storm, he woke and stayed awake. The fear muted now into something harder to define, and before it could rouse itself or he could think too hard, he sent his email, finally. At the same time, like a counter-weight, his brother sent a text message, angry that Kit had forgotten his wife's birthday. Kit stared at the words, thinking of cards winging across the ocean, foundering, sinking, thinking of his sister-in-law who he had always suspected of wearing a façade like a shield. She reminded him of Rachel, now he thought about it. He left his phone on his unmade bed and went out into the garden, standing hunched beneath the starved branches of a pine, counting his breaths and willing them to stay steady, for the world to stay steady, weighing this small failure against his brother's callousness and not knowing whether either mattered at all. Two children and an adult passed through the garden and up towards the tombs and his heart twisted against his ribs until he saw they were carrying nothing larger than a bundle of branches. He realised what he'd been expecting, and why he was counting the days at all.

The fifth day. There had been talk over dinner the evening before – small, dry words like neonatal tetanus, drug resistance, rapid mutations, endemism. Reducing brutality to a problem and a challenge. But Kit heard only *nine days*. Nine months of promise, and then a nine-day life. His own profligacy disgusted him all of a sudden, standing here being stalked by fires and the cliffs, proxy-relieved that a baby hadn't yet died. No wonder Sisi had looked at him condemning and bewildered, him choosing to throw away what they were fighting so hard to save.

But these three, the children, the non-binary other whose name and title both eluded him, what were they doing going beyond the house into rocks the colour of faded wine? Giving thanks? Asking for help? He had no idea how their faith worked, but he wanted to ask Sisi. He wanted to listen to her low voice slipping in between story rhythms and brevity like a moth. He wanted, stupidly, to tell her about his brother and watch her face for his answers.

Sisi would be down in the village, though, and didn't wildfires, sea levels and storm surges make his brother insignificant? And besides, curiosity was dangerous, if curiosity meant stepping through the storm debris that had unleashed that awful breathless panic, the imagined flames. Better to stay here weaving a path in the grass like just another ant, following his own footsteps until it felt like he was moving backwards, the long fall to the sea whispering in his ear.

You didn't realise that you'd begun to climb until you feared the fall, he thought, pausing between one footstep and the next as a dark lizard darted across the ground where his foot had been poised to land. The animal stopped just beyond the line of Kit's shadow, looking up at him and then S-bending towards the path leading down to the bay.

Skink, he remembered. Sisi's voice in his ear louder than the sea. He stood where the skink had stopped him. 'A skink,' he whispered. 'A skink told her not to let me jump.'

But he wasn't brave enough. He didn't want to know if he'd be welcomed, didn't want to know if the storm baby was well, or to see Sisi's heart breaking if it wasn't. Pain in his chest again, panic or prescience, if there was any difference. He breathed, took a step, breathed. In a gap between trees he caught movement on the beach and realised that for the first time it was not people tidying or repairing, but people preparing the boats. What unspeakable bravery, to still throw yourself out on the sea in those tiny vessels after it had taken so much. Was that faith, or only necessity? Did they forgive the sea that they worshipped? Did they even see the need to do so? Or did they really see it as kin, someone who you loved and were loyal to, even when it betrayed you? Was that, he thought bitterly, what kin was meant to be?

*

Something about his own bitterness, and their unbroken bond with the water, pulled him finally out of the garden. He slunk past the village like a pariah and was almost at Les Hautes when he found Sisi standing silently as if lost. He stopped, waiting for her to spot him in between low, tangled trees, the leaves thick, their undersides mink-grey.

'Hi,' he said, half-expecting her to know what it had taken for him to leave the garden. But of course she didn't.

'Kit,' she said. 'All is well with you?'

The words were only a formula, he remembered, but then weren't most conversations? 'Yes, thank you, and with you?' Trying to catch her eyes where they drifted to him and then away.

She smiled emptily. 'Yes.'

'But I heard... How are you really?'

Sisi lifted her face to look into his properly for the first time. The quiet was all around them, and he realised that he'd come up here to confront the cliffs. To prove to himself he'd still step back. Her eyes were old pools and autumn. 'What did you hear?'

As if she had no idea which of her nightmares he was referring to. 'Matt, Dr Freshman, said that...' He trailed off because her whole frame had braced itself for the blow. 'Sorry,' he finished lamely.

'Yes,' she said, but she was shaking her head, lifting a hand to readjust the knot of her wrap. 'Why are you sorry, Kit?' The question holding a strange challenge.

'I... I don't—'

'Are you culpable?' She said it while gazing down on the roofs of houses and the boats just now being floated in the surf by brown, anonymous bodies. 'And if you are, regret changes nothing, n'est-ce pas?' Looking back at him in time to catch his own tiny flinch, then frowning as if he perplexed her as much as she perplexed him. She shrugged, the straps of her backpack shifting against her collarbones, their shadows like the wings of a bird tattooed onto her skin. Kit looked away. 'It is with those doctors now, I think,' she said. 'They are our hope now, no?'

'And your Mother Sea,' he said. Partly because it was suddenly terrible that the child's life was being entrusted to friable, fallible humanity. Partly because of the cliffs and wanting to know that there were things to stop you from falling.

She was frowning again, this time at a point further out, the offshore dock with its splash of orange that was the tied-up rib.

'Mother Sea wishes for us to help ourselves,' she said. 'This is why we went to the doctors.'

'Right,' Kit said, watching her frown. 'That makes sense.' Then he said slowly, 'I'm sorry about the other day, you know?' She looked at him blankly so he added, 'Me running off like that – you must think I'm crazy.'

'I think...' she began, half a smile forming and then dissolving. 'I think it is fine.' Turning again. 'But actually, I must go. I have work.' She stepped over a lip of rock, looking back over her shoulder to say, 'Take care, yes?' and then passed around a tree, leaving him alone.

'I meant,' he said to the rocks, 'that I'm sorry I haven't helped you repair your homes. I'm sorry I'm a mess when you have way more going on than I do.' The sun made his skull paper-thin, and no one answered him. Perhaps he wouldn't go to the cliffs after all, but instead to the island's hidden, hypnotic heart. He wanted to lie on a skin of rock and look down into the green sea, watching forgiveness and forgetting himself by thinking about Geo's secret deals and the price of a future.

Chapter Nineteen

Sisi

Sisi was barely aware of having met Kit, barely aware of anything other than her own flesh and that today was day five. The babe was five days old.

Mama Anouk had sent Sisi away, telling her with uncommon cruelty she had played her part and her vigil now only risked her own child.

She had played her part. Sisi had seen the same thought, less subtly, on Mahena's face, and Luc's, even sometimes on Nuru's. She had taken Manon to the doctors; she had played her part, she had been certain. So when Mama Anouk sent her away, she came to the weather station and leaned against the outside wall with her laptop resting on her thighs. Then she uploaded the data from the thin baskets of soil lying in the hollows around her, the need to *do* co-mingling with the need to *prove*.

When she had started the study, testing moisture retention, salinity and pH, carbon and nitrogen levels, it had felt incredibly important. To know whether there was any scope at all for farming the hard land up here. Olives, she had thought, something that might survive the dry, because if they could eke food or a trade crop from this, then they would rely less on the salt-spoiling earth down in the bay. And now, with their harvest washed away, it had become only more important, no?

Perhaps Les Hautes was where their hope lay, and if so then the path to it was through these numbers on her screen, and her knowledge.

But taking food to Luc and Manon this morning, Sisi had watched the babe pull away from his mother's breast after only a few mouthfuls. Dozing fitfully, puckering his brows and mouth into discontent when Manon switched him to the other side, trying to make him feed again. Manon and Luc had not looked at each other or at Sisi, their eyes sliding from the babe to the floor to the light from outside, and Sisi had been grateful. This terrible thing might not become truth if she did not see it in Manon's eyes. She wondered again whether Antonin would have died more fiercely or more gently if he had known what lay ahead for them, for her.

'He is only slowing down after making up the early weight loss,' Sisi said. 'Tired from all this attention.' She reached out to Manon's hand where it cradled her son, but her fingers shook like a plucked string and she pulled them back. 'I will find Dr Adler,' she said, leaving the three of them in the sun-red room with their silence.

Then Mama Anouk had sent her away, and Sisi had gone, leaving her heart down there in Manon's lap, beating fierce prayers to the sea and to science and to the sky.

*

'Oh, Mother,' she said, pushing the laptop aside with too much carelessness and rising to her feet, walking away from the building into the bruising sun. Her wrap caught the wind, fluttering before her towards the point where Kit had stood poised with one foot on land and the other above the sea.

There, with only the Devonian sea and a thin-skinned sky, Sisi carefully unbound her thoughts.

Manon's boy was sickening.

The doctors that Sisi had convinced Manon to believe in had four more days to find him a cure.

And Sisi? Sisi would give up the blood in her veins, would cut the fingers from her hands, if it would save him.

*

She had been sent away for the safety of her own child, and there was such deep irony in this, because Sisi had never really wanted Antonin's child who would be Jomo's kin. It was terrible to admit this truth, and with Antonin gone it made *her* terrible. But Manon *did* want this child. Oh, how she wanted him.

Sisi sighed, then turning away, she felt it.

A flutter twist.

Butterfly wing, fairy skip, bird breath.

Cataclysm, earthquake, tsunami.

'No,' she whispered, placing the palms of both hands over her womb, gently because the skin and muscles of her stomach were suddenly foreign. There, there again. A playful thing, a skip-hop of sensation. Her whole heart sank and sank again.

'No,' she said again. 'Oh, not now.' But there *was* no more denial now as it unmade its isolation. The wind pressed against her as if it wanted to bear up the weight; Manon's babe lay sickening below, and Sisi began to weep.

*

It was her laptop that pulled her back, the tinny, incongruous sound of an email, and she used a corner of the wrap to wipe her face, pushing her hair back from where it had stuck itself to her skin. There were things she needed to do, and she would do none of them standing here crying over futilities. Waking her laptop screen, above the email about the studentship she found the one she had been waiting for. Its own small cataclysm, not sorrow this time, or hope, or at least not something quite so simple as either. Jomo had written:

I'll come on the next boat, so guess I'll be there in two weeks? It will be good to see you, Sisi.

Sisi turned her laptop off, closing the lid slowly and slipping it into the backpack. Two days ago, Nuru had said that surely he was not coming as he had not replied. They had said it calmly, but there had been a hardness there that could have been either anger or hurt, so she had said, *No, he will come. I know it.* And then had to turn away so that Nuru could not read her face.

And now he was coming, just as she had known he must. She thought, privately, that his return was not so much to say his farewells to his brother but to show his sibling that they neither of them were now alone. For a moment she wanted nothing other than to go up to the red cliffs to tell Antonin that his little brother was coming home. He would have been glad for Nuru's sake, she knew, and probably even for hers.

Jomo had been in Durban, last she'd heard, so if he were there, he would first fly to the Seychelles, then await the mailboat to carry him here. Two and a half thousand miles north-east, and only the very last part something that Sisi had experienced herself. How odd, she thought, to have Jomo back here when he would surely be so changed. How odd, to have him say it would be good to see her as if he had forgotten the last words that passed between them. How much more complicated it was now, although they had thought it was the end of the world back then. She wondered how much she still loved him, and whether it mattered, and knew that she would only learn the answer to both questions when he was standing in front of her, real and whole and returned. She did not wonder whether he still loved her. He had loved her once, and left her, so whatever was in his heart now carried no water at all.

Lifting the bag, she sighed, scrubbed at her dry face again and closed the door of the station against creeping dust or birds looking to nest. Last year a pair of tropicbirds had claimed the corner inside the doorway, so she had shared the whole season with the angry gaze of the parents and the chicks' somnolent chatter. It was nearly lunchtime now, the apex of the sky burned away, shadows on the ground as dense and as perfect as spilled ink. Sweat gathered in the curls of her hairline and along her vertebrae. But Sisi had never minded the heat up here, the way it crawled along the ground and reared up at you from the white rock. It was so different to the saline shore, the hill forest and the baobab forest that it made the island manifold, climate zones in infinitesimal shades of heat and humidity. Large enough, she had promised herself, to contain her.

She walked more gingerly than before, testing footholds on the ragged path down the cliff as if the body that she was bringing down to the village was not the one she had taken up. Perhaps it was not – it had definitely ceased to be hers. The rocks were watchful and she looked for geckos in their shadows but found none, realised she was also looking for Kit and not finding him either.

Chapter Twenty

Sisi

Sisi went to the doctors in the evening, but they were bent over their microscopes and the thrum of a centrifuge filled the concrete space, so she found herself only watching instead, reading hope into their industry. This was what she had wanted to see, after all, their expertise and mysterious tech all bent to one thing, one life.

But the next day, the sixth, with the babe pulling away from Manon's breast and whimpering listlessly, with Manon's eyes raw from sleeplessness and terror and Luc leaving the room when Sisi entered it, Sisi went back again. She followed Dr Adler up through the village to where the clinic sat like a scar beneath jacaranda trees. Her grandparents had attended the missionary school here, when it was no longer French but English; how cold it must have been for them enclosed in there rather than in the open sea-breeze shade of the village hall where the Sacere taught.

'Doctor,' she said when the other woman reached the clinic door and Sisi was still twenty metres behind. 'Dr Adler.'

'Geraldine,' the woman said, turning with a smile that drew shadows beneath her eyes. 'Please, call me Geraldine.'

'Is...' Sisi's words were stacked like books in her throat, each one filled with thousands of others, nested questions. 'Your work is going well? You are close to finding a working immunoglobulin? This is what you are working on, yes? The antitoxins?'

Dr Adler stood with one hand on the door handle, looking at Sisi without speaking, then she pushed the door and moved aside to let Sisi pass in before her. Sisi did so, eyes adjusting to the light, her muscles bunching then relaxing again as she registered the male doctor's presence.

'Hello there,' he said, looking sharply between Sisi and Dr Adler, Geraldine. 'Have they agreed?'

The airlift. Manon had refused. Sisi had begged and Manon had said that it was *these* doctors she had agreed to, and *they* must be the ones to help. But Sisi saw the weight in both doctors' eyes and shuddered.

'No,' Geraldine said and Dr Freshman bent his head, his hands setting down the pipette and vials, then after a moment picking them up again.

'Have a seat,' Geraldine said. She lifted the sealed box Sisi had seen before and handed it to Dr Freshman without speaking. Then she leaned back against the table, facing Sisi with her hands resting on the wood behind her hips. 'Yes,' she said, 'to answer one of your questions, it is the immunoglobulin we are focusing on at the moment. Trying to find a form that might be more effective against the tetanus.'

'And?' Sisi said.

Geraldine flexed her arms without moving them, the thin bones of her wrists almost visible through the skin. Her hair was pulled back harshly from a face made wan and ghostly. Sisi swallowed down frustration.

'And,' Geraldine repeated slowly, 'you probably know that the immunoglobulins don't act strongly against toxins that have already bound to the nervous system. That's why the disease is most effectively dealt with via immunisation.' She hesitated, either waiting to see how much Sisi had understood, or wrestling with what to reveal.

'But there are other methods,' Sisi said. In the corner of her vision Dr Freshman lifted the syringes of Manon's and the babe's blood, setting them in racks, changing his gloves. Her lungs hurt, as though his averted gaze and the workings of his hands were sucking oxygen from the room.

'Yes,' Geraldine said, tendons rising again on her hands. 'But the endemic bacteria here are resistant to most antibiotics, and the... the patients just don't seem to be able to develop their own toxin antibodies after vaccination. It looks like either there's a mutation in the islanders' gene pool that suppresses immune response, or the bacteria itself is suppressing it.'

Had Geraldine forgotten Sisi's own pregnancy? That in a few months she too would be holding a 'patient' in her awkward arms. Subject B. 'So what can you do?' she asked. It was a puzzle, she told herself, like the farming of Les Hautes. A matter of problems and solutions that simply needed the correct alignment. 'Intravenous immunoglobulin? Would this not work?'

Dr Freshman stopped whatever he was doing, looking up at her again with eyes bright as a hawk's, and as angry. 'Are you the biologist?' he said before Geraldine could answer. 'I didn't realise.'

On any other day, she would have resented the adjustments she could see tickering behind his eyes, but today she only nodded.

'It's the next step,' Geraldine said, answering Sisi. 'Now that the... patient is showing symptoms, I'd like to have him on a regular IV infusion. We can give him muscle relaxants as well, to buy us time.'

Sisi balked, then cursed herself for doing so because she wanted this honesty. She wanted to parse assurance from Geraldine's face and hands and words. 'You can do that here?' Looking around the room, the equipment lined along the tables, piles of paper and the slow hum of electricity.

'In the big house, I thought. There's more room.'

'And you will start today?' Sisi leaned forward in her chair. 'Because this will work, yes? It is providing the immunity directly and not relying on the babe to produce it.'

She saw Dr Freshman's face move, Geraldine's pale eyes grow a shade paler, and the small room closed in around her. 'What?' she said.

'It doesn't work like that—' Dr Freshman said.

With a slight shake of her head that might have been meant for him, Geraldine interrupted. 'It might. It should give us time, and time is what we need now.'

But Sisi could see the man's face and Geraldine could not. 'What do you mean?' she said to him. 'Why does it not work like this?'

Geraldine pursed her lips and there was that look in Dr Freshman's raptor eyes that was surely anger, although for what she could not guess. For her, for them all? Or *at* her, for demanding repayment for her faith?

'Geraldine said it just now. The immunoglobulin attacks the toxins, but only those that aren't already bonded to neurones. IV treatment will' – he shrugged so sharply that Sisi expected the things in his hands to fall – 'press the pause button. But the body still needs to develop its own immunity. Tetanospasmin is... it is one of the most lethal toxins known.'

Sisi looked into his eyes with her own anger rising. 'I know,' she said. 'I think that I know this better than you do, no?' Pushing to her feet. 'But this is exactly why you are here. So solve it. All of this you knew before you came, so give us something new. Give us an antitoxin that can kill it in the nerves. Give us something that *works*. You are doing *what* in here all day?'

'I'm *trying*—'

'Matt,' Geraldine interrupted, moving so that her body was closer to both Matt and Sisi than they were to each other; behind her the island's paltry tele-medic set was pushed into a corner. 'Matt is working to isolate the toxin, the tetanospasmin, and create an inactive form that will be a vaccine specific to the strain we are seeing here.' She tried a smile but there was so little blood in her lips that it looked rictus. 'I am testing existing drug combinations against our blood samples to try to find the most effective combination. None of it is quick, Sisi. I know this is not what you want to hear, but none of this was ever going to happen quickly, and we did not know about Manon. But we are trying our best.'

They truly were, going by the clutter of water bottles and coffee cups, the bruise-blues around Geraldine's eyes, the bin overflowing with discarded gloves like dead sea creatures. They were, but it did not matter.

'You have *days*,' she said. '*Days*. Tell me you can do this.' Her hands fisted in her wrap and she felt it again, the quickening, the child within her making her heart lurch with horror and something else she could not define.

The doctors looked at one another briefly, and Sisi stared at them without blinking. When Geraldine spoke, it was not an answer. 'Get Manon to agree to come up to the house so we can start the IV. Please, that's what we need to do now.'

Sisi looked at the blind-eyed machines and then at her own hands. 'Yes,' she said. 'Get everything ready. They will be here in an hour.'

*

Nuru was there when she returned to Manon's house. She told them all the news and her sibling led her back out into the ferocious heat of the sun; the tide was out, the beach vast as a held breath. 'You still believe this is the right thing?' they said.

'Yes.' But her eyes skipped from Nuru to the distant water and back again. 'Yes,' she repeated. 'I know that you do not—'

'It is Manon's choice – my thoughts do not matter.' Their eyes were dark with strain and she wondered if they too lay awake at night paralysed by the importance of the next few days.

'I thought we were one people, with one heart,' Sisi said sadly. Because it was a terrible thing that this choice existed at all, but given that it existed it was surely cruel to put it on one person alone.

'We are,' Nuru said, and the fierceness in their quiet voice made her look up at them. 'We have to be.'

Within the house, the babe mewled and mewled again, and both of them stiffened as if the sound were a blow. Nuru turned their head away, then shook themself and looked at Sisi instead. They had, she realised, been about to look up at the red cliffs.

'Come, then,' they said. 'Let us pack for them.'

*

Hours passed. Hours that became days.

In the great white bed in the foreigners' house, the babe began to fit, muscles convulsing with a pain that the drugs dulled but did not stop. Manon sat, holding him when she could, stroking his head and fingers when she could not. She saw neither Luc nor Sisi, even when they touched her, when they held food or drinks out until she took them. Luc crouched in corners unspeaking, or he went out to sea and came back with his eyes slitted and ghostly. Sisi floated in the space between Manon's heart and the real world, and waited.

They waited.

Dr Freshman did not sleep and Geraldine's hands shook handing over syringes although Nuru's hands did not. Mama Mandisa rested her fingers in Manon's hair; and they waited.

The hours counted themselves off deafeningly, the sun flickered like a candle, or like the end of days. *Not again*, not spoken but in all their eyes. *Not again. Not again.*

They waited.

*

Only when Nuru whispered in the false cool of a morning, 'Eleventh day,' did Sisi realise time was a measurable thing. And it was a point that might have been a miracle if she did not remember Matt Freshman's words. *The pause button*, he had said. They were all paused, she thought, all of them apart from that microscopic chemical lacing ruin.

So now the hours were grains of sand; blurred voices, breaths, a heartbeat like a bird's. The sun crept onward, and Manon's eyes refused to blink. Luc fled back to the sea. Sisi stood at the window as evening slipped over the water like a dropped veil, the sun falling behind the far end of the bay. She watched these things, the white sails of the pirogues turning amber, a gecko beneath the eaves, heat rising blood-red from the rocks; everything surreal with insignificance.

Life flickered in her womb and Sisi closed her eyes, but then, and because it was all she had been listening to for days, she heard Manon's breath change.

A hitch, a rasped inhalation.

Such infinitesimal sounds.

Sisi ran, her ribs opening like a chasm. *No,* she thought, falling to her knees at Manon's side. *No, oh Manon, no.* Denial drowning her whole. *Not yet. Not yet. Don't take him, don't take him from her.* 'No,' she whispered. 'Oh Mother, no.' Hope broke and promises broke; she folded herself around Manon and her child like a shield as the whole world bled. 'Manon,' she whispered, 'Manon.'

*

'Sisi,' someone said from a thousand miles away, from flesh and blood and bodies that did not deserve their heartbeat as much as Manon deserved her son's.

If he had lived another twelve hours, he would have had a name.

'Sisi.'

'I know,' she said. 'I know.' Tearing herself in two, leaving half of herself here, on this floor, rising to her feet because she must leave the dead for the sake of life. But if the world could do this to Manon, then the world deserved to die.

Chapter Twenty-One

Sisi

The twelfth day, and the first, and also the second time that Manon had endured this. Sisi cut a strip of cloth the colour of the evening sea from one of her wraps and scoured the tideline until she found a yellow-gold shell with a hole already in its rim. She threaded the cloth through the hole and then wound it around her fingers, the shell in her palm like a heart.

Few people were out at this time, and those who were, Sisi did not look at. She walked heavily on the sand towards her friend's house, her hands cold despite the rising heat.

'She is here?' she said to Nuru who was standing just outside the door, caught in the act of entering, or departing.

Nuru looked at her with their eyes haunted and black. There were things they wanted to say, Sisi thought, but in the end they simply moved aside from the doorway as if it hurt them to do so. Antonin waited in the silence, but in this moment, just for this moment, Sisi could not care.

*

Manon was sitting in her kitchen, the table already cleared and Luc putting dishes away in the far corner. They both turned to look at Sisi as she came in, and all the words she wanted to say dried in her mouth.

'You!' Luc said, the word an explosion.

'Go, Luc, would you?' Manon said quietly, not looking as he turned that hot gaze on her, and then he was brushing past Sisi, his footfalls fading quickly into the wider voice of the sea.

'Manon,' Sisi said, coming forward with her hands outstretched. 'I am here with you, I know—'

'Leave,' Manon said. She did not meet Sisi's eyes, instead looking around the kitchen as if searching for something lost. Her voice was flat. Sisi finished the words silently: *your sorrow. I know your sorrow.*

'Manon, I brought...' She held out the hand wrapped in oceanic cloth. Unravelling it until the strip and its shell dangled from her thumb and finger. 'I wish—'

'*No!*' Manon said in an unknown voice. 'You do not speak! What use to me are your words? Or your' – flicking fingers at Sisi's offering like a curse – '*gifts?*'

It was the grief, Sisi told herself. It was horror and loss and a bleeding heart pushed beyond bearing. She stumbled to her knees at Manon's feet, her face turned up like they were children again, only this was not a game and a part of her that she'd thought already broken was breaking all over again.

'Manon, my love, let me—'

Manon's hand slashed the air and Sisi broke off, tried again. 'Manon.'

'*No!*' Manon said. 'No! Do you hear me, Sisi? It was *you* wanted me to go to them, and now see? You *promised* me, Sisi. You promised, and yet he is dead. Why did you do this? Was it for yourself and not me? Yes, Sisi? This is why you wanted so much for me to go?'

Sisi's whole body jerked. 'Manon! No! Never! How could you think—'

But Manon cut her off. 'I do not care. It comes from you wanting so desperately your science and your *independence* –

you have always done this. And of it all this is the worst that you have done.' She looked at Sisi finally. 'You and your doctors, you changed *nothing*, but you *stole from me*. You stole all of the hours that he did not spend in my arms. You took them from me, Sisi – you *stole my child*.' Her hands like claws on her chair, her face wracked and tearless, and Sisi tried to reach for her, coming up on her knees to wrap her arms around her friend, but Manon pulled away.

'*Get out!*' she said as if she were not weeping but holding a knife. 'You do not know what it is to love. You do not know. You *stole him from me* and I *will not see you*, Sisi. You are no part of us.'

Her eyes were on the opposite wall, Sisi already erased, and although she sat there, her hands curled like shells in her lap, her mouth open and empty, Manon did not look at her. She did not look at her, and she wept.

*

Sisi did not remember getting to her feet or to the doorway, although she must have done both. She walked directionless, stumbling and blind. It was the grief, she told herself, over and over and over. It was the grief. And Sisi was a safe target for her anger, because who would forgive her quickest but the friend who was almost a sister?

It was only the grief. But a gecko was waiting on the wood beside Sisi's door and it licked one eye as if pleased with the taste of her lies.

*

She remembered this feeling. The thing in her womb fluttered but she ignored it because she remembered this, this *severing*.

Then, the first time, she had been sitting with Jomo on Pointe Basse where the ridge came down to the sea. The wind had been strong, tugging at their voices and their clothes, sending the scent of cinnamon out to the open water.

'Would it be so bad,' she had said, 'to stay?'

'It was you who applied to universities in South Africa and England. Won that Commonwealth scholarship too. What has happened to that?'

'I cannot go now,' she had said, not explaining because Jomo knew Manon was newly pregnant, and this argument was old. 'Can you not wait? It will be less than a year.'

He had moved as if in pain, cotton shirt shifting against his shoulder blades and her aching to touch him. 'If I miss this job, do you think another as good will come again? It is what I wanted, Sise. I have to take it.' Looking at her pleadingly. 'Sise, come with me, please.'

'Jomo...' Her hand defeated her, crossing the space between them, his meeting hers halfway, their fingers tangling together in shapes she knew with her entire heart. No one else called her that; no one else fitted her so perfectly as he did.

'Then come as soon as the babe is born, as soon as it... as it lives.' His fingers tightening around hers, his face twisting. 'Come, then, say yes.'

She looked away, out to sea, blues drifting across it like dyes. 'You know what the Mothers have said.' The words stuck in her throat and made her shudder, because she had hurled refusals back at them, defiant and in love, fighting duty like a child.

He shed himself of her hand. 'You must marry. If you do not go to university now, then you must marry first and perhaps go later. Because the island needs mothers. And if I go now, then you will still marry.'

'Jomo, I will never want this!' Could he not see that? Could he not see that the only marriage she wished for was one with him? Could he not see the empty spaces where all the lost children ought to be, or how heavy the burden of their hope was because she was young and healthy and unwed? That his departure was one less pair of hands, one less part of the whole, but that hers would be a betrayal.

'Then say no. Come with me.'

As if it were so simple. The softness of his face all gone now, hurt and bitterness making his bones sharp beneath his skin.

'I cannot leave Manon, not now. She is terrified – she will not say it but it is true, you know this. Jomo, Jomo, we could' – dredging courage against the bulwark of his face – 'we could marry. Then you could go on ahead, and—'

'We are *nineteen*, Sise! To marry at nineteen only because the Mothers tell us to? For the *whole*? I won't do it.' Seeing her eyes widen and flood, he made a noise deep in his throat and grabbed at her hand again, holding on so tight her bones wept, reaching out to press his other palm against her cheek. 'I *love* you, Sise. But I wish for us to marry when *we* choose it, not when we are told.'

And so that was it. There was no middle ground to be found, because the middle ground between them would soon be the sea. 'When you have gone...' she said, pressing her own hand over the one against her cheek, closing her eyes because she could not bear to see his face. 'When you have gone, and do not come back, the Mothers will choose someone for me, because my only choice has said no.' She felt him flinch, his hand dropping away, making her open her eyes. His entire heart was there in his face, she thought, and she carried on in a voice that sounded as if it were coming from very far away. 'They will choose someone for me to marry, and I will have to say yes because we need marriages and we need babies, and because there are only so many times I can say no before it becomes hateful of me to do so.'

And then, so quietly he had to bend his head to hear, the words dying in the waves at her feet: 'Jomo, please, will you stay?'

He had not answered her. Instead, after a long moment with the sea and the cries of terns as the only sounds, he had pulled his hand from hers and she had listened without turning as he walked back up the rocks and away.

She did not watch the boat leave the next day. She did not write, because what would she have said? When the Mothers chose his own brother and she thought perhaps they were punishing her, she sent one cruel, desperate email, and he did not reply.

*

And now she had lost Manon.

*

She was at the clinic before she knew it was where she had been heading. The door was open so she shouted, her voice echoing warped off the hot concrete. Sweat stung her hairline and when no one answered, she wanted to scream, pound her fists against the door until her knuckles bled.

'Sisi?'

Dr Freshman was behind her and Sisi realised that probably they had been at lunch. The thought painted her whole vision red.

'You said you could help,' she said, spitting the words at him like seeds, like seeds that would grow into hex and poison and strangling vine, climb his pale limbs and choke the undeserved life from his lungs. 'You said you would help her.'

He did not answer, staring at her as if those vines were binding his tongue. And she stared back, her eyes coals in her skull as devastation and pity and shame played themselves out on his face. Eventually, he moved forward with all three emotions still there as plain as the sun where Geraldine Adler would have hidden them. Sisi did not know which she would have preferred, but she hated him most of all for the pity.

'Sisi, Madame Mathilde, Sisi.' He frowned, flailing. 'I know how you must be feeling, but I promise you we did everything we could in the time we had.'

'You *promised her*.'

He shifted, put his hands in his pockets and then pulled them out again, blood making his neck and ears darken. 'We hoped to be able to improve things, you are right. But the development of a... do you want to sit down?'

'No.'

'No.' Coming another step closer, almost within touching distance, but even though the fady meant that she ought to step back she refused to give him any ground at all. 'Okay,' he said, 'but you understand what Geraldine said before, that the development of a new antitoxin can take months, usually years. It was never something we'd be able to do at such short notice, given the... timescale of the disease.'

Timescale of the disease. 'You mean between the time of a babe being born and of it dying? You mean that timescale?'

'I am so sorry.' He lifted his hands and dropped them, looked in through the doorway of the clinic as if searching for something other than defeat. 'I am so sorry, Sisi.'

'So what is it you have been doing, if this promise of antitoxin is still a... a nothing?'

This question seemed to give him safe territory, and that angered her all over again. He deserved no safety. Not when Manon's every breath was a wasteland, not when every one of her people's hearts were breaking, their future bundled up yet again, *yet again*, in soft cloths and incense in Brother Island's maw.

'I had to isolate the toxin first, then Geraldine tested it against other available compounds. There was a possibility we'd find a match that way, you see? It would have meant immediate treatment – it would have been the... the optimal result. But as that was unsuccessful, we have a few months' window, for you, I mean. The best thing now will be for me to take the isolated toxin back to the university and...' He hesitated, tried a smile that frayed around the edges, turning a hand palm up towards her. 'My aim is to have something viable by the time you are... in time for you.'

In time for you.

In time for you.

Had she known this?

Oh Mother, had she known this?

'You mean...?' But she could not speak.

Manon had said this. She said Sisi had made her do this for Sisi's own child. And Sisi had said 'No,' and 'Never.' She had thought, *It was only ever for you.*

But had she known this, a little?

She stepped away from Dr Freshman, putting space between them because the air was all lead and fire, his words bucking the ground beneath her.

'Manon's... you are saying that because of her babe, it is more likely you will save...' Stopping again, pressing a hand over her mouth, the life in her womb still and listening. A keening sound broke from her before she could silence it.

They hungered for blood and with blood we sated them so that they turned away from our children.

In time for you.

Manon was right.

Right to accuse her; right to reject her. How could anyone forgive this?

The doctor was speaking again but Sisi turned away, her lungs spasming. His hand stretched out as she passed, fingers brushing the folds of her wrap but not catching hold and the fady shuddering over her body like a live thing. And then she was past him, down under the trees, out onto the beach, the weight of the island crushing her shoulders. *How?* she thought desperately. How could she possibly have betrayed Manon?

You do not know love, Manon had said. But she did, she did.

She loved Manon. She loved Jomo, and had chosen Manon over him, proudly martyring herself for her friend, for the whole.

Sisi sank to her knees right on the very cusp of a coconut tree's shade, the line between light and shadow so sharp across her knuckles that it ought to draw blood. She wished that it would. She wanted to crack open the universe between flesh and bone, sun and shadow, innocence and guilt. Crawl into a folded infinity where those she loved could not exile her because her beliefs had not betrayed them.

You are always so certain. Mama Mandisa's voice whispered in her head. Her fatal flaw. To always choose and to always act. She bent forward, shattered by the awful impetus of her arrogance and by Manon's broken trust.

Chapter Twenty-Two

Kit

Kit was sitting on the veranda steps in the quick dark after sunset when he saw torches coming up the path from the village. Bats were emerging from the eaves of the house like manifests, intersecting the lights and the sky.

'Oh, dear god,' Rachel said.

They had been comfortably silent together, her sipping wine at the table, both of them watching the stars.

It was the tone of her voice that told him what the torches were, although he should have guessed as he'd seen them before and thought they were for him. The song now reaching up through the trees wrung his heart out like a rag. Perhaps he should have gone inside, but that would be like turning your back, so neither Kit nor Rachel moved, or suggested moving. They stayed there at the edge of the pool of light and watched the funeral pass them by. Sisi was not there, Kit realised, and he couldn't understand why that would be. He scanned the fire-burnished faces, looking for hers but also looking for... he didn't know what. An answer, perhaps, to how they carried on singing.

*

Once the garden returned to shadows and bats, Kit leaned against the rail post, angling his body towards the half-concealed cliffs.

'They looked angry, some of them,' Rachel said.

He'd not noticed, looking for other things, but realised she was right. 'Can you blame them?'

'No.' The sound of her shifting in her chair. 'But what are they angry at?'

'You think they might accuse the docs of something?'

'Could you blame them?' she said with a trace of sad humour. Kit was glad he couldn't see her face. What on earth had she been thinking, coming to this place, carrying her own childlessness so quietly? He remembered his mother sending flowers after the first round of IVF, shaking her head in disapproval after the third. *Benedicts ought not fail*, he thought.

The air smelled of warm earth and the sea, with a faint, fading trace of the torches, resinous and clean. It drew a question from him that he'd not imagined asking. 'Did you know about Geo's agreement with that company?'

A bat flicked past his face close enough for its wings to brush his hair. The silence must be full of their calls.

'Did you?'

She sighed. 'Yes, I know about it.'

'And? Do you think it's okay?' The muscles of his arms flexed and Kit realised just how much he wanted to know her opinion because he didn't trust his own.

'I... Ah, Kit, you should just stay out of it, honey.' He turned his head so he could see her, and although the angle of the light obscured her features, he could tell she was watching him. 'You're doing so much better,' she said before he could speak. 'You really are, so why not just leave all that stuff to Geo? Let him worry about it.'

'I'm supposed to be working with him.'

She made a sound like a tiny, abbreviated laugh, and Kit didn't know whether to take it as mockery of him or of Geo, or as weariness. 'Yes, Kit, sweetie, but not if it's going to upset you. Find something you enjoy doing. Help that scientist woman – she seems nice.'

'I could help her by telling her what Geo's up to,' he said, his voice more confrontational than he felt.

Rachel pulled back a little in her chair, then leaned forward again. 'You could, darling, but would it help? Don't they have enough to worry about already without adding in the fate of this place once they've left it?'

'Don't you think it would matter to them? It's their home.' His throat squeezing on the last word like a traitor.

'Oh Kit, honey,' she said, and he turned away from her again to look up at the black rocks and the stars. 'We should never have brought you here, should we? It seemed such a perfect idea when your parents asked. Space and freedom and somewhere beautiful where you could perhaps heal. I didn't think.'

'No,' he said, although she was only repeating thoughts he'd had himself. 'No. I'm glad I came. I've found...' What had he found? A hidden heart, colours he had no names for, a woman with eyes like forests. The long fall to the sea and the stepping away. People who sang despite everything. 'I'm glad I'm here.'

'Oh,' she sounded pleased. 'Oh, well, that's great, darling. But you must put yourself first, you know? Don't get into anything that's, you know, hard for you.'

Turn your back, he thought. *Spare yourself the discomfort.*

'Have you heard from your parents?' she said and he wondered at the link she had drawn between her two thoughts, whether she was conscious of it.

He'd had no reply to his email. He'd texted a *Sorry* to his brother. 'Charlie's mad at me,' he said. 'I forgot Jen's birthday.'

Rachel laughed softly. 'He probably forgot as well.'

It was possible, but he'd half-expected chastisement and its absence silenced him.

'Don't worry about your brother, darling,' Rachel added. 'You only need to look after yourself.'

The words from anyone else in the family would have sounded very different to the way Rachel said them, but still, they were the same words. Tipping his head back against the pillar, Kit mapped constellations, and his voice now wasn't confrontational at all but listless. 'So you think it's okay that Geo wants to sell this place off for mining and push the people out before they're ready?'

'Oh, Kit, really.' Like he was exaggerating. That was how they got you, he thought. You expressed a truth and they made you feel childish for doing so; they made honesty and emotion things to be ashamed of. *You're overreacting. You're too young to understand. You're being naive.*

He didn't speak again and perhaps Rachel could hear her own words repeating in her head because after a long time she said, 'You can't fight climate change, Kit, not like this at least. They'd have to leave eventually and Geo will get them an excellent deal, you know he will. It must be so hard for them to see this logically, but it's for the best, in the end.'

They'd said that too, *You're not being logical*, and Kit wondered who got to decide that a secure life was better than a happy one. Was it the same people who got to weigh the merits of exile over hardship, tally sunrises and tidelines and give them a price?

We just drift, then, he wanted to say. *We let others decide so they will let us belong.*

He rose, walking barefoot through the darkness. There were scorpions in the rocks here, but they could only hurt him, not kill, so it would have been hard to fear them even without the sense of deathlessness he carried now.

At the point where the path climbed, he stopped, spotting a gasp of firelight between the trees, high up the cliff. He thought he could still hear the islanders singing. There were so many reasons to give up, he thought. And so few reasons to fight. If only he knew how to weigh them, to set a price against powerlessness, and another against hope.

*

He might have refused when one morning Rachel came to invite him swimming, out of some tiny spite for the opinions she'd refused to hold the night of the baby's funeral. But the heat today was a forge melting his clothes to his skin and solidifying his lungs, so he couldn't resist. If he'd fallen, he'd be out there on the reef already, fish-nibbled and crab-shaped. But that alternative self seemed distant and faintly repulsive, which turned the act of swimming into a victory.

The tides and the islanders had turned the beach back into what it had been before the storm, but the postcard perfection was a veil, he thought, a lie tapping at his conscience like stones. As soon as the water reached his thighs, he pushed down and forward and down, the sea on his skin just on the decadent edge of cold, and he came up smiling.

Rachel was already just the tube of a snorkel, further out. He didn't try to reach her, instead swimming west to the village hall on its promontory, opening his eyes underwater and remembering his brother mocking him for not liking doing so. There were fish beneath him, convict-striped and surrealist yellow, but he was looking at the sand. The rippled lagoon floor extending away from him made jade by the sea. Somewhere away to the side, completing the caldera of the island, the reef rose up to the surface. But here there were just the darting movements of fish in water so clear it was like air; the fish suspended, and the sand.

*

Back at the surface again, eyes stinging, Kit trod water, turning in place to look back at the village. The boats weren't out today, but a couple of figures were sitting in one up beneath the trees, perhaps fixing something. Longing caught him unawares and he gasped, sank and rose again, wondering what they would do if he asked to join them, if he asked to help. They didn't need him – no one here did – but still he wanted to ask, and to slip out over the water beneath their sails, learning the capricious will of these unfamiliar boats and being laughed at for his ignorance. He pushed the thought away, studied the arc of the bay again, and realised that perhaps they did need him, after all. The worst thing... no, not the worst thing at all, but still terrible, was that he had no difficulty picturing it; bulky excavator barges, shipping containers, prefab staff accommodation, the smell of engine oil, cargo vessels pulling gingerly up against the scaffold of a hastily extended loading dock on the spine of the reef.

He dived under and up again, wiping the scene clean. Just like it always did, the sea was shifting the weight from him, buoying him up. Like the iron in the island's heart, the tarnish was being erased by each wave. The sea would never tire of cleansing, Kit thought, but then he remembered oceans of plastic and oiled birds, a pilot whale mourning its poisoned calf. There was as much shame in swimming in her water as there was in walking through the village with his insignificant griefs.

A wave flicked up into his face like chastisement and he grimaced; he was so tired of shame and so tired of doubt. His mother had emailed again, his father copied in, and her email was like a script they had memorised long ago. He didn't think there was any point in replying because it was a play he didn't have the will to perform anymore. Rachel's silhouette was heading towards him and he swam not quite away but tangentially to her, closing the distance between himself and the low western headland, the sand rising up to meet the shore. Climbing out to sit on a rock with crabs skittering away, the returning heat on his skin a crescendo, water droplets on his skin like tiny mirrors slowly shrinking.

People were talking behind him, he realised, and one of the voices was Sisi's. He ought to announce himself, or move away, but it was just too easy to sit here in front of the measured tonnage of sand in the lagoon, set his feet into the surf that the crabs were dancing with, and listen.

'Luc, please. I need to take the buoy out.'

'Ask someone else.'

'I have – they will not take paid work away from you.'

'I do not wish for your money.'

'It is not my money. It is your contract with the university. Please, Luc.'

'No.'

'Luc...' Her voice quieter like she'd turned away or bent her head. Kit's eyes narrowed on the sharp edges of the waves and now he didn't dare move, even if he'd wanted to.

'*No*, Sisi. How can you not understand this? How can you not respect this?' His voice louder.

There was a silence full of the waves and a sound that Kit could not identify, cloth or rope being handled.

'You are right,' she said, just as quietly as before. 'I was wrong and... How can I... please tell me what I should do, Luc.'

'Leave us alone, for once. Leave Manon alone.'

Kit thought he heard her gasp, and the muscles of his legs flexed, his body responding to some urge to rescue. But he spread his wet hands on his knees instead, pressing down into the joints like he was holding himself back, although it was more to remind himself who he was, and what he knew.

'Ah, Mother. Sisi.' Luc again, raising his voice in a different way as though Sisi had begun to walk away. 'Give us time, yes? Give her time. It was our choice too, but it is... to remember this is hard, now.'

Then quiet again, and Kit bent his head forward to press against his knees, the skin there cool and hot in patches. They had lost so much already.

And that thought made his decision obvious. They had too much to bear, so he wouldn't tell them.

Better to do nothing at all than do more harm. It wasn't about being led by Geo, he told himself, because Geo was right about one thing: they all knew the island would die, in a way, sooner or later. So what good would it do for them to worry about their island's fate if the end result was the same?

They had so much to carry already, he should surely spare them this.

Yes, he thought again, and breathed out, all his vertebrae relaxing.

Such inexpressible relief, to realise it was better to lie by silence than be the messenger of another betrayal. Anyway, perhaps he was completely wrong. They might look at the maths the same way Geo had and decide that money for their future was worth more than their past. It would probably come down to a choice between better care for their babies, or their island. And who would ever choose the island, in their place?

You can't go back, he thought. To burned homes or old selves; or dying islands. Once gone, this island would exist only in their minds, like childhood, so did it matter that it was going to be torn apart while they dreamed it whole?

Chapter Twenty-Three

Sisi

It was late, closing in on midnight, but Sisi could not sleep. She had left a light on to hold off a darkness full of faces that she loved and that no longer loved her. The shutters were open, but despite the night breeze her skin itched and she could not settle, could not concentrate on her book because the words on the page morphed into the words Luc had said, and Manon, and the hawk-eyed doctor. How could she sleep when she had been so wrong? There was an innocence to sleep that she did not deserve, and so she turned over again, thumping her hands into the pillow and pulling the edges of the sheet off her angry skin.

'Sisi?' In the yellow light Nuru's skin was molasses. 'You cannot sleep?'

'Sorry,' Sisi said, the word monumental, 'for waking you.'

Nuru pushed the door wider and came to sit on the edge of the mattress, rubbing a hand over their face. 'You did not. There is no sleep for me as well.'

Sisi could not remember ever seeing her sibling like this, bowed. It made her reach out to take their hand, their skin cooler than hers but still warm. 'Lie here,' she said, tugging gently. 'If neither of us can sleep then together we can be awake.'

With a quiet laugh, Nuru moved, stretching out beside her, and for a moment, Antonin was present in the room again, his sibling's body lying where his own used to. It could have been strange but was not, and some thread in between Sisi's ribs relaxed. Antonin was another person she had failed, but they had failed and forgiven each other, and perhaps Nuru loved her anyway. Did they? She had taken so much for granted.

For a minute or two neither of them spoke, listening to the crickets, the wind in the palms and shearwaters purring as they returned to their nests up in the rocks. Sisi turned on her side to face Nuru and said, 'There is nothing I can do to make amends.' Not asking, because the answer was obvious.

Nuru's chest rose and fell before they spoke. 'We all have been wrong, n'est-ce pas? So we, the whole of us, must make amends. We must find our way back to what we have lost.'

They were thinking as a Sacere, Sisi realised, not as a sibling, and that fact hurt. But what personal care did she deserve? She had believed that her training and her eyes on the horizon made her wiser, yet that arrogance had done nothing but harm. So perhaps she needed to learn to think as Nuru did, as a people, as plural. Make amends by remaking herself. If that was what it took, then she would do it.

'How?' she said. 'Tell me how.'

Nuru turned towards her, their knees touching. 'I have been thinking,' they said, 'about how we have changed – how we have *been* changed.' Their black eyes were reflecting enough lamplight for Sisi to see in them her own silhouette. 'We must cut away everything that our ancestors strove to escape and that we have, in our weakness, allowed back in. Cleanse ourselves.'

The words sounded rehearsed and as if Nuru were speaking more to themself than to Sisi, but the certainty in their voice unnerved her. She had also been so certain that the doctors would help, that Mother Sea would help if they only fought for themselves. 'But we follow the old ways still,' she said slowly, testing the words.

'The old ways?' Nuru smiled and reached out to touch Sisi's cheek briefly, the shells around their neck clicking softly together.

'This is it exactly, Sisi. They are *old ways* in your mind. They should not be so; they should be *now*, they should be in everything. We put ourselves, our ambitions, our wants, before the whole and forget everything Mother Sea taught us. Would she be so wrong to be angry?'

'Then what is it you think we should do?' Yesterday, she would have said, *If Mother Sea can do this, then she does not deserve us.*

'Cut it all away,' they said, still quieter than the crickets but also ferocious. 'Cut away everything tainted and wash ourselves clean.'

Their shoulder loomed in the darkness and Sisi could see enough of the line of their jaw, their neck, to know how tense they had become. *Tainted* said like a curse, and Sisi's breath caught. Nuru was all she had left.

'You are angry with me?' Hesitating. 'You would be right to be so.'

Their frame softening again, their voice gentler. 'Not with you, Sisi. Or if I was, then I could not stay that way for long. You are carrying my brother's child and if you were blind then you were blinded by hope. We are all tainted by the outside – we go away to school, we buy their goods and sell ours to them; for this job, or that one, we have all of us accepted their money and made them welcome when they come. You are not the only one.'

She lifted herself up onto one elbow, their words sparking fireflies in her mind, even now. 'We... Nuru, we cannot *stop* dealing with the outside just like this. Stop children going to school? And the Climate Plan... and my job, I have nothing else now that—' Cutting herself off just in time before speaking Antonin's name. Nuru turned their face just a fraction as though adjusting for the blow, and she was swamped yet again with that strange concoction of sorrow and regret, terrible absences that were her own form of grief.

'We will find a way,' Nuru said stubbornly. 'Our ancestors did so.'

'Yes, but also they had neither medicines nor electricity. We cannot go back to that, Nuru.' Yet the medicines had failed Sisi, and Sisi had failed Manon.

'Were you right about the doctors, Sisi?' As if they had read her mind. Sisi did not answer, could not.

'Sleep,' they said. 'The child needs care, and this means sleep.'

'Nuru—'

But they lifted a hand again, cupping Sisi's shoulder this time and squeezing gently. Strength in their fingers turned into comfort. 'We shall find a way together. Trust me.'

They settled themselves more comfortably, showing no inclination to move, and with them here she could believe that forgiveness was a possibility, listen to the sea and sleep. But even once she slept her dreams were full of blinkered eyes and the threat of hunger, uneasiness stalking her like a shark, tasting the air for failures.

*

The meeting was at dusk because the fishers had come in on a late tide. The lights hung moth-baubled from the ceiling and the raised screens were letting the day's dreaming warmth slip away.

Sisi sat against a pillar at the side, isolating herself by avoiding anyone's eyes, but even without looking, she knew the moment Manon and Luc arrived because the pattern of voices faltered momentarily – a hitch in the breath, a snagged thread. They came nowhere near her and Sisi ached as she looked over to them on the far side of the room.

'Thank you,' Mama Anouk said, coming to her feet as nimbly as a much younger woman and smiling while the room quieted, those last few standing either leaning back against posts or settling on the benches or the floor. 'Thank you,' she said again.

A gecko laughed from the shadows of the roof and everyone shivered, spooking themselves with the territorial cries of a reptile smaller than their hands. But this was Sisi's other self, she remembered, this cynicism; her wrong self full of vain certainties.

'First,' Mama Anouk said, 'we all together are here with you, Manon and Luc. Yesterday and today and tomorrow we are here with you and we will share your sorrow.' She paused and everyone murmured; Sisi could not bear to look across the hall but did anyway.

'And now,' continuing quietly, 'the boat will be here in six days. If you did not yet hear, Jomo de Sabah is coming to say the farewells to his brother.'

The life in Sisi's stomach burst into flight as if responding to Jomo's name. Nausea rose with it, then fell.

'Also,' Mama Anouk said, 'we all know of the Administrator's… proposals, and so now is the time to think and choose. In eight days we shall meet here again and vote on what it is we wish to do.' Voices rose, lapping against her upheld hand and then dying away. 'Remember, we decide for the whole, and not for ourself alone,' she said, the Mother and not the mother. 'We vote, and we move forward as one.'

The hall stayed quiet and Sisi felt Mama Anouk's words like a blow, wishing Nuru were beside her.

Mama Mandisa spoke next without rising. 'Three choices, we will have. First, to leave our island and find a new home among outsiders, just as we prepared for but hoped never to do. Second is to continue with our Climate Plan as we have been doing; and third…' She paused, turning her head to where the Sacere always gathered, and Sisi saw Nuru straighten, looking back at the Mother as if the two of them were sharing words no one else could hear. 'And third, to change how we live in the hope of regaining Mother Sea's blessings.'

How definite the choices sounded, Sisi thought, without holding any structure at all.

'We have eight days to talk on how we would do all of these things,' Mama Anouk said as if reading Sisi's thoughts. The silence hummed and Mama Anouk raised her hands, palms pale as the inside of a shell. 'As I said, we are six days from the boat coming. Until this, because the harvest is damaged, and also our stores, we must each be careful of the rice we use, and the sweet potatoes. There is much unripe fallen fruit, so we must now preserve what can be preserved. The vanilla is unscathed, thank the Mother.' Her smile was a conclusion and everyone began to talk again, not about the food because they had known already, but about the vote.

Sisi watched Manon and Luc rise to leave, and this time the talk did not map their progress, which was natural, perhaps, but also cruel. They were just into the mauve-green light beyond the building when Berhane's voice called everyone's attention back again.

'My apologies,' they said. 'We wish to add our thoughts, before you go.'

Those who were standing did not sit again, but they grew still and over the heads of those on the floor, Sisi watched Nuru watching Berhane, remembering the comfort of their presence in the night, the unearned gift of their absolution.

'It is our role, we Sacere, to guide us closer to Mother Sea,' Berhane said in the voice they used for storytelling, tonal pathways they were all trained to follow. 'And so, we say now that Mother Sea took us in as her children because we strove to escape the poison of the outside world. We escaped slavery and caste, poverty and the wars of greedy men, and Mother Sea saw that we were different, brought us here to Brother Island and fed us from her waters.' Their shoulders shifted, pushing backwards beneath the loose cotton of their shirt. 'We have turned more and more to the outside in tiny ways and in large ones since the time of our grandmothers.' They glanced down to their fellow Sacere, met Nuru's gaze. 'We must consider if this is why we are now cursed. However we vote, we must search for a way to return to what we were.'

'Speak with your ancestors,' Nuru said from where they sat, their voice carrying. 'Speak with Mother Sea, and search also in your heart for the places where you have left her behind and let the outside in. This is what we ask of you.'

Sisi looked at Berhane, and at Isolde, Sable and Krish, the way their disparate faces were the same, and their utter unity turned her cold. Because her own faith had been wrong, and it hurt to know that. Such a terrible wrong, to betray someone you loved because they were loving enough to trust you.

Nuru was not looking at her so Sisi bent her head, studying the way the light made her interwoven fingers into a mosaic of skin and shadow, not listening to people talking because they were too contradictory and all she wanted was a certainty in *something* to replace the certainty she had held in herself. A way to make herself forgivable, to be able to cry for Manon's son without remembering Dr Freshman's words, or Manon's.

*

'Sisi.' Nuru appeared beside her, resting their hand on her shoulder. 'Sister, come home.'

Sisi rose, grateful.

Chapter Twenty-Four

Kit

The next time Kit saw Sisi she was back up on Les Hautes, and his lack of surprise told him he'd come to think of this place as hers – hers and a little bit theirs, despite the occasional meeting with goats and their guardian, or with someone come to gather brushwood. Those people were passing visitors; he and Sisi were not.

Or at least it gave him a small, silly burst of warmth to think so. He walked slowly up to where she sat against the wall of the weather station. There was a laptop on the ground beside her, but her hands were curled into loose fists in her lap and when she looked up at him, the sadness in her face made him rush the last few steps.

'Sisi, I'm so sorry.' Crouching, not touching her but wanting to, tears in his throat that surprised him and tasted of self-pity. 'About the baby. I'm so sorry.'

Her eyes were awash but she wasn't crying, her hands tightened and then relaxed.

'I can't imagine,' Kit tried. 'None of us can, but if there's anything I can do...'

She blinked rapidly. 'Thank you. But...' Looking away from him. 'Thank you, Kit.'

'Are you working?' Perhaps she didn't want him there, but he couldn't walk away when she looked like this.

Glancing at the laptop and reaching out a hand to brush over the mousepad, rewaking the screen but doing nothing else. 'Sort of, yes. I am supposed to be.' A half-smile in his direction, although she didn't meet his eyes.

'What on?'

She shrugged. 'Only some experiments testing the soil up here.' When he didn't speak, she shrugged again. 'It was to see if we could grow anything up here, you know, away from the salt inundation.'

Kit scanned the land around them. The knife-ridges of pale rock, the cacti and knotted shrubs, hard-edged shadows turning the landscape brutally surreal. 'Up *here*?'

That got a more convincing smile, although it hadn't been his intention. 'Yes.' She touched the laptop again, looking at the spreadsheet that appeared, half-full of numbers that Kit found himself angling forward to try to understand. 'We must be prepared to lose much of the land that is down in the bay. I was testing if the soil was good enough up here to try drought-tolerant crops.'

'But?' he said, frowning at the numbers and then at her.

She looked at him, a strange expression on her face that he thought might come closest to shame. 'But I will not continue, I think. Not for now. I... I need to' – she took a breath – 'not make such decisions.'

Kit lowered himself to sitting, his spine against the tepid wall, stretching his legs out beyond her own and into the first of the encroaching plants, their tough little leaves leathery against his ankles. He wanted to tell her that the work sounded hard and hopeless, that he understood why she was doing it but it was too late.

'You... you think you will all stay here that long?' he said, the deceit sour in his gut, his voice tinny.

She turned her head sideways against the wall, looking at him and then past over the chiaroscuro rocks to the sea and the sky. 'It is our home,' she said.

Kit had to swallow hard. He wanted to tell her so he didn't have to lie, but *Don't do it*, he told himself. *You've made your decision. It's kinder for them not to know.*

'But why wait?' he said eventually. 'It's just going to get harder. Why do it? Stay, I mean.'

Tears gathered again in her eyes, the browns multitudinous. 'We must,' she said, as if it was an answer. 'We must find a way. Because this, here – it is all we have.'

No, Kit thought, she was wrong.

She must be, because they didn't have a choice, and they *weren't* just a place or a past, that was a terrible thing to think. But how could he say that? He wished he'd never met her, never learned about the babies or the sea, never seen the wreckage of the storm or read a document that wasn't meant for him. Because Geo had to be right and Kit just wanted to be alone, away from this horrible empathy and attraction and awe.

He said something to her although he wasn't sure what, and rose. He would never understand her; she would never even want to understand him, so why did it matter what her choices were or which future she would choose, one free from the past or one trapped in it? Walking quickly, he reached the cliff path and went down into the village.

The calculations and the map in Geo's office were a complexity reduced to a sum. *This is life*, he thought. *We begin with a map but sometimes it only leads us to the cliffs.*

*

'Kit?' It was Geo, just on his way out of the house with Euan, both of them looking distracted and hot.

'Hey,' he said, stopping in the sun.

'We're off to tackle those Mothers again – terrifying bunch.' Geo hesitated. 'You all right, mate? Look a bit pale there.'

Smiling, because he ought to. 'Yeah. Just thirsty.'

'Think there's a beer or two left in the fridge. Get yourself one before they're all gone. Won't be any more till the boat comes at the end of the week. Hard times, mate, hard times.' Geo laughed, then cut himself off abruptly, realisation and shame contorting his face.

Kit simply nodded and went on into the house, but he did get a beer, because he *was* hot, and because Rachel was not there to worry that he shouldn't drink on his meds, and because even if she *was* there he half-wanted to drink in front of her anyway. For lack of anything else to do he checked his email, staring at the new, unread one from his mother. She would email Rachel, he suspected, if he didn't reply to this one. There were others too, from people who still, unfathomably, treated him like a friend, and one day, one day soon, he needed to write back. But not today. Rolling the bottle over his forehead and thinking of Sisi's fingers resting on her laptop, the unfamiliar apathy in her voice. The research she'd begun.

There was a lecturer from his university who'd encouraged him when he went to her about changing degrees, before he'd found the bravery to tell his family. Supported him afterwards as well, although he remembered that less clearly. He could see her shrewd eyes and pensive smile, and without really knowing why, he found her last email and wrote a reply. Perhaps to check his own reckoning of futility.

I have a friend who wants to set up a research project testing crop growth in limestone karst ecosystems, and in soil that is salt-contaminated. I remember your lecture on extremophile mutations in plant evolution and wondered whether you think a project like this has any potential.

He paused with the arrow over the send button. What would she think, Dr Reinwald, receiving such a strange email from the student who had vanished from her class last semester? She'd have been told at some point: *Oh, Kit Benedict? Suicide attempt, you know, on the psych ward. Weird, hey?*

She'd ignore him, or worse, she'd pity him, but his finger moved without him and the message was gone. Dismay and completion warred in his head, a slow fizzling panic making his eyes dry, but the beer helped. Pressed over his eyes and cool on his tongue, it helped a lot. He might never see her again, so did it matter what she thought of him? What harm was there in confirming that Sisi's experiments were pointless and thus his inaction mattered less?

*

Dr Reinwald emailed Kit back two days later. That simple fact surprised him enough, but the tone of the email was startling. She said she was glad to hear from him; she asked if he was returning to his studies next semester, said that she looked forward to teaching him again, that if he were worried about anything at all to come and speak with her.

Kit read those words once, then again, then a third time. His fingers shook very slightly and he could hear voices in his mind arguing over her sincerity, her motives, her exact meaning. He was frowning, and then he wasn't, pressing his fist to his lips and measuring his own smile.

Then he read on. She loved the sound of the project – it was a major theme right now and she wondered if Kit and this friend would be interested in building it into something bigger, developing the island as a study site, and perhaps Kit might want to use this as his dissertation. She mentioned industry collaboration and studentships.

'Oh,' Kit whispered.

He pushed the laptop lid down and got to his feet jerkily, wanting to talk to someone, to tell them that his first instinct in Geo's office had been right, and that he'd been wrong to silence it.

He had no idea why that fact mattered so much, but it did. Euan was in Geo's office, working on the computer and wearing a pair of glasses that Kit hadn't seen on him before. The thin frames made his face even more fox-like, the reflective glass like shutters. Kit came into the room without pausing.

'Euan,' he said, 'can we talk?'

'Sure.' Euan pushed away from the table and smiled thinly, white-toothed. Kit wondered what it might be like, to be a good person with a face built for cunning.

'What do you think about the agreement with the, um, aggregates company? For the sand?'

'Ah.' Euan rose to his feet, looking past Kit to the doorway and then coming around from the desk to sink into one of the padded chairs at the side. Kit sat in the other one, watching his face. 'So Geo told you, then.'

'Not exactly.'

Euan shot him a slantwise grin. 'I see.' The grin vanished and he rubbed a hand over his forehead, hard enough to leave imprints of his fingers. Then, dropping the hand and looking squarely at Kit, he opened his mouth as if about to speak. But there was movement in the hall and Geraldine and Matt came into the room quietly.

'Looks weird out there,' Matt said, gesturing to the window. 'Thunderstorm or something.'

Euan grimaced at Kit, the expression melting into an effortless smile at the doctors. 'Nothing like the last one, don't worry. Just a bit of rain and noise, I imagine. It's the time of year for them.'

'Oh, I think I knew that,' Matt said, frowning abstractedly.

'I found some limes,' Geraldine said, holding them up in her hand. 'Fancy a G and T? We'll lose the power again if there's a storm, so we won't be able to do much work after lunch.'

Kit knew, he *knew*, that this was all at least partly false. That being pleasant company didn't mean they weren't devastated by the child's death. Everyone was fighting to parcel off their horrors, and these doctors had even more to wrestle with than most. But still.

'No thanks,' he said, barely civil, not moving.

Euan looked at him and then at Matt, Geraldine already gone and opening cupboards in the kitchen. 'Sure,' he said again. Placid, sharp-eyed. 'Kit, all done too soon for my comfort but more than my job's worth, unfortunately. You might do something, if you wanted. Open things up a bit.' He walked out of the room, patting a hand on Matt's shoulder like they were friends, like friendships could form at all in between death and the sea.

'Open things up a bit?' he repeated to himself. Could he? Geo couldn't be so completely justified if Euan disagreed with him. And there was Dr Reinwald, seeing futures where Kit hadn't. Kit wavered and stayed where he was, in his uncle's office and frowning.

*

If a thunderstorm was coming, Kit decided eventually, then he wanted to be out in it. He wanted to watch lightning carve up the sky and be charged to the point of sparking.

'I'm off for a walk,' he said, passing the three sitting on the veranda. There were clouds on the horizon, gathering mass into one spot, a dense column of white that was nothing at all like the last storm, not angry but gravidly, jubilantly alive. He couldn't remember ever understanding the moods of clouds before; it was something this place had given him.

'Now?' Geraldine said, raising her eyebrows.

Kit didn't answer, looking at her then at Matt. Before he could think too hard about it he asked, 'What impact does it have on people, relocating? What does it do to them, to their culture and stuff?'

The three at the table looked at each other fleetingly, not in collusion, Kit thought, more because it was him asking such a question than because of the question itself. There was something to be ashamed about in that, he realised, but he pushed the thought away.

'It screws them up,' Matt said succinctly, with an edge.

Geraldine tipped her head back and forth, moderating or thinking. 'There's always loss of culture,' she said. 'And a dilution of the population, more mixing with other people, that sort of thing. It's just not feasible to remain isolated when you aren't, geographically.'

'And depression,' Matt added, still biting at the words. Euan ran a hand over his forehead again but stayed silent. 'An increase in drug use, suicide, loss of self-sufficiency, language, traditional knowledge.'

'Well, I guess. I wouldn't know about that, so much,' Geraldine said. 'But it sounds plausible.' She pulled a face. 'It's all a bit hellish really, isn't it?'

And there at her words, that tiny life was present again, the baby that Kit had only caught passing glimpses of. Black hair in whorls on a small head, tiny nut-brown fist escaping from blue cloths. He'd avoided the room while they'd been in the house, not wanting to inflict his presence on them. But now the baby was here again, in between them all. *The lost live on in the silences,* Kit thought, *in the pauses between all the noise we make to prove we are alive.*

'Yeah,' he said quietly. 'It really is.'

Chapter Twenty-Five

Sisi

'Mama Mandisa.' Sisi dropped the mango she was slicing and rose to her feet, taking the old woman's hand to guide her into a chair.

'Hiding still, Sisi?' Mama Mandisa said, and Sisi felt blood rush up her neck, her cheeks. It was not hiding, as such, but the difference was so slight it barely mattered.

'I thought it would be kinder.'

'It would perhaps be kinder to give her the catharsis of not seeing you, rather than the responsibility for your absence.' Mama Mandisa accepted the slice of yellow-gold flesh that Sisi handed her, juice on her fingers as she ate it slowly, her eyes closed. Sisi wanted that. She wanted, when she became old, to be so at peace that all her tiny moments were full of joy instead of regret. But how did you get to that place when you had so many penances to pay?

She did not answer Mama Mandisa, because she was not meant to. *I do not want your words*, she said to every child caught disobeying, *I want your thought*. So Sisi thought, and stayed silent, holding her protestations wrapped in among her grief and her guilt like a tangle of wool.

'Child,' Mama Mandisa said after a while. 'Be careful with Jomo, yes?'

It was not what Sisi had been expecting. 'Mama?'

'He has been away a long time, Sisi. Outside. And now you carry his brother's child. You are neither of you who you were when he went away, n'est-ce pas?' She reached her mango-sticky fingers out and patted the back of Sisi's hand, leaving behind the imprint of her touch. 'Guard yourself, child.'

Sisi inhaled slowly, smelling mango, hot earth and the overripe lychees beneath the tree. 'Mama,' she said, 'why did you choose his brother as my husband?'

Mama Mandisa did not answer immediately and Sisi watched a small gathering of hermit crabs tussle over something at the base of a tree. Such small, vital battles, she thought; so full of certainty. She expected to be told what they had told her at the time – that she and Antonin both had strong blood, that there was no one else who was not already attached or gone outside, that she was the last of her mother's line. But Mama Mandisa surprised her.

'Because you were both so lonely,' she said.

Sisi looked at her, trying to fit this statement into the terrain of her marriage. 'But he—' She stopped when Mama Mandisa lifted her opal gaze.

'I know, child. But how could anything be wrong that has given us this?' Her bent hand gesturing at Sisi, her stomach. 'There can be no wrong in this.'

Sisi put her hand there lightly, testingly. Two weeks ago, every cell in her body would have disagreed, but that was before the child had quickened, before they had fluttered within her skin, responding to her heart. Now, she did not know at all. There was resentment and there was failure and, most brutally of all, there was Manon. How did you reconcile all those things?

Mama Mandisa let her think her thoughts again, although honestly Sisi was not thinking coherently, everything an extension of the babe in her womb and Manon's babe in the tombs, loss and complicity and a dread she barely recognised because every time before, it had been for other people.

*

People were talking, of course. Sisi heard them from her tiny isolation outside her house and when she passed them by. They murmured about outsiders and money, gifts from the sea, the wells, the storm. Mahena, Clémentine and Oni shelling beans, worry becoming opinion becoming argument. Oni, who was their electrician, saying the outside help would save them; Mahena, whose babes had died, wanting to drive the outsiders into the sea.

Old Abasi, overhearing, laughed and said, 'Will we also tear down the solar panels and the clinic? Will we do these things, Mahena?'

'How hard has anyone tried to help us, really?' Clémentine said bitterly, her hands working savagely. 'Even ours who stay outside, how many have helped? How many have come home?'

'Jomo is coming home,' someone answered. Sisi closed her eyes.

Clémentine laughed, short and hard. 'Lured by death like a bad spirit? We should tell him not to come. Nuru should tell him he is too much of the outside and is not welcome.' And then silence, because they remembered that Sisi was there, and who Sisi was.

They were defiled or they were adapting; they were faithful or they were naive...

It exhausted Sisi. And yet Nuru was always present and full of patience, tilting their head and murmuring. At sunset, they sat beneath the tamarind trees, telling old stories with new emphasis. *Oh, Nuru*, Sisi thought. *You are so sure*. Awe, gratitude, doubt.

*

The next morning, she woke beside Nuru again because Nuru had heard her crying. They were still sleeping when she woke, their face lit by the curtain-filtered light to a brown subdued by gold and amber, the shadows only half-present. There was a fine stubble on their cheek and the tightness in their jaw had vanished for the first time perhaps since Antonin's death. She had nearly forgotten it *could* vanish, until this moment.

'Good morning,' they said without opening their eyes. 'I can hear you worrying, sister. Stop it.'

'I am not...' She paused. 'Good morning.' Lying back to stare at the ceiling and gathering the energy to get up.

'Yes you are. It is not good for the babe.' They breathed in enormously, rubbed a hand over their face as if to scrub something away, then sat up, slipping out of bed and wrapping a lamba around their waist. 'Crêpes for breakfast?'

'Hmm.' Sisi smiled and they went into the kitchen. She had not realised they were capable of being so gentle and yet so intent at the same time.

*

'Will you help me with the stock-take?' Nuru said as they ate. 'It must be done before the boat comes.'

'Of course,' Sisi said, but at the same time thinking, *What if she comes? What if she comes to the store while I am there and the sight of me hurts her further, or the sight of her hurts me?* She had not been up to the weather station in days and the buoy was still sitting waiting, gathering meaningless data that she had not uploaded and soon someone at the university would notice, and would email her. The deadline for the studentship had passed.

*

It was simpler now, and more comfortable, to wrap a lamba beneath her arms rather than have the pressure of a waistband on her abdomen. A new solidity to her flesh reminding her of her near future; it would remind Manon also, if she came, and if she saw. But it was easy in the end to stay out of sight, leaving to Nuru the customers who came to seek their counsel and tell the Voice their thoughts as much as to buy anything. Sisi counted tins and boxes, and listened, wrestling against her own opinions on the vote, because there was no more trusting herself, and it had taken her a very long time to realise that. She would be as neutral as a Voice now, and would learn how to belong.

'You are the Voice, Nuru.' Berhane's voice made Sisi realise that the two Sacere were alone in the front of the store. 'You need to *reflect* the whole, friend, not be *pushing* like this. It is too much.' Echoing Sisi's thoughts, and yet Sisi's thoughts were wrong.

'I am the Voice only to outsiders. Among ourselves I am simply Sacere. And is our part not to guide, Berhane?'

But that was not what they had said before, n'est-ce pas? Before Manon.

'Nuru.' Weightedly. 'This might be so. But I am not convinced that you are *guiding*, so much as *driving*.'

Sisi set her stack of notepads down on the shelf and took two steps closer to the dividing wall.

Nuru laughed. 'Berhane, we agreed that it is insidious, this pull of the outside, yes? If we *do not* push against it, then what will happen?' Not waiting for an answer. 'We will continue drifting off course. You agree with me, I know this.'

'No, I do, but...'

The shelf in front of Sisi held rechargeable batteries, low-energy bulbs, replacement water filters. She rested her fingers on them and thought of the thousands of miles they had been shipped and shipped again before arriving here.

'I do agree. But you go too far. This is not the century that our ancestors lived in – we cannot cut away all ties with the outside world.'

'Why not?'

'What of your sister? Would you take her job, her passion from her? She has worked so hard—'

'She has, this is true.' But their voice was all wrong, and she was already braced for the blow before they spoke again. 'She has tried, and her way, the outsider's way, has failed us. Now is our turn to try, to fight, instead of only to hope and wait. I am done with waiting, Berhane. Are you not also?'

'You…' Berhane's voice lowering, becoming less combative and more kind. 'You are grieving, Nuru. I know your sorrow. You have lost your brother and then a child under your care – you fear for Sisi's child. But my friend, we are Sacere. In the support we offer our people, we do not also put forward our own wishes or our own pains.'

'You think that I am putting my grief before the whole.'

'I… Yes, I do. I am sorry.'

There was silence again, full of birdsong and the sea, chickens protesting loudly but far away.

'I think that you are putting your comfort before your faith, Berhane. And I too am sorry.'

Sisi drew in breath between her teeth. Never before had she heard dissent between the Sacere, and she was only hearing it now as a spy. Was there any certainty to be had, then, she wondered, if the unity they presented to everyone else was a lie? All of her mind said Berhane was right, but all of her heart was whispering, *She has tried… and her way has failed us.* And perhaps it was cruel, but it was also entirely true. So her mind was wrong, and Berhane was wrong, because Nuru had never once put themself before the whole, and they would not begin now. Not when they had barely forgiven Sisi for doing so.

*

Later, long after Berhane had silently gone, after Chicha and Katura came scavenging for frozen juice, and Philippe delivered a batch of soft cheese that filled Sisi's hands with the smell of goat and wood and rocks; after all of this, Nuru poured mango juice into a glass that they passed to Sisi. 'Come and sit,' they said. 'Tomorrow I can finish the rest.'

Sisi drank gladly. 'Thank you.'

Nuru did not answer, pouring their own drink, adding a touch of mellow rum and drinking it in silence, the day's river of words finally run dry.

'Everyone is so angry with each other,' Sisi said eventually. There were clouds on the horizon again, just visible between Pointe Rouge and the trunks of coconut trees. They would stay distant and be gone by morning, raining on a stretch of unwatched sea. Beneath them the ocean was the same silver as the sky, so that the clouds were suspended against nothing, landscapes that only they on this island would ever see.

'It is difficult,' Nuru said quietly. 'To accept that you must change, knowing how hard it will be.' They took another slow drink. 'It is also difficult to believe, after all this time.'

'Yes,' Sisi said. Both these things were true. She wondered if she had been meant to overhear their words to Berhane or if they had only forgotten in that moment that she was there. 'Do you think it will be enough, then, to change and to believe?'

They turned their glass within their palms, studying it. She thought that if they lifted their gaze to hers it would be full of the red cliffs and Manon, just as hers was. 'It was you, sister, who said Mother Sea wished her children to fight for our survival. She meant, I think, for us to fight our way back to her. This has always been our truth, yes?'

Sisi turned to face the direction of her best friend's house, the absence within her chest like a constant, endless falling. How could you ever tell truth from hope?

As if reading her mind, Nuru tilted their head. 'Do you trust me, Sisi?'

She looked at them. 'Yes,' she said, 'I do, but—'

'So trust me,' they said. 'I can only protect your child if you put your faith in the whole.'

She gave a soft, wary laugh. 'Is that all it will take? Your promise, my trust?' It might have sounded scornful if she did not want so desperately for it to be true. *I trust you, Sisi*, Manon had said. *You stole my son from me*, she had said.

Nuru shook their head very slightly. 'It is what is needed of you, Sisi, just as I am needed to be the Voice. We must all play the part given to us.' They paused, their shoulders shifting slightly. 'Have you talked to your ancestors? You may go up to the cliffs as long as you do not enter the tombs. You should do so. Your grandmother was very wise and your mother will be worrying.'

'I will,' Sisi said quietly.

'Let yourself belong at last. That is what we need of you. You are so terribly clever, my sister – it must be hard to trust in anything but the power of your own mind.'

Sisi winced, searching Nuru's face for insult, but there was only sympathy and seeing that, she said, 'I trusted the doctors. But they did not change anything.'

Shadows flickered in Nuru's face, but their voice did not alter. 'That is why you must let go. Ma chère, there is no need all of the time to stand alone – it is good sometimes to let others show you the way.'

What had been anathema sounded wondrous now. To hand her life and its awful scope into Nuru's sure hands, to do nothing with her own fickle mind other than tend the house, help restore the fields, pick vanilla pods and dry them in the sun; go up to the red cliffs and speak into the darkness. Be subsumed. It would be so nice, like being held or feeling sunshine on your skin after a long storm. There would be no blame and no doubt because those things belonged to the whole, to whoever chose for her. And perhaps it was cowardly; it was definitely cowardly, but it would be such a relief to be beyond blame.

Sisi sighed and finished her drink. She smiled at Nuru and her heart stumbled once or twice. 'I will see you at home, sibling,' she said and walked away, her mind, that terribly clever traitorous mind, full of challenge and found flaws, but her heart silent.

Chapter Twenty-Six

Kit

Both Rachel and Geo were still eating breakfast when Kit came down. He'd been skirting around them for the past couple of days, but there was no avoiding them this time. A lingering weightlessness in his stomach expanded, one full of Euan's words and Dr Reinwald's email.

'Morning,' Geo said around a mouthful of toast. 'You all right, mate?'

Rachel smiled at him, lifting a hand like an unfurling flag but saying nothing.

'Hey,' he said, sitting and pouring coffee with his eyes on that rather than them.

'I was thinking you might come with me today,' Geo said, holding his mug out expectantly. 'Euan and me, we're meeting with the Mothers and Sacere again. Thought it might help if you came along, friendly face and all.'

Kit filled Geo's mug then set the pot down and frowned at his uncle. 'Friendly face?' he said.

Geo shrugged, grinned and then shrugged again. 'You're friendly with that woman, the scientist, aren't you? It's more than I've got.'

Rachel made a soft noise at the other end of the table, and Kit caught the look she threw at her husband, the nerves in his gut turning into a kind of sick, guilty anger. 'It's hardly a friendship,' he said. 'How can it be?' His voice was cold in the warm air and he held tight to his coffee, staring at its rising steam.

'Kit, sweetie,' Rachel said. 'Do you mean the mining deal, or...?' She shrugged and tilted a hand to suggest the island and the wide sea.

He made a noise in his throat and lifted his mug, the coffee almost as bitter as the words he wasn't saying.

'What?' Geo said, setting coffee and toast both down, leaning forward, his elbows on the pale wood. 'The land lease? I thought we'd talked about this. What is it? You worried she'll blame you, is that it?'

Yes. And no, because that was more than a little pathetic, wasn't it? And it wasn't really about his own tangled wants anyway, or his memories. It was the view from here; cerulean bay and indigo ocean, a tower of cloud burgeoning in the eastern sky again, the scent of frangipani and jasmine. There was having choices, and having conviction.

Kit sighed. 'No,' he said eventually, meeting Geo's eyes. 'No, it's not that,' he repeated. 'It's the whole thing. Profit over environment... and the *corruption*. You're saying that just because they'll have to leave sometime, they may as well go when it benefits you most. I think you're wrong.'

Geo blinked, and in the corner of Kit's eye he caught Rachel smiling fleetingly. He remembered how the doctors and Euan had looked, when he'd asked them about the relocation. It was amazing, he thought, how poorly he knew himself.

'Jesus, mate,' Geo said eventually. 'You're really hung up on this, aren't you? I didn't figure you for it.'

A month or so ago Kit wouldn't have said these things, so it was no surprise Geo was baffled. But there were many things Geo wouldn't grasp, like the fact that Kit had been foisted on him because Kit's parents were ashamed. The fact that they were ashamed of him because he'd tried to kill himself, but also and equally because he'd seen more value in climate science than law. What else, what else would Geo never understand? How about the fact that there was no single reason that had pushed Kit over the edge, there were a dozen messy, tangled, illogical things; or maybe nothing other than exhaustion. But somewhere in among the tangle was also the burned house, the home.

'I wanted to ask you something, actually,' Rachel said, raising her voice just slightly, like she'd expected to have to speak over someone although the only sounds were a group of birds passing through the palm trees, a cicada and the subliminal sea.

Kit wanted to ignore her. He wanted to formulate an answer to Geo before his confidence failed him.

'Darling,' Rachel said and he looked at her, frustrated.

'What?' he said.

He saw her falter at his tone so repeated more gently, 'What is it?'

'Well...' She tilted her head and smiled. 'The boat is coming, you know? And I was wondering if you might like to be on it when it leaves.' Carefully inquisitive, pressureless. 'You've done so well out here, and I wondered if maybe you're ready to go home. Back to your real life. What do you think?'

What did he think?

The thunderhead that had been a faint smear was now gathering mass like a whirlpool; he thought he saw lightning flicker.

What did he think?

That they didn't like him disagreeing with Geo's plans, and perhaps wanted him gone before he said anything. That they couldn't quite approve of whatever it was between him and Sisi, if there was anything at all.

But also this – that he couldn't picture himself anywhere but here with the red cliffs watching him and the sea like a thousand jewels. That he still wanted to go out in a pirogue and find out if his body remembered how to sail. And besides, he didn't know what his real life was anymore, let alone whether it was something he could step back into.

He rose. His hunger gone and the whole island swaying beneath his feet. 'I don't know,' he said. 'I'll think about it.' The colours of the garden seemed too bright so he went into the house, wanting shade and to be back before he'd had to imagine going home.

*

From his bedroom, though, with the curtains drawn but the window open, their voices were still clear.

'Bethany ask you to send him home, did she?' Geo, about his mum.

'No.' Rachel paused, and Kit realised he had never replied to the last email. The last two. They were so much easier just to forget.

'No, she hasn't said anything about when he might go home, actually.'

'Not in any rush, I'd imagine.' Kit winced, but Geo carried on: 'He should go home.' And Kit realised the mockery in his uncle's voice hadn't been aimed at him.

'Oh, G, I don't know. If all this other stuff weren't going on, I think it would be good for him to be here a bit longer. He's come so far but it's still so soon.'

'Yeah, but getting all up in arms about this isn't going to help sort his head out, is it?'

'No.' A pause filled by the sharp song of a magpie robin. He knew its call now, he thought. Rachel spoke again, differently. 'Do you think it'll resolve itself, the upset in the village?'

Geo gave a single barked laugh. 'With them holding a vote? God, I don't know.' Kit could picture Geo shifting his big torso uncomfortably. 'I haven't got a clue how to reason with them, and Euan tries but he's not making any headway at all, far as I can see.'

'They're frightened.'

'And angry. I don't like it. Perhaps you should get on the boat, too, Rach.'

'I don't think so,' Rachel said mildly. 'I doubt it'll go that far. Perhaps I can help, actually. They might listen to me more than you. I'm not official, after all.'

'You're still an outsider.'

'I can try.'

A noisy sigh, another creak of furniture. None of them were wanted, Kit thought, it wasn't just him. He leaned his head against the wall. The day was building to a furnace and if the storm reached them, he wanted to be suspended in the lagoon with lightning arcing overhead. Was that dangerous? He couldn't remember the probabilities.

'All this talk of ancestors and whatever. They won't listen to the practicalities of it. They act like financial security doesn't mean anything to them at all.'

'Perhaps it doesn't.' Rachel sounded like she was smiling, smothering laughter that would only aggravate her husband. 'You need to speak their language, Geo, darling. If their ancestors are more important to them than money, then make your arguments about them, somehow.'

'How do I bloody do that?'

A proper laugh this time. 'Euan will think of something. He's good like that.'

'I don't see the humour, Rachel. This is my career on the line here,' Geo said, then, almost threateningly, 'I could tell them the whole deal, like Kit wants. Make it clear this is a time-limited offer and if they turn this down then there'll be no help when things get desperate. That should sober them up.'

'I'm not sure that's...' Rachel stopped talking and Kit heard footsteps approaching. 'Morning, Euan. I was just hearing about the challenges you two are facing.'

A tiny breeze lifted the curtains and let them fall, and Euan said something, but his voice was too soft for Kit to hear. There were three thousand miles between him and home; between not understanding and not wanting to. His phone buzzed and Kit grabbed it as if to stop those outside from hearing. It was his brother.

Call Dad re your tuition fees.

Kit put the phone down, grabbed hat, water bottle and sandals, then picked the phone back up again.

I'm busy. He can call me if it's urgent.

The reply came immediately. *How much more time are you going to take off?*

I'll let you know when I decide.

Turning his phone off carried no guilt. He'd go up to Les Hautes instead of the sea, not seeking Sisi but if he met her, and if her forest eyes were not quite as empty as they had been, then perhaps he'd tell her. He hoped he would. Courage and informed choices, valuing things that other people did not.

Chapter Twenty-Seven

Sisi

In the end it was Mahena who drove Sisi finally back up to Les Hautes. Despite her not being able to work. Mahena and Agathe were at the store, raising their voices against something that Ghede was saying, and where before this argument would have held laughter and wry affection, now it did not. And the way Mahena shot looks at Sisi, her eyes narrowed to black crescent moons, made Sisi want to shout, *I am trying! I am trying to do things right this time.*

'You must be pleased, Sisi,' Mahena said. 'That Jomo will be returned soon, because he will surely agree with all the things you have done.'

Sisi held her anger within her because she had no right to it. 'I am glad that Jomo is returning to say his farewells to my husband,' she said softly, and saw the flicker in Mahena's eyes that spoke of shame quickly pushed away.

Then Nuru said something to Ghede as if Mahena had not spoken and Ghede frowned, and Manon's absence was like an empty well.

So she retreated from both the divisions and the contempt. Escaped the reminder that she was grieving Manon's friendship more acutely than she was the death of her husband, whose brother would be back soon and whom she had no idea how to face.

*

Her feet carried her unthinking all the way to the weather station. There was dust in the room and on the monitors. It slunk ceaselessly in as if Brother Island was seeking to erase the building, and Sisi went to brush everything down the way she had done a thousand times before. But instead, her fingertips drew lines in the white coating, nothing particular, just swirls and curving lines that might have been the sea or the pattern of her thoughts. Easier to focus on her fingertip and the path it made than do any of the overdue work.

This job had never quite been enough for her, however much she had tried to convince herself otherwise. But if they decided now to do away with it completely, she would let them, and then she would be lost. Her life could perhaps be divided into two: *before*, so proud of her own separateness, her mind, the significance of the sacrifices she had made; and *now*, having betrayed both the memory of her husband and her best-loved friend. And her people; the work she thought she'd done for the sake of the whole, had it instead done harm? Some of them thought so.

Her breath was loud in the square room and she let her stained hand drop. Why had she come up here?

She left the station and walked towards L'Ambre. A sunbird flushed from the scrub and Brother Island's heart was crying out today, maybe speaking to her, or speaking *for* her, transferring her own heart into the tidal anguish of his own. She found the place where she had once knelt with Kit. There, with the heart beneath her, she curled into a wind-hollow in the rock and closed her eyes, listening to the terns cry and the island moan as if the whole world were tallying her life.

*

Kit was beside her before she even realised she was no longer alone, but she felt no surprise at all. She watched as he lowered himself to his knees and peered through the honeycomb rocks at the sea. His hair caught the light like old gold, or like dry sand in the evening, and she realised she was thinking of Jomo again. Comparing the two in a way that meant nothing good at all.

'Hello,' she said. 'All is well with you?' She was not sure she had spoken aloud until he sat back and looked at her steadily, without smiling.

'Are you? Okay, I mean.'

She looked away from him to L'Ambre, aware of the tombs just out of sight the way perhaps you always were, wherever you were on the island. There were many lies, she thought, and only one truth, and so it was almost always easier to lie.

'No,' she said. It hurt just as much as she had expected it to. 'I do not think I am.'

'No,' Kit repeated, shifting his weight backwards until he was sitting cross-legged, surprisingly graceful.

'And you?' Sisi asked, watching his sea-glass eyes and thinking of the cliff face by the station. Wanting to know, and wanting to avoid other thoughts.

He was silent for a minute, his lips pursed and pensive; then he said slowly, 'I'm better than I was. But that feels wrong. To be better, I mean, what with...' Gesturing with one hand at Sisi and the island.

'Why were you... like that?' Not asking so much from boldness as desperation.

He shrugged, colour appearing above his collarbones and beneath the fair stubble on his face. 'Why does anyone get to that point? I don't know.'

It was a rebuffal, and although she thought the deflection might be more about shame, still it stung. 'Because of death and poisoned soil and the truth that your people might be dying out?' she said. A flinch made the muscles of his shoulders move beneath his shirt, for which Sisi was both sorry and not sorry at all.

'Will you leave, do you think?' he asked, looking at the rock that was the skin over Brother Island's heart. 'Will you vote to leave?'

He meant them all, she thought. In French it would have been obvious, and that thought led to another, so that her words that did not sound like an answer at all honestly were. 'Do you think it not strange that we have only one word for "time" in English?' she said slowly. Watching the palms of her hands and feeling the child within her flex their tiny body. 'But in French we have three.' She could feel his confusion, his frown, like ripples in a pool. '"Temps" and "fois" and "heure",' she tried to explain. 'How much time do we have left? How many times must this happen? At what time will this one die?' She shrugged, still not looking at him, not expecting him to understand.

Out over the cliff, where the sea washed in and out of the heart, a frigatebird hung in the air like a miracle made angular and black. Sisi watched it and it watched her, then it tipped a long wing and was away.

'I tried to kill myself three times,' he said eventually and she turned sharply to look at him, but this time it was him watching his hands and her watching his bent head. 'I got better at it, and the last time I nearly succeeded.' He shot a sliver of a smile at her from beneath his hair. 'When I got here, I hated them for stopping me. I don't anymore.'

Sisi blinked away sudden starbursts, searching for words. 'We cannot leave,' she said, feeling the island listen to her. 'Even with everything, sea levels and the tetanus and the salt, we cannot leave.'

He met her eyes and his were achingly sad. 'You can. You might survive it. It might be okay.'

Looking back towards the tombs, Antonin in her mind alongside both Manon's daughter and her son, her own mother and grandparents, even Afiya because Antonin had loved her so completely, she said, 'We will never vote to leave. All of our people are here, and we cannot leave them.' She saw he understood but she wasn't sure how much.

'It's your home,' he said, something in his face making her heart twist painfully.

'Yes,' she said, wanting to reach out and touch him, wanting to tell him about the man coming back on the mailboat and how frightened she was that he might have changed. But Brother Island's heart boomed beneath them, so loudly that tremors passed up through the bones of her hips and spine to echo in her jaw. 'However broken it is, it is who we are.'

He looked towards the bay and the village, his mouth narrowing. How familiar he had become, she thought, so alien and so known. The dust shivered with the beating of the heart below, but in the narrow space between them there was only stillness. Which she would not have minded, only it let other thoughts crawl back to the surface that had been quieted by Kit's presence. Jomo, out there somewhere on the sea, coming back but not to her. Manon – *oh, Manon* – and her unimaginable pain. And the child inside her, Sisi, pushing their limbs out again, timorous as a new butterfly as if knowing how the thought of them overwhelmed her. She did not know what had taken Kit to the cliff's edge, she thought, but she also did not know what had brought him away from it again.

*

'I heard from a lecturer at my old university, Dr Reinwald,' Kit said, as if they had never stopped talking. 'I... I mentioned the tests you were doing and she's interested in working with you on some resilient crop research. Salt tolerance and whatever.' He was frowning but not at her, colour again beneath his skin that she suspected was blood from some internal battleground. 'I thought, if you want to stay, it might help, you know?'

His eyes were still not quite meeting hers and her breath hitched. 'You did that? You asked, for me?'

A vanishingly quick smile, a slantwise glance at her and then away, she could hear her own pulse in her ears. 'I just thought it would be useful to know, one way or the other. Honestly, I thought she'd say it wasn't feasible, but...' he shook his head and turned his hands palm-up on his knees as if his own words bewildered him.

'We could do that,' she said, options and hopes ravelling in her mind. 'It could be... if it worked it could be *huge*.' For her people, for their future. He still would not meet her eyes, though, and the sun shone off his own, making them close to silver, like the surface of the sea when it was full of secrets. She found herself scanning the rocks for geckos, but there was only the two of them and Brother Island's heart growing quieter as the tide fell.

'Kit?' she said, and his jaw tightened as if his own name hurt him. 'Kit, did you mean it?'

'Yeah,' he said, shifting in the dust. 'I'll give you her email.'

And then she could talk to this woman far away – they could formulate projects and trials and... and she would have to seek consents from the Mothers and the Sacere, and they would say... they would say...

Her whole body curved, bled of whatever this feeling had been. *Let yourself belong at last*, Nuru had said, *You are so terribly clever*, but her cleverness had not made her wise so she had decided that yes, she would do as Nuru said. She would listen to their words and Mama Mandisa's, and Manon's silence, and she would try, belatedly, to be a part of the whole.

She spoke to her hands and her own shame, Kit leaning forward to hear her over the sea. 'I do not see how we can survive here if we say no to these things.' She shrugged, the movement hurting. 'I cannot see how we can reject anything that might make life here possible. We are none of us blind – we know the world is changing, the seas are changing. How can we live if we ourselves do not change?'

'But they don't want to? The others?'

She looked up at him. 'It is the curse, the tetanus. They say if we are to break that, we must return to the old ways and rid ourself of taint.'

Kit's face moved. 'And we are the taint, we outsiders.'

'Yes,' she said.

He sighed and straightened, putting distance between them. 'But you don't agree.' Still not a question, but more of one than the last.

'I...' She reached to tug frustratedly at the ends of her hair, the sharp, distinct pains almost soothing. 'It does not matter what I think. Before, I was so wrong, Kit. There are a lot of things I have got so wrong.'

Perhaps Kit knew that the doctors had seen Manon's babe as a... a *testing* for Sisi's own, that Sisi's words and Sisi's friendship had made Manon go to them so that Sisi may as well have proffered up Manon's beautiful son like a sacrifice for her own. Perhaps he knew, or perhaps he only guessed; it made no real difference in the end. He reached out a hand as if to touch her but didn't, and she could not know about that either, whether he knew about the fady, or whether he did not.

'Will you tell them,' he said instead of whatever he was thinking, 'about the crops?'

'No,' she said without having to think about it. 'Everything is too... everyone is too upset at the moment. And also' – her own honesty surprising her again – 'they will distrust it, coming from me.'

'If you knew beyond doubt it would change things,' he said, strangely insistent, 'would you tell them?'

She hesitated this time, made unsure. 'No,' meeting his gaze, 'because I do not think it is about *facts*. Not truly. It is about who we are, and were, and will be.'

Kit turned his head away and Sisi fell silent.

Chapter Twenty-Eight

Sisi

She met Kit up on Les Hautes again two days later, at Brother Island's heart as if this place had become somehow their own. Just the two of them and Brother Island watching. The boat would arrive tomorrow and Sisi had come up here to escape a furious row between Mama Anouk and Luc and others who Sisi had not stopped to listen to. It was about Mahena pushing Oni so that she fell into the sand, and Luc saying it was Oni's own fault for being so faithless; about where passion became spite, and it was all so terrifyingly *wrong*, her people like this. Despite a lifetime resisting the primacy of the whole, seeing it shattering was *wrong* and frightening and the island felt smaller than her skin.

But also, Manon had been there, grey-faced and silent with her arms clutching empty spaces to her body. Her hands and those spaces were barely noticed, though, because she was not the only one cradling emptiness and hers was no harder than theirs. How cruel, Sisi thought, and how forgivable.

Manon had looked right through Sisi unblinking and then turned away.

So now Sisi was up here, running away again rather than be invisible, and rather than be asked for an opinion. The heat up here, even with the sun slipping westward, was sharp as the rocks, tight against her skin like a giant's fist, but she did not mind it. Far better this dust-haze furnace than the village and the sea. She was wearing a pair of Nuru's shorts, belted low below the tiny curve of her belly, and if from here she might also keep watch on the empty sea, she was not looking, not really.

*

'Were you at the store?' Kit asked her. They were walking this time, perhaps because it was too hot to sit in among the limestone hollows where the frail sea-breeze would not reach them. 'Were they still fighting?'

'Yes,' Sisi said, answering both questions, watching her feet find traction in the jagged earth. Two tiny asity birds were dancing through the thorns of a flowering bush, the sun catching the blues and greens in their feathers, bleaching out the yellows. 'I hate it,' she said. 'All this anger.'

Kit was a little behind her, a little to one side. His hands in his pockets and his face, like hers, turned down from the glare of the sea to the rocks. 'It must have got like this before,' he said eventually. 'None of this is new, is it?'

Green lentils and sweet potatoes dug withering from the salted earth, the babes. 'No, but...' How did you explain the way it had been up to now? How tragedy could happen in so many parts that the whole stayed unreal. 'Now it is different, with you... with the Administrator here and setting out these things with such... finality.'

Ahead and beneath them, the sea washed into the heart on a changing tide, the beat of the waves losing their rhythm and then finding it again. 'We should have decades, but now he gives us a deadline,' she added when Kit said nothing. 'He cannot see that this decision is not one we will make only because someone else says we must.'

Kit stopped walking so she did too, turning to face him with the sun throwing his shadow towards her.

'But if no one pushed you to a choice, do you think you'd ever make it?' he said, his hands curling into fists. 'Or would you just carry on as before, always putting it off, burying it?'

She recoiled.

'Oh, Sisi,' he said, stepping towards her but then stopping, 'I'm so sorry, I didn't—'

'It is fine,' she said, lying to both of them. 'I do not know. This has been coming for a long time, yes? I think all this anger, it has been waiting to be allowed to speak. We... the more that we lose, the harder it is to find the words, n'est-ce pas?' She took a long breath. 'They are not separate for us, Kit. The island and our children. You think they are, but it is not so.'

She saw his eyes drop to her stomach and then up again, and the simple fact of him linking her tiny babe to the ones already dead hurt her like a knife. She could not bear it, so she turned away from him, spinning on one heel. Stepping forward, weight swinging.

Rocks trapped her foot; her ankle twisted, slipping; she gave a small shattering cry, and her hands were reaching out, whole body flexing, trying to curl inwards, and *my baby* screaming in her mind, wrenching her body sideways so that she hit with hands and forearm and shoulder, a knee, a *snap* in her ankle.

The scream, and that snap; the world dividing in two.

*

Then stillness. Sunlight filled her eyes with white and the dust in her lungs tasted of horror.

And the pain found her.

'Jesus, Sisi, Jesus,' Kit was whispering, kneeling beside her, lifting her up to sitting, his arm around her, brushing her tumbled hair and headwrap away from her face. His touch was warm and strong and she knew, distantly, that he ought not touch her but could not remember why. She leaned into his shoulder, panting with the hurt of it.

'The babe,' she said. 'Kit, my child.' Her ankle was a lightning strike and there were a thousand fires along her arm and leg and the palms of her hands, but there was something else in her stomach. An ache, soft and softer but terrible, and her whole heart was at once ablaze.

This was the hidden fear and *this* the end of the world, and *this* was the life that she carried becoming finally real. *Oh Mother,* she wanted to howl. *Oh Mother, please.* 'Kit, I cannot—'

'It's okay,' he said. 'Are you... does it hurt?'

Her hands smearing scarlet on Nuru's pale shorts – oh, how hard that would be to wash out, and Nuru so fastidious. Kit's fingers wiping her tears from her face so gently, pressing the edge of his shirt against the blood on her hand. She whimpered.

'Sisi? What hurts? Your ankle's—'

Sisi shook her head, and that ache rose again. 'My babe,' she gasped; it was all she could say, but her bloody hand touched her stomach, shaking, and Kit's eyes widened.

'I'll go and get help,' he said. 'I don't want to leave you, but—'

'Yes. Quickly. Please. It hurts. Please go.'

He frowned at her, half-risen. 'Don't move,' he said. 'You mustn't move.' Fumbling with the bag on his back: 'Here, here's water and have my hat, and promise me, Sisi. Promise me you won't—'

'I will not move,' she said. The ache in her stomach was there again and she didn't dare weep because her muscles were newly and terrifyingly vital. 'I will not.' Wanting him gone, wanting him running to Nuru and Mama Mandisa and Manon; anyone, someone to make this all right. But as he stood she clutched at his hand, remembering now why she should not but doing it anyway. 'Kit,' she said. 'Oh Mother, Kit.'

'I know,' he said and bent swiftly to kiss her hair. 'We won't be long.' Then he was turning and running perilously over the rocks, his legs the same colour as the dead corals and his long stride surprisingly sure.

*

Time slowed. She was almost too scared to move at all, but the blood was still welling on her arm and knee, which would be bad too, n'est-ce pas? Blood loss? A tiny child gasping for her blood, reaching nubbed hands out, and *Oh Mother*, she thought over and over. *Oh Mother, I did not know. Please, please, I did not know.* Bloody handprints on her shirt. *I am so sorry. I did not understand this thing, but please.* Someone was keening – perhaps it was her. *Let me keep them, this tiny thing. I am sorry, I did not know, I did not know.*

She made herself drink water, she made herself pour more onto her headwrap to wash grit and sweat and blood from her skin. The sun drying her in seconds, dust resettling on her skin like ashes, and every movement made her ankle shriek demons. It was swelling already, the straps of her sandal cutting in, so she bent forward to take it off, not sure if she was meant to but needing to anyway.

Then there, curled over the nexus of her womb, she felt it again – cramp slipping through her abdomen in a wave – and she froze, her hands reached out, ankle pleading. Three breaths or four breaths, then it eased and she leaned back, sandal forgotten and all of her mind, all of her heart on the muscles of her stomach and the tiny life she had been refusing to see.

How could you ever buffer yourself against *this*? How did you save your own heart from *this*?

'I will save you,' she whispered to them.

The world had snapped in two, and that cold, tight unwanting she had carried from the start was gone and gone and gone.

*

Beneath her the sea sucked out of Brother Island's heart and the rocks sucked at her blood, dust climbing her limbs. Someone breathed beside her, hot inhalations, and she opened her eyes, thinking, *Nuru, Kit.* But there were only the red cliffs, her own blood, and the ragged landscape watching, the heart beneath.

Alone. Unalone. Was it Mother Sea watching, or was it love?

'I will save you,' she repeated. 'Only, stay with me now. Please, stay with me.'

She had been saying this her whole life. But never like this.

Never with such surprise and tenderness, such fury. And there *was* someone else here, the hair at her nape prickling and the ache in her womb sweeping over her again, not strong but terrible. The sun was falling from the pinnacle of the sky towards the sea, the tide licking at Brother Island's heart like a snake. Unalone, not a comforting presence but a malevolence, a hunger.

'You cannot have them,' she said without thinking, her voice high, her stomach contracting again. 'The babe is mine and you will not have them.'

There were black starbursts swimming across her vision and blood running again down her shin. She did not know who she was talking to, but the island stained itself with her blood and Mother Sea coiled beneath them. She whispered to them both, 'Please, not this one,' and nothing else mattered at all, she knew it now. She would become anything at all so that this babe, this child within her, would be saved.

Chapter Twenty-Nine

Kit

Kit didn't know who to get, but he knew where Nuru would be. He reached the store already calling, Nuru coming out, the hostility in their eyes turning to horror, then they were grabbing things, shouting to someone Kit couldn't see, and running up the path Kit had just come down.

Three steps into following them, Kit stopped and turned the other way. Running again, along the beach and up beneath trees to the clinic. They were there, thank god, and thank god Geraldine was used to people stumbling up to her, incoherent.

'Matt,' Geraldine said, on her feet and stuffing things into a bag. 'The stretcher.' Then, Kit taking one end and Matt the other, they were off.

*

Even from a long way away, Kit could see the people standing around Sisi, although she herself was hidden by the rocks and their bodies. Nuru had gathered more after Kit went to the clinic, and as they got closer, Kit thought he recognised two as fishermen, and the other two kneeling beside Nuru he thought were more Sacere.

Nuru was holding Sisi in just the way Kit had done, talking to her in a low voice, and something in Kit's gut turned over even though he knew it was ridiculous. Another Sacere was dressing the cuts on her leg and arm and hands, her ankle already bound in a scaffold of plastic and straps.

'Sisi,' he said over their backs, and the smile she gave him, wavering but beautiful, made him lurch forward and then stop short. 'Dr Adler's here,' he said, and Geraldine *was* there beside her already, opposite Nuru, saying something to Sisi.

Nuru reared up. 'Get away from her,' they said, pushing Geraldine's hand from Sisi's shoulder so hard that Sisi quailed.

'Wait,' Kit said, louder than he'd intended. 'Don't be stupid. Let the doctor examine her.'

Nuru looked up at him, then at the faces of everyone gathered around, one corner of their mouth lifted in a grimace as they looked back at Geraldine, and Kit knew what they were about to say.

'This same doctor who let Manon's son die? You think we will trust you with Sisi's?'

Sisi closed her eyes, and Geraldine grew paler than she already was, but her hand touched Sisi anyway. 'I am still a doctor,' she said quietly. 'I am on your side.' She looked at Sisi, who opened her eyes and looked back. 'Sisi, will you let me help, please?' All the colours of Sisi's eyes and skin were translucent, as if pain was draining her away from within.

'No,' Nuru said. 'The taint was brought here by you outsiders, the disease carried on your boats. The greatest danger to Sisi and her child is you.' Laying their hand on Sisi's belly, blunt fingers spread protectively, possessively. 'Leave us alone.'

'Sisi?' Geraldine asked again. But Sisi looked at Nuru, her eyes very wide.

'Sisi,' Nuru echoed and Kit breathed in sharply. Matt swore under his breath. Sisi leaned against Nuru's shoulder and turned her face into their neck.

Geraldine sat back on her heels, her own face bleak, and Matt said, 'At least use the stretcher. At least have the sense to do that, will you?' He dropped it beside Sisi, lurid orange and Sisi's blood vivid against the rock.

*

Geraldine and Matt withdrew but didn't leave, and Kit hovered between them and Sisi, all their shadows lengthening like an unspooling darkness. The fishermen did lift Sisi onto the stretcher eventually, although Nuru was frowning. *How would you have done it instead?* Kit wanted to shout. Slung hands beneath her shoulders and ankles? Jolting and bruising her rather than using something they must have used before?

He followed after them as they carried Sisi back across Les Hautes, watched the stretcher begin its slow descent to the bay. Wiped sweat from his palms and face that was only partly from the slow-falling heat.

'Will she be okay?' he said to Geraldine.

Her face twisted with frustration. 'How am I supposed to know?' she said. 'Ah, Christ. I couldn't even tell whether her ankle was broken or not, although at least they'd braced it properly.' She hesitated, stepping over a ridge of stone that was sharp as a knife. 'They do know what they're doing,' she said slowly. 'But still, I wish they'd let me help.'

'They're frightened,' Matt said impatiently. 'So they're being stupid.'

'You saw her fall,' Geraldine said to Kit. 'Did she hit her stomach, did you see?'

It had happened so fast. 'I don't think so,' he said, then more certainly, 'No, she landed on her knee and shoulder. That's where she was bleeding worst.'

Geraldine puffed out a breath, walking silently for a while, and it was Matt who asked. 'That's good, right? For the pregnancy?'

'Yeah,' she said, lifting her shoulders. 'Yes, it is. It should be. You said she was experiencing cramps?'

My babe, she had whispered with her eyes like a cataclysm. 'I think so,' Kit said.

Geraldine nodded slightly. 'It can be the muscles responding to shock. She probably just needs rest.'

'She was bleeding a lot,' Matt said.

'It's this rock,' Kit looked down at his feet, cross-hatched with scars from his mad-blind run up here an age ago. Hating Les Hautes suddenly, hating himself more, although he wasn't sure why.

Geraldine grimaced. All three of them skirted a thorn bush and didn't speak until they'd clambered down a series of steps. It would be fully dark by the time they were back and Kit couldn't bear to imagine how Sisi had fared, carried over this. 'It's brutal stuff,' Geraldine said eventually, perhaps just about the rocks, perhaps not, but she stopped then and turned towards Kit. 'Actually, Kit, do you think they'll let you see her? I could tell you what to ask, what to check for. If she's still having cramps in the morning, I could give you some meds.'

Kit looked on down the path but saw no one. The sweat on his shoulder blades turned cold. He wanted to help, but god, how could he persuade anyone – least of all Nuru – of anything?

'I'll try,' he said. Weren't those words the worst? *I'll try. I tried.*

Chapter Thirty

Sisi

The pains in Sisi's stomach had slowly eased that night, the night after she fell and was carried down from Les Hautes shaking. They eased, but they did not stop. Night fell but still, every ten minutes, they would come. A soft ache too gentle for what it was, lesser than menstrual cramps but loaded with horror.

Sleepless in the time after midnight, her whole body hurting and the muscles around her womb tired, tears clogging her throat because the darkness around her was ravenous and fear was in every chamber of her lungs. She had not wanted this child, but now – before they had any chance at all – she might lose them, and she knew, finally, that she could not bear to do so. She was glass around a gemstone, inadequate to the task of protecting this thing within her.

She must have made a noise, because beside her Nuru said quietly, 'You must try to sleep, Sisi. It will do more for you than lying there listening to your body.'

There was no answer to that, and another cramp drew her muscles down.

'I cannot give you passionflower, I'm sorry. It's not safe.' Their hand came out of the shadows, brushing her hair from her forehead, testing for fevers, retreating. 'Sister?'

Sisi took an uneven breath. 'I cannot lose my child,' she said.

Nuru made a low crooning sound that was both understanding and reassurance. 'You will not.'

'I might!' Shifting against her pillows, wanting to sit up and not wanting to move at all. 'Nuru, how can you promise this thing? No one can. Even if I am well now...' The words catching, breaking. 'Even if I do not lose them now, then I will lose them afterwards, n'est-ce pas? I will carry them and birth them and then watch them die. And how have they all borne this knowledge, Nuru? I do not think I can.'

'You can, Sisi,' Nuru said, finding Sisi's hand in the dark and squeezing it until her wedding ring was pressing against her bones. 'You can bear it because you are strong, and because you must.'

'But Nuru...' Sisi turned her head away, wanting to believe them but almost bitter. 'I do not have...' *Anyone*, she wanted to say. Meaning Antonin, but meaning Manon too.

'You have me,' Nuru said, understanding, then adding slowly, as if reluctant, 'and tomorrow, Jomo will be back.'

They were the right words to say. But they were also, and completely, the worst. She stopped crying, her face still turned away but her eyes open now, watching the sway of the curtains lit by the moon and the moon's eye on the sea. A gecko laughed.

'I will fight for this,' she whispered.

'I know,' Nuru said, 'and I will show you how.'

Sisi held her breath and then released it slowly. 'How are you so sure?' she asked, not as a challenge but in wonder.

There was a long silence, as if they had misinterpreted, but then they sighed and said, 'Because that is what is needed of me. Because it is right.'

Whereas she had been wrong. She closed her eyes, and after another silence, said, 'I thought there was someone there. Before you arrived.'

'Oh?' The bed moved and Sisi looked at Nuru, barely making out silhouettes and the thrice-reflected moon in their eyes.

'It was… it was only my fear…'

'But?'

Fumbling for words because this was not like her, the island's scientist, the island's reluctant returner. 'It was as if a thing was watching, and was hungry.'

'Oh,' they said again, but drawn out into a spoken breath rather than a word. 'Mother Sea.' As if giving an answer to a question.

'I am not sure,' Sisi said, thinking of the heart's pulse beneath her, glass-edged rocks peeling away her skin, staining themselves red. 'It was only my fear. And the pain.'

'I think not, sister,' Nuru said and the speed of their certainty made them inviolable. 'This is a message, Sisi. It is Mother Sea telling us that I was right. I *am right*! For *you* to fall, to shed blood… Ah, ma chère.' There was quick movement and then the press of their lips against her temple. 'I will go now to see if the others are awake.' Meaning the Sacere.

'In the middle of the night?'

'Yes, but we have been listening so hard for Mother Sea to speak to us. We will talk with the Mothers in the morning, but Berhane at least will be awake now.' They were rising off the bed even as they spoke. Sisi wanted to clutch at the shadows and beg them not to leave her, but she did not and then they were gone.

*

Cool air pulled itself into the room and across her limbs, and Sisi lay limp, thinking about hunger and her own desperation, which was its own sort of hunger. When the next wave of cramps came, she realised it had been longer since the last one, and this one was gentler. She wove her fingers together over the dome of her womb, making a fortress of her own bones and listening to the sand-hustle of crabs outside, the single sharp barks of a gecko again, the tide, ebbing away from her in slow degrees.

Two truths, she thought, watching the angles of the moon change, still listening for someone else's breaths in the dark. Two thoughts. That yes, she must trust Nuru to guide her where her own instincts had failed. But also that she had been too passive, not only letting others guide her, but *waiting* for them to do so. She had been waiting, and now she would demand.

Four months. Four months and then the nine days. There was too little time and she could not resign herself, not to this.

Chapter Thirty-One

Kit

Early the next morning, as soon as he reasonably could, Kit left the house and walked down to the village. The sand slipping into his sandals was cool and the sky held strange colours, none of them blue. Quartz and moonstone, he thought; as a kid, he'd loved geology, palaeontology, a vast narrative he wanted to be a part of. Studying climate science was the same thing, he realised. The wish to step into the world's story.

The door of her house was open and Nuru sat on one of the chairs outside in the blue shade of the trees, busy with something in their hands. They looked up at Kit already frowning.

'You cannot see her,' they said before he could speak.

'Is she okay?' he said, coming to a stop beside a coconut tree, one hand on its rough trunk. 'How is she?'

'She is better, but resting.' They were still staring at Kit, holding his gaze with so much animosity it scalded. Kit hadn't expected this to be easy, but still...

'I just want to see she's okay, ask if I can bring her anything. That's all. I won't stay long.'

'No.'

'Why not? I was with her yesterday.' His fingers moved on the tree trunk, searching for holds, and his pulse thrummed beneath the skin of his face. It was an effort to sound reasonable.

'Yes, you were, this is true.' Nuru blinked as slowly as a cat.

'What?' Kit took half a step forward, stopped. 'What are you suggesting? Don't be ridiculous.'

Nuru looked away finally, their eyes narrowed and on the sea. They looked, he realised, pleased – like his anger was all they had wanted.

'Will you even ask her?' he said to Nuru's profile. 'Will you ask her if she wants to see me? Or are you her jailer?'

That word found some sort of mark, which pleased Kit in return. Nuru's body tensed and relaxed again like a bow being drawn and then not. 'I am her family.'

Kit wanted to shake them until that untouchability was wiped from their face; to punch them. His own violence startled him, but he hoped it showed on his face anyway.

'And what are you, Kit Benedict? What is it you think you have with my sister?'

The muscles of his jaw did not want to let him speak. 'I'm her friend.' He thought he was; he thought that was what it was between them in among the rocks and thorns. 'I'm her friend, and I just want to know if she is okay.'

Nuru rose to standing and Kit repositioned his feet in the sand. They put down whatever they'd been holding and brushed their hands together. 'So, now you know. She is well, and you may go.'

What could he do? Wrestle his way into the house? Shout for Sisi until she emerged? Anger was a lump of coal in his lungs, but there was nothing he could do other than pivot on one heel and walk away.

'You know who the boat is bringing today?' Nuru said to his back. Kit stopped but didn't turn – there was something in Nuru's voice that Kit didn't want to see on their face. 'You know it brings Jomo back to her? She has, of course, told you about Jomo, yes? Who she wished to marry? Who comes back to her now she is widowed?'

There was a trail of black ants in the sand just in front of Kit, most of them heading right in an almost continuous line, but the occasional one was going the other way, blundering through the lines and fighting against the tide. Kit didn't turn; the question didn't need an answer. He stepped over the ants and went through the houses, down to the beach, not stopping until he knew he was out of Nuru's sight. Walking away from his own house and away from Sisi's, round the curve of the sand towards Pointe Basse and the island hall. He sat where the last tide had left rock pools, studying the water for tiny wonders. Anemones and seaweeds, shells he couldn't name.

Both intent and anger were crushed out of him by Nuru's words and his own retreat, so he sat counting colours in the water, waiting for the tide to drive him away. Was this Jomo the same Jomo as her husband's brother who was also coming back? And how on earth had that come about? He wondered if today Geo would tell the islanders about the deal he'd made. It would be so much easier if he did, because Kit had dared to imagine himself stronger and yet had still failed. First he'd allowed Sisi's doubts to silence him and now he'd allowed Nuru to do the same.

*

The tide reached the pool he was probing with his fingers, and voices came down to him from the building above just like they had before. He froze, seawater running down his wrist, thinking *not again*, half-amused.

'It is a clear message, Mothers. We Sacere are agreed we must act on this.' Nuru, Kit thought, fingers tightening.

Another, female, older but not old. 'Sisi falling was an accident only. It means nothing.'

'Mama Anouk,' – Nuru again – 'her falling perhaps was only chance, but that she fell with the outsider, and what she felt up there, these are not chance. To ignore this would mean being deliberately blind.'

'We are… jumping at shadows, I think.' The voice of Mama Anouk, the youngest of the Mothers.

'Beloved Mama, we would be wiser perhaps to listen and be mistaken than not to listen at all.' This one was a voice that Kit recognised as another Sacere, although he didn't know their name.

'I agree.' Yet another voice, so old and so quiet it sounded like the wind. Kit put his hand back into the water, the cold of the tide against his skin. He'd have to move soon, up the pointe and away from the sea, but then they might know he was here and think he was eavesdropping. Whereas he… was doing exactly that, and whether it was deliberate or not probably didn't matter. He was where he didn't belong.

'Mama Mathilde, thank you.' Nuru again. 'Mama Mandisa?'

'What exactly are you proposing, Nuru? We are not children, believing without question.'

Kit's lips pulled back into a sort of smile.

'Our Mother hungers,' Nuru said. 'We have been distracted and starved her of our love, and now we must sate her. It is the only way forward.'

Someone sighed softly. 'It is,' the other Sacere said, 'a message that we cannot ignore, however we choose to interpret it.'

'And so…' Mama Mandisa said.

'And so, Mama Mandisa,' Nuru said, sounding just a touch too patient. 'We make sacrifice. We give her blood.'

'So that she takes no more children.' Mama Anouk sounded dubious. 'It is barbaric.'

'As is the sea, sister,' Mama Mandisa said, her voice calm and soft. 'And would this be more barbaric than those who destroy the world and then hide behind their walls so they can pretend ignorance?'

Mama Anouk did not answer, and then Nuru said, 'At least we are honest.'

'If we do this thing,' the other Sacere said slowly. 'We must yet decide how. What form it will take.'

'Before, it did not work,' came the whisper of the oldest voice. 'With Manon's babe.'

'Then, we did not give of ourselves.' Nuru again.

A wave hit Kit's shins, startling him and making him scurry backwards.

'Et bien, we shall think on this,' Mama Mandisa said. 'At this time, we must be patient and not add to the storm. Sisi has time.'

Just as two or three voices began talking at once, Nuru's voice rose over them. 'I fear that we do not have the benefit of time, Mama Mandisa. The mailboat comes today and will be gone this evening. If the outsiders do not leave on this boat, then it will be another month or more before we can begin to reclaim ourselves and recover what we have lost.'

Someone made a hissing sound, and someone, not the same person, said, 'What does it matter if they lurk in their house on L'Ambre? We have so many more important things to think of than the presence of outsiders who do nothing but repeat themselves. They are nothing to us.'

Another wave broke over Kit's feet but this time he didn't move. *They are nothing to us.* But he didn't want to be nothing, he thought. Unable to move because then he'd be able to see them gathered on their mats in the shade, and they'd be able to see him. Or, worse, what if he moved and they didn't see him? What if his presence, his existence was so barely relevant that he was invisible?

He hadn't felt invisible earlier, confronted by Nuru's loathing, but wasn't that loathing simply because of the colour of his skin, because of the way he spoke and who he lived with? It wasn't for *him*, Kit Benedict; and now he wished it had been. Because better to be *anything* than be negligible, surely. *It is about who we are, and were, and will be,* Sisi had said, and whatever he wasn't, he wanted to be more than his failures, more than nothing at all. He wanted to choose that.

Chapter Thirty-Two

Kit

After he returned to the house Kit watched the boat arrive, a growing mass moving down the gradient of the sea, dwarfed by the ocean. By the time the shadows were shrinking from the veranda steps, its ugly bulk was mooring against the floating dock on the far side of the reef, crates lowering down beside the rib, and boats racing out from the bay to meet it, their white sails butterfly-like and anachronistic against the ship's hull.

He was sitting at the table on the veranda, his laptop in front of him, re-reading Dr Reinwald's email, trying and failing to forget the newly arrived one from his father. The first words from him since the hospital, and Kit wished he'd stayed silent.

I've spoken to Student Support at the University, and arranged for them to hold your place for a semester. You'll have to make up the courses, but it won't be insurmountable. In the meantime you can intern here, perhaps with Heinrich. I am confident it will do you good to spend time learning the ropes in a practical sense before returning to your studies.

I hope you are getting back on your feet and making the most of your time away. Your mother and I look forward to seeing you when you return. You are of course welcome to stay with us.

Your father.

It didn't seem to matter how many times Kit read other emails – this was the one that echoed inside his skull, like it was alone in there, surrounded by darkness. In his dad's eyes, he guessed it was both olive branch and support, giving Kit time to recover and reconsider. As if he would simply *forget* how he loathed law and wanted oceanography, ecology, climate change, meteorology; some wider, fundamental *meaning*. What would they do, his family, if he did forget? Went home, worked the internship, returned to his former degree and pretended contentment. What would they do? Be proud of him? Paint over all of this and make it unspoken, unspeakable? Yes. Of course they would.

Rachel came out from where she'd been clattering in the kitchen, wiping her hands dry on a dish cloth and looking at him with one hip canted. 'You have till five to change your mind, Kit, darling. I still think it might be a good time for you to move on.'

Kit looked at her without smiling, then through the hibiscus at the boat, closing his laptop with his gaze still averted. Go home and straight back into the life that had nearly killed him, or not? What might change? He might in time learn to accept it, like it even. Who he was, and who he would be.

He pushed to his feet and said, 'I'm staying.' Found himself reaching out to touch Rachel's forearm gently. 'I'm not ready yet,' he said. 'But thank you.' Then he went on down to the shore.

*

He stood at the top of the beach in the shade of the coconut trees, goat's foot vines tangling around his feet. From here he could see the boats returning, sails collapsing and the hulls driving up onto the sand. Men leaped into the water, bare-skinned and shining either from sweat or the sea or both, and Kit envied them the ease with which they used their bodies, the way the sunlight turned all their shades of brown into riches, but for once didn't envy them the water, because...

He only realised who he was looking for when he spotted him. Broad-bodied, wearing a T-shirt and board shorts, sunglasses pushed back on his head. He had been helping to unload, but now jumped out of the boat, leaning his weight into its flank to push it back out for another journey. Then, wading inshore, he stopped with the water around his ankles and looked at the village, his face from this distance nothing but the identical dark of eyes and skin. Kit had braced himself for antipathy, but it wasn't there. Instead he wanted to walk into the furnace of the sun until he could read this man's face, and it wasn't about constructing a Venn diagram of the two of them in someone else's eyes, but about knowing what it was like to come back to a life when you yourself were irrevocably changed.

It was too easy for Kit to tally how far he thought he'd come in his time here, where the old him had never been. But Jomo was doing what he must do too: coming home to face the ghost of the self he'd left behind. The ghost his family still saw.

How did Jomo see his old home now? How much courage had it taken to leave; how much to come back? And did he regret either?

*

Oblivious to Kit, Jomo began to walk up the beach. There was a holdall slung over one shoulder and when he was at the strandline, Nuru came down the sand to meet him. They hugged, kissing cheeks, both of them laughing, but then Jomo looked past Nuru, tilting his whole body into a question that Kit knew the answer to. And Nuru was shaking their head, making calming, slowing, backing-up gestures with their hands, speaking quickly. Even though Kit couldn't hear them, he knew what this was, too. *She is ill, she is resting.* Then the moment when Nuru said, *She is carrying our brother's child.* Jomo rearing back, his head coming up and both feet moving backwards, searching for balance like you might do in an earthquake. He shook his head, going to push past Nuru. But even though he could have swatted aside his sibling, he didn't, stopping at the touch of Nuru's hand on his chest. Their voices rose enough for Kit to catch the meter of them, heat-flattened, and he finally turned away because he wanted to think about that other moment, Jomo on the sands looking at his old life, instead of this, Jomo's hurt.

*

Nearly back at the house, he met Geraldine on her way down to the clinic. They were packing up, ready to board the boat, and Kit was only just realising he'd miss them. Not only as a buffer between him and his uncle, or because they sounded like home, but also because they were separate from his own demons in a way that nothing else here was.

'Do you need a hand?' he said, realising he could have done the same at the beach, although he'd probably have been turned away.

'No, thanks. We're almost there. You can help get it all down to the boats later, though.' She smiled and Kit expected her to move on past him, but she hesitated.

'They wouldn't let you in to see her?' she asked, and when he shook his head mutely, added, 'Would you do something else for me, then?'

'Sure,' he said, thinking, *Why do you have faith in me?*

'Can I give you a package for Sisi? I've sent her an email, but there are some things I wanted her to have. I'm hoping to keep her updated on Matt's antibody work, you know.' She grimaced. 'I want to try to get her over to the mainland, before the baby comes.'

Which seemed a forlorn chance, the way Sisi had been talking. But Kit wasn't about to say that – there was something sacrosanct about their meetings up above the sea cave, and he wouldn't violate it. He thought of Nuru's antipathy towards him, them holding Jomo back with just the pressure of their hand, and it made him say, 'You might be better off asking Rachel. I think they'd be more likely to let her get close than me.'

'Nuru? He acts like he's her guard dog?' Geraldine's shoulders rose and stayed risen, her face disapproving.

'They,' Kit corrected automatically. 'They're a they. But yeah.'

'I wish I could stay, but I'm not doing any good just sitting here watching Matt work. I can at least try to do something from home, and perhaps email will be a... safer way of communicating with Sisi. Less interference, don't you think?'

She was genuinely asking, he realised. Trusting his opinion. He thought about being back on the mainland emailing Sisi, and reading her words in reply. It was incomprehensible and he realised for the first time that when he left, he'd be choosing to *leave* just as much as he'd be choosing to *return*. More so, in a way, and *oh god*, he didn't know how to do either. The scent of the flowers switched from fertile to cloying in his throat, crushed petals and fallen fruit.

'Yes,' he said eventually, but she misinterpreted his hesitation.

'Well, between you both, can you see she gets it?'

And he said yes again, then pushed on through the trees into the garden to stand there with the sun bleaching his thoughts. *Forget about going home*, he thought. *There's no point thinking about it at least until the boat goes and comes again. Forget about how far you've climbed, and how brittle the ladder feels.* Instead he thought about being here alone with Geo's confidence and Euan's slantwise expectancy; and Sisi, isolated and not isolated, even more lost than him.

*

By the time they had loaded the doctors' gear into the boats, Kit's clothes were a clinging second skin. The ship was waiting for the doctors and the rising tide, so Geraldine and Matt said their goodbyes, shaking hands with the three Mothers who stood in the sun like jewels. Kit hugged the doctors goodbye too, hating his own sweat, apologising even though they were little better, them all laughing and everyone fighting almost physically to be cheerful, but it was hard and they were failing, because at the top of the beach a gathering of islanders was watching the two doctors leave. They watched, and they didn't move or talk, their faces blank and queerly hungry, as if in the doctors' retreat they were not only counting victory but envisioning catastrophe. Kit kept checking the horizon for clouds, the sea beyond the reef for white caps that weren't there, Geraldine and Matt's eyes for the fear that the villagers' awful watch was stirring in him.

Jesus, he thought, *Jesus*. Even indirectly, even though it wasn't aimed his way, this collective, expectant animosity was chilling. It hadn't been personal before – the arguments he'd half-heard walking through the village had been pointed more inward than out. *They are nothing to us*, they had said, but this was different. If he had the courage he'd turn to where that group waited and say, *They were helping you! They still are! How can you treat them like this when you so desperately need that help?*

'They are frightened,' Matt had said yesterday. But it was more than that. *They are something strong*, Kit thought, *finding out that they are also fragile.*

He hunkered into the grim embrace of his own T-shirt. The loaded rib churned water as it reversed, turned and began to pull away, the sound of the outboard drowning everything else in the wide bay until it was distant enough for other sounds to slip back in. Birds screaming out over the water somewhere, Rachel murmuring to Euan and the wind in the palm trees, hissing.

*

Again, Kit saw the bay the way it would be if Geo's deal came through. Girders and slicked water, rusty shipping containers and strangers everywhere. The houses bulldozed out of the way and the red cliffs looking down at something ugly and unrecognisable.

The image dissipated, overlaid on the now like a hallucination, or the memory of a nightmare. *Jesus*, he thought again. *Jesus*. He didn't even know what he meant – pity or self-disgust or just someone else to blame. He wanted to be more than nothing and he didn't want to go home, but what was the point of staying here if he wasn't going to act?

Chapter Thirty-Three

Sisi

Sisi rose late in the morning, obeying Nuru's instructions to rest. But the tendons of her ankle were wrapped; those awful pains had stopped and there had been no blood, so now Sisi wanted only to escape into sunlight and the clean air coming in on the tide. Away, too, from the sense of being watched in the dark. And besides, the boat had arrived.

Once Nuru had returned from meeting with the Mothers, she walked with them to the store, carrying her laptop because she had promised not to do any work but still needed to find the words to let her colleagues know. There was low conversation under the trees off to the right, and she felt unfamiliarly clumsy, like her body was too delicate for its own strength, more present and more precious than she had ever been before.

She turned her head at every footfall, though, every voice, because even though her whole heart was bent to the life within her, it was also, somehow, straining towards one particular life without.

'Where is Jomo?' she said eventually, sitting in the chair that Nuru pulled into the slim shade of the store wall, her feet and the bare skin of her calves stretching into the sun.

'Helping unload. He will be staying with Mama Anouk,' Nuru said. 'And the pirogues are going out later, so he will go with them, I think.'

'Oh.' Trying hard for this news not to hurt, and knowing that she had failed from the level look that Nuru sent her. They were pulling crates of vegetables out from the shade of the store to where they could be scrutinised and smelled and squeezed. Fresh mainland stocks; potatoes, short-lived oranges and tomatoes that would be devoured amorously in the next few days. Sacks of rice and flour, of course, and how they had ever survived the long years between shipwreck and outside trade would always be mysterious to Sisi. Scraping a diet from coconuts, wild fruits and the sea. There was celeriac; stripped stems of lemongrass that freed the air of flies; chilli peppers lying luminously next to fat white butterbeans. And also a crate of mangoes, gathered by whoever had found the time, to be taken by whoever had the need.

Nuru picked up a tomato and inhaled the bright scent of it with their eyes closed, their face inscrutable, and when they did not seem inclined to speak, Sisi pressed the power button on her laptop where it sat at her feet, and said, tentatively, 'Mama Mandisa warned me away from Jomo. Did you do the same, to him?'

'She did?' Nuru said without answering. 'And will you listen?'

Sisi watched the waking screen of her computer with unnecessary focus. 'How can I, Nuru? But then... what is there to say? How can we even know each other anymore? What if he never forgave me for marrying his brother?'

'Hmm,' Nuru sat beside her and looked towards the red cliffs even though they were hidden. 'If he has become a good man, then he will have understood. If he has not, then... Alors, he might no more be a person you can love. He has spent so long outside.'

As if the one would perforce lead to the other. They were right, though, and Sisi did not know what she felt or wanted to feel for Jomo, other than that she wanted to see him so this first meeting was over. Once they had met, and been polite and said at least some of the things that must be said, then she could slip him back into her past because she had other things that were more important now than him.

'Nuru?' she said, again tentatively and hating how that sounded.

'Hmm?'

'What do we do now? To save them.' With a hand on her belly, her eyes lifted up to the leaves above her, to a drongo perched at the apex of a branch. Her looking up so that tears did not fill her eyes, him looking down to search for prey. 'I did not...' She sighed. 'There must be something I can do.'

Nuru paused in their work and Sisi might have leaned forward to push answers out of them if the mound of her belly felt less blown-glass.

'Not *I*, sister. *We*,' they said gently. 'We have been talking this through and there are things we think we must do.'

'What things?'

Nuru looked at her as if weighing her commitment or her faith, but then reached to hold her hand. 'You felt Mother Sea's hunger when you fell. This was a message, I think; she was telling us what she needed from us. We must sate her.'

Sisi felt again that crawling, ravenous watchfulness that had slipped over her as she lay on the rocks alone, and she frowned at Nuru's hand where it held hers. Her other self repeated that it had been only revelation and shock and loneliness. But if she said this then Nuru would pull away. 'How in all the world do we sate the sea?' she said helplessly. 'And why is she so hungry? Why take so much from us?'

Nuru smiled at her in the same way they smiled at children who asked good questions but too often. 'Is she not being broken on the spine of humanity? Is she not being poisoned and cluttered, deafened and pillaged? Have we not also become a part of that? Alors. That she needs sustenance is no wonder; it is a blessing that she does not ask for more.'

'*More?*' Sisi straightened in her chair, pulling on Nuru's grip. 'What more is there than our own children?'

'Sisi, you were to trust us, yes? Trust me?' They held her gaze, but their dark eyes were shuttered and she could read nothing in them other than determination. 'Be guided by the whole and together we will soothe our Mother, and she will save your child, yes?'

Spare my child, Sisi corrected silently. *Not save but spare*, and she wanted to ask when Mother Sea had become vengeful and rapacious. But then Manon's grandfather Kiran came asking for cumin seeds and to pick through the boat goods with his calloused fingers, sparing Sisi the need to fight herself silent. He surprised her by bending to kiss her cheeks as he passed. To cover her gratitude and tears, she lifted the laptop and logged on.

Dear Sisi, the first email began, from an address that should have been obvious but was not until she'd opened it.

I am leaving a package for you with Kit. It has some medicines I'd like you to think about taking. There are instructions with them, but please ask me anything you want.

Sisi looked up, furtively repositioning the screen, a queer mix of gratitude and shame making her tremble. They had not forgotten her, and it was awful how much that comforted her, even now. No wondering what it was that might delay this letter, though, because Nuru was there as both shadow and answered prayer, smiling at her even as they spoke to grandfather Kiran over the oranges.

Dr Adler continued:

I hope that we can stay in touch this way, so I can keep you up to date on the treatment development Dr Freshman will be working on. His work will go much faster once he's back at his lab, with access to better equipment and more useful staff than me!

A smile flickered in the muscles of Sisi's jaw, then faded.

*I also hope that you might let me know how you are doing. I am
sorry to be leaving you but I hope I can be of some use remotely.*

She closed the email window without registering the sign-off,
because it was one thing to know that she was not forgotten, and
another to be asked once again to collude.

'You are well?' Nuru asked. More people were coming now;
the store would be busy today so Sisi would soon have to help,
which would be a good thing. But just for now Sisi neither rose nor
set her laptop aside. She did not know which she wanted: Dr Adler
and Dr Freshman to have put her aside, the way everyone thought
Sisi had done with them, or this, them offering her their foreign,
traitorous hope despite Manon, despite Sisi's promise?

Because Nuru was watching, and Jomo was not here, and
because she was missing Manon as if her absence was a knife,
Sisi moved her fingers again on the touchpad and returned to
her emails.

There were a couple about her work. Asking how she was in a
way that instead meant, *Why are the buoy data not uploading? Why
have you not sent the latest calibrations? How are you, but more
importantly, where are you if not on the sea or in Les Hautes or online?*

There was also another, from an address that made no sense
to her even though she took the time to check. Dr Freshman was
her first thought, but no, it was a Dr Reinwald instead, Alice
Reinwald from the University of Cape Town – and then it made
sense. This was where Kit had been, so this must be the woman he
had mentioned. Another foreigner offering her things the old her
wanted and the new her was meant to refuse.

*I am making contact following discussions with a student of
mine, Kit Benedict, who I believe you know? He mentioned
developing a research project into climate-resilient crops using
your island as a case-study hostile environment.*

Hostile environment, Sisi thought, wanting almost to laugh. Above, the drongo carved a black parabola flight, catching food.

If you are interested, there are several potential sources of funding for such a promising project but which ones we go for would depend largely on the scale of experiments you have the capacity to establish. I am thinking in terms of space, as other concerns such as staffing and logistics can be incorporated into the funding proposals. I see from your details online (sorry for the inquisitiveness!) that you have a degree in ecology and now work primarily in meteorology and coral reef restoration?

It went on. Not much longer, but talking about research trips and studentships. Sisi stopped reading. How brutally unfair it was to have the world suddenly hold out treasures to her just when she could not accept them.

She closed her laptop without answering any of the messages at all, and said to Nuru, 'I am going to the beach. I will be back soon.'

It was fully hot now, the sun high and sticking her wrap to her legs as she walked, the ache in her ankle not the only thing making her tread more gently. The tide was turning, the pirogues lined along the water's edge with fishers bending into their hulls as if in worship. The mailboat was still there but would be gone by nightfall. And on the shore was Jomo.

She realised then that seeing him would always hurt even if another three years passed, or thirty, or a hundred, before she saw him again. She sat in the silver sand, watching him until he felt the weight of her gaze and turned. She knew from the movement of his shoulders that it hurt him too, and also that he had been told about the babe. Her heart ached and her feet shifted in the sand with the wanting to run to him, but she saw his fists open and close against his thighs and knew he wanted to run to her too, yet would not.

Because the life in her womb hung between them, and she lifted her chin and thought to him, sending the words out of her eyes like stars, *I choose them*. Realising it was true only as she thought it. *If there is a choice to make, then I choose them over you. And I am not sorry.*

Which was not true, but there were different forms of sorry and some of them were more byzantine than others. Pardonne-moi, je suis désolé, je m'excuse, je regrette, je me repens. They each had their own borderlines.

He turned back to the boat, not coming to greet her or lay kisses on her skin like he once would have done, so she did not let herself bend her head because she would not let him see her do so and understand. His pirogue slipped into the water like a freed eel, and Sisi watched the white sail bright against the pale-noon lagoon. She thought again of the hungering she had felt, and of Antonin, who would never hold his child, and who had lived more of his life mourning love than possessing it.

She had not believed that his death might be a tithe for Manon's child, but she had been willing to agree. The Sacere had been wrong about it, though, n'est-ce pas? Unless of course they had only been wrong about who the tithe had been for. Unless this was another of Sisi's thefts.

Did they think of Antonin, the fishers? As they cast themselves out beyond the lagoon to where the larger fish swam, did they think about Sisi's babe, and their own blood and bones suspended above the sea? Did Jomo?

They were far enough away now for Sisi to rest her forehead on her knees. Patterns of baobabs and zebu becoming a soft kaleidoscope in front of her half-closed eyes. She must go to speak to Manon, she thought. If Manon was too proud and too full of grief to come to Sisi when Sisi was fearing for her own child, then Sisi could either let that become its own rift, or she could reach out, and hope for forgiveness.

Chapter Thirty-Four

Sisi

But first she had once again to weave a doll from strips of cloth and palm fibres twisted into thin, coarse rope. It was like the one she had made for Antonin, but without anything of a known person. It had no gender and nothing in its shape or clothing to suggest a person known, because she did not know this person yet, not in that way.

It was instead all of them. Dark hair in black silk threads; brown skin; strong legs and narrow waist but genderless hips and torso. She gave it treasures. Tiny black-purple pearls for its eyes, a sliver of abalone for its mouth, and wrapped around it all the shades of blue that she was gifted. Some of these tokens were given with kisses on her cheeks, others dropped into her lap from stiff, reluctant hands.

Her fingers shook because the ritual was one of mourning, and in this pre-emptive sacrifice she saw only prescience, carnivory. But Nuru had said, and the Mothers had said – and even Berhane, who she had heard disagreeing, now agreed – that this must be done. As soon as possible and with Sisi's own hands so that Mother Sea would trace this unnamed gift back to her own unnamed child, and be content.

Manon had not come. Sisi had not yet found the courage to go to her.

'It is finished, I think,' she said to Mama Mandisa, who had sat by her through the whole long task, sorting fibres and cloths by touch onto her lap for Sisi to pick from.

'This is well done,' Mama Mandisa said, running her fingers over the doll's clothes and limbs and hair. 'You have done well, child.'

'What do you think, Mama,' Sisi asked quietly, 'of this thing?' Meaning the ceremony rather than the doll, meaning more than that.

Mama Mandisa's gaze roved over Sisi's face and then lifted to the sky. 'Are these your doubts asking, or your fear?'

'My fear,' Sisi said quickly. Too quickly. Her heart skipped and ached.

'Hm-mm.' Mama Mandisa shook her head, looking wearier than Sisi remembered. 'Neither we nor Mother Sea can help you unless you truly wish to be helped, child.'

It was a warning and a slap; Sisi wanted to cry, her fingers shaking where they held the terrible surrogate doll. 'I do!' she said, reaching forward to touch Mama Mandisa's arm. 'Mama, I do.'

Mama Mandisa patted her hand, her face still drawn. 'Then we will give you everything it is in our power to give.'

Sisi breathed out slowly and leaned back, flexing fingers that ached from their task. It was that mid-afternoon point when the heat stopped rising, the air of the bay stalling in between one moment and the next. Birds in the thick sky were voiceless and even the hermit crabs were somnolent, but it felt like it ought to be much later. As though she ought to have looked up from her completed sacrificial proxy child and seen the night all around her. Bat wings and starlight, the smell of charcoal when it collapses into embers.

Believe and belong, be safe, be loved. It was the simplest of equations.

*

Mama Mandisa pushed herself to her feet, her hands tight on the arms of the chair. 'I will go to tell the others,' she said, and began to walk away, her sandals and stick shuffling in the sand, slow but not cautious. Sisi tried not to look at the doll now that she was done making it – she did not wish to think of imbuing this thing with part of her child's life, and then casting it away. Stark shadows edged her vision and everything felt too... predatory. But she would do anything at all. She shivered and brushed her hands clean.

Tidying up the scraps and threads that had gathered around her chair, she had to bend at the knees because her child's small ocean no longer let her bend at the hips; and she was thinking of Manon again, her only mirror to hold up to her daily changing body. *Now*, Sisi thought, straightening with a fistful of fibres. She would go to Manon now and make her see her, even if only to speak more loathing. It would at least be words and not silence.

But coming back out of the house, she stopped, one hand going to the doorframe, smooth wood beneath her fingertips almost like skin.

'Sisi,' Jomo said. Standing a little too far away and yet still too close. 'I... All is well with you?'

She wondered if it was strange to him, to speak the ritual words. She wondered what it was he said now, greeting friends. 'All is well,' she said, carefully. 'And with you?'

'Sisi,' he said again, coming forward out of the shade, into sun, squinting so that she herself moved forward to read his face.

'I thought you would not come to see me,' she said, reassured by her own calm voice that yes, she could survive this, despite her heart. She sat where Mama Mandisa had been and tilted her head to Jomo to see if he, too, would sit. He hesitated, but he did. Studying his hands, then the house, and then the trees as if the entire village and he himself had changed in his years away. Perhaps they had.

Sisi said gently, 'Have you been up to the tomb?'

'No.' The feel of his eyes on her was so familiar she was relieved when he looked away. 'Not yet. It is tonight, but Nuru said they must do something else, for...' gesturing at her and what she contained, his voice bland but his fingers angular.

'I am sorry for delaying it,' she said, and meant it. His hand back on his thigh curled slowly, becoming a broken fist. 'They believe it is urgent, I think.'

He still would not hold her gaze, and without reason or pause she was frustrated. 'It cannot be such a great surprise, Jomo. That I am pregnant. It has been more than long enough.'

A shift of shoulders that she remembered holding against her own skin. 'I know. But I thought... Don't worry, it is not important. How are you? Nuru said—'

'I am well. I fell, this is all. Nuru is taking care of me.' His jaw twitched and she was glad. 'You will be going back on next month's mailboat?' Asking because she wanted the fact of his leaving again to be as stark between them as her pregnancy and the spirit of his brother. Asking because it would remind her of her anger towards him, and she so needed that reminder now, in this moment.

He looked out to sea, where the boat had been and gone. The pirogues were drawn back up on the beach, quiescent.

'I have work,' he said. 'They were good to give me this much leave in one go.' He met her eyes properly for the first time since he had sat down, smiling slightly. 'And I have university. Did you know? I'm finally starting a degree.'

'Oh,' she smiled back, thinking, *Am I pleased? It is what we planned, him to find a job while he decided, and I to go straight to university. Am I pleased that his life has moved along the single trajectory he wished it to, whereas mine has had to shift and bend and warp to fit the needs of others? Is this what it means to be truly separate from the whole, and is it forgivable?* For the first time she wondered how much of her love was for him, and how much for the dream they had shared. But she said only, 'Well done, Jomo – this is wonderful. Engineering, yes?'

He nodded. 'But you beat me to it, Nuru said. Distance learning in two years? Well done, Sise. I bet you sailed it.'

Sise. A name that made her want to cry. *I bet.* A phrase from another world.

'I had few choices,' she said, more harshly than he deserved, and he looked away, blinking against the light and making her ashamed. But part of her, the part that knew her life was changing yet again, being bound by others again, was not sorry at all. Was in fact angry that he got to act wounded.

'I hoped to do more,' she said, the words stinging her tongue. 'A master's. But of course this will not happen now.'

She realised from the way he looked at her that he had not thought about this from her perspective at all. Seeing only himself returning to a tangled love, perhaps with hope, and finding that the tangle had not gone at all, but was worse. It turned all her bitterness into an ache so sharp she gasped. 'Oh, Jomo,' she whispered. 'Did you think of me at all?'

His eyes widened and filled with heat and hurt and bewilderment, as if even now after everything, they were still each other's mirror. 'Sise,' he whispered, and she could not bear to hear what his answer might be. There were none that were not terrible, and she should never have asked.

'You have seen the outsiders?' she asked without thinking, and then realised why they had come to her mind at that moment, and winced.

He stared at her for another long minute, but then a magpie robin called from the roof and he looked away, rubbing a hand over his face and frowning in the direction of the Administrator's house. 'No. But Nuru told me.'

What, she thought, *what did they tell you, and how did they word those things?* But he spoke again, before she could find a way to ask.

'I thought you might be wishing to leave. They said the hospital in Cape Town is leading the research.' Not looking at her, not looking at anything anymore, she thought, other than all their griefs. 'Nuru says you are staying, but I thought you would...'

I did also, she thought. *Oh, Jomo, I did too.* 'You thought that I could choose now?' she whispered. Her hands ached to touch him, but she held them still. 'Now, with everything that is happening? It is a good thing, though, I think, given how badly I do with the choices I have made. No, I will stay and fight to keep my child. Your brother's child.'

'How can you do that *here*?'

There were tears stinging her eyes like the sea in a wound and she so much did not want them to fall. Within her, the babe spun a slow circle. 'How can I do anything else?' she asked him, herself, and all their broken promises. Then, more firmly: 'I must stay and make this right. And you will go. This is how it is, yes? Just as it was before.'

'You could have chosen differently,' he said quietly.

How did he do it? Turn her inside out in five small words. Anger and disbelief piled up like a storm surge in her stomach, and her child danced in the eddies, thrusting their hands and feet out into the rage as if wanting to hold it, consume it. Chosen selfishness? Chosen to abandon Manon, pregnant and afraid? *No*, Sisi wanted to argue yet again. But what if Nuru or Luc had already told Jomo of how Sisi had, after all, betrayed Manon anyway?

Then, before she could speak, Kit walked into view between the coconut trees, seeming just then so much more familiar than Jomo, with all the ways he had changed and yet not changed at all.

*

'Oh, hi,' Kit said, stopping. 'Um, not interrupting, am I?'

Because Jomo was about to say yes, Sisi spoke first. 'Not at all. Kit, all is well with you?' Gesturing to another chair and smiling more widely than she might have done if Jomo had not been there. It was both petty and stupid, but still.

'All is well,' he answered. 'And with you?' Truly asking the question, his eyes scanning the scrapes healing to blackness on her arm and hands, her bare knee.

'It is well,' she said gently, meaning it and seeing him relax. 'Kit, this is Jomo de Sabah, the brother of my husband and Nuru. Jomo, this is Kit Benedict, who has become my friend.' Not meaning it the way Jomo took it, and beginning to regret this game because Jomo looked poised for violence, and too much of her wished to know whether that was because of his brother's spirit or because of her. 'Jomo. Please. He is a friend.'

Kit smiled and held out a hand, which Jomo stared at for a deliberate minute before taking in a brief grip. Sisi breathed out and wanted them both gone so that she could stop *longing* and instead think only of tonight's ceremony, and of conviction.

'I was wondering if you wanted to come for a walk,' Kit said to her, excluding Jomo even without the more useful pronouns of French. 'If you're well enough?'

'She can't,' Jomo said.

If Nuru had said it then Sisi would have done differently, because Nuru would have spoken from concern and love rather than territories and sanctity.

'Thank you, Kit,' Sisi said. 'Yes, I will come.' She would go, but to Manon rather than for this walk, not only because it was time but also because the Sacere's new fady forbade her even being close to this outsider. Although Jomo, so much more recently outside, should surely be just as worthy of fady, despite his kinship which so neatly exempted him. She rose, avoiding Jomo's narrowed eyes.

Going into the house to find sandals and a headwrap, she turned at the footsteps behind her, half-blind but knowing who it was anyway. 'Jomo,' she said.

'Can we talk?' His voice pulled her forward helplessly, his bulk blocking the doorway so she could see his face, drawn and suddenly uncertain. 'Not about us. About what's happening here?'

She thought he meant Kit, but then changed her mind. 'Do you mean the vote?'

'Yeah.' Another new word. 'And all the anger. Some people won't come near me, you know? Luc would barely speak to me, because I am *tainted*! Did you know that? What's going on?'

She put her hand on his forearm, comfort rather than intimacy although his skin beneath hers, after all this time, reverberated through her blood. 'But of course we must talk. Later?' The child within her stirred. 'People are frightened, Jomo,' she added. '*I* am frightened. We will talk, though.'

'Luc said...' He paused, inhaled sharply and said something quite different to the thing he had meant to. Sisi could perhaps guess, though, and wanted all over again to weep. 'Nuru said I must be careful of what I say, that I shouldn't talk too much of the outside. That's crazy, Sise. When did we ever silence each other?'

She looked up into his face and sighed. 'They wish to protect you. That is all. It is not that they are silencing you.'

'And yet that is how it feels. And you? What—'

'Kit is waiting,' she said quickly, her fingers tightening on his arm and then letting go. 'We shall talk later, yes?'

He nodded, his face blurred just enough by shadow to make the movement exactly that of his brother, and Sisi knew that even if things had been very different, even if she had been free now, there was no erasing that. Loss hit her brutally, and perhaps he saw it on her face because he said, quick and low, 'Were you happy, at least?'

Wrapping her arms around her waist, she did not know what to say. Who to protect him from, his brother or herself? 'I was not unhappy, Jomo. *We* were not unhappy.' She smiled to show that this was less condemning than it sounded. 'He loved Afiya. I understood that.'

Jomo moved closer, and she so wanted to know what he intended, what he was acting on – the lovelessness she had lived with, or the love she had confessed? But her body acted without her, slipping sideways and past him, turning to smile at him from the safety of the open door. 'Tonight we can talk. After the ceremony?'

'Yes,' he said, her old lover who she had once loved so boundlessly. She left him in her house and walked into the sun.

Chapter Thirty-Five

Kit

'Will you show me the vanilla vines?' Kit said. 'It's flatter that way.' She was keeping more of a distance between them, more than an arm's reach, and he was trying not to wonder why.

'I must go to Manon,' she said, stopping.

'Will she speak to you? I thought...'

Sisi looked at one of the other houses – Manon's? 'She does not see me.' It carried a meaning he wasn't sure of, and her hands were clenching and unclenching at her sides. She was silent so long he said her name, then finally she sighed, looked at him and said, 'Come, I will show you something else.'

They walked past the fishing boats and the mats that had been slung over rope lines to air but still reeked of fish and brine from the gutting he'd seen the islanders doing before. He'd seen the speed of their knives, both metal and shell, and briefly wanted to know how those two things would feel against the skin of his wrist. But then he didn't, and shuddered at the shadows he thought were fading, but that sometimes weren't.

They walked up towards the house slowly, Sisi moving gingerly, and it was only once they were within the gardens that Kit realised where she was taking him. 'The red cliffs?' he said. 'I thought I needed a Sacere. I've wanted to go, but... I didn't like to ask.'

'It is no problem,' she said, throwing the words over her shoulder at him like confetti. 'You need a Sacere to go into the tombs, and we will not. To go up to the cliffs, you need only kin.'

'Kin?' He measured the distance between them, wanting to close it.

'Someone the ancestors know, to introduce you.' He could see the edge of a smile, there and gone. 'Otherwise how would they know you are a friend?'

'Oh.' He thought about it, this theology of theirs. 'I like that,' he said, hoping she heard it the way it was meant. Free of condescension.

She looked over her shoulder at him four paces behind her, then she stopped, so he did too. 'Kit,' she said slowly, 'you understand the fadys?'

'Yes,' he said, 'I think so. Kind of rules, taboos – is that right?'

'This is close enough, yes,' she said. 'I keep my distance from you because of a fady.' She tilted her head as if to measure his response, but he said nothing, waiting. 'To touch an outsider, it is fady for a pregnant woman; this is normal. But now' – she lifted her shoulders and then dropped them – 'the Sacere say this fady is not strong enough, that I must not be alone with outsiders, yes?'

He frowned at her. 'So, you shouldn't be here now? With me?' He thought of Jomo, and the look on the man's face. 'Oh, Sisi, if you want to go back, if it was just to get away from... I'm sorry...'

Doing exactly what he least expected, Sisi laughed. 'No, Kit,' she said, one hand splayed over the small dome of her stomach. When he'd first met her, it had been flat. 'I was not escaping from Jomo.' Her smile was sad, a little self-mocking. 'This is not possible, I think. There is something I wish you to see, and understand' – gesturing to the space between them – 'and soon we will not be alone.' She turned away again on the bare earth pathway. 'My ancestors will be with us, you see?'

His turn to laugh, quietly. 'Yes, I see. Lead on, then.' And she did.

*

He'd seen them from a distance, of course, but it was very different to be here, standing on a ledge of red rock with the air so clear that it played tricks with distance. On his right, because he didn't dare turn his back on the drop, were rectangular caverns all along the ledge as far as he could see, the cut rock a different shade to the uncut, like muscle beneath skin. Each tomb a slightly different size and spaced out not quite regularly, as though the people who'd made them had chosen spots for the natural inclinations of the rock rather than for symmetry.

And the tombs breathed.

The sun shone full onto the face of the cliff, simmering through the soles of his sandals, the air on the ledge like a slice cut from a kiln. But from the tombs cool air puffed out, stopped, then puffed again. Now near-metallic dark-wet-rock scent; now baked earth and furnace. Repeating.

'What's...' He stepped to the side of an opening, then back in front of it again. The tomb breathed. 'What's that?' he said, not looking at Sisi but watching the darkness.

She turned like the drop wasn't there at all. 'Brother Island's breath,' she said. As if that were an answer, and comforting. He thought about the sea cave with iron leaching into the water, and the fact that these tombs had probably been caves long before they were anything else, fissures in the rock. Still, it was hard to be scientific about it, knowing what lay within.

'This one here is where I will lie, when it is time,' Sisi said from up ahead and he came up to her slowly, suspended between the edge and the openings.

'They are each a family's?' Where the light ended sharply, he could see bundles of plants hanging from snags in the rock, the suggestion of platforms further in.

'My mother lies in there. And my aunts and my grandmother, and her siblings and her mother and her mother also…' She put a hand on the edge of the cutting but made no move to enter. Perhaps she couldn't, he thought. Unable to touch her dead the way she was unable to touch him. 'If… My children will lie here someday, with me.'

The tomb breathed and Kit's eyes filled with tears.

'This is why we will not leave,' she said, looking at him fully. 'I wanted you to understand.'

He did. That was the worst thing about it all, because of course he understood. What he'd lost had nearly finished him, his place within his family and then a home he'd already left. So how much worse would it be to lose this? Your home and your mother's, and your mother's mother's, all the way back to when you first became a people; and all the way forward too. But they had one thing he didn't, and the mining contract and Geo's bullishness raged in his mind, so he tried one last time. 'Your people came here, though, right? So they survived that change – they built their own future here. Why couldn't you do that again? You could start again, make something new. You still have each other.'

She sighed and dropped her hand from the rock, saying quietly, 'Would we not lose who we are, though? We were not us, before we came here. We were Malagasy and French and Indian, slaves and slavers and lascar; we were not us. How can we remain us if we leave?'

Turning her back on him, she walked further along the ledge and he followed helplessly, thinking, *No, we can* choose *to be ourselves – we can do that and survive it.*

'What about you?' he said to her back. 'And Geraldine. She can help you if you come to South Africa – you know she can. It wouldn't be forever. I'd have thought you'd be desperate to go.'

It sounded like judgement although it felt more like frustration. With her, with them all, with himself.

'I cannot. You do not understand.'

'I do,' he said. 'I understand that you're frightened, you all are, and that you're letting fear make your decisions for you. Sisi. Sisi, look at me and tell me you honestly believe that getting rid of modern medicine and electricity is going to help you treat tetanus.' He closed the distance between them and reached to grab her hand, suddenly too exasperated to care. But she pulled away from him, turning on the ledge so fast he saw images of her falling again.

'Modern medicine and electricity have not yet saved our babes, Kit. Why would they now save mine?' Her eyes were opaque as polished wood.

'Is that really what you think?' he said viciously. 'Or is it something else? Do you think you *can't* let Matt and Geraldine save your baby because they didn't save your friend's? That's it, isn't it?' It was; he could see it was. 'Are you really going to let your baby die out of some fucked-up guilt? Would Manon really want that? Because that is totally insane.'

'Stop it,' she said, stepping back with one hand up between them and the other on her belly. 'Stop it. Stop saying these things. Who do you think you are?'

'Who do I think I am?' Throwing up his hands: 'I'm the best person on this island to talk about how completely stupid we can be when we're desperate, or hurt, or frightened of getting lost.' He stopped and rubbed a palm roughly over his face, forced himself quieter. 'Sisi. Sisi, I'm sorry. I just... Don't do this, Sisi. You're stronger than this and you're giving up.'

'Fuck you,' she said. The words shocking. She turned, moving rapidly away along the cliff path, limping heavily but unslowing, and he listened to her unsteady footsteps until he couldn't anymore.

Chapter Thirty-Six

Sisi

Sisi thought, if she thought at all, that he would walk back down past the mouths of the tombs to his house. Away from the woman he thought was cowardly and foolish, who he believed was better than either cowardice or foolishness. What right did he have to believe such a thing of her? What was between them at all? Other than a few quiet moments, small joys at the way he comforted her, and at how the light made the muscles of his forearms into gold.

She walked fast, despite her ankle, the fear for her own flesh relegated. Up and up to where the ledge narrowed past a spur of rock then widened again rough and craggy, and from here below the summit of L'Ambre she could see the whole island, the lagoon, the broken line of islets and coral that marked out the reef. The westering sun casting shadows dark as ink on the ocean's long swell, and one of those shadows was the departing mailboat. At the point where the path split to either ascend or wend down onto the tsingy and Brother Island's heart, she stopped to gather her breath, resting her throbbing ankle. She could see the furthest half of the village, the tall afternoon shadows of the baobabs beyond, her own weather station, square and outlandish. She had never felt further from home.

When Kit had taken his aborted half-step into the air from the cliff edge, perhaps he had wanted to close that distance. Was that it? Had he thought that if he fell from his own solitude into the sea, he would be taken up, accepted and embraced? That he would belong again.

She could understand that now. But that did not mean he could also understand her. She went slowly now down to her brother's heart.

*

The vote was tomorrow.

She kept trying to forget that it was happening at all. Walking away from the arguments, the vitriol like fires, the animosity a constant creeping presence. Not once had anyone asked her what she thought or which way she would vote. But was this because Nuru had warned them away, or was her vote assumed because of Nuru's proximity? Or was she still, despite the babe and Nuru, only and forever the one who had trusted in science and been wrong? She did not know which way Manon would vote, although she would have known before, and even if they had differed they would not have fought. Not like Clémentine and Oni. Not like Jomo and Luc.

If Manon had not already cut her out, Sisi would not have believed it possible for Luc to fight with Jomo, and in among everything else she was aware of a slow, sad pity for Jomo, who had come home grieving and found instead of comfort that he was a symbol of a taint for which he was surely no more to blame than anyone, certainly less than Sisi.

She knelt gingerly by the heart and listened to the sough of restless waves beneath her. Nuru said Mother Sea needed the babes to feed her wounded self, blood to wash herself clean and bones to strengthen her. Sisi put her hands onto Brother Island's sharp rocks, old fossils from long ago when he had hungered for the sky. *Such wreckage*, she thought.

You're letting fear make decisions for you, Kit had said, and of course she was – how could she not? It was fear, but it was also long litanies of failure. And Nuru's love.

The heart whispered; movement caught her eye and she looked up to see Kit picking a path down from L'Ambre towards her. He had followed, after all. He was still a mystery, she thought, because it had not once occurred to her that he would have the... the audacity, the loyalty, to come.

To avoid watching him, she bent down to the hungry heart of Brother Island, feeling herself rise and fall with the sea. She did not wish to talk to Kit, or to Jomo. She did not wish to vote, or to listen to her people fight. When she went down, Manon would not see her and Antonin would still be gone, so she wanted only to float here, oscillating over the heart of her home, curved around her babe.

*

'Is it the same thing?' Kit said from beside her. She ignored him, falling into the heart. 'The leaching iron here, and the salt-water incursion below?'

The heart sucked at the air. Sand shifted beneath her fingertips, fitting itself to her pores.

'Dr Reinwald said she'd emailed you,' he said into her silence. 'She says she's found a really promising call for proposals, or something. The deadline isn't for a few months, but she's keen to talk, if you are.'

Another person Sisi did not wish to talk to. Why could the world not leave her alone with her child and the sound of the sea? But this was the problem, n'est-ce pas? The sea, in her blood and her child's blood and the earth. How could she belong so completely to something that had betrayed her?

Why did everything come back to betrayal?

'Sisi,' Kit said, weary and sad, and she wished to unhear those things in his voice. 'I didn't mean to upset you. Or... I did, I guess. I wanted to make you listen. Make you see. But I should know better than that, shouldn't I? And anyway, I was being a hypocrite.' His low, wry laugh grounded her in a way she resented.

'This is all I do,' she said to the sea and the heart. Not to him. 'Listen. Let others decide. This is now all I do.'

A solitary gull called above them, riding a wind that was swinging east and cooling.

'What would change, if you didn't?'

How odd a question. Not who was she listening to, or why, or why not stop. But what would change? What was she changing by listening and not choosing?

Such a careful man. She wondered whether he had been like this before the cliff, before the hospital, and whether it mattered when this, here, was the person he was now. She looked up finally, feeling dust at her hairline and the imprint of rocks against her jaw like a memory of flying.

'It would be my fault,' she said. Was it the heart or his presence that made her honest?

He nodded, his face in profile to the sun half ochre and half ivory, masked.

'Did you know I'm supposed to be studying law?' he said. 'It's what my family do. Law or politics. I hated it.' He smiled with his lips but not his eyes. 'I did it because I wanted... I don't know, their approval, their love, validation. I wanted not to rock the boat.'

She watched his unsmiling eyes. 'You said already I am a coward, Kit. You do not need to say it again.'

'I didn't say that.'

'You did,' she said, and this time he did not bother to deny it.

'Okay,' he said, meeting her eyes. 'Then I'm calling myself a coward too.'

She studied him gravely. The sea in the heart was a bated breath.

'And on that subject,' Kit said, grimacing and looking straight at the sun until it must have blinded him. *Why*, she thought, *why do that?* Because he wanted some of its fire, or because he did not wish to see her face? 'I have something to tell you, if you'll listen.'

How did he make her smile when she still wished he was not here?

'You know the vote?' he went on. That soft huff of breath. 'Of course you know the vote. I'm... I found something out. I...'

And then he told her truths.

*

When he was finished he fell silent, and she was silent, and the island's heart was silent, too, other than the hissing of the sea. Somewhere nearby claws scrabbled over rock, and Sisi knew that it would be a skink.

'They...' Her voice was dry as ashes. 'They will come to dig... They will dig out the lagoon. For *aggregate*? For buildings?'

'Yes.'

'This is agreed? It is signed and... Your uncle has agreed it?'

His face twisted again, but this time she was spread so thin over the acres of her home that she could not interpret it.

'Not quite. It's agreed in principle. That's where a lot of the money is coming from, for the relocation. But it... could be stopped.'

Pulling all of herself back to herself, she gathered the folds of her wrap like armour. 'When did you learn this? The research project, was this to help us stay? Or... But you try always to say we should leave.' Cotton stretched within her fists and at least he did not look away. 'Kit, when did you know?'

'Too long ago,' he said. 'See? I am a coward. I figured it wouldn't make a difference if you were leaving anyway... But also, I couldn't bear to... hurt you more than you already were.'

It was so unfair. That he admitted to this unimaginable betrayal, and also to love.

'They cannot,' she said. 'They cannot do this.' Fists against her belly, the two merging in her mind. Her island and her child. Both would destroy her if they were destroyed. 'Kit, they cannot.'

'We can stop them,' he said. 'But you'll need help, Sisi. You see that, right? This isn't going to go away after the vote. None of this is going away, and you can't fight it all alone.'

Herself and her people, alone in the wide, wide sea that had stopped being wide enough to save them a very long time ago. 'I cannot tell them,' she said at last. But silence would make her no better than him, hiding secrets because she was scared of hate. Besides, how could she *not* tell them, when it was overspilling her already, toxic and torrid and foul?

Her babe rolled within her, fearful, so she undid each fist to cradle them. *No, my child*, she thought, unfamiliarly fierce. *Never fear. I will keep you safe. I will save you.*

But how? How, when the world was full of traitors and she herself was one of them?

'I must go home,' she said, and rose. Kit stood quietly beside her, but she scarcely saw him.

'I'll follow down after you, so they don't know,' he said. And he did.

Chapter Thirty-Seven

Sisi

Sisi went to Manon first, because she should have done so before and needed to do so before facing Nuru. Her friend, her dearest and closest, was updating the records for the clove harvest just sold. She was alone.

'Manon,' Sisi said.

Manon did not look up.

'Manon, please.' Sisi did not know what to do with her hands. Wished she could hide the curve of her womb, but could not. The whole island around her felt breakable. 'I did not know,' she said. Manon's fingers tightened on her pen. 'I know this does not make it better, but I never thought of myself, of any of it helping me. I wanted to believe... I would have given anything for you...'

She fell silent. Manon had lost weight, shrunken in on herself; the skin of her hands was cracked and grey.

'Manon...'

Manon rose as slowly as an old woman and for a second, for two, Sisi hoped. But then those beautiful, shattered eyes passed over Sisi and she went into the shadows of the storehouse. Sisi stood there for a long time, watching the empty doorway but not seeing it at all.

*

Nuru found her as the sun passed down below the house. She was sitting on the bed she had shared with her husband, thinking of Kit's gentleness, the hunger she had tasted in the air; Manon and the price of sand. Struck dumb by hurt and fury. It was still bright but very soon would not be, and Nuru led her to the water. Jomo and Mama Anouk were already waiting on the shore, although there had been fights over Jomo being a part of this. His blood belonging but his spirit soiled.

Soiled, Sisi thought. She needed to tell, but had no idea how. It had been the other Sacere, not Nuru, who had argued for Jomo, but Luc and Mahena and others had muttered among themselves, teeth bared. Now, as if he had never doubted, Jomo's hand rested on the side of the pirogue, and Sisi remembered that he had wanted to talk to her, but that she had not gone to find him. Her love for him sat inside her like a well, but above it barges and excavators were clamouring in her mind. Jomo smiled at her and her ribs ached, but she still could not speak.

By the time they pushed out from the sand, the darkening ocean was spilling evening upwards into the sky. Everyone stayed quiet as the sail whickered and ropes creaked, tiny waves clapping against the hull, and Sisi held the doll in her hand while her babe spun as if they sensed the surrounding sea.

'Here,' Nuru said, and Mama Anouk nodded her agreement. Jomo pulled the sail in, but instead of throwing down an anchor weight, he let the pirogue drift. They were in Mother Sea's arms; they would go where she wished. Sisi dared not look beyond the boat. *This*, she told herself, *think only of this now.*

She handed the doll to Nuru and held out her wrist, skin tinted damson by the deepening sky. Nuru used the edge of a shell so sharp that she only felt the cut afterwards, as she tipped her hand to let blood fall onto the doll.

This was new. If the body was in the sea, then the gifts were for Brother Island; if the body was in the tomb, then the gifts were for the sea. But this was new, pre-empting death by sleight of hand. She tightened her fist and raised it away from the doll that was proxy for her child. Her blood as the mother, Nuru's blood as Sacere, Jomo's uncle and both of the siblings' for their brother who was not here.

Mama Anouk took the figure, all their blood staining her fingertips as she lifted it to her lips and kissed the raffia of its forehead. 'Beloved child,' she said, her voice carrying over the waves to the terns on their sandbars and the fish in the sea, 'you are here with your family, and you must sleep now with the Mother of us all. Sleep well, beloved child.' Reaching over the side, she rested it on the sea's skin as gently as if laying a real child into their bed. It floated there for a second or perhaps two, and then with a murmur the water swallowed it. Sisi shuddered.

The sun flashed a last burst of crimson-orange over the rocks and all the dome of the sky turned lilac, the sea olive and indigo and black. Sisi pressed her hands over her child and imagined the doll leaching its blood into the sea, fish nosing it and knowing it, Mother Sea smiling. Love like heartbreak filled her, for this precious sea and this precious sky, and if she could translate that love into faith then this ritual might have brought her relief. But love instead meant only fury. They had been taught that their Mother was both justice and life, so for her to crave her child's death this way – it went against all the stories Sisi had been taught, rousing all her doubts, and she was so full of secrets that she curled forward over her womb to hide her face.

Someone laid their hand on her back, but she did not look up to see whether it was Nuru or Jomo; it should not matter and she was too lost just now to conceal the truth that it did. Then the sail unfurled and the pirogue lifted like a beast coming alert, and they were all silent as they returned to shore.

*

'What is that?' Jomo said, as he and Nuru hauled the pirogue up alongside the others, screwing his face up.

The breeze had died with the sunlight, which was perhaps why they could smell it now, and not before. Something rotten – salty and fetid.

'The turtle nests did not hatch,' Mama Anouk said, shaking her head, her eyes catching skylight. 'Those poor children were drowned in the storm.'

Of course. Their full moon had passed without sand-whispering sea-bound hatchlings, the night cries of birds hunting blindly along the beach. In among everything else, Sisi had not noticed, and her own obliviousness stung.

Jomo matched his stride to Mama Anouk's, and someone, Ghede, coming to meet them was talking with hands and indistinct words. Sisi frowned, but Nuru took her elbow to stop her following them towards the houses.

'Sisi,' they said, their face serious, 'you went walking with that outsider, the nephew.'

Of course they would know.

'How could you, sister? How could you be reckless enough to break a fady? What were you thinking?'

'We were with the ancestors. I had to tell him about the fady. No one else had.' She could see the holes in her own argument but it was hard to care with her babe and Kit's words burning within her.

'Do you think that will save you? Why does it matter if he knows? What do you feel for him, Sisi? This outsider?'

Sisi stepped away, needing the evening air to cool the furnace in her heart. 'I feel nothing. Tiens, if I did it would not matter. Nuru, I must—'

'So then, you do. How could you? With Jomo here, and with...' Gesturing to her stomach but not saying *Antonin's child*, because that would make their mention of Jomo wrong, and this, their manipulation of truths, made Sisi throw her hands up in the dark.

'You wish for me to care for no one, n'est-ce pas? First Jomo and now Kit. I must always love no one, is this your wish?'

'This is not about love. It is about putting the whole above yourself as you promised. Your babe and the island, Sisi. These alone are what matters.'

Alone, Sisi thought. *Alone?* Her child and her home cut away from the rest of the world, and from her own heart. As if anything could ever be pared back to isolation. She wanted to shake Nuru, or to cry.

'Listen to me, Nuru! Please, this one time. Kit told me something today, something we needed to know, we the *whole*' – her words coming in a torrent – 'and I would not have known this truth, *we* would not, if I had not gone with him. So I was meant to go, yes? Mother Sea perhaps wanted me to go so that I would learn this outsider secret. Do you wish to know it, Nuru? Even though it comes from such a source?'

Nuru was silent, arms folded and their face painted inky dark by the trees and the night. Sisi's own face must have been darkened too, and knowing that made the words easier to say. A mutual breaking of hearts concealed.

'They will lease our island to a mining company, Nuru. The new money for us to leave – this is where it comes from. They will give us this money, pretending it comes from the government and out of charity. Then they will come to dig out the lagoon, blast the limestone and the coral and the sand, and take it away. This is the truth Kit told me today, so that I could tell you.'

She stopped, made herself speak more softly. 'He says that we can stop this, Nuru.'

Nuru still did not speak. She waited for them, her breath singing high in her throat, aching with tension and tenderness and the memory of her own shock when she had first learned of it. She was so frightened, she realised; of their condemnation and her ancillary blame.

'Dear Mother,' Nuru whispered.

Away towards the houses, fruit bats began to squabble and feed and Sisi said quietly, 'What will we do?' And she was frightened of this, too, of them not having an answer. But the air around Nuru was a storm coalescing.

'Sister,' they said in a terrible, slow voice, 'you must go home and rest yourself. Do not speak to anyone. You have told this truth and it is enough.'

'And you?' She wanted to go home. She wanted to lay herself into her bed and close her eyes so that the whole day was over, with its truths and silences and drowning of proxy children. But first, 'And you, Nuru?'

They had not moved but still seemed vast with momentum. 'I will tell our people. This is too urgent a thing to be unknown.'

'You will go to the Mothers, and Berhane and—'

'Them, everyone. This betrayal must be known before the morning.'

Sisi breathed in; the bats fought.

'Go home, Sisi. I must begin.' And they did, leaving her to follow along the line of coconut trees and into the pools of light that gathered like floodwater around each house.

*

The day still would not end, though. Jomo was waiting for her and deserved to be told so many things, but she was so tired. She took Mama Anouk's wrapping from her arm, where the cut was vivid but closed, and poured them both drinks, which she carried out to where Jomo was sitting. They had sat here so often when Sisi's mother was alive, even when her father was still here and they were so young their feet could swing freely beneath the chairs, their toes carving furrows in the sand. The two of them, and Manon, and Luc.

'I missed this,' he said eventually. For a moment she thought he was talking about them, but then saw the sweep of his gaze, the way he breathed so deeply his ribcage swelled. 'It is strange to be back. *I* feel strange, being back. But I missed it so much.'

There were things he was not saying, obvious things, and Sisi was glad because she did not know anymore how to answer.

'It has not changed so much,' she said. 'It is you who have changed.' Not as a criticism, the way Nuru might have meant it, but simply as a fact. High school in Mahé changed you; South Africa, and alone...

'Mmm.' Jomo sounded like Nuru, and Sisi smiled even though he could not see her. 'That's not quite true, though, is it? Something has changed.'

'The vote,' she said softly.

'Ghede said someone had graffitied the clinic wall. People...' He hesitated, which was so unlike him that she turned to look into his face. 'They act like I am not a part of us, Sise. Like they want me gone. They have said... Even Luc, even Manon. Even *Mama Mandisa*.' He looked at her, the black of his eyes visible only as reflected light from other houses. 'Only because I went back outside.'

'Yes,' she said. 'There is so much upset, arguing over what to do. I do not... You must not let it hurt you too much, Jomo. It will pass.'

'Luc and Manon,' he said slowly, and did not need to say any more.

'Yes,' she whispered. The babe flexed within her, then fell still. 'Yes, I know.'

Just beyond the light, something rustled in the palm tree and Sisi knew, she *knew* that it was a robber crab come again full of omen. Perhaps they two had summoned it with their silent, shared heartbreak.

'You did nothing wrong, Sise.'

The crab shifted in the papery bark again, and Sisi's eyes filled with the sea. She did not realise how much it would hurt to have someone, anyone, tell her this.

Jomo leaned forward, elbows on knees, the lamplight sculpting the hollows and planes of his face. 'I said this to Luc. That they were being unfair.'

'Oh, Jomo,' she said, and knew from the way he moved that he had heard the tears she refused to shed. Of course he had heard them. 'What of any of this is fair? They are permitted their anger, I think. They all are.'

He watched her, unconviction in the silhouetted muscles of his jaw. Nuru had told her to tell no one, but surely they had not meant Jomo. So she told him now, glad again of the dark. A tiny, unfair voice asked in her ear whether he could understand what it meant anymore, whether he had been taught to value money more than the sea.

'Fucking hell,' he said, slumping back in his chair, and that tiny voice died. 'That's... It's corrupt. It cannot be legal that they haven't told you. It is not their land to sell.'

So it *was* different, the way he saw it, but not in the way she had feared. Not once had she thought about legalities. 'It will be hidden somewhere in the contract we sign for the resettlement deal, no?' She frowned at her own words. 'But really, it does not matter – we will never vote to leave, so we will not sign. It is more about the... the dishonesty of how they have dealt with us. The lies.'

Jomo grunted and turned his face towards the sea. 'I think it does matter. These companies, they are relentless. If they've decided they want this place, then they will not let us stop them, not so easily.'

Was that true? *None of this is going away*, Kit had said.

'What can we do?' she whispered, to Jomo and the listening sea, and to Kit, who she should have asked earlier.

Pushing to his feet and pacing between trees, bounded in by trunks, Jomo woke an ache in her sternum because she had forgotten this, his restlessness when he thought. 'We place objections, appeals, formal complaints with the government – we get legal help, we sue them for... I do not know, for *something*! We get it in the newspapers, online, we get petitions and crowdfunders, and... we can *do* this, Sisi. We can fight them. Only we must do it their way, not ours.'

Yes, she thought, and then *no*. In her lungs, the air turned to water. 'But we will vote with Nuru, I think. To go back to the old ways. Especially now, with this. The world has become our enemy in so many ways, they hope that if we shut it out, it will leave us be.' The words came to her slowly. The night breathed against her neck. 'We have had to carry so very much, n'est-ce pas? It is a relief to have something to blame, to be given permission to hate... So I do not think they will believe you, Jomo.'

'They would believe you.'

'No,' she said, 'they would not.' And besides, Nuru thought she had set herself aside, and Nuru had forgiven her.

'Sise, of course they will. You can speak against this crazy stuff Nuru is saying, yes? I know they are Sacere, but they, we...' He took a breath. 'We lost our brother. And they feel responsible for the child, too, and the babes before. They know it would be a disaster to... to shut ourselves off, but they are not themself. You will say something, yes? They will listen to you.'

Sisi closed her eyes and tried to tell herself that if she stayed that way for long enough then Jomo would cease to be there, waiting for her to answer. She thought of Kit, up on the red cliffs, saying, *You're stronger than this, and you're giving up.*

'Sisi?'

'Jomo, go to bed,' she said, standing up with one hand on her stomach and the other reaching for the doorframe. 'I am tired and tomorrow will be awful. Go to bed.'

'Sise,' he said, but she went inside and left him with the rabbling bats and the stars.

Chapter Thirty-Eight

Kit

Euan walked in while Kit was getting his breakfast. Bagel and fresh coffee, because the boat had brought both.

'Might be wise if we all stayed out of the way today,' Euan said. Kit looked at him sideways.

'When's the meeting happening?' Rachel said from where she was folding night-dried laundry into piles on the table. She ran her hands over each item in the exact same way, smoothing them.

'They're gathering already,' Euan said. 'Is there coffee left?' Kit handed him the jug and Euan poured his own, adding milk until the mixture was silty and pale. 'They usually hold their meetings in the evening but they decided to hold this one early.'

'To get it over with,' Kit muttered. Had she told, he wondered, and *how* had she told?

'Or to strike while the iron's hot,' Euan said. 'Where's the boss?'

'In the shower,' Rachel said. 'He said they'd found out about the proposed deal. Do you know how?' She said it lightly, with her eyes on Euan across the room, and Kit had to force his face smooth.

'Yeah,' Geo said from the hallway, rubbing a towel over his hair and then slinging it across his shoulders as if he'd just emerged from the gym. He couldn't help it, Kit thought. He was like his brother, and Kit's brother, and probably every other male in the family since physicality and drive had been a survival strategy.

'Did you find out, Euan? Was it those doctors? I wouldn't have thought it of Geraldine, but Matt could have done it.'

Euan looked at Geo and no one else, then shrugged his thin shoulders. 'It hardly matters. They know, and they're furious, so we should give them a little space for now. The Mothers will settle them, once they've voted.'

'It does matter if it swings this ridiculous vote,' Geo said bullishly. 'We can't have them haring off in indignation right now – it's the worst timing possible.'

Kit set his coffee down and pressed his teeth together hard. Rachel looked his way fleetingly, and then again, and although she tried to mask it, her expression made Geo spin around like he'd only just noticed Kit was there.

'Kit!' Hands braced, face shocked. 'Mate, tell me you didn't.'

Kit set his plate down beside the coffee, thinking regretfully that they were both getting cold. 'You should have done it yourself.'

'Why in god's name—' Cutting himself off and frowning at Kit in a way that might have been dangerous if Kit had enough in him to feel threatened. 'Kit. I can't believe you did anything so idiotic. It better not have been just to impress that girl.'

'Woman,' Kit said. 'They had a right to know – you know they did. They wouldn't be so angry now if you hadn't kept it a secret. It wouldn't have changed the vote anyway.'

'I was keeping it a secret because it isn't official yet, and because information in the wrong hands can be bloody lethal to a deal like this.' Seeing Kit about to speak, Geo raised his voice. *'It's for their own good, Kit!* Are you so high on your own morals that you think you know better than the *entire fucking Territories Office*?'

'Maybe the entire fucking Territories Office is wrong.' His hands were shaking but his voice wasn't. Something was soaring in his lungs like birds. He looked at Euan. 'What do you think, Euan?'

'Euan agrees with me!' Geo wheeled around to look at his assistant, who raised his eyebrows infinitesimally.

'I think a lot of the decisions we've made have been perforce a little rushed,' Euan said, and Kit wanted to laugh. 'I think what to present to the islanders, and when, are very sensitive issues and needed a degree of consideration that the timeline didn't permit.'

'What?' Geo said. 'Stop talking like a fucking robot. Do you agree with me or my idiot nephew?'

Euan smiled. 'I agree his actions were catalytic, but I also think they were... understandable. Perhaps it would be wise, though, to deal with the fallout, rather than focus on what can't be undone – don't you agree?'

Kit turned and walked out into the garden.

He wouldn't listen to Geo and Euan turn morals into politics. He'd done the right thing, the first right thing he'd done for as long as he could remember. Even if Geo never saw it that way, or Rachel... He faltered. The birds in his lungs were pride, or something very close, and he clung to that feeling, the brightness.

Did it matter that this belated bravery was for someone else? *Just to impress that girl.* For Sisi? It was... He didn't know what it was, but he didn't belong with her, however easy it was to think so. If he left – *when* he left – she would stay in his mind the way she was now, a point of compassion and connection when he'd needed it most. Someone whose memory would become a thing he could look back on and remind himself that, yes, even when things were at their worst, there had been something good.

He'd stayed for her, perhaps, but mostly for a secret and to see if he could find courage, so now there were no more reasons not to leave.

*

At the hedge, he reached out to touch the petals of a hibiscus flower, translucent in the morning sun. God, but if he was capable of this rebellion, this certainty, why did he still feel breakable? Was going home really so terrible?

Yes, it was. But how ridiculous. Look at Sisi with her child growing inside her, living every day with the knowledge that the baby might die, that her home would eventually die. If not quickly for money, then slowly because of a climate being destroyed for the exact same goal. He'd called her a coward. And been a hypocrite.

Kit took a breath that was salt, ozone and nectar. The heat was already rising, and the cloudless horizon blended seamlessly with the sea, making the island into an oasis inside a vast blue sphere.

He went inside, ignoring the two men at the table, going on into his bedroom where he opened his laptop and waited, watching the curtains billowing, reminding himself of confronting Geo with birds in his lungs. You could salvage strengths from your old, dead self without resurrecting your failures; and he had been brave once. When he'd changed his course, and again when he'd told his family. When he'd hiked out into a rising swell; when he'd dived deep enough for the light to be reduced to a whisper in the indigo-black.

He typed.

Hi Mum and Dad.

There was so much he might say, and so little he could, and up to now he'd settled on saying nothing at all, or nothing real. But if he could tell Sisi one hard truth, then he could tell others. And if he could rage against her unearned shame then he should also rage against his own.

Thank you for your emails and I'm sorry for not replying sooner. It's amazing how time slips away from you here. I've loved spending time with Geo and Rachel, even though I think I've got in their way sometimes.

Somehow he was smiling.

You should see this place – it's insanely beautiful and peaceful.

Aside from griefs, the storm, the threats of hunger and destruction.

I guess I need to think about coming back soon, but I'm in no real rush.

   Dad, thank you for your offer of an internship, and please thank Heinrich for me as well. But as it happens, I've been in touch with one of the ecology lecturers who taught me last semester. She says my place is still open, if I want, and

– one deep breath –

that is what I want to do. I will stick with the Ocean and Atmosphere BSc when I get back. I am more certain than ever that this is what I want to do and I hope you can be OK with that.

Now. I hope you can be OK with that now.

Love to big brother.
   Kit

Chapter Thirty-Nine

Sisi

The screens were all raised in the island hall to let in the morning, but the shadows beneath the roof were still sharp and dense. Sisi sat on the floor with her back against a pillar beside the Sacere: Nuru, Berhane, Isolde, Krish and Sable, even young Katura, the Sacere presenting themselves united. But if they were, then they were the only ones. Sisi had pulled her knees up as far as was comfortable, wide around her new shape, as people clustered into groups, murmuring, hissing, their words and elbows and ankles jostling for some territorial primacy. There was even a uniform. This group here in T-shirts and cut-off jeans, those over there in printed cotton wraps – and she realised with a shiver that she herself had come in a wrap of blues and reds. She had sublimated the two faces of the argument and picked out her clothes in the dark of morning led not by comfort but by the need to belong. The thought made her heart hurt almost as much as seeing her people this way, every glance knife-edged, every word hard. Hunger and bated breath stifled the air. How had so much damage been done to them? Or had they done it to themselves? Had she even understood, until now, how bad it had become?

'Nuru,' she said, leaning forward until her babe flexed in protest. 'Nuru.'

The Sacere, her sibling, turned and smiled at her with their eyes sharp, their teeth shining in the gold-tinted light, and Sisi hated seeing this in them; the fractured room and their faith.

'This is bad, Nuru,' she said, reaching out to grip their arm. 'We must stop this. Everyone is too angry, and look at all of us – we are *broken*.'

'Sister, it will be well.'

'But—' she began.

'Those who live outside should not be allowed to vote,' someone said, and Sisi turned her head sharply. Luc stared at Jomo; Jomo stared back. Perhaps it was only ever those you loved most whom you could learn to hate.

Mama Mandisa shook her head slowly, her moonshine eyes scanning the room, searching and not finding. 'We are one,' she said. 'We each of us will vote.'

'Why should—'

'Luc de Fantine,' she said, and Luc fell silent, his shoulders curling forward like a child's. Someone beside him murmured and he shrugged, sat down heavily without looking again at either his oldest friend or Mama Mandisa.

Sisi wanted to go to Jomo, to lay a hand upon his arm and say, *You are not alone, and you will always belong.* But what right did *she*, who was not sure of either of those things, have to say them? And she wanted to go to Manon and Luc, too, but there were no words for that, only longing. She turned to her sibling instead, but they spoke before she could find anything to say.

'He is surely entitled to his anger, sister. And it will pass.' The muscles around their eyes were taut and Sisi thought, for a moment full of hope, that they doubted too; but then whatever shadow she had seen was gone.

'It is not only about those two, though, n'est-ce pas? Nuru, look at us all. How can we have let ourselves become this?' *You*, she thought traitorously. *How did you let us become this?*

'*They* did this with their lies,' Nuru snapped. '*The outsiders*, Sisi. *We* now will make it right.'

'How can we when we are caught up in blaming each other?' And it did not occur to her until she spoke that she might be talking about herself as well as Jomo, but she could not think about that now. 'How will we make this right unless you defuse this? The Sacere and the Mothers could do it, now. You said we would be well, Nuru – this is not well. And it is not the deal alone. People have been saying...' But Nuru knew well what people had been saying. 'Delay the vote,' she said. 'Please, do something.'

That shadow flickered again in their eyes, but they braced their shoulders as if taking a weight and put their free hand over hers, comforting a child, making Sisi bristle. She did not need their protection, or their confidence; she needed them to *see*.

'We are wounded, Sisi,' they said, 'and do not wounds need to be cleansed before they can heal? We need this vote done, and then things will be good again. Have faith.'

Drawing her hand out from beneath theirs and leaning against her pillar again, Sisi felt her heart skipping beats high in her throat. Whatever was in Nuru's heart, they were burying it deep. Perhaps it was the only way – perhaps this would all become far worse if the Sacere, too, wavered. But did it truly again come back to faith, and her own lack of it? She closed her eyes, then opened them again, looking for Manon, looking for Jomo. Manon as worn thin as a tendril of smoke in a yellow wrap that jaundiced the greys in her skin. Jomo in his jeans, leaning against the pillar opposite hers with his eyes hidden beneath a baseball cap, but she could feel his gaze anyway, its latency. He did not appear to care that many of the whispers were about him, but it must have hurt him too, the distance between him and his friends, his sibling. She held her fingers in fists in the tiny space between womb and thighs, measuring the universes between her loves.

*

Mama Mandisa and Mama Anouk rose to their feet, either side of Mama Mathilde, who was seated and listing a little to one side as if she were teetering on sleep. It took an age for people to sit or retreat to the edges and for the muttered conversations to subside; and even then the air beneath the rustling roof stayed as brittle and dangerous as kindling.

'Ce matin, there shall be two votes,' Mama Mandisa said. 'First we ask this question: do we stay on our island as written in our Climate Plan, or do we accept the... deal... offered, and move now to somewhere else? If we vote for leaving, then there will be time to decide where, and how, but first we must know this simple thing: do we stay, or do we leave?'

Mama Anouk raised her right hand, the palm facing out and pale as a moth. 'Those for staying.'

Hands rose like a wave, a sunrise, a blossoming after rains. They hardly needed to count, because the answer had turned the air into a sea.

'Those for leaving.' Faces turned and the space above everyone's heads was empty, but sharpening and sharpening, pressure beating against Sisi's eardrums because this had been the easy vote, and now came the terrible one. Shoulders were shifting, feet bracing beneath benches, every body in the room bound by tension and festered hurt. Jomo unfolded his arms and resettled his weight. Nuru's entire body vibrated with the pulse of the waiting crowd.

'Oh Mother,' Sisi whispered, a prayer and a disbelief all in one. 'Nuru, please stop this.' They had promised safety and love, not this. Not this. 'Nuru,' she whispered, but they did not turn.

'So we stay,' Mama Mandisa said, serenely, her eyes like moons. 'Et alors, the second vote.'

Sisi could not watch her, could not tear her eyes from the crowd as it morphed and shuddered, muscles taut and shining with heat. Manon's head was bent as if none of this mattered at all; perhaps the future did not, if you had already lost the very thing you most wished for. But Luc – Luc's head was not bent, and Sisi felt his gaze slide over her like a flame.

'We choose today between pathways that promise hope for overcoming the curses that have come upon us. Both the deaths of our children and the rising of the sea are burdens we must bear as one people, and will overcome as one people. So today we choose our path, which *we will travel together*.' Mama Mandisa did not raise her voice but it thundered anyway. 'Our votes are cast openly because we are all parts of one whole, the children of our Mother. I remind you, then, of this: we are raising our hands with love.'

It was too little, Sisi thought, too little and far too late.

The hall was silent, the air like the moment before a lightning strike.

Mama Anouk turned from watching Mama Mandisa, and raised her voice even though there was no need. Nuru leaned forward. 'The choices are: that we seek help for our burdens from doctors and scientists and the government of Britain. Or that we trust instead in Mother Sea to restore us, return to the foundations of our faith, the principles that call all things outside tainted as the lives of those who became our ancestors were tainted before they came here.' She raised her hand. Sisi's heart deafened her and she wanted to grasp Nuru, wanted time to stop.

Please, she thought. *Please*.

'Raise your hand if you vote to embrace the outside.'

Nuru leaned sideways as if about to reach for Sisi or block her from view. The air crackled. Jomo, across the seated crowd, raised his chin and his hand; other hands rose in the pocket around him. People began talking, cursing – there was movement, bodies rising, shouts, a bench toppling over. Sisi shrank back against the pillar, pressing her spine so hard against it that her muscles slipped like snakes. Mama Mandisa called out; Mama Anouk's raised hand vanished behind someone's broad back, and they *surged*, the people, the dam broken, hate and rage and fear, they *heaved*.

And Nuru *was* in front of her now, hands on her shoulders and their eyes black and aflame. 'Get out, sister, get away.' She pushed herself up the line of the pillar, Nuru pulling her arms.

'Sise!' Jomo's voice, asking her the way he had asked last night, but it was too late and too late and Nuru's shaking grip tightened as if they, too, had heard their brother's call.

People were moving behind them; more shouts from across the hall, Jomo and Luc, a woman, another man all blurring into one ravenous baying as though there was more here than just people. Something old and raging, drinking up the anger like it was water or blood.

'Nuru,' Sisi gasped. 'You must stop this.'

'Oh, Mother. I cannot,' Nuru said.

Perhaps it was true. Mama Mandisa shouted again, barely heard. 'You can,' Sisi said. 'You must.'

Someone knocked Nuru, pushing them into Sisi, and she gasped. There were fists falling now, the heavy sounds of bone and skin, and it could not be happening, she thought desperately, not this. But then a new noise clearly among the shouts, a bellow of pain. Her babe kicked; she screamed and fought Nuru. 'No!' she said. 'Nuru, that was—' But they were stronger than her, pushing her away and away from everything she belonged to there in that tangle of punches and shouts and all the terrible angers of the last eight years. Out under the raised screens, under the eaves, Nuru tugging her further until she was on the grass. She keened; her voice broke.

'Go!' Nuru said then turned away, bracing their shoulders like they must hide her. But that voice and its pain, the madness and ululations, and Mother, there were *children* in there – Sisi could see Katura held tight against Berhane's side, and she leaped beneath the roof again to grab their slim arm.

'Come, Kat,' she said, meeting Berhane's fixed, frightened gaze and pulling Katura into the fold of her arm, three steps back out from the hall, four. 'Come away with me.'

'But Chicha,' Katura said, leaning towards the violence as if they, too, were incomplete and could not leave until they were whole.

'Chicha will be away too, and safe.' Sisi did not know if it was true, but others were leaving, watching as disbelieving as her, backing away as she was from the wild beast. Women and men, and someone cradling Mama Mathilde like a child, and there were tears on her cheeks but she was shivering. Pulling Katura another step away, and then another, she would have turned and gone then. She would have. But a woman screamed not in pain but horror, and her whole body resonated.

And still she could not move, held fast by the child in her belly and the one beneath her arm, held back from the place her heart had leaped to.

'Jomo,' she whispered.

Nuru had left her and she could not move, Katura trembling against her. 'Jomo,' she whispered again.

Chapter Forty

Kit

It was the hottest part of the day, the house breathless despite the white caps beyond the lee of L'Ambre. The floor and walls emanated heat, sucking it in from the scorched garden, but Kit wished he was out there, with the smell of rock dust and flowers on the turn, the quiet calls of birds waiting for the air to cool. Not here at the table with Geo and Rachel and Euan all breathing the soupy air and each other's exhalations, drinking water in long gulps before it became tepid.

Geo was on the phone again. He'd had the last call in his office with only Euan to hear, but now they'd come out and as Geo spoke, leaning back in his chair, Euan updated Rachel and Kit.

'The office has been informed and Geo is phoning Mahé to see if the mailboat captain can take on an airlift delivery then turn around.' Euan drank water and pressed fingertips to the skin just above his right eyebrow, leaving marks. 'They'll helicopter a Seychellois doctor on board for Jomo. And I've emailed through an emergency food order.' He looked at Geo, listening to the half-conversation as Kit frowned at the heat and at Euan. He wanted to go down to the village to check that Sisi was all right, but also because it felt craven to be hiding up here from their own wreckage. Euan had brought news of the vote and the fight, passed on to him in the shade of the clinic by the youngest Mother, Mama Anouk. She had pressed his hand, tearful, and told him that they would do better to leave, to come back soon but be gone now.

'Boat needs to get within chopper range of Mahé, but they'll rendezvous tomorrow then turn straight around,' Geo said, putting his phone on the table and wiping his hand down the side of his shorts. 'Jesus wept, this is no weather for crisis management.'

'Why the emergency food?' Rachel asked. 'The boat only came yesterday. Is it a... a token of goodwill?'

An insult, Kit amended, if that was the reasoning behind it, but actually he thought Euan's reasons were more pragmatic and much sadder. He was right.

'No, not that.' Euan smiled lopsidedly and shook his head. 'They are facing shortages, as they lost their harvest in the storm. We'd do well to remove that as a concern as soon as possible. I was going to do it for the next boat, but it might have been wise to act more quickly, in hindsight.'

'So,' Geo said sententiously, looking around the three of them, 'boat will be here in three days, and we'll be ready to leave. Give these guys time to sort things out among themselves. If the boat gets here early enough, we can unload and get going the same day.'

'I think' – Euan studied his fingertips and then tilted his head – 'that you and I might consider staying, actually. Rachel and Kit could leave, but there's much we can do, once the islanders are ready to talk. Even if the relocation is off the table, there are still decisions to be made.'

'They've just tried to kill one of their own!' Geo glared at Euan. 'What the hell do you think they'll want to say to us that they won't say via a fist?'

'They've shocked themselves, I think. They'll calm down, and we should be here when they do.'

So Euan did have lines he wouldn't cross. Not the lines Kit had drawn, but at least there were some. Geo puffed and puffed again.

'We've done the best we can, Euan. There's no point putting ourselves in danger when it won't achieve anything.'

'Actually,' Rachel said slowly, 'I agree with Euan.'

'You what?'

Kit lifted his empty glass, tipping it until the very last drops of water gathered into a trickle, enough to wet the tip of his tongue. Just outside the open window a cicada wound itself up to a monotone that was as relentless as the heat.

'I think you and Euan should stay, dear.' Rachel got up to refill the jug, ice cubes crackling as they hit water. She returned and poured into everyone's glasses, unflustered by Geo's stare. 'You need to show success, Geo. Remember? We all know the situation here has been difficult, but they don't know just how much in the Department, do they? It would be... a setback, darling, don't you think? To go home so soon.' She patted his arm, then rubbed her thumb back and forth across her palm. Kit couldn't tell if it was distaste bred simply from the temperature, or something else.

'I don't—' Geo began, but Rachel interrupted him.

'We know how important this posting is for you, and, well, we need to get it right for them too, don't we? Listen to Euan, dear – he knows this place best. If he thinks they'll be ready to talk once the air has cleared, then they will be. And if you stay, despite all the challenges, and manage to achieve progress?' She made it sound like a question, but she'd won. Geo shifted, his hands on the table curled into fists held on end.

'True, Rach.' He smiled as if he'd not protested at all. 'Voice of reason, as always. Euan, buckle up, mate, we might be in for a bumpy ride!'

Kit leaned back, sweat on his legs and the air hotter than his own blood.

'But you two are going, of course,' Geo added and Rachel looked at Kit. Kit met her eyes, then looked at Euan, who had woken his tablet and gave every appearance of paying no attention.

The cicada's drone clawed at his mind. He could smell his own body beneath the flowers and wood polish.

'I don't know,' he said. 'I might be able to help.'

Euan glanced up at him, then away, his face unreadable and wan in the woody light.

'Don't you think you've helped enough?' Geo said, but Rachel spoke over him.

'Well, I'm going, dear, and I hope you come with me. I'd like the company.' Which might not be a lie, but was one slantwise. He got to his feet, taking his glass and going out onto the veranda, his thoughts swimming through insect noise and the desire to sleep.

*

The magpie robin was perched low in the lantana, and when Kit emerged it cocked its head to better study him, but did not move. He found some shade and sat, looking out at the line between calm water and roughening sea, the wind shadow of the island an ellipsis beyond the reef. He wanted to be out on the water, far enough from land to catch that cool, gusting air; feel the skip and pull of the waves that would dry the sweat from his skin and cleanse his head.

'I hope that boy's all right,' Rachel said from behind him, making Kit realise he was worrying too. Suspended calamity not just for Jomo, whose bulk and presence made serious injury seem preposterous, but also for all the islanders. What would it do to them to know that they could do that – have one of their own come close to murdering another of their own?

Kit turned his back on the robin and the sea to look at Rachel, noting that even she looked less than immaculate for once, her white blouse hanging limp and sticking to her ribs. 'They know what they're doing,' he said. 'Nuru and the others, they're well trained.'

'Oh, I know, darling. But still, what with all this, I do hope they don't… you know… take risks.'

He hadn't thought of that, but surely even Nuru wouldn't risk their own brother for their principles, especially after today. He hoped Sisi was okay. He wished he knew how badly hurt Jomo was, and how badly she feared for him.

'You aren't staying for Sisi, are you, dear?' Rachel said and Kit stilled.

He didn't answer quickly enough to lie, so she spoke again.

'Only, I don't want to see you get hurt, Kit, darling. You are doing so well, and we are so proud of you. I worry, you see?' Coming forward to put her water on the table and smiling at him in the same patient, gentle way she had right at the start. 'I worry that at the moment she perhaps cannot see this the way you do. She is widowed, after all, and pregnant, and you will leave.'

'I know that, Rachel. And you don't need to worry.' Kit smiled at her but looked away again out to the line on the water. Underneath the hedge, the female magpie robin hopped through shade, tossing aside fallen flowers as she hunted. Kit thought he'd sounded relaxed and honest, which was good. If he was going to carry this muted, unexpected heartache with him, then he wanted to do it privately.

Besides, it honestly wasn't Sisi – it was the place he'd been in before, waiting for his return. 'I emailed my parents,' he said, still hoping for casual. 'They replied just now.'

'Oh.' Rachel watched him carefully. 'How are they?'

Kit smiled; she'd been a near-stranger before and she wasn't now. His affection surprised him. 'They're fine. I said I would be coming back soon and that you're looking after me wonderfully.' She shook her head, demurring. 'I told them I would go back to uni, but to do science, like I was before.' Remembering the hospital, and trying not to. Wanting a shower or a swim, to go up to Les Hautes where he'd become someone new. He added, 'They said we would *discuss it* when I get back.'

Rachel looked out at the garden without seeing it, and then back to Kit. She spoke very gently. 'Am I allowed to say that I think there's not much to discuss? That you are brave and good, and this is *your* life, Kit, dear; *your* choice.'

Kit put a hand out to touch the rail beside him, breathing through a quick, sharp pain. 'You are allowed, and thank you,' he said, meaning it more than he ever had before. 'I guess it will take time, right? They aren't used to losing.'

Perhaps he hadn't been used to losing either. Around the far side of the house, the cicada wound down, coughed, then started up again.

'They almost lost their son,' Rachel said eventually, 'and they are regaining him. They should be grateful.' She opened and closed one hand, and Kit might have hugged her then, if they weren't both too hot to bear it. He hoped his pity was nowhere on his face; he hoped all she would see was the love.

'I'll come with you,' he said eventually. 'When you leave.'

Chapter Forty-One

Sisi

Sisi sat beside the bed watching Nuru and Isolde work over Jomo. She was supposed to be peeling and cutting sweet potatoes for the evening meal but kept forgetting, her hands dropping tubers so they lay shedding earth on her wrap.

'We might perhaps make our own suture thread,' Nuru said quietly, possibly not to anyone other than themself. 'A traditional material.'

'Bird guts? Truly, Nuru,' Isolde said, 'we need proper thread.'

'We can think of something,' Nuru insisted. They were stitching the long cut that crossed Jomo's chest, the black knots like flies lining up from the far edge of his left collarbone across his ribs. Their hands were not entirely steady so they were bracing them on Jomo's ribs, but even though Isolde had offered to take over, they had refused. 'A plant glue, perhaps? It will take effort to become less dependent, but we should try, no?'

Jomo muttered and shifted, tossing his head against the pillow either at a dream or at the tugging of his skin. Sisi held his hand, shuddering at the sight of his familiar body stretched out helplessly. One of his eyes was swollen and closed, blood in the corner and the skin a red-edged black, yellow over his eyelid like a secondary gaze, and her own body ached with him, as if it still knew his, its pains, its vulnerability.

Isolde swabbed silently as Nuru worked, then stepped back and passed Sisi on their way to the kitchen, their hands held out delicately in front of them, gloved and bloodstained.

'Alors,' Nuru said, straightening slowly. 'It is done. He will heal well.'

'Will you give him antibiotics?' Sisi said, her voice surprising her because she had been silent so long that she had mistaken her silence for calm.

Nuru looked at her narrow-eyed, holding their own hands just the way Isolde had done, white gloves and the skin showing through as inverse shadows. 'He has no need of them. He is strong and healthy, and the wound is clean.'

Sisi ran a hand soothingly over her belly although her child was resting now, and Isolde came back into the doorway, pressing clean fingers onto her shoulder. Sisi tilted her head up. 'Are you sure? It looked deep.' She had seen ribs. In the mess of blood and splayed muscle, his brown skin bled black and shining, she had seen teeth in the wound.

'Hmm.' Isolde frowned down at Jomo as he moaned again and his hands twitched at his side. Perhaps he was still fighting, trapped in that moment in the hall when he became the enemy. But whose face was it he saw?

'There is no harm, perhaps, in waiting a day,' Isolde said, but they were still watching Jomo when footsteps and voices told them the Mothers were coming.

'Aie, our poor child,' Mama Anouk said, coming to the bed in quick, tiny strides and bending over to kiss Jomo's cheek, brushing his stubbled hair and then straightening with his free hand in both of her own. Isolde found a chair for Mama Mandisa, and Sisi rose to push her own forward for Mama Anouk, then went to stand by Nuru in front of the window, their two silhouettes blocking enough of the sun to make the light in the room aqueous. Here, the smell of blood and sweat and her half-peeled vegetables was replaced by lychees and ozone, the sea picking up offshore. She felt watched again, fighting the urge to check behind her or up in the shadows of the ceiling.

'Who did this?' Mama Mandisa said, her voice hoarse. 'Pulled out a knife in that place?'

'Does it matter? We are all of us responsible, and must all ask forgiveness,' Nuru said, but they watched the Mothers and not their brother, and it was not enough. The long muscles of Sisi's arms flexed and she did not dare speak, because there was anger rising in her like the sea, as hot as the midday sand.

'It matters,' Mama Mandisa said heavily. 'It matters and there must be justice.'

Mama Anouk nodded, stroking Jomo's hand. 'This is the truth,' she said.

'It was a moment of madness,' Nuru said, and Sisi pressed her teeth together until her jaw ached. Her child uncurled within her, tasting rage in their shared blood. 'It was a symptom of how deeply we all care about making the right choices.' They spread their hands. 'We are all hurt, and we must all heal. That requires forgiveness, does it not? For the sake of the whole? ...And a decision, of course.'

Sisi jerked, stilled, felt shadows shifting.

'Ha!' Mama Mandisa said. 'Et bien, you suggest that we call a vote now, while one of our children lies injured?'

'Would this not be the best time? When we are shocked back into unity by our angers?'

'We cannot do it,' Mama Anouk said. 'Not until Jomo has a voice, as it was his that they sought to silence.'

Sisi tensed. Because *who was it* who had sought to silence Jomo, and *who was it* who had refused to step in? And this could have been prevented, she thought. But it had not been.

Mama Mandisa was nodding slowly, but her pearlescent eyes turned towards the light and Nuru as she waited for them to speak.

'We know Jomo's vote,' Nuru said. 'We can count it without him.'

'It is not a question of how he would vote, child,' Mama Anouk said, almost sharply. 'But of him being a part of us when we do so.'

Nuru shifted beside her. *Dear Mother, enough*, Sisi thought, wanting to push away from the window and shout it. *Enough*. They had to stop using Jomo as a tool in their arguments, because he was *right here* and *bleeding*. There was thread holding his chest together and he would carry the scar forever. How could Nuru, *Nuru*, be doing this so wrong? Their brother halfway to death, and they had said they knew what to do. They had said that if Sisi trusted the whole, trusted *them*, then she would be forgiven and loved and *protected*. And she had silenced herself and she had trusted, so why was Jomo lying here and why was Nuru choosing *anything at all* over Jomo, and over love?

Pressing herself against the window frame, she counted out her breaths. *Nuru*, she thought, *Nuru, please*.

'Come,' they said. 'We should go to Mama Mathilde.' And with eyes that reflected too much light and would not meet Sisi's, Nuru left with both Mothers, leaving only Isolde and Sisi, who wanted to claw them back and beg.

After a moment, Isolde bent to pick up the sweet potatoes and a knife. 'Shall we?' they said. Then, 'It will be well.'

'This is exactly what Nuru said at the meeting,' Sisi said. She had meant to speak only mildly, but failed.

Isolde nodded, tilted their head to study Sisi where she still stood silhouetted against the light. 'So instead I will say *he* will be well. Do not fear for him. And for the rest of us, well... Mother Sea tests us, does she not?'

This was, Sisi thought furiously, a Sacere's way of avoiding a truth. She made a soft sound that stung her throat and averted her gaze from Isolde's, wanting to argue but knowing that her anger and thus her words were not for this Sacere here at all.

'Come,' Isolde said again, holding out a knife, the blade towards themself. 'Sit with me. There will be time enough for all of that.'

Sisi moved very slowly, sat and worked beside the Sacere in silence, half-watching Jomo, guarding him. A part of her, somewhere, was weeping, but most of her was not. Perhaps she would become calm while Jomo slept unquietly.

*

She did not.

All night she was restless, her child writhing within her and her own mind playing over the fight at the island hall again and again. Hearing again Luc's words and Nuru's, seeing again and again the shadow of doubt that Nuru had wiped from their face. Sometimes she was herself, standing out beneath the sky with Katura; sometimes she was in there, in a maelstrom of muscle and contorted faces, metal entering her skin. Sometimes she was crouched among the roof beams, up with the geckos and bats, hanging mantis-like and ravenous, taut with glee.

Waking one last time, she rubbed the hunted night from her eyes and went to Jomo's room. Nuru was there; they might have been there all night.

'What is it?' she said, seeing them bent over Jomo, lines between their brows black in the slanted light, a cloth in one hand and the other braced against the mattress.

'It is nothing,' Nuru said. 'He is only a little—'

But Sisi had reached the bed and it took no training at all to understand the sweat on Jomo's skin, the flicker-skitter of his one visible eye beneath its lid. 'He has a fever. The cut is infected.' She looked up at Nuru, who had straightened and folded their arms. 'N'est-ce pas?' Pulling back the sheet over Jomo's chest, laying her fingers gently on skin that was like the edge of a fire. 'Nuru!'

They sighed, but did not unbend, their face all lines and shadows. 'C'est ça, he has a fever.'

Pulling the cloth from Nuru's fingers, Sisi reached for the water they had been using and wiped Jomo's face, the intimacy strange now, but also lovely. As if with her touch, she might heal the space between them. And apologise, because he had asked her to speak and she had not.

'So, you have given him antibiotics, yes?'

Silence as Sisi wiped carefully around the swollen eye, cleaning away pink-shot tears.

'I am awaiting Isolde.'

Sisi's angers had fed on shadows and hunger in the night, the wind swinging to the north-east, full of blades, thorns, blood. Now it was morning, her sibling's face was sharp with darkness, and she was poised on the very edge of something terrible.

'And perhaps you must wait also for Berhane and the Mothers, yes? Especially Mama Mathilde, who no longer rises early? Perhaps even little Katura, when they have finished their schooling, yes?' She leaned on her palms, angled forward over Jomo like a bird on eggs. 'Do you need a vote on it, Nuru? To decide which is better or worse: the outsiders' antibiotics, or Jomo *dying*?' She threw up the hand holding the cloth, water spraying spots of darkness on Nuru's clothes. 'You told me to trust in you, Nuru, but who *are you* now? To do this, who are you?'

'I am the Sacere. I am what I must be.'

Sisi straightened. 'And if he gets tetanus, Nuru, in the name of your beliefs? Because you, *his sibling*, would not treat him.'

Their hands were gripping Jomo's bed so hard the knuckles shone, but their voice was utterly level. 'He will not, it does not—'

'*You do not know this!*' She was shouting – everyone in the houses beside hers would hear. 'Nuru, *where is your heart gone?*'

Then a hand touched her arm and Isolde said, 'It will be well, Sisi. Come now, it will be well. Let me see him.' They were red-eyed with fatigue, shadows purpling their skin, but they moved her gently, went to stand beside Nuru, their fingers finding Jomo's pulse and stroking his forehead. And Sisi cradled her stomach where the muscles pulsed in time with her anger. Her whole body quaking but her child lying still within the bell curve of their womb.

She knew this ache.

'Oh,' she whispered, trying not to bend, trying not to give in but to watch Isolde and Nuru. 'Oh, please,' she whispered, 'not now.' But now here was someone else, murmuring in the room at her back. Mama Mandisa putting an arm around her strong as a bird's wing and Sisi wanted to crumple into that touch, but she wanted to throw it off, too, because Jomo was gasping for breath like a man drowning, which was how his brother died; and her own child who was both of theirs differently was tenuous within her. Muscles cramped again and she moaned.

'Sit down, Sisi, child,' Mama Mandisa said. Berhane was there too now, their fingers doing exactly what Isolde's had done, and she wanted to scream at them, *How many hands must count a heartbeat before you will act? How much must Jomo endure before you will act?*

Mama Mandisa pushed Sisi into a chair, placing her bent hand onto the top of Sisi's belly. 'Mmm-hmm,' she murmured, 'it is because you are upset, child. Be calm and your babe too will be calm. Your muscles are stretching and they listen to your heart to know whether to fight their change or not.'

'We must,' Berhane was saying.

Nuru looked at Berhane, then shook their head. 'Their drugs do not help us. And there assuredly is no need.' Jomo opened his unhurt eye, seeing nothing, or seeing the one thing that no one else could see. 'This will pass. He can fight it.'

Isolde peeled bandages from Jomo's chest and Sisi curved over her womb, her wrap ruching beneath her hands. Fire shone around Jomo's stitches, the cut like a claw, and he bucked against the bed at Isolde's touch.

'Nuru,' Berhane said, holding Jomo's shoulders as Isolde cleaned his broken, raging skin.

'*Nuru!*' Sisi said, the word twisted by Jomo's moans and by her own muscles. Nuru looked up, then in half a heartbeat they were kneeling at her side as if the rest of the room was empty.

'It will be only stretching pains,' they said, placing their hand over hers. 'You should go and lie down, sister. Rest.'

'*How*, Nuru?' she asked, gasping as Jomo gasped. He was her once-lover, her first love, her family, her mirror, and he thrashed against Isolde's gentle touch like a broken animal.

'Oh,' someone said.

Sisi's whole body turned towards the part of herself it had been missing.

Manon stood in the doorway to the room, her hand pressed to her mouth and her beautiful, night-sky eyes wide.

'Manon,' Sisi said, lifting a hand from her womb to her friend. Nuru rose to their feet, standing just a little in front of Sisi, but Sisi did not want their protection, not from what was happening to Jomo and not from Manon. Never from Manon.

But still Manon did not see her, going forward to the bed, looking between Isolde and Berhane. 'He is... I did not know,' she said slowly.

'Manon,' Sisi said again, her stomach contracting, and she could smell the tombs, rock and herbs, but it was only because Jomo was so ill and Nuru would not help; it was only because she was so frightened. 'Manon.'

'I did not know,' Manon said again, reaching a hand towards Jomo's chest and then letting it drop. 'Luc...' Her lips were an unsteady line and her worn face was hollow.

'Luc?' Mama Mandisa said, her voice deep as water. 'Why has Luc not come to see his oldest friend, Manon, child? Why is he not here?'

'No,' Sisi whispered, aching. She had known, but knowing had not made it any less impossible. 'Manon, no. Not *Luc*?'

The room was silent aside from Jomo's hissing, moaning breaths.

Manon backed away from Jomo, a broken-nailed hand stretching behind her for the doorframe; it hurt Sisi all over again that she had not reached for *her*. Manon whispering, 'He will be well, n'est-ce pas? He will be well, yes?' Then she was gone, and Mama Mandisa made a humming sound that held the sorrows of the entire island.

Chapter Forty-Two

Sisi

Sisi stood abruptly, momentum shoving Nuru away. All hurt and fear and fury. 'You *will* do this, Nuru. This is not a choice you have. If you love your brother, and if you love me, then you will do this. There is no choice.'

Nuru reached for her and Sisi stiffened, but when they turned, she followed them out into the gold-edged morning. The wind picking at her hair smelled of storms.

'You are wrong, ma chère,' Nuru said to her, reaching out again, touching her arm. 'There is always a choice. But this one is yours.'

'What do you mean? I choose to treat Jomo with the best you have. Of course I choose this.' Pulling away to put more distance between them because Nuru's eyes were no longer calm but full of sorrow and fervency.

'Sisi, do you not see what it means that Jomo was cut down? That *Jomo* of every one of us was cut down?'

'It means Luc—'

'It means Mother Sea is watching.'

Sisi stared at them. The doubt she thought she had seen in them was gone now, burned away by the sleepless night and their brother's blood. She did not know how she was not screaming. 'What—'

Nuru interrupted her. 'Sister, this is your babe, and your love; your science and your faith. Do you not see?'

Somewhere far away a woman was weeping. It was not Manon, and nor was it Sisi. 'It is *your brother* fighting for his life, and *your faith* standing in his way,' she said.

'But still it is you who must choose,' they said as if her words had not touched them at all. 'Who must prove how united we are in our desire to change. These drugs or Mother Sea.'

She could have borne it if they were forceful or evangelical, but they were only intent and full of grief. Believing their own words more deeply than Sisi had ever believed in anything.

'Nuru,' she said, pleading and furious. Her stomach spasmed again and she gasped. 'Nuru, you cannot believe this. Mother Sea would not do this to us. Do what you wish tomorrow, hold your vote or make your sacrifices, only treat Jomo today, please.'

'And what if you are wrong, as you have been before?' Nuru said, shaking their head and lifting their hand to touch Sisi's hair with famine in their eyes.

She jerked away from their touch. 'This is about Jomo, not about me.'

'Sisi. Sister, I am so frightened,' they said. And it was true, it was finally there to be seen, but she did not care. 'I cannot be the one who endangers your child. Not after...' Not after Antonin, not after Manon's son. They shook their head, blinking too rapidly into the wind. 'I cannot risk your child, Sisi. If I gave Jomo the outsider's drugs and... Sisi, I could not bear it.'

What could she say to their shared ghosts? Was this what faith was? To take your griefs and build them into a world. To hold conviction more tightly than love.

'Mother Sea would not ask for this,' she repeated. The island listened, the sea. 'I will fight for my child,' she said. '*You* must fight for Jomo, now, when he needs you.'

They hungered for blood and with blood we sated them.

'I cannot.' Nuru was pleading. But there was pain in her stomach and pain beneath her ribs and all of it she could lay at Nuru's feet. She breathed in sharply.

'But you promised me,' she said and they flinched and she did not stop. 'You promised that all would be well and I *believed* you, Nuru. How can you make *this*' – a hand flung towards the house, the broken man – 'about faith when it is *love*, Nuru? This is about *love*.'

'But the child is...' Their voice fractured. 'Sisi, *this is my duty.* Say you understand.'

'No,' she said, too loudly, 'no, I do *not* understand this. You said you would find a way, but this is not it, Nuru.' Bending over her child, and baring her teeth at the sand. '*How can this be faith, Nuru? Where is your heart?*'

They hungered for blood.

The wind's teeth snagged her skin and she staggered backwards. *You are wrong*, over and over in her mind. *You are wrong, you are wrong.*

Nuru reached for her and she shied away. 'Sisi, no—'

She could hear her own voice reciting stories to Kit above a furious heart. *In his hunger and his anger he rose up again, taking her children up into the air with him so that they died.*

And Nuru's voice: *They hungered for blood and with blood we sated them.*

And it all made a terrible, impossible sense.

'How could Mother Sea be so hungry for blood, Nuru?' she said. Escape – she wanted to escape. This thing had been stalking her for days. *They hungered.* A hunger and a greed that made no sense but filled her with terror and revelation. *They* hungered. *He* rose up. The elder siblings, the Brother Island – they were the ones who hungered for blood, and who defied Mother Sea in their hunger. Oh Mother, *it was a lie.* Nuru believed a lie and they wanted *her* to believe a lie and they would let Jomo die for it.

'How could you believe that of her?'

Nuru stared at her, but her fury and her hurt were drowning her, vast as the ocean. 'Where is your faith, Nuru? You told me to trust you and yet you believe *this*.'

What was faith worth if you believed the wrong thing?

'What do you—' Nuru's hands were fisted, and Sisi threw her arms wide.

'You told us the wrong stories, Nuru. You blamed the wrong god, just as you...' Just as they had blamed her, and Manon had blamed her, and Jomo was dying for it. She spat out a laugh full of brine and glass. 'It is the brother, not the mother. Why did you not see that in your stories that you *told me to trust my babe to*? Is it because you are like him, sibling?' Stepping backwards, wanting to stop now, because this was too much and their face was as wide open as a broken sky. Wanting to stop and unable to. 'You will drag us to our deaths with your heart full of anger, and now you want me to give him Jomo? Never, Nuru. I will not give him anyone.'

'Sisi,' they called. She took another step away.

'But will you?' They came towards her and she asked again: 'If you believe this so much. Will you give Jomo to Brother Island? Your home or your blood, your faith or your brother.' Mocking their own words to her, not recognising her own voice. 'Which one are you willing to betray, Nuru?' Not waiting for an answer but turning away, taking four steps then stopping, looking over her shoulder and saying far more quietly, 'You treat Jomo, or I will not see you, Nuru. I will not know you unless you do this.'

Then there was nothing but the need to be *away*. Almost running, cradling her womb, the storm tide of her heart pushing her onward.

*

She thought she was heading for the lighthouse, for her old self, or perhaps the cliff and Kit's unfathomable bravery, but instead she stopped where she had fallen, where the rocks had lapped at her blood and she had learned to love her child. Where she had first felt the hunger that had watched her in the night, that had waited in the island hall with its teeth bared. Nuru had told her to believe, but no mother would demand the blood of her children, so Sisi should have known. Nuru should have known, and she had no idea why she had come up here, but if Nuru could bury their heart beneath faith then she would not watch them do it.

Her own heart was a storm within her chest and if she would not watch Nuru choose, neither could she do *nothing*. Fierceness turned her bones to fire. She *would not let anyone* have her child, and she would not let them have Jomo, because to lose either would take too much of her heart for her to survive. All the fury she had not allowed herself was towering within her like an unbroken wave.

If Mother Sea wanted her faith, then she must also have her anger, and Nuru might be willing to choose, but any choice here was a betrayal. Brother Island had betrayed them in his anger, and Mother Sea had betrayed them by choosing to forgive, and Sisi was not so easily appeased.

What does it mean? Kit had asked when she had told him the story of Brother Island's heart, and she could not remember how she had replied but she knew what she would say now. She would say, *It means that hollowing out your heart does not undo the hurt you inflict. It means that the gods are flawed. It means that they are careless with our lives so we must not be.*

Or perhaps she would say only this: *It means nothing, Kit. We have nothing now but tetanus and loss; too much grief and too much anger.* It was only a wonder they had not come to this before, breaking themselves open. Sisi gasped, tears and wildness scalding her eyes. It did not matter what you believed – but it did matter whether you believed more than you loved.

'You cannot have them,' she said to the rocks and the heart beneath. She needed suddenly to confront this story, the one Nuru believed so desperately and wanted *her* to believe completely because they were mourning, and full of fear, and mistook sacrifice for hope. She wanted to climb inside this story's skin and tear it open. Reaching the slope above the heart, she turned to face the rock with hands and feet and teeth gritted against the wind filling her eyes with salt, and against the pains in her womb that matched the waves. Jomo's blood and hers and her proxy child's had run into the sea, and she would lose her child, she would lose them if she did not *change everything.*

Feet slipping and rock biting her palms, she shivered in the wind, reaching down another step and another, the heart opening up beside her like an eye, a doorway, a mouth. And perhaps he was dying too, her Brother Island, this no longer his heart but his grave; perhaps he had reason to hunger for life. But she would not let him have *these lives,* because he had taken enough. He had taken enough and enough, from Mahena and Agathe and Célestine and Manon, and every single one of her people was hurting. And if Mother Sea and Nuru were both too wounded to stop him, then Sisi would. She knew it made no sense but was far beyond caring; the sea hurled itself at her feet as she climbed along rock ledges and handholds into the heart, the tomb, the flesh of her brother, and she clung there with the sea pounding at the rock.

'You cannot have them!' she shouted. The sea snatched at her words and the wind swept them into the heart. 'You will not have Jomo and you will not have my child!' Waves sucked at her legs, but Sisi clung on with her fury and laughed, teetering on madness. No science or logic or outside world; none of her terrible cleverness or sacrifices or broken promises. Only her and her fierceness and the cave that was a heart clamouring for blood. A wave surged and her hand slipped; the rocks sliced her wrist and *Oh, Mother,* the pain. The sea fell away again, and she watched blood in rivulets cross her hand to drip into the water. She laughed again, furious and terrified all at once.

'So, then,' she shouted, holding her arm out, 'take this and be content. Take it, for it is all I will give you.'

But he drank and drank, and what would it take to sate an island? *Please*, she thought, her arm bleeding and her heart. *You will not have my child. Enough.*

*

'Sisi!'

She twisted, slipping, grasping at the rock.

'Nuru! What...' Dropping her arm, blinking salt water. The wind roared, thunderclap waves rattling her bones. 'Nuru?'

'Sisi, are you here?'

It *was* Nuru, appearing with their teeth bared against the wind and sea. She realised that she had been waiting for them. Of course she had. *Where is your heart?* she had said and then come here to this heart knowing they would follow. *So is this faith, then*, she thought, *or is it love?*

She had trusted them and they had failed her, so now she was in a demigod's heart, tearing her own faith to pieces because she was done with twisting grief into anything other than defiance. And now she clung on with one hand, watching her sibling, her carer, friend, judge, with their eyes wild. *Is this faith?* Her blood running across her palm, scalding her fingertips. The heart beat around her; their brother moaned and wanted and craved. Pain in her stomach, her child whispering distress.

'Nuru,' she whispered, close enough now for them to reach out, gripping her arm bruisingly.

'What are you doing?' they shouted. Waves engulfed their legs and she had no answer. Which story? It was a god demanding tithes. It was a cave and an epidemic and fear, and what was she doing here, bleeding into a sea full of hunger and broken hearts?

'How do we sate an island?' she said too quietly, Nuru reading her lips. Sisi lifted her arm, vermilion and salt, weak from loss and fury. '*They hungered for blood and with blood we sated them.*'

Nuru shook their head. 'Come back. This is not the way.'

Sisi's clothes were shoaling around her calves, and *Is this faith?* They were willing to let Jomo die, and to let her carry his death. *Is this faith, or is it despair?* 'How do you know?' she said, her voice echoing. 'Do you really believe we must choose?'

Nuru met her eyes, Antonin's death between them, and Jomo's wounded skin, Manon's poor, poor babes. Her own. 'A broken heart for a broken heart,' she said. 'Is this what Brother Island wants?'

'Not like this,' they said, and their voice cracked; their eyes were wide at the blood on her arm. She wanted to shake them until the battlements of their faith fell, if that was even possible.

'Why not?' she shouted. The sea was like ice against her now, or she was ablaze, and she should stop, but she had thought they loved her. Yet how could that possibly still be true? 'If you truly believe that sacrifice will save us, then why not here, now?' Mother Sea burst over them, and what would you believe to save a child? Anything. It was so forgivable, and so terrible.

The sea fell off Nuru. They reached for her wounded arm, twined their fingers into hers, blood between their palms. 'I do not think—'

'Tell me, Nuru.' She cut them off, and their brother's heart paused so that they heard her. 'You promised you would save my child. Is this what you meant, Nuru? A life for a life?' Their fingers were crushing her bones. 'What is it you believe?' she said. So cruel – so angry and desperate and cruel. 'Will Jomo's death save me? Would anyone's? ...Would yours?'

'Sisi, I do not understand—' they began.

'Do you not? It is simple, Nuru.' The sea bellowed, throwing itself at their faces. Sisi gasped, but she had given herself up to them and now she wanted herself back. 'Surrender is not faith – how can you not see that? Why could you not believe in *me*? Why can you not choose *us*? We *fight for the things we love*, Nuru – we do not give them up.' She was so terribly angry, and only a part of it was at Nuru, but more than enough. 'If you believe someone must die, then why Jomo, Nuru? Why your brother and not yourself? Why is it always someone else who must sacrifice for your faith?'

The tears on her cheeks were like fire; fury and helplessness and redemption. Her heart or the god's, the sibling or the Sacere.

*

But then her babe turned and made her forget everything.

Oh, my child, she thought. *My precious child.* She had to get out, leave her blood in the sea but take her babe to safety. Nuru was staring at the sea as if she did not exist, and she was too tired suddenly to batter herself against their faith anymore. *Away*, she thought, *come away, child*. She crept forward, Nuru pressing against the rock to let her pass, their body heat alive against hers, all their hearts roaring. A wave wrapped around them then pulled them apart, and Sisi went with it. Her child flexed; her muscles cramped. Turning back: 'Nuru, please,' she said, pleading. But for what? Pleading for what?

They did not move, staring into the heart.

Her babe turned, and she carried them away.

Chapter Forty-Three

Kit

Kit had come up to Les Hautes simply to be out of the house – to imprint this place into his soul, because leaving would be harder than he'd ever imagined. But then Nuru was there, running, freezing at the edge of the cliff then, insanely, swinging themself down and out of sight.

Kit's ears were full of wind, and the sea beyond the cliff was striated white, all hollows and broken peaks, but Nuru had thrown themself down towards the heart.

What... Was it some ritual? But there'd been no dignity, only frantic haste.

'Jesus,' he whispered and moved in spite of himself, or in spite of one of his selves. 'Jesus.'

*

He was twenty metres away from the edge when someone appeared where Nuru had vanished, but... but it wasn't Nuru. It was Sisi. Soaked and bloodstained, one hand on her stomach. He ran the last few steps, reaching and pulling her up onto flat ground. She looked through him blindly, so he bent to catch her gaze. Her arm was bleeding.

'Sisi. Jesus, *Sisi*, what's happened? Are you okay? What's—'

'Kit,' she said, eyes focusing, and they were dark as moss, brown as autumn.

'Are you...' Holding her hands, and damn the taboos because she was shivering, half-dissolved by the sea. 'Sisi, you're hurt... Did Nuru—'

'Do you have faith?' she said. Like he'd said nothing. 'Kit?'

'Your wrist!'

She wiped the blood onto her sodden clothes without looking. 'What do you believe in, Kit?'

'What's happening, Sisi? Are you okay? Why are you—'

'You are leaving,' she said.

He took in a breath, the wind a vacuum in his throat. 'I'm sorry,' he said, not sure what he was apologising for. 'Yes, I am. I think I need to.' He wanted to explain but couldn't think. 'Sisi, please—'

'Why?' she said, looking up at him both intent and far away, and Nuru hadn't come back up. Should he be angry at them or worried? What had happened? What was happening?

'Because I need to face everything,' he heard himself say, straightening so that he pulled on her hands, and she looked up at him. 'To... have some faith in who I am. Who I want to be.'

Her hair was whipping around her as if possessed and pain rippled in her face, her hands pulling away from his to cradle her stomach. Why, for god's sake, were they talking about this? 'Sit,' he said. 'Sit down, please. You need to...' But he didn't know what she needed. He didn't know what any of this was, other than that she was in pain and he couldn't help her.

'Faith in who you are,' she echoed. 'Kit...' Trailing off, turning to look back at the sea and the cliff, and *Jesus*, the sea was crazy and he kept forgetting Nuru. 'That is what I lost, what they took away. No... no, they did not take it. I gave it to them because I was frightened. And that is only...' Her arm was still bleeding.

'Is Nuru okay?' he said.

She shook her head roughly, as if awakening, eyes widening. 'I must get them out.' She tipped forward. 'I told them... I should not have said it. It was not fair – they only did exactly as I did. Oh Mother, I must...'

She took two steps forward. 'Sisi,' Kit said, reaching for her. 'You can't.' Her hands were curving around her child. 'Please, Sisi. I'll get them. Stay here – I'll go.'

She turned her head to look at him like she'd never seen him before. 'I told them to choose, Kit. I told them to choose between the two halves of themself and it was... Oh, Kit, it was wrong of me,' she said, her voice rising. 'Get them. Please, Kit. Please. Before they...' Leaning out over the rocks.

Before they what? Kit stood on the edge seeing nothing other than a maelstrom. 'What's happening?' he demanded. Her and the sea equally terrifying.

'I was so angry,' she said. 'I was so angry but they... What if they choose the sea?' Her eyes desperate, her voice shrill. 'Please, Kit. Stop them. Tell them...' Her fingers smearing blood on his arm. 'Please go. Oh, Mother, what have I done?'

'I'm going.' Already looking for the first foothold, bending down. Disbelief making his hands and feet numb, but he climbed. The waves reached up for him, and he climbed.

*

'Nuru?' he shouted as he reached the cave; shouting again, still climbing down. '*Nuru!*'

They were abruptly there, dark and solid, creeping into view around the edge of the rock. Their head was bent so Kit didn't know if they'd even heard him, but he slipped and scrambled down into the waves. 'Nuru, this way,' he called. Nuru came towards him, still looking down, water over them both. Kit reached out, found cloth and pulled, then pushed them up ahead of him. They climbed, Nuru slipping, stopping, slipping again, so Kit was almost shouldering them up the rock, and he didn't have the breath to speak or do anything other than manage the next step and the next. Until finally they scrambled over the lip and sank to their haunches beside one another, water darkening the dust around them, the sun already drying their skin. Kit wiped a hand over his face and looked up.

Sisi was a few metres away, half bent over, one hand on her stomach, the other against her mouth. She didn't move and the horror on her face made Kit say, 'Go, Sisi. I'll stay with Nuru – you need to look after yourself. Go.'

Nuru was weeping.

'God, Nuru,' Kit said helplessly, reaching out a hand that Nuru didn't reject, shocking Kit more than the tears. They wept, raw and ugly, sobs wrenched from their gut, their face twisted, Kit bending forward to wrap both arms around them. The wind in the spaces between them was almost words; Nuru turned their face into Kit's shoulder and howled.

Sisi took a step forward and Kit looked up at her, utterly bewildered. 'They asked me to give myself up,' she said, almost pleading. 'And they were wrong and now I have asked them the same. Nuru,' she said, stumbling, trembling from a pain he couldn't see, blood on her fingers and fear hitting him again.

'Go, Sisi. Go. You have to. For the baby.'

'Nuru,' she said, reaching them, touching the Sacere with bloodstained fingers. 'Nuru, it will be well. We will find a way, yes? We will find a way that does not destroy us, yes? I know it.'

But Nuru only shuddered and wept in Kit's arms, and Kit wondered if they had ever let themself weep for the babies or their brother or the island. He suspected they had not. He brushed a hand over their coiled hair. 'Find a way with what?' he said.

Sisi flinched, but not at the question; her hand on her stomach was shaking. *Oh god*, he thought.

'With everything,' she whispered. 'Oh, Nuru...' She flinched again.

'Sisi, go home,' he said, aching. 'You have to go. Please, Sisi. Get Isolde, or one of the Mothers.' Because god knew he wasn't qualified for this, but neither could he bear to watch her bleeding, hurting, endangering herself all over again.

'I cannot,' she whispered.

'You have to.'

She lifted her gaze from Nuru to him, and finally, slowly, she backed away. He couldn't watch her leave, so he tucked Nuru against himself and closed his eyes.

*

After a long time, an eternity, Nuru straightened away from Kit, no longer exactly crying, but not really anything else either. Kit had no idea what to do.

'I could not,' Nuru whispered. Kit leaned forward to hear them over the wind and the sea. 'It is all lost.'

And abruptly Kit's own ghosts were crowding closer, the cliff singing. 'What have you lost?' he asked slowly.

Nuru laughed, or tried to, and rubbed both hands over their face roughly. 'Everything,' they said. 'I am Sacere, and I have failed in my faith.' One hand tugged hard at a string of shells around their neck, but it did not give; they made a soft, anguished sound, and dropped their hand.

Sitting back a few inches, Kit watched them carefully. 'Your faith...' he tried. 'What's happened?'

I told them to choose, Sisi had said, *between the two halves of themself.*

Nuru shook their head, gathering themself like you would gather all the pieces of a shattered cup. 'I have demanded sacrifice of others, outsider,' they said eventually. 'I demanded it of Sisi, my own sister – that she must love nothing so much as the whole of us. Neither her convictions, nor her heart.'

They took a breath. The wind scooped fistfuls of dust and raked it across both their faces. Out over the rocks, a seabird called, high and eerie.

'And now I am asked to do the same and I cannot.' Nuru met Kit's eyes for the first time, almost stern but mostly broken. 'Tell me what I am, outsider, if I cannot do for my faith what I have asked of others? What am I without my faith?'

The lines in Nuru's face were like a broken song, and their mouth twisted with despair. *Oh god*, Kit thought. He knew this; he recognised it. Pills and cliffs and loneliness. The terrible finality of exile. He took Nuru's hand in his own, not speaking because he couldn't, because it wouldn't help.

Benedicts do law, someone whispered. *Otherwise they wouldn't be Benedicts.*

I need to have faith in who I am, he'd said to Sisi. And Rachel had said to him, *They are regaining a son.*

'You are a sibling,' he said eventually, cautiously. 'She asked you to love your family, and you do. There's nothing wrong in that, or weak.'

'Sacere must be more than this.' Shaking their head, barely listening, and Kit recognised that too.

'But you are Nuru as well,' he said. 'And that is who Sisi loves.'

'Does she? I took away the work she loved. I told her she was to blame.'

Kit hesitated, but then said very gently, 'Yes, you did. But that isn't where this ends. And you were only doing what you thought you had to.' Did that make it forgivable? Beneath them the sea wept within its heart.

'I did it from fear,' they said bitterly. 'And told myself it was for this.' They scraped dust into their palms, lifted it up, their hands shaking. The island, they meant, and the whole of what the island held. The wind caught the dust and lifted it into the air. 'And even then I was wrong; misunderstanding, misreading. I have believed our Mother cruel. Why did I do that? Because it meant *I* could be cruel? Because penance is easier than bravery?'

'Because you are grieving,' Kit said. The seabird cried again and Nuru shuddered. 'And frightened, and we all make mistakes when we're frightened.' He had not, he realised, been nearly this kind to himself.

'You cannot understand,' Nuru said slowly, but they looked at him as if the words were a form of prayer.

Sisi had said the same, on the red cliffs. 'Not everything, no,' he said calmly. 'But I understand how we contort ourselves to be what other people need, and I know that sometimes we break.'

Nuru was frowning. 'But I must be more.'

Kit closed his eyes again.

'Why?' he said to both of them and to everyone. 'You are yourself. Does anything else matter?'

And he realised he was almost smiling, unspeakably tender, a warmth beneath his ribs where he hadn't even noticed there'd been nothing at all.

But Nuru straightened, lifting their gaze from their empty palms, eyes like black holes. 'Yes,' they said. 'It does.'

*

One of the other Sacere found them eventually. Krish, who slipped an arm around Nuru's waist even though Nuru would not meet their eyes, and together they walked down to the village, to the house they shared with Sisi. Mama Anouk was there, and Kit didn't fear for them nearly half as much as he'd done in those first terrible minutes. Then, once Kit left them, he walked down to the shore, his feet in the incoming surf and his mind full of wings and possibilities.

He was himself and there was nothing wrong in that. Perhaps he didn't know yet who he could become, but this was enough. It was a start.

Chapter Forty-Four

Sisi

Sisi was sitting outside with Mama Mandisa in the evening when she heard someone approaching. Looking up through the gold light, she watched Kit coming and thought that he was walking with a buffer of air between him and the sand, like it was impossible for him to fall because he just might learn how to fly. She felt herself smiling at the thought.

'Sisi,' he said, stopping beneath the coconut tree, his shadow long behind him and the amber sun in his eyes. 'Mother.' He met Mama Mandisa's eyes warily. Within the house, Mama Anouk said something and someone else, Isolde perhaps, answered. Not Nuru. Sisi had not tried to speak to them yet, but she was not sure who she was protecting. Isolde had started Jomo on intravenous antibiotics; his fever was still raging.

'Kit Benedict,' Mama Mandisa said, leaning back in her chair. 'Child, all is well with you?' She gestured at another chair and relief made Kit's face soften, his eyes aflame.

'All is well,' he said, meaning it, Sisi thought. 'And with you both?'

Mama Mandisa did not smile, but it was there in her voice. 'All is well. Thanks, I believe, to you.'

'Are you okay, Sisi?'

'Isolde says I must rest,' she said. 'But I am fine now – it is well, yes?' She touched the curve of her stomach and marvelled all over again at how much her babe had forgiven her, how they had ridden out the tempest of her rage and her wildness, and were now resting as if she had never been anything other than a safe harbour. Kit let out a breath and she marvelled at that, too, that he cared.

Mama Mandisa tilted her head, sunlight painting the knot of her hair umber. 'What happened with Nuru, child? They will not talk.'

Kit leaned forward, elbows on knees and his head bowed, just as Jomo had done... was it truly only two days ago? Oh, how easily a world could change. Mama Mandisa waited. What *had* happened, Sisi wondered, after she had left, torn perfectly between terror for her child and horror at Nuru, at *Nuru*, weeping. She had tried to explain the sea cave and her anger to Mama Anouk and Isolde, but faltered and they had hushed her.

'It matters not,' Mama Anouk had said. 'You are all three returned to us safely, and we shall make this well between us all.'

How? Sisi had thought. *How do you make so many betrayals right? How do you reconcile all your contrary parts?* But she was beyond worrying about such things today; tomorrow was soon enough for that. This evening was about watching the sky turn emerald and damson when she was not watching Jomo, and waiting for the bats to come squabble in the tree above them. For listening to the sea breathe against the sand.

*

Kit met Sisi's eyes now, and only once she had given him a small nod did he turn to Mama Mandisa. 'Nuru believed they had to save Sisi, all of you, through sacrifice. I think... I think they have realised...' He faltered, took a long breath in, then simply said, 'That they are only human.'

'Hmm,' Mama Mandisa murmured and Kit lifted his gaze. Sisi turned. 'Our strength must come from who we are, and not from who we are trying to be, is this what you mean, child?'

The tears in Kit's eyes turned them the exact colour of the lagoon, and Sisi's own heart shuddered at the words. He wanted to speak, she saw, but could not; tried to smile, but could not. She found that her own terrible hurts mattered just a little less in the face of his healing, perhaps because he gave her hope. Mama Mandisa reached over to touch her palm to his cheek briefly, because of course she would know when there were tears waiting to fall. She was a Mother.

'We are very lost, I think,' Mama Mandisa said, and Sisi thought that she was talking of themselves, and Kit, and perhaps the whole of humanity. 'But we are not yet broken.'

Kit blinked several times and looked out at the sea with the very edge of a smile showing. Sisi watched him, and then the sky that was changing shades between each breath. The cut on her arm stung but she thought she deserved it, saying what she had to Nuru.

'What is it you are wishing to do now?' she said.

He looked back at her and surprised her by laughing. 'I would love to go out with your fishers, try sailing one of those boats.'

Mama Mandisa laughed too, the sound full of the sea and surprise, as if she had not expected to laugh, and was welcoming back an old friend. 'You wish to sail a pirogue on our waters?'

'Yes, I really do,' he said, and there was colour on his skin that was nothing to do with the somnolent heat of the day. 'Sorry, is that not—'

'I think perhaps we can arrange this thing for you. When you have shown us kindness.'

'I didn't—'

'Yes, you did,' Sisi cut him off, thinking not so much of his arms around Nuru as about all the truths he had told her, large and small.

He shot a glance at the doorway beside her, then lifted a shoulder in a shrug. 'I'd like to help more, if you'd let me.'

'Why?' It was another voice, Berhane come to the corner of the house and leaning their shoulder against the frame like they might otherwise fall. They looked so weary, Sisi thought. But the word had not been said the way it might have been a day ago.

'Because Sisi helped me,' Kit replied. 'I didn't think anyone could, or would want to, but she did. And you did.' Turning his palm up and gesturing at the village, the island, the sea.

Berhane and Mama Mandisa looked at him for a long time, and Kit looked back. 'I don't think you need my help,' he added, 'but I'm offering it anyway.'

'We shall see,' Mama Mandisa said eventually. 'We thank you. It will not be easy, I think, or quick.'

No, Sisi thought, it would be far from easy, and perhaps never-ending. Mama Mandisa pulled herself slowly to her feet, and Sisi rose to help her. 'And now, Berhane, you are come to tell me I must go home and rest, n'est-ce pas?'

Berhane smiled. 'Yes, Mama,' they said, and took her hand in theirs like it was a precious gift. They walked away slowly through the mauve light, and somewhere a drongo sang the day to sleep.

*

'You are glad now, that you stepped away,' Sisi said after a while. She was too tired to mind the silence, but she wanted to know this too.

'Yes,' Kit said. He might once have evaded this question, but he studied the movement of hermit crabs at his feet and said quietly, 'We aren't defined by the cataclysmic moments, are we? Not really. It's not the stepping away that shapes me, it's the… laughing in the rain.' He looked at her steadily. 'The choosing to sing.'

She remembered too many funerals, remembered braiding Manon's hair in the dark and Kit's hands holding hers above an island's heart. 'All will be well with you, I think,' she said.

He nodded. 'I think so. I'm okay today, and I hope to be okay tomorrow too, and that's enough.'

She did not know if this could be true of herself, not with Nuru so silent and so many fears unresolved. She wanted to tell Kit her hopes, but they were still too fragile for words, and perhaps Mother Sea knew she needed time, because Isolde came to the doorway of the house, the lamplight casting their face soft and glowing.

'Jomo is stirring, Sisi. Come to him.'

'Yes,' she said. 'Oh, yes.' She rose, and Kit rose like some ancient courtesy, and they smiled at one another just as the first fruit bat landed noisily above them.

'I should go back to the house, anyway,' he said. 'Rachel will be worrying. I'll see you tomorrow.'

*

Sisi sat in the chair beside Jomo's bed. Nuru was not there, and she realised she had been hoping that they would be. There was not enough bravery in her to think about the island's heart, not yet, so she only took Jomo's hand in hers and said his name.

He turned his face towards her, the undamaged eye opening, narrowing against pain or the light. There was sweat on his forehead and she lifted the cloth Isolde had left to wipe it away. He watched her, unfocused and then focused. Something terrible that had been coiled within her relaxed just a little, just enough.

'Sise,' he said. 'What's wrong?'

Everything, she thought. She had absolved herself of responsibility because she was first lost and then angry, but finding herself again was no less terrifying. And she had perhaps,

perhaps, rediscovered parts of herself, but she had done it by breaking Nuru. 'Nothing,' she said. 'I am glad you are awake. You frightened me.'

He shifted and winced and closed his eye again. There was a moth circling the ceiling light, the sound of its soft wings audible even as the crickets were starting to call outside the open window.

'You will not lose me so easily, Sise,' he said without opening his eye.

And she studied his strong, wounded face, so familiar and so beloved, so like his brother's. *No,* she thought, *I will not lose you, but also, you are no longer mine to keep, just as I am no longer yours.* It hurt, and it would always hurt, but not as much as fearing for her child, or Nuru, or Manon. Her eyes filled with tears and even though his eyes were closed, he knew, and tightened his fingers around hers.

'It will be well,' he said. 'We will be well.'

She was not sure she believed him, or even that he knew what he was saying, but still it helped to hear the words, to know that here was someone who might have left her but who had never once stopped believing in her.

'Sleep,' she said, but he already was.

Chapter Forty-Five

Sisi

The next night, Sisi's dreams, begun in thunder, would finally end in the sea. All her fears and hopes and loves strewn over the sand in the shapes of cone shells, clams, sea-pens and glass-footed shrimps. She was a jewel anemone and a manta ray, and when she woke in the early morning of that final day she stretched, her child stretching within her, and her body felt unspeakably beautiful, the way her skin met the world, the way her muscles gave and held and did not hurt.

She went of course to Jomo's room where Nuru was sleeping in a chair, worryingly limp the way awake they were worryingly quiet. Jomo's swollen eye was yellowing at the edges and every one of his heavy muscles was relaxed, but differently to the way Nuru's were. She did not know what Nuru was thinking. She had failed them, and it was not their whole self that had come back from Brother Island's heart, but last night they had changed Jomo's IV bag as Sisi watched, then sat there not meeting her eyes. When she had taken their hand in hers, though, their fingers had been warm.

*

Going to the window now, she saw that the boat had come. Felt the same fleeting shock as always, seeing its bulk there in the dawn, huge against the lace-work sandbars, violate and foreign and familiar all at once.

Things happened quickly after that. The rib brought the doctor across – a small Hindu man who spoke quietly but very fast, and whose hands were completely steady, completely gentle as he unwrapped Jomo's bandages, lifted eyelids and took his temperature. Sisi followed him outside to listen as he said he would be happier if they took Jomo to Mahé for observation because although, yes, he hoped that the infection was responding to the current antibiotics, the wound was still worrisome and they were not, he cautioned, quite out of the woods.

So Jomo went, carried on a stretcher even though he was awake again, slurring insistence that he could walk on his own – what did they think of him, that he was weak? Sisi told him to shut up and watched as the rib took him away over the lagoon.

It was nothing like last time, and yet somehow similar. This time it was concern and not heartbreak that ached in the column of her throat. And she missed Antonin because he would be feeling now what she felt, and they should have allowed themselves more of that, before.

The sun slid loose from L'Ambre, up into the expanse above in a moment of change that she always sensed, the tethered becoming free. Walking back up the beach, from smooth cool sand to soft and warming, she had so little time, and so much to do. She was not sure when she had reached this moment. Had it been with Kit above the sea cave, Nuru still below and possibly dying because of her own words and their conjoined desperation? Or had it been later, at Mama Mandisa's words, or as Nuru had treated their brother with a foreigner's drugs?

*

The village was quiet. It had been quiet a lot since the vote, and the fight. People spoke in whispers, touched one another's hands, and everyone, in ones and twos and silence, went up to their ancestors to apologise. Luc had gone out in his pirogue alone and come back last night long after moonrise. It was more of an admission than anything else had been, but Jomo had asked the Mothers for leniency and they would give it.

When Sisi reached their house, Nuru was sitting in the shadows with their shoulders bent. Her words had done this, she knew, and that was a terrible thing to bear. 'Nuru,' she tried. 'My Nuru, you know I was wrong, yes? Wrong to—'

They lifted a hand but did not look up. 'I was also,' they said, their voice all husks and sand.

She did not answer, because it was true and besides, they had both been so deeply wounded already. Forgiveness was such a slow miracle, she thought, but she had to believe that they would find it. What was love, after all, if not the promise of refuge?

'He is gone, then,' Nuru said eventually.

'Yes,' she said, laying her hand on their shoulder and then stepping away to begin cooking.

'We have lost him.'

She turned to look at them, profiled against the light, and realised that after all she did not need to forgive them for what their griefs had driven them to. Their hands had carried too much for far too long. Antonin was here and watching; they were losing Jomo all over again, and of course she understood this. She understood being lost.

'Not quite,' she said and Nuru shook their head very slightly. Coming back away from the stove, she reached down to take their hand in hers. At first it was heavy and lax, but then their grip tightened, making her a spar in a shipwreck, a ledge in a heart. 'Not truly,' she repeated. 'He might come back, or he might not. But he is ours and we are his. You would not want him here, and not himself.'

Nuru smiled up at her, a terrible, alien little smile. 'Who is the Sacere here, you or I?'

Sisi held their gaze. 'You know the truth,' she said quietly. Which was a strange thing to say, because no one knew all the truths, apart from Mother Sea. Sisi herself knew only a few of them, none of them particularly important to anyone other than her. But this had to be enough, she thought.

'Alors, Nuru, Jomo will go, and be happy. And you will stay, and help our people to be whole again.' It was as much of a challenge as she dared give them, but if her words dug a little at an open wound, then maybe they needed to. Better the sharp pain that made you move than the slow surrender. Becoming fallible was dreadful for someone so proud, and terrifying, Sisi knew this. But they were stronger than Brother Island, and they would heal.

Her child stretched out their fists, so she laid Nuru's hand on her skin, seeing tenderness slip tidal across their face and wishing that there were decisions to be made which did not involve sorrow.

'So you will leave also,' Nuru said, watching their hand on her stomach, not looking at her.

Sisi studied their bent head, familiar and changed and so incredibly loved. 'Yes,' she said. Nuru tilted forward, spine curving until their forehead rested on their hand, on her skin and her child. They did not speak, and Sisi did not make them, but they stayed there for a long time as the air swam around them, and the drongo above called and listened, called and listened.

*

She left in the evening with the sun hanging amber-tinted above the island hall. Luc would carry her to the boat in his pirogue, and he must have asked to do so, because Mama Mandisa and Mama Anouk stood on the tideline watching him instead of her. He did not talk, but his eyes were narrowed in pain, and Manon did not come. Even now, she did not come. It was understandable and deserved, because a few months and a few tragedies did not erase the children who slept up in the tombs. But still it hurt. Sisi looked and looked again, but her friend was not there and it hurt.

Kit, Rachel and herself. No harvest, because none was due, and just a couple of packages for those outside whose home waited here for their return. Nuru held her, and Sisi felt the effort of letting go shudder through them. But for the first time since the heart and the choice not made, or made and cataclysmic, their eyes were as steady as they used to be. Sisi met their gaze and answered it. 'I know,' she said, 'and I will.'

*

'Will you be taking care of Jomo?' Rachel said as Luc raised up the sail and the boat skipped away from the beach.

Sisi closed her eyes to fix the people on the sand into her mind, and then looked at the outsider woman. Kit was watching her in his quiet way and his eyes perfectly matched the sea. 'Of course, yes,' she said. 'But this is not my only reason for leaving.'

'Ah,' Rachel said, and although the sea was silky and quiet within the reef, her fingers were tight on the wood. Her eyes dipping to Sisi's stomach and back. 'Dr Adler? I'm glad.' They heeled into another wave, and Kit leaned backwards as unconsciously as Luc did, but without shifting his gaze from Sisi.

Sisi nodded. 'Yes,' she said. 'But also...' Looking at Kit directly for the first time and smiling, and it was wonderful to smile like this. To look at him and know that of everyone in the whole world, he would understand what her next words meant. 'But also to meet a Dr Reinwald, to talk about a job.'

With the narrow width of the boat between them, she could have sworn she felt Kit's touch. Or perhaps it was not his – perhaps it was Antonin's, and her mother's, and her grandparents'. Perhaps it was even Manon's from wherever she was cradling her grief.

'Then, when it is time,' Sisi said, 'I will bring my child home.' And she turned away to watch the sea.

Acknowledgements

First and foremost, thank you, reader, for spending time in my world. It is a never-ending wonder to me that I get to share my stories with strangers, and I appreciate all of you!

Building an entirely fictitious island in the real world started with my own experiences and grew into a whole lot of research. So I should begin by thanking all the many islands where I've lived and worked, from Shetland to Madagascar – their people, wildlife, history books and storytellers all made me who I am, and I will always be grateful for the experiences I have shared with them. Those islands, and many more, all shaped this book in various ways, and I hope this story shows my love for the wondrous, liminal, fierce places that they all are, however tropical or sub-arctic. My endless appreciation to the climate warriors of vulnerable nations too, especially the youth activists raising your voices. You shouldn't have to be fighting this fight. Thanks also to the authors and publishers of books about remote islands or forgotten places – you know full well I am your target audience and that I will never be able to resist you! The very first seeds of this book were found in two fine examples: *The Life and Death of St Kilda* by Tom Steel, and the *Pocket Atlas of Remote Islands* by Judith Schalansky (read the entry on Tromelin).

Huge thanks to my agent Robbie Guillory for his belief in me – I am so delighted to be sharing this whole shebang with you. And everyone at Fairlight Books: it is really something special to be supported by such a wonderful team and I'm so glad this book found its home with you. Laura Shanahan, your tireless and insightful editing absolutely made *Mother Sea* shine and I love that so much! And Daniela Ferrante and Sarah Shaw, your vision and enthusiasm (and patience with me asking random questions) is a wonderful thing, thank you. Thanks also to Louise Boland for all your support and to Rebecca Blackmore-Dawes for your fab early work on the cover, and Beccy Fish who picked up that baton so brilliantly. Boundless gratitude and awe to Gill Heeley who created a cover that made me gasp at its sheer gorgeousness. Many thanks also to Gary Jukes for his meticulous eye, and to everyone who contributes to this book after I've been told I really can't change the text anymore – believe me, I am sending you my gratitude by the bucketload.

I am forever grateful to be part of several immensely supportive writers' communities, most particularly the Scottish BPOC Writers' Network, the Society of Authors' Authors with Disabilities and Chronic Illnesses group, and the Edinburgh SFF group. Thanks to all of them for their support and the sense of belonging. Earlier versions of this book were immeasurably improved by critique from Garry MacKenzie and his University of St Andrews Open Access Creative Writing group, and also from my indomitable beta readers Shell Bromley, Fiona Erskine, Karen Ginnane and J. A. Ironside. And Francesca Barbini – I owe you so, so much. Thank you all – you are the best.

The cats, as always, deserve special mention. I'm not sure what for, but they assure me they do. We lost our old kitty Marley during the final stages of this book, so please raise a wee glass to the best and gentlest of boys. I miss him.

And finally to my family. Mum, sorry for upsetting you! Thank you for being fabulous. Jennifer, Len, Stu, Nina and all my family and friends who have cheered me on, said nice things about my books and been so incredibly supportive – you are all wonderful, thank you. Living with disabling illnesses while building a career as an author is tough, and it is my husband and daughter who bear the brunt of the compromises I make. I couldn't do this without their support. So thank you, the pair of you. I consider myself very lucky.

About the Author

Lorraine Wilson is an ex-conservation scientist who writes fiction influenced by folklore and the wilderness. With a third-culture heritage, she is drawn to themes of family, belonging and the legacy of trauma. Her debut novel *This Is Our Undoing* (2021) was shortlisted for the Kavya Prize and for the British Fantasy Society's Best Newcomer and Best Fantasy Novel awards, and longlisted for the British Science Fiction Association's Best Novel award. Her second novel *The Way the Light Bends* was published in 2022. She won a British Fantasy Award for her short story 'Bathymetry' in 2022. Lorraine currently lives on the east coast of Scotland with her family.